P9-CKB-903

PRAISE FOR
IRIS JOHANSEN AND *HIGH STAKES*

"[A]n enthralling, keep-you-on-your-toes read. Enjoy these *High Stakes*! You won't get a moment to rest!"
—FreshFiction.com

"Logan is a well-written character, who is smart, sexy. and a badass…He fits in perfectly in the Iris Johansen world of characters. Here's to more Logan books."
—RedCarpetCrash.com

"Page-turning virtuoso Johansen is a master at character development, and *High Stakes* does not slack in that department. She has another series in the making that her many old—and new—fans will find addictive."
—*Florida Times-Union*

"*High Stakes* will remind readers how talented [Iris Johansen] is in writing gripping characters. Per usual, she puts her heroines through the wringer but has them come out on top and with more strength."
—CrimeSpreeMag.com

"[A] gripping dive into the world of high-stakes gambling." —MysteryandSuspense.com

"This was another fast-paced, action-filled story that I have come to love from this author. Having Logan come from a gambling background provided a whole new set of skills that added a new level of intrigue to the story. It made the cat-and-mouse game that we have come to expect in these books just that much more exciting."   —AlwaysWithABook.com

"Iris Johansen is an award-winning, bestselling author, and with this new release, it's easy to see why. *High Stakes* is a sinister, edgy, action-packed page-turner that is intricate, entertaining, and undoubtedly extremely satisfying."   —WhatsBetterThanBooks.com

"There's no one like Iris Johansen!"
     —Tess Gerritsen, *New York Times* bestselling author

"[Iris] Johansen keeps readers on the edge of their seats."   —*Booklist*

"Just by seeing the Iris Johansen name…you know [it] will be an explosive, unforgettable story."
                    —*Suspense Magazine*

"[Iris] Johansen knows what readers like and doesn't hesitate to give it to them."   —*Kirkus Reviews*

"A bestselling writer whose talent is out of this world."
                    —*San Francisco Book Review*

HIGH STAKES

STANDALONE BOOKS BY IRIS JOHANSEN (IN ORDER OF PUBLICATION)

The Ugly Duckling

Long After Midnight

And Then You Die

Final Target

No One to Trust

Dead Aim

Fatal Tide

Firestorm

On the Run

Killer Dreams

Pandora's Daughter

Silent Thunder (Iris & Roy Johansen)

Dark Summer

Deadlock

Storm Cycle (Iris & Roy Johansen)

Shadow Zone (Iris & Roy Johansen)

The Perfect Witness

No Easy Target (featuring Margaret Douglas)

Vendetta

Chaos (featuring Margaret Douglas)

For a complete list of books by Iris Johansen, as well as previews of upcoming books and information about the author, visit IrisJohansen.com.

HIGH STAKES

IRIS JOHANSEN

GRAND CENTRAL
PUBLISHING

NEW YORK   BOSTON

Copyright © 2021 by IJ Development

Cover copyright © 2022 by Hachette Book Group, Inc.

Grand Central Publishing
Hachette Book Group
1290 Avenue of the Americas, New York, NY 10104
grandcentralpublishing.com
twitter.com/grandcentralpub

First published in hardcover and ebook in September 2021

First Premium Mass Market Edition: April 2022

Grand Central Publishing is a division of Hachette Book Group, Inc. The Grand Central Publishing name and logo is a trademark of Hachette Book Group, Inc.

The publisher is not responsible for websites (or their content) that are not owned by the publisher.

The Hachette Speakers Bureau provides a wide range of authors for speaking events. To find out more, go to www.hachettespeakersbureau.com or call (866) 376-6591.

ISBNs: 978-1-5387-1311-2 (premium mass market), 978-1-5387-1309-9 (ebook)

Printed in the United States of America

OPM

10 9 8 7 6 5 4 3 2 1

HIGH STAKES

CHAPTER

1

I t's time, Lara," Maria said gently from the doorway behind her. "They'll be picking you up in thirty minutes."

Lara didn't look up from the piano keys. "Screw them. I'll be done here soon." She finished the concerto in a final glorious flourish. Then she drew a deep breath and sat there letting the music soothe her, letting its beauty take away the ugliness to come.

"How are you?" Maria walked across the room to stand beside her. "Rachmaninoff's Third. Quite a challenge. But you did it well. Would you like to tell me why you chose it today?"

It was the last thing she wanted to do, Lara thought. There was no use bringing her mother into the situation when she would not be able to do anything but worry. Maria always did anything she could to help her, and she often suffered for it. "I believe it's the most difficult concerto. It demands every technical skill. I wanted to conquer it. I *had* to conquer it. As you say, I wanted to challenge myself." She got to her feet and brushed a kiss on Maria's cheek. Maria's skin was silky soft, her dark hair shining in the firelight. Lara had always thought her mother beautiful, and she was just as lovely in maturity as she'd been when Lara was a little girl growing up. "I'm glad you think I did it well. Now I have to go pick up my gear and wait on the steps for them." Her lips twisted. "I know you don't want to invite my kind, loving father into your house."

"It's only my house as long as he permits it to be," Maria said bitterly. "But it won't always be that way, Lara. We'll find a way out."

"I know." She took her in her arms and gave her a quick hug. "It's just difficult right now. As difficult as that Rachmaninoff Third. But I've got a few ideas." She turned to go. "I should be back in a few days. I probably won't be able to call you." She headed for the parlor door. "But don't worry."

"Lara."

Lara looked over her shoulder.

"Why shouldn't I worry?" her mother asked hoarsely. "What weapons?"

Lara froze. It was the one question she wished she hadn't asked her. Lie? No, they never lied to each other. They'd made that promise long ago. There were too many lies surrounding them. She braced herself. "No weapons. Bare hands."

"What?" Maria's eyes were suddenly glittering with anger. "That son of a *bitch*."

"It's okay," Lara said quickly. "I'm ready for them. Volkov warned me six months ago it would be coming."

"How kind of him." She was across the room, her arms enfolding Lara. "I'm sorry," she said huskily. "I should have run away when he set it up. No, I should have run when it first started. I thought I'd be able to fight them. I had no idea they'd use you for their damn games."

"How could you know? You were caught, too." Lara took her by the shoulders and shook her gently. "It's all right. I've had the music and I've had you." She grimaced. "And look at all the things I've learned. Aren't I lucky?"

"Don't even joke about it," Maria said curtly. "Those bastards. What hell they put you through."

"I wasn't joking. I did learn a lot." Her lips tightened. "And most of the time I won. And if I lost, I learned something from that, too." Her hands fell away from Maria. "It made me stronger."

"Yes, it did," Maria said bitterly. "No one can argue that."

"And *you* made me stronger, too," Lara said. "Because you've fought them all these years and never stopped."

"I couldn't save you," she whispered. "Not since the day Volkov talked Anton into that damn bet. All I could do was try to make it easier for you. But there's no way I can make these next days easier."

"No, I'll do that," Lara said. "He won't win this one. I'm ready for anything that—"

"What are you ready for, Lara?" Anton Balkon asked mockingly as he came into the living room. "I hope it's to perform better than you did with Oleg a few evenings ago in that barn. He was not impressed."

She stiffened. "I was trying something new with him. He still didn't take me down."

"And Volkov's men won't even attempt to take you down. They'll have permission to make it permanent. Life or death, Lara. Volkov is going to send two of his best men, and they'll be much more skilled than Oleg and very used to hunting down prey."

"Stop it, Anton," Maria hissed as she took a step forward. "You're going too far. She's your daughter, for God's sake."

"Then she should try to please me. She knows what's expected of her. Volkov upped the bet on this weekend's Trial. I'm not going to lose." He leaned forward and stroked Lara's cheek. "It's your first real blood challenge. Are you excited?"

"No." She wanted to step back, but she knew his hand would only tighten and his nails would dig into her cheek. "But I'll do what you want me to do."

"Yes, you will." His hand fell away from her face. Then he whirled and his hand was suddenly on Maria's throat. "How have you been, Maria? You're still beautiful, but you're a little old for my taste these days." His grip tightened until she began to choke. "I prefer the little girls Volkov keeps me supplied with. So young, so fresh. But I do remember how talented you were. That's why I kept you around even after you were stupid enough to get yourself pregnant."

"Let her *go*," Lara said with set teeth.

Anton's grip grew tighter on Maria's throat. "Please?"

Lara swallowed. "Please."

He released his grip. "You see, politeness is everything. I'll even forgive her for forgetting her place in our arrangement…as long as you don't forget yours. I will win, won't I?"

"You will win." She was cursing herself for not

being outside when he'd arrived. She wasn't sure if it would have done any good, but the longer she stayed the more dangerous it would be for Maria. She had to get out of here. Say anything, give him anything he wanted. "Is that why you're here? I promise you I'm ready for anything that Volkov's men will throw at me."

"Of course that's why I'm here." He smiled. "I thought I'd add a little incentive to the mix. Incentive can often be the final ingredient that makes a masterpiece." He patted her cheek. "You know about masterpieces, don't you, Lara?" He pushed her toward the door. "Let's see if you can create one that will keep our Maria alive."

"Lara!" Maria started to follow her.

"No!" Lara quickly put up a hand to stop her. "It will be fine. I promise."

"That's what I like to hear." Anton pushed her out the door. "See that you keep that promise." He followed her out the door and down the stone steps. "I have to win, Lara. Volkov is entirely too sure of himself. Now go over and tell him how ready you are."

"What?" She froze as she saw her father gesturing down the street. Boris Volkov was leaning against his Mercedes, and he was smiling at her. Her heart skipped a beat. "What's he doing here? I wasn't supposed to have to see him until after it was all over."

Anton shrugged. "He said it was a special trial and he wanted to see if he had anything to worry about. Go over and talk to him so that I can get you to the forest."

There would be no use arguing with him. Anton always gave in to anything Volkov wanted. She dropped her backpack on the ground and ran down the street to where Volkov was waiting.

Don't let him shake you.

Look him straight in the eye.

He wants you to be afraid so that he'll have the advantage.

Don't be afraid.

She stopped in front of him and lifted her chin. "You wanted to see me?"

"For one last time," he said softly. He reached out and touched her cheek. "I always forget how fragile you look. But you're not fragile, are you? Between Anton and me, we've made you into almost as tough a bitch as your whore of a mother. Maybe even more." He smiled maliciously. "But you're not going to be tough enough to survive what I've planned for you this time. I've been very careful to load the decks against you."

Don't let him see the fear. "May I go now?"

If anything, his expression became even more malevolent. "And if by some miracle you do survive, it will only be to face what's been waiting for you all these years. Are you ready for that?"

She had to keep her face impassive. "I'm ready. It would just be another Trial. I'd win that one, too. May I go now?"

He muttered a curse and for an instant she thought he'd strike her anyway. Then he pushed her away and got into his Mercedes. "By all means, you wouldn't want to keep my men waiting. They're primed and eager for you."

She didn't wait for him to start his car. She didn't answer. She turned on her heel and headed back toward where Anton was waiting for her.

Don't look back. Don't be afraid of what's coming. It will be difficult, but so was Rachmaninoff's Third Concerto.

Close everything out but Rachmaninoff's Third and the challenge waiting for you in that forest.

CASINO MILAN, ITALY

Josh Mallory stopped Logan Tanner before he got on the elevator to go up to his suite. "There's something you should know. You have a visitor."

"I didn't get a text on my phone. Now I wonder why not?" Tanner gazed at him quizzically. "Particularly since you seem to be getting such a degree of sardonic pleasure from telling me about it. Would you care to tell me why?"

Mallory scowled. "You've been in a terrible mood ever since you got here and have been giving my dealers hell. I figure you deserve a little trouble for making me up their salaries just to keep them from walking out on me. I have the best dealers in Milan, and I don't want them going to some other casino."

"They're not alert enough." Tanner grinned as he punched the elevator button. "I could have taken them to the cleaners before they took their first break. I'm just looking out for you, Mallory."

"You're just too damn bored," Mallory said, disgusted as he got into the elevator and punched the button for the penthouse. "And I can look out for myself. I run this casino better than any other property you own, and you know it. It wasn't fair to expect them to know you were counting cards when you were so good, you were barred from half the casinos in the world by the time you were sixteen."

"No, I was so *bad*. They wouldn't have caught me if I'd been good enough to keep them from knowing what I was doing. I was always too impatient when I was a kid." He tilted his head. "But I had a good run."

"No, you got bored and took too many chances with the wrong casino boss," Mallory said. "And you had to find a way to get away before you got your throat cut."

"Did I tell you that? I must have been drunk."

Mallory nodded. "Stinking. But it was the first week we were in the special services together, and you thought everyone was your best friend. I even had to keep you from confiding your murky past to the sergeant."

"Which goes to prove that you *were* my best friend," Tanner said lightly. "Because I don't believe I came out of the service with more than one." He shrugged. "And I won't be bored at the poker game tomorrow night. It's high enough stakes to even interest me. Has everyone accepted?"

"Why wouldn't they? You're a target for every player who wants a name for himself among live high stakes poker players. That pot you won last time was higher than most state lotteries."

They had reached the penthouse floor and the door started to open.

Tanner reached out and pressed the STOP button. "I know you're anticipating getting some sly pleasure by making me uncomfortable about my 'guest,' but that wouldn't have caused you to come up to the suite with me." His eyes were narrowed on Mallory's face. "So I'd bet that you're a little worried that I might need help in making him feel welcome. Who is it, Mallory?"

Mallory was grinning. "Nikolai."

Tanner stiffened. "Shit." He paused. "Kaskov?"

"Not with him." His smile widened with mischief. "Yes, that's the expression I wanted to see. It's almost worth giving those dealers a raise." His smile faded. "But where Nikolai is, Kaskov is sure to follow. Unless you've done something to annoy Kaskov and he just sent Nikolai to take care of you. With you, there's always that possibility." He tilted his head. "But I don't think it's the way Kaskov would handle you. I thought you'd reached an understanding after you saved my neck in Moscow."

"I thought I had, too. But Sergai Kaskov is an enigma, and you can never take him for granted." He smiled wryly. "Not that anyone would take one of the biggest mob bosses in Russia anything but seriously."

"If it has anything to do with me, I won't—"

"It won't have anything to do with you," Tanner interrupted. "We worked out the payment on that, and Kaskov never breaks his word. It has to be something else." He smiled faintly. "You were going to face Kaskov to save me? I'm touched, Mallory."

Mallory snorted. "Asshole. I just didn't like Nikolai showing up. I remember him too well."

"Let's see if he remembers you." He pressed the button and the door slid open. "But after you say your hellos, I think you should go back downstairs and soothe your dealers."

Mallory shook his head. "I'll stick around. You've got a great view of the city from this suite. I'll go have a drink on the terrace until you're finished." He moved toward a giant of a man dressed in a very expensive-looking navy-blue suit. "Hello, Nikolai, I thought I saw you in the lobby. Anything I can do for you?"

Nikolai shook his head. "No, Mr. Kaskov says you're no longer of interest to me."

"Thank God," Mallory murmured. "Then may I ask why you're here?"

"Mr. Kaskov is going to have a discussion with Mr. Tanner and wanted me to check out the premises." He turned to Tanner. "Everything seems to be in order. I've notified Mr. Kaskov and he's on his way up. I was just in the kitchen preparing coffee. May I get you a cup?"

"By all means. Thank you. Make yourself at home." Tanner glanced at Mallory. "I believe it's time you went out on the terrace and had that drink."

"You're certain?"

"Nikolai says you're not needed. But evidently I am." He turned back to Nikolai. "And I'm sure you've chosen the place where Kaskov would want to have this discussion?"

"The library seems to be comfortable and secure. But Mr. Kaskov said that he'd be happy to accommodate you if you prefer another location."

"He did? Interesting." Tanner headed for the library. "The library is fine. I'll wait there for him. You can show him in when he arrives."

Nikolai glanced at the elevator. "I'm sure it will be any moment."

Tanner was certain it would be, too. Kaskov's schedule usually ran smoothly with absolutely no glitches. Since he was head of one of the most powerful mafia groups in Russia and had any number of enemies among the lesser mob hierarchies of the

Russian underworld, he wouldn't have lived this long and gained his present dominance if it didn't. Tanner hadn't had any dealings with him since he'd worked out the payment for Mallory's indiscretion, but he was sure that hadn't changed. He'd never met a more intelligent or dangerous man nor one he'd more prefer to keep at a considerable distance.

But none of Nikolai's signals had indicated threat, and Kaskov had ordered those signals. So assume dominance until he knew what the hell the bastard wanted. First, sit down behind the desk in the library and make Kaskov come to him.

He didn't have to wait long. Sergai Kaskov swept into the library only a few minutes later. He was dressed in a faultless tuxedo and tossed his coat on a chair beside the door. "Hello, Tanner. Thank you for seeing me. I meant to be here earlier, but I just flew in from Rome. I had tickets for a concert at the opera and there was an artist I didn't want to miss. Superb. You'll understand, you go there frequently when you're in Italy, don't you?" He dropped down into a chair beside the desk and smiled. "Life can be so tiresome; one must take advantage of every minute of beauty." He looked almost exactly the same as he had when Tanner had last seen him several years ago. He sat there perfectly at ease, powerful, magnetic, totally dominant, gray-streaked dark hair, somewhere in his late fifties. He chuckled as he continued, "But then you know that about me. You investigated everything you could find regarding who I was and how you could get what you wanted from me. I expected it." He leaned back in the chair. "I even admired it."

"I could hardly blame you for not coming earlier when I didn't expect you at all," Tanner said dryly.

"I assume you mean Pierre Lazco. He's a wonderful violinist. I saw him last night after I arrived in Rome from New York."

"I didn't think you'd miss him. I told Nikolai I'd bet him you'd come in at least a day early for your big game. I thought I might even see you there tonight. I have a box at the opera house, and we could have enjoyed the concert together."

"Why doesn't that surprise me? You very generously fund both the Bolshoi Ballet and the Tchaikovsky Concert Hall in Moscow. Why not spread the largesse around to Rome?"

"Why not?" Kaskov repeated with a wry smile. "And you very neatly sidestepped my gracious invitation to share my box. But you're probably right, you wouldn't have enjoyed it as much if you'd had to concentrate on outside influences. I saw you at the Tchaikovsky Concert Hall one night, and I might have been looking at myself. It was good to know. The dossier I had on you hadn't mentioned that passion for music. I immediately dismissed the investigator."

Shit, he didn't like the idea that Kaskov knew anything but the bare basics about him. "There's no way you could use that as a weapon. I like all music from Bach to jazz, but it's not a passion. It was understandable that your man skipped over it." He shook his head. "And I'm sorry to disappoint you, but you wouldn't have been that much of a distraction. I could have closed you out."

"Could you?" Kaskov asked thoughtfully. "Yes, you might have had the willpower, but you would have had to make an effort. Sometimes the smallest things are the ones that take us down. At any rate, as I said, I admire that you researched me so thoroughly. It shows how determined you were to save your friend. You wanted me to use my influence to get Mallory safely out of Moscow before Narzoff took a contract out on him for luring his mistress into bed. But I don't know many men who would have come to me about it."

"Neither do I," Tanner said. "Believe me, I was out of options."

Kaskov shook his head. "Mallory made a bad choice. Narzoff is a very possessive man, and he wasn't even one of my family. I'm usually careful about not interfering with the members of other families as long as they accord me the same courtesy. You caused me a good deal of trouble before it was over."

"But you still did it." Tanner's lips twisted. "And I paid your price. I extracted that man Putin was after. That makes us even. So why are you here?"

"I did it because I'd heard enough about you that I was intrigued and wanted to know more. I'm always looking for men with the right qualifications, and you were very, very good. I thought I might hire you. That extraction was necessary, but it was still in the nature of an audition."

"Then I must have failed it. I never got an offer from you." He sighed. "Too bad."

"By that time, I'd assessed your capabilities and I knew that I wasn't going to be able to persuade you to come over to the dark side. You were moving too quickly out of range of either bribery or intimidation. You'd already had your sights set on your first leap into the big leagues. You'd become an extractor after you left special services, but you knew it was only going to be temporary until you earned a big enough stash for your first casino." He smiled. "So I decided I'd just take advantage of those capabilities on a one-shot deal and then file you away for future notice. But even if it was temporary, you'd made the right contacts and you did my job superbly. And you were smart enough not to want any connection with me after that one extraction." He lifted his shoulders in a half shrug. "Why should you? You're quite probably a mathematical genius, and you've already bought several casinos in the U.S. as well as here in Milan and Macao. You're a fantastic gambler—no one's better at judging the odds than you. Then you started playing the market and you opened an entirely new chapter. I've increased my net worth enormously just watching and following."

"I'm glad I could be of help," Tanner said dryly. "Is this going somewhere?"

"Oh, yes." He took the cup of coffee Nikolai was handing him. "I seldom waste my time on reminiscing. I just wanted you to know that I wasn't going at this blindly. I've studied you and I have faith you can give me what I need."

"And yet you already know that I don't want to do another extraction for you. It *is* an extraction?"

Kaskov nodded. "An extremely difficult one that involves a multitude of complications that might suit your talents. So I pulled you out of my file and dusted off all the info I'd gathered about you. You might actually want to do this one. Not only will I promise to give you whatever you wish in return, but it might bring you a certain amount of satisfaction. From what I've heard, I think you're probably restless and bored and ready for a new challenge. Plus, you didn't have to save Mallory, but you did. Which indicates a softness that may be rather naive but is an integral part of your character. You didn't like your friend being bullied by

Narzoff." He frowned. "It's lately been brought to my attention that I don't like bullies, either."

"May I point out that your life is devoted to enforcement and criminal activities? One might even call you a bully."

"Not to my face," he said softly. "I'd suggest you change your phrasing."

Nikolai had turned back at the door and was looking at Kaskov.

Kaskov made a motion. "It's all right, Nikolai. Tanner is feeling a bit pressured. We'll either come to an agreement or we won't."

"We won't," Tanner said flatly. "I'm not interested. Who is it? Another scientist you're trying to get out from under Putin's thumb?"

"No, though that was a case of bullying in the extreme and would have ended very badly if you'd not gotten him out of Russia." He paused. "This is more personal. Lara has nothing to do with politics. She's just trying to survive." He reached into his coat pocket and drew out a large manila envelope. He opened it and spread a group of passport photos on the desk in front of Tanner. "Lara Balkon." He pointed to a beautiful dark-haired woman with high cheeks and slightly slanted eyes. "She's the one I need you to extract."

"Your mistress?"

"No." He pointed to another photo of an attractive older woman. "Maria Balkon, her mother. She's English, and she and Lara are very close. Lara probably won't consent to be extracted without her." He pointed to a photo of a dark-haired man in his forties. "Anton Balkon, Lara's father. A total son of a bitch. He's head of his own family business in the south Georgia area and does moderately well. Mostly drugs, he's no problem for me. But Boris Volkov might be a different matter. He's boss of a neighboring family and has recently taken over several other syndicates in the area and become a close friend of Balkon." He threw down another photo of a tall, smiling man with sun-streaked brown-gray hair. "Volkov. He now controls the south territory except for a small area he allows Balkon to run. He'd like to move in on me in Moscow if he had the nerve."

"Which he doesn't?"

"No, but he keeps testing me. I think Lara might be part of that test."

"You said she wasn't your mistress."

"But he knows I've stopped by the Balkon house and listened to her play every now and then over the years."

"Play?"

"She's a pianist. Remarkable. I heard her play at a recital in Moscow when she was eleven. She won first prize, which was a grand piano and a scholarship at the Moscow Conservatory. I thought she was a prodigy then. But she never used the scholarship. Her father took her back to the country the next week, and she never performed after that."

Tanner's eyes were narrowed on Kaskov's face. "And therein lies the tale," he said softly. "You couldn't stand to see a talent wasted."

"I won't deny the idea makes me angry. But it's a bit more involved than that." He added curtly, "And it's not been wasted. She's still brilliant. She practices four or five hours a day when she gets the chance. She's twenty-one now, and I heard her last year. I'd judge, if allowed another few years, she'll be one of the top pianists in the world."

"You'd be a good judge if you weren't swayed by other factors." He glanced at the woman in the photo. She wasn't smiling but there was an intensity, an eagerness, an odd expectancy in those dark eyes that was fascinating. "She's beautiful. You're sure she's not your mistress?"

"No, and I'm not swayed by anything other than her ability." He thought for a moment. "Or perhaps her courage. Those are the two things that impressed me about her. She reminded me of someone…"

Sentiment? Not likely, Tanner thought. Kaskov's expression was as hard as ever. "Why don't you get her out yourself?"

"I told you, it's not my custom to interfere with the decisions of other families. It's not good business and sets a bad example."

"And?"

He didn't speak for a moment. "I have to get her out right away. She has to totally disappear for a period of time so that I have time to rearrange her circumstances. That disappearance must not be connected with me."

"You'd rather it be connected with me?"

"If you're so clumsy that you make that kind of a mistake. I don't believe you will."

"I don't believe I will, either. Because I have no intention of doing this extraction. Find someone else."

"If you weren't perfect, I'd take your advice. But there's no real reason why you shouldn't do it. You're bored, and this would be something to fill in the time until you move on to your next project."

"I'm *not* bored."

"You set up one of your poker games for tomorrow night. You usually only do that when you're—"

"I'm not bored. And the poker game is another good reason why I can't do it. You said it has to be done right away. The game is tomorrow night."

"Cancel it."

"Absolutely not."

"You have to get her out of there right away," Kaskov said quietly. "It's a priority. You can set up another poker game anytime."

"Priority?" he asked impatiently.

"She might not be alive after this weekend. Volkov's men are laying bets she won't be. The odds are against her."

Tanner went still. "The odds?"

"I told you that Anton Balkon is a son of a bitch." He shrugged. "Volkov is far worse. He's a sadistic bastard, and he never forgets an insult. I don't know the details, but Lara managed to make him furious before she went to that recital in Moscow. It was Volkov who ordered Balkon to bring her back. He had plans for her."

"Plans?" His hand clenched on his cup. "She was only eleven."

"Not sexual. At least, not then. He had something more long-range in mind. He came up with a punishment that could amuse both her father and him for years to come."

"He wouldn't let her take the scholarship."

"Oh, that was definitely gone. But he was still going to permit her to play the piano as long as she agreed to go along with the rules of the bet he'd made with her father."

"Bet?"

Kaskov smiled bitterly. "I told you this extraction was perfect for you. Volkov and Balkon don't have your talent, but they do have a passion for gambling. Particularly Volkov. So why not set a master gambler to spoil their very dirty games? It seemed Balkon wouldn't have minded having a son, but he was disgusted with not only having a daughter, but having one who could do nothing but pound a piano. Which also caused him trouble with his boss, Volkov, who seemed to be impatient with everything Lara did. He grabbed at the chance to earn his approval when Volkov told him his idea of letting Volkov choose certain goals twice a year for Lara to reach to make her into the kind of person they both wanted her to become. Then they'd make a wager as to whether or not she could meet each goal." His lips tightened. "I don't have to tell you what kind of punishment she'd have to take from her father if she failed him and he lost a bet. I'm sure that Volkov made those goals very difficult for her to reach."

"But you don't know?" Tanner was gazing at him. "And if you don't interfere with other families, how do you know so much about this particular horror story?"

"Word gets around. I didn't hear about it for a few years, but then both Volkov's and Balkon's men started to make their own bets on Lara. It was bound to happen after she started not to lose all the time. You know gamblers will bet on anything. You've made some crazy bets yourself." He was studying Tanner's face. "But I thought this setup would turn you off. You don't like bullies, and a kid isn't exactly fair game."

"I didn't say it turned me off," he said coolly. "Life's not often fair. You've got to accept that and go on." He looked down at the photo again. "She looks...fragile. You said she began to win?"

"So I heard."

"That's right, you kept your distance. Which is what I intend to do."

"Oh, like you did when you and Mallory and a few of your men broke up that dogfighting ring in the backwoods outside your casino in Atlantic City? I understand you inflicted serious and permanent damage."

Tanner carefully kept his face without expression. "It seemed the thing to do at the time. I like dogs."

"And you have problems with bullies. As I said, some gamblers will bet on anything. Not you. You have a passion for the game, but it annoys you if the rules are ignored. Or if there are penalties to anyone but the opponents involved." He shrugged. "But if I'm wrong and you've made up your mind, then I suppose I should tell you what you're turning down so that you can compliment yourself on staying away from it. Lara's goal this time is basically just keeping herself alive for this weekend. Her father is turning her loose in the forest outside Avgar. Volkov is sending two of his best men after her with orders to take her down. Which means that to live, she'll have to kill them. No weapons allowed. She's not as fragile as she looks and she's trained herself, but what do you think her chances are?"

"I think if Volkov and her father have been enjoying their game, they'll back off or they'll lose the mouse they're toying with."

"We'll see. They haven't backed off before." He nodded at the manila envelope. "I've included the principal hoops that Volkov made her jump through in the past and the results. It might interest you. But the hurdle this weekend is a step beyond. It's clear that this 'game' has become an obsession with Volkov over the years. Yet lately he's been losing too often, and he might be getting frustrated. He has a reputation for hating to lose. There's a chance that he'll want to end it." He paused. "Or to damage her so badly that it will happen anyway."

"But then you'd lose your prodigy, and you don't like to lose, either," Tanner said mockingly. "I can't believe you won't find someone else to accommodate you."

"I think I'll wait for you to change your mind. I hate making do when you're so perfect, Tanner." He got to his feet. "If you need my help, I'm at your disposal as long as you keep it confidential. You'll find additional information in that envelope that may assist you. It's only fair since I realize it's short notice and you've had no opportunity for preparations." He took his coat off the chair. "There's also a copy of the DVD I had taken of Lara Balkon last year so that you can understand what they're killing." He headed for the door. "Nikolai will be in the lobby all night. I hope you'll be in touch."

"I won't be. If time is of the essence, I'd suggest you start making a few calls."

"I rarely take suggestions." He smiled at him over his shoulder. "I tend to make a decision and then roll the dice. Like you, Tanner." Then he hesitated as he reached the door. "But you're being more stubborn than I thought, so it might be wise to give you another incentive to please me." His gaze narrowed. "How about Antonio Sandrino?"

Tanner stiffened and inhaled sharply. "I'm listening."

"Your reason for coming to Moscow the first time was because of business, but you sent me a message about six months ago and asked me if I had any information about Sandrino."

"And you told me you didn't. It was a lie?"

"No, not at the time. And I had no reason to explore the matter." He smiled. "But there's not much that I can't find out if I go to the trouble. People seem to want to tell me anything I want to know. And I decided I wanted to know when this unfortunate matter of Lara appeared on the horizon. I'm sure I'll have your information when you've finished taking care of her problem."

Then he was gone. Tanner heard him speaking to Nikolai in the foyer and then the sound of the elevator.

The next moment Mallory was standing in the doorway. "Am I in trouble?" He came into the library and dropped down in the chair that Kaskov had occupied. "He didn't stay that long. I hoped that was a good sign." His gaze was on Tanner's expression, and he gave a low whistle. "But I gather it wasn't."

"He stayed long enough," Tanner said dryly. "Too long. Kaskov doesn't know how to take no for an answer."

"Not many people would dare to tell him no." He sat forward. "Look, if there was a problem with anything to do with my—"

"It had nothing to do with you," he said curtly. "I told you I'd taken care of that. He's crossed it off his books. This was something else."

Mallory leaned back again with a sigh of relief. "Good. So what's on his mind? Another extraction? Did you tell him you'd moved on and weren't interested?"

"Of course I did. He wasn't listening," Tanner said

through set teeth. "He didn't care. It's personal. He *wants* this. He said Nikolai would be downstairs in the lobby waiting if I changed my mind."

"Oh, shit."

"That's not going to happen. He can find someone else to get her out." He pushed the photos on top of the manila envelope aside. "I don't take his orders. I have a life. He thinks he can just dangle the damn name in front of me and I'll jump and do his bidding? He didn't even care about the game tomorrow."

"It would have had to be an immediate extraction?" Mallory was picking up the photo of Lara Balkon and gazing at it. "That's bad news."

"No, it isn't. I'm not doing it."

"Yes, you said that. What name was he dangling in front of you?"

Tanner didn't answer for a moment. "Sandrino."

"Shit." Mallory inhaled sharply. "He knows something?"

"No, he only said he could find out. And I'm supposed to trust the bastard? Kaskov's one of the biggest crime bosses in the world. If I haven't been able to turn up anything during the last eighteen months, why would he be able to?"

"You tell me. You went to him in the first place. He's powerful as hell." His gaze returned to the photo of Lara Balkon. "Personal? Is she his mistress?"

"No, it's something else. He's hard as nails, but somehow she managed to…reach him."

"That could be even worse." Mallory reached over and picked up the manila envelope. "This is the extraction info? Do you mind if I go through it?"

"Be my guest. But it's a waste of time. We aren't going to use it."

"It's my time to waste." Mallory glanced up from going through the documents. "Look, you wouldn't have even been involved with Kaskov in the first place except for me. I put you through a hell of a lot of trouble, and there was a chance I could have gotten you killed. I still feel guilty about it. And now he's pulled Sandrino into it, and that's going to rub you raw and might be even more dangerous for you." He grimaced. "I'd far rather this extraction you've refused was Kaskov's sex object. In my experience, people get more emotional about the 'personal.' I just want to be prepared for anything that comes along." He'd pulled out a DVD. "What's this?"

"I assume it's the DVD that Kaskov ordered me to watch," he said caustically.

"And you're fighting doing it." He tossed the DVD on the desk in front of Tanner. "Because you're pissed off with Kaskov, and you don't want him to pull your strings. Well, it's *me* pulling your strings now. *Watch* the damn thing." He got to his feet. "I'm going to settle in the living room and go through this file. I'll come back after I've finished, and we'll talk about it." He suddenly grinned mischievously. "Am I fired yet?"

"Very close," Tanner growled. He took the disk and slid it into his computer. "It's still a waste of time."

"And you're a stubborn asshole," Mallory said as he headed for the door. "I don't know why I'm trying so hard to keep you from getting killed."

"Because you don't know if you're in my will yet." Tanner waved him out of the room. "Go away. I'll watch it."

He settled back in his chair and glared at the computer. It didn't help that Mallory was right. Too many of the chords Kaskov had struck had made an impact, and he hated being manipulated. He had an idea that Kaskov wouldn't have included this disk if it wasn't designed to do the same thing.

"Play it!" Mallory called from the other room.

Tanner muttered a curse and punched the button.

Lara Balkon appeared on the screen, dressed in jeans and sweatshirt, her long hair in a ponytail. She looked much younger than she had in the passport photo. She was sitting at a piano. Then she started to play Rachmaninoff's Concerto No. 2.

Tanner froze. "Holy shit."

He tried to be objective, to criticize her technique, to stop Kaskov's words repeating in his mind.

So you can understand what they're trying to kill.

Then that was all gone.

Everything was gone but the music.

"You've played it four times." Mallory was leaning against the doorjamb. "Not that I blame you. I'm not even a fan of classical music but I can tell she's something special. How good is she?"

"Phenomenal. No, magical. Kaskov was right, damn him." Tanner reached out and turned off the DVD. "I can see why she might have had that effect on him. But why the hell didn't the bastard yank her out of that situation when she was a kid? Why wait until now and leave it up to me?"

"Maybe he didn't have a choice," Mallory said quietly. "Or maybe he thought there would be an opening for him to do it down the line somewhere." He held up the manila envelope. "I could see they kept her pretty busy from the time her father brought her back from that recital in Moscow. Some of it is pretty rough. Are you ready to read it?"

"No." He got to his feet. "I don't have time now. Take it with you." He moved across the room and past him into the foyer. "You don't have time, either. Call Jordan in London and tell him to get the crew together and be ready to head out for Rome within the next two hours." He was striding toward the elevator. "I have to go down to the lobby and tell Nikolai what I'm going to need from him."

Mallory followed him. "I take it that we're going to Russia?" He smiled with sly malice. "Oh, my, I guess I'll have to cancel that poker game tomorrow night."

"Don't push it," Tanner said sourly. "I'm pissed off enough that I have to do this, and try to make it happen in the space of a few days." He got into the elevator. "And if Kaskov thinks he's going to get off scot-free and not tell me everything I need to know about Sandrino after this is over, he's very much mistaken."

CHAPTER

2

Volkov's smile was more of a smirk when Balkon strode into his study late that evening. He'd known it was only a matter of time before he'd be scampering here to see him. "You look a bit edgy. I told you the odds were against her. You shouldn't have taken the bet if you were this scared."

"I'm not scared. She's made it through the last twenty-four hours, hasn't she? And you made sure that I'd take the bet. You doubled the stakes." Balkon took the glass Volkov handed him. "You knew I couldn't resist the chance to take it away from you like I did the last time." He took a swallow of his vodka and dropped down in the easy chair by the fireplace. His gaze shifted away from him to the burning logs. "Have you heard from either Razov or Gregor today?"

And that's why Balkon was really here, Volkov thought cynically. In spite of what he said, he was terrified that he was in over his head and the bitch would end up dead. He had a right to be panicky. When he won the bet, he'd squeeze the little prick dry. Volkov had known Balkon couldn't afford the bet, but he'd been so frustrated that he'd wanted to hurt and humiliate him as Lara had humiliated him. "No, I told you that they checked in last night. They'll call me when they've put her down."

"I wouldn't be too sure." Balkon forced a smile. "They might be stronger, but as soon as the bet was set, I started working with Lara. She's better than you'd think. And I guarantee she wouldn't want to make me angry."

"I wouldn't think so." Volkov lifted his glass in a toast. "You've had all these years to train her. Or should I say we've had all these years? You have to admit that I've done my part. Not that I haven't enjoyed every minute of it. There have been times when it's been quite satisfying." He smiled. "I suppose we should consider this weekend as graduation?"

Balkon's eyes widened in bewilderment. "What do you mean?"

"Well, you can't actually believe she'll come out of this alive. Our little experiment had to end sometime." He shrugged. "I would have preferred to finish her myself, but this will do as well. I find that I like the idea of thinking about her facedown in the forest with a broken neck. I've been getting sick and tired of your Lara lately. Those last two times that she managed to win our little challenge, it was a bit humiliating for me." Now to flick the whip and make him feel it. "My men didn't dare to laugh in my face, but I heard their bets and I saw how they looked at me after she won. That's not going to happen again. I believe this is where our paths part. I enjoyed our little games, Balkon, but we'll have no further business once she's gone."

Balkon's jaw went slack. Then he recovered. "You can't be sure you'll win."

"Sure enough. I chose my best men, and she's only a woman."

"What if you're wrong?" He moistened his lips. "And even if you're not, I've been valuable to you in other ways over the years. No one has been more loyal." When Volkov didn't speak, he added quickly, "And you might be bored with the game, but you've said a few times that you might have a use for her later. What if we continue with our usual business arrangements, and I just give her to you as a gift for any embarrassment she might have caused you?"

Yes. But Volkov kept his expression impassive. "You've always refused to do that before. You said that because she was your daughter, it would look bad to the other families."

"I'll find a way around it."

Volkov pretended to think about it. "If she wins, you'll still deliver her to me?"

Balkon nodded. "But you'll have to pay me what you owe me. That's only fair."

"Then I can hardly lose, can I?" Volkov took another sip of vodka. "Have I ever told you how I admire the way you've kept your Maria in her place all these years? A perfect combination of sex slave and meek servant. Lara might keep me amused indefinitely in that role." He smiled at him. "How clever you are, my friend. You might have come up with a way to salvage our relationship…"

AVGAR FOREST
THIRD NIGHT

Volkov's men were still together, Lara realized in frustration. Gregor and Razov were hunting as a pair, and there was no way she could take them down as long as she had to face that double threat. She'd hoped they'd split up to go after her tonight.

Yet she would find a way, she told herself instantly. But not if she allowed herself to lose confidence or let herself be intimidated by the odds. Forget being tired. There was always a way to succeed if she kept her mind clear and fear at a minimum.

"Where are you, bitch?" Razov had stopped on the trail to shout out into the darkness. "We'll get you tonight. Volkov doesn't understand why it didn't happen last night. I told him that you were so scared of us, you were probably burrowing in a cave somewhere. But he liked it when I described all the things we're going to do to you when we catch you. Do you remember what I told you last night?"

How could she forget? Ignore him. He only wanted her to speak so that he could zero in on where she was. *Don't let it get to you. It's almost over.*

When Volkov had given her this Trial six months ago, she'd realized that she'd be lucky to survive it no matter how many martial arts lessons her father had put her through. It would be two against one, and she wouldn't have their strength or experience. But she did have the advantage of being fit, lithe, and very, very fast. So she'd concentrated on learning this forest like the back of her hand. Her father had told her that Volkov would almost certainly choose Gregor and Razov, and she'd spent several nights spying at Volkov's compound watching them so that she'd know their strengths, the way they moved, how they reacted to each other. She'd been as ready as she could be when her father had dropped her off at the forest two nights ago. Her only plan was to keep out of their way and keep them moving. Let them catch glimpses of her and then vanish and make them hunt her. She'd wanted them tired and frustrated enough to make mistakes so that she might get her chance. It hadn't been easy, but she'd evaded them for the last two nights. Though she hadn't counted on how tired she would become herself or that the curses and foul descriptions about what they were going to do to her before they killed her would make her this afraid. She'd thought she could block the ugliness out, but the more exhausted she grew, the more difficult it became.

She'd done more difficult things.

Though she'd never taken a life.

Yet if she didn't take their lives, Maria would not survive. Her father had made that clear. He had no more use for her now, and he had only one use for Lara.

"It wasn't supposed to be like this." Gregor was suddenly cursing as he strode ahead of Razov. "She's only a woman. I thought we'd track her down the first night when I saw her down by the creek. I told you we should split up then and each take a different direction. I'm not going to spend another night wasting my time. I'm heading east toward the creek. You go west and circle back to meet me. I want this over."

Yes. It was the break Lara had been waiting for. She moved down the trail toward the east, taking a

shortcut so that she would arrive at the creek before
Gregor in order to position herself.

There he is.

She froze on the other side of the trail, watching
as he moved toward the creek and then bent to check
the bank for footprints. He would find them: She'd
deliberately left prints leading deeper into the woods
to the west before she'd swung up into a low tree
and moved through the branches until she was close
enough to the creek to jump into the water and wade
toward a stone bank.

Gregor had straightened and was following the trail
to the west.

She drew a deep breath. Then she was silently
moving forward. *No noise. Don't breathe. Gather your
muscles for the blow.* Precision was all-important, but
when she struck, it had to be with all her strength to
have the needed force. He was in the trees now. She
could see the beam of his flashlight on the ground as
he looked for footprints.

Then he bent lower to examine the area.

She leaped forward and struck a karate blow to the
back of his neck!

He slumped forward and she followed it up with
another blow. It wasn't necessary; the first one had
killed him. Most of the time it was impossible to kill
with a karate blow. You were lucky if you could knock
the other person unconscious. But that would not have
saved her. So she had practiced balance and precision
for hours until she could do it.

And she felt sick.

Don't be this weak, she told herself. She hadn't the
slightest doubt that he would have killed her if he'd
had the chance. Only he wouldn't have made it this

quick or easy. She turned away. She couldn't keep standing here and staring at him. It wasn't done yet. She had to go after Razov.

He should be coming from the west...

Move swiftly.

No noise.

She wasn't sure how close Razov was, but she figured she had at least ten to twenty minutes before she'd encounter him.

Move faster.

Keep an eye out for the beam of his flashlight. It was the principal thing she had to worry about. She could defeat him only if she took him by surprise.

Twenty minutes later, she saw Razov heading down the trail toward her. He was moving fast, and she had to duck to one side into the bushes to avoid the beam of his flashlight. He was ahead of her now. How to take him out? Another karate blow? Or a karate chop to stun him and then go for the—

What!

Suddenly, out of nowhere, a dark-clad man came between her and Razov!

Lara stopped, stunned, as the man's arm encircled Razov's throat and he gave a jerk that broke his neck. Razov crumpled in a heap on the path.

Dead? How could he be dead? She couldn't understand it. No, this couldn't be happening. She was the one who had to do it. It wouldn't work otherwise. He couldn't do this to her. She instinctively took a step forward with fists clenched. "What do you think you're doing? Who are you? There was only supposed to be two of you and I—"

"It's okay, you're safe." He whirled to face her. "Everything will be okay."

He was speaking in English instead of Russian and she instinctively switched to it, too. "The hell it will. You've ruined everything." She braced herself for the attack to come. "You can tell Volkov that he can't get away with cheating me like this. Come on. I'm ready for you." It was a lie. She was trying to desperately think of a strategy that might get her out of this. No surprise, and he had taken Razov down with dazzling efficiency. He was facing her, and if she could just make the strike to the jugular absolutely perfect, it might work. No choice. She could see his muscles begin to tauten and he'd be coming for her! She darted to one side and then spun and leaped toward him.

But he'd already anticipated the move and was whirling toward her, moving swiftly. Dammit, he was so fast...No time for the jugular. She spun again as her leg lifted in a kick to his abdomen. She heard him grunt with pain but then he grabbed her ankle and flipped her to face him. She had only a glimpse of a lean, taut face and glittering light blue eyes before his hand was pressing her carotid artery.

Darkness.

———◆———

Tanner was kneeling beside Lara giving her a shot when Mallory came down the path from the creek. "Gregor's down?"

Mallory nodded. "I didn't have to do it." He nodded at Lara. "She took care of it before I got the chance.

Very clean. Very neat." He looked down at his phone. "Jordan says the helicopter is on the way. We have seven minutes to get to the edge of the forest for pickup."

"Then let's move." Tanner settled Lara in a fireman's lift on his shoulder and started trotting down the path. "I want to be at the airport and on the jet by the time she comes out of the sedative. She wasn't in the least grateful about getting a little help with a nasty job. And she wasn't in a mood to listen. She tried to come after me."

"Maybe she was scared."

Tanner remembered her dark eyes glittering with fury as she'd leaped toward him. "Somehow I don't think so…"

———◆———

Something was wrong.

She was lying on a bed of some sort…a bed made of the softest leather she'd ever touched.

And she was on a plane!

She shouldn't be on a plane.

She should be in the forest.

But there was something wrong about that, too.

Something about Razov…

"No!" Her lids flew open and she jerked upright.

"Easy. No one's going to hurt you." English again. A man in his middle or late thirties. Light blue eyes, high cheekbones in a lean face, dark hair. Black sweater and black jeans. He was sitting in a seat across the aisle and straightened warily. "There's nothing wrong. You're safe."

It was all coming back to her. "The hell I am." Her

voice was shaking. "You said that before, and then you knocked me out." She got to her knees, prepared to leap at him. "You killed Razov. I was supposed to do it. Why did Volkov send you? It wasn't fair. I would have brought him down. He can't go back on his word."

"I imagine he does that quite a bit. Though I've never met him. He certainly didn't send me." He got to his feet. "And I knocked you out because I was short on time and you impressed me as not being willing to listen without taking up too much of it. But I'm ready to explain everything to you now, if you'll stop threatening me and let me do it." He added, "I'm going to go get you a cup of coffee. While I do it, I'd like you to sit there and look around and pull yourself together enough to be able to react reasonably when we have our discussion."

"You patronizing son of a bitch."

He suddenly chuckled. "It probably did sound like that. But I'm trying to handle this situation with tact, principally because I want to avoid having you leap at me and try to take me out the way you did at Avgar Forest."

"You're not succeeding."

"I was afraid of that." He made a face. "But just go along with me, Lara." He bowed mockingly. "You might feel better if you know who you're dealing with. I'm Logan Tanner and I have nothing to do with those bastards who sent you into that forest. I was sent to bring you out of there alive because I'm very good at it. I have two other employees on this plane. The pilot is Les Jordan, and Josh Mallory works with me and was down there in the forest with me." He smiled faintly. "Mallory admired the way you took out Gregor. He said it was neat and clean. Neither of them will hurt you, and they have nothing to do with Volkov or your dear papa, either." He started down the aisle. "I'll make sure that it takes me at least ten minutes to get your coffee to give you time to think about the situation and get your questions in order. The bathroom is in the rear of the plane, and you won't find any weapons. There are some parachutes in the closets, but I wouldn't advise you jumping out. You have a much better chance with me, as you'll see when we talk." Then he disappeared from view.

She stared at the door for an instant before she slowly swung her legs to the floor. She closed her eyes and took a deep breath. Think. Absorb the situation. Consider Tanner and anything she had picked up about him. She didn't know enough about what was happening to fit him into the scenario, but that wouldn't stop her from analyzing, comparing him with the men she knew. Razov hadn't had a chance with him. She hadn't, either, though she might have done better if she could have taken him by surprise. So excellent warrior skills. Clever? Probably. He'd handled her as diplomatically as possible considering the situation. She got to her feet and headed for the bathroom. Explore her surroundings. Just because Tanner had said there were no weapons, it didn't mean that was the truth. If possible, she had to find a weapon to fight him if he was as good as she suspected.

She went into the tiny bathroom and quickly relieved herself. Then she washed her face and hands to take off some of the mud and sweat of those days in the forest. It didn't do much good, but it made her feel a little fresher and better able to cope. She checked the cabinets, but there were only towels and cleaning products. No weapons.

She left the bathroom and opened the door of the closet she'd passed on the way down the corridor. Four parachutes, a first-aid kit, some rations. Nothing really useful unless she wanted to jump out of the blasted plane. Not practical until she was able to figure out how to use those parachutes and found out where the plane was heading. For all she knew they might be over the ocean.

The thought frightened her. She didn't know where she was or how much time had passed since Tanner had knocked her out. Did Volkov know about Gregor and Razov yet? What about Maria?

"Considering the parachute exit?" She whirled to see Tanner standing in the aisle behind her. He had two cups of coffee in his hands. "I really wouldn't, until you hear what I have to say. You're much better off with me."

She tensed. "And what do you have to say?" she asked. "What time is it? Do my father and Volkov know what happened with Razov and Gregor?"

"It's a little before dawn. Since I was told you had all night to dispose of Razov and Gregor, I assume Volkov won't know yet how efficient you were. But they should very shortly. We didn't have time to dispose of the bodies."

"Damn you." Her hands clenched into fists. "Why couldn't you have kept out of it?"

"Because I was given an extremely good reason not to do that. It was an offer I couldn't refuse." He stepped to the side and nodded at the seat across the aisle. "Now why don't you sit down and drink your coffee and I'll explain."

"I don't want to sit down. I want you to take me back. You've probably ruined everything, but maybe I can convince Volkov I did the kill." She ran her hand through her hair. "But if he paid you, that won't work. Maybe I can think of something else. What can I do to get you to lie to him?"

"Stop." Tanner put the coffee cup in her hand and pushed her down onto the seat. "Now listen to me, and then you can try to bribe me. Volkov didn't send me into that forest, your friend Sergai Kaskov did. He didn't like the odds you were facing and thought that you might need help."

"Kaskov? He's not my friend." Or maybe he was, but Lara had never been sure. "He should have stayed out of it. He might get Maria killed. I didn't ask for help."

"Kaskov evidently didn't care whether you wanted help or not. I've never found him to give a damn what anyone else thinks in the scheme of things. He just decided that he wanted you away from a bad situation and tapped me to get you out of it." He took a drink of his coffee. "I have experience in extraction, and my job is to whisk you away from here and out of the country. I'm to settle you somewhere you'll be safe from both your father and Volkov."

"Why you?"

"He knew I could do the job, and he offered me something that would give me enough incentive to go to any lengths to do it well. Which I will do." He smiled crookedly. "So get used to me. I agreed to take this job, and you're stuck with me until I finish it."

"You're supposed to take me out of Russia?" she asked slowly. His words were gradually sinking in and her gaze flew to his face. "Truly? You're not joking?"

"It's no joke. Kaskov said that you wouldn't be safe from Volkov while you were still in Russia. My deal was to get you out and then somewhere he wouldn't find you."

"Yes, I'll be safer out of Russia." It was difficult to believe. It was too good to be true. But she mustn't get this excited. "But that doesn't mean Volkov will stop searching for me. He never lets go of anything that he owns."

"Owns?" Tanner repeated slowly. "I don't believe I like the way that sounds."

"I don't care what you like. Volkov is what he is. He practically owns my father, so he owns me, too. It's been like that since the games started." She leaned forward, her gaze focused on his face. "But this could be a way out. If you're not lying. If Kaskov isn't playing some kind of game. He's very…strange. I've never been sure about him."

"I'm not lying, Lara," he said quietly. "I can't vouch for Kaskov, but he's going to a lot of trouble and expense if this is a game to him."

"That wouldn't matter to him. Men don't care about pain or money or trouble when it comes to their games. It's worth it to them."

"Is it?" His gaze was narrowed on her face. "I suppose there's something in what you say, but not in this case. I fully intend to get you out of here."

She met his eyes. "You really mean it," she said in wonder. She drew a deep breath and then let it out. "But it's not that easy. I can't go with you. Not unless you find a way to take Maria with us."

"Maria?" he repeated. "Your mother? I'd hardly leave her behind. Kaskov already told me that you wouldn't go without her. I had two of my men pick her up before I went after you. She should be over Finland by now. She'll be meeting us in Stockholm."

"Finland." He'd rattled off those words so casually. Why not? He had no idea what they meant to her. Or how often she'd dreamed of flying away anywhere to freedom. She'd almost done it once before, but she'd been caught…and punished.

"I hope that's okay?" Tanner was staring at her quizzically.

"I don't know if it is or not. It might be. If it's the truth."

"Would you like to talk to her?"

"Yes." She moistened her lips. "Could I?"

"I don't see why not." He smiled as he took her cup from her. "You didn't drink this. I'll get you a fresh cup when I go get Nash's phone number from Mallory. He took your mother's phone away and got rid of it so that she couldn't be traced. It's standard operating procedure. I did the same with yours. We'll replace them in Stockholm."

"It seems like a smart idea," she said absently. Then as he turned away, she suddenly called, "Tanner."

He looked back at her.

"No one's ever done anything like this for me," she said awkwardly. "If it's true. If it really works, I'll always be grateful to you. There's nothing I won't do to pay you back."

"I'll keep that in mind," he said lightly. "I'd much prefer gratitude to the fate you had in mind for me when you first opened your eyes."

"I thought you were just another enemy," she said. "I'm not used to having anyone do anything for me. It was…strange."

"But then so is our entire encounter to date." He smiled. "We'll just have to become accustomed to it, since we're going to have to be around each other."

He was gone again.

She leaned back in the seat and tried to relax. It was either a lie or the truth. She was still leaning toward thinking he had lied to her. As she had told him, she couldn't see why anyone would want to help her. She and Maria were alone in a world that had seldom shown them mercy. Why should Kaskov or this stranger bother themselves to interfere with her life?

So don't want it too much. Don't expect it to be true.

It was safer like that.

———◆———

Tanner came back fifteen minutes later and handed her his phone. "She's going to call you right away. She's fine. She gave Nash an argument, but she finally went with them without having to be persuaded. I told them I'd prefer to have it that way."

"You mean they didn't have to knock her out?" she asked sarcastically.

He nodded. "She was much more reasonable than you. She didn't go on the attack. I had to protect myself, didn't I?"

"Yes, you did. I was going to kill you if I could."

"I thought that was where you were headed."

"I still will if you're lying and they hurt Maria."

"I'm not lying." He sat down across from her. "Why do you call your mother by her first name?"

"My father didn't like it when she got pregnant. Then she compounded the sin by having a girl. I learned when I was very young that it was better for both of us not to remind him of that terrible mistake. I've always called my mother Maria and my father Anton."

"What a son of a bitch," he said softly.

"Yes, but we learned how to survive him." She was gazing impatiently down at the phone. "When is she supposed to—" The phone rang and she pressed it to answer. "Maria? Are you all right?"

"A little bewildered and suspicious, but that's all. I've been so worried about you for these past days. And then these men showed up and told me something about Kaskov and that you weren't hurt and would stay that way as long as I went along with them. Are you okay?"

"Yes, I haven't been hurt. Are they treating you well?"

"Insistent," Maria said. "But very polite. What's this all about? What does Kaskov have to do with it?"

"I have no idea about Kaskov. We hardly saw anything of him except those times he'd stop by and you'd have me play for him. He wouldn't speak more than a few words to either of us and then he'd be gone again. I don't know why he'd interfere like this. He doesn't care about anyone but himself. Maybe it was just a random impulse. Anyway, I'll take it."

"Interfere? You're not being clear, Lara."

Her mother was right. Nothing was clear at this moment. It was all guesswork. "Kaskov did something that might change everything for us. I can't promise, but there's a chance." She looked at Tanner. "We're leaving Russia. We're not coming back. You're going to be safe."

Maria was silent. "Thank God. But you're the one who has to be safe. Volkov was getting…I've been afraid for the last month. But you know Volkov isn't going to let you go."

"He won't have a choice. Once I'm free, I'm going

to stay free. If Tanner gets us out of Russia, I'll find a safe place for you and then just disappear."

"Tanner?"

Lara looked Tanner in the eye and said defiantly, "Kaskov's errand boy. But Kaskov wouldn't have sent him if he hadn't thought he could manage to get us out. You know how afraid everyone is of Kaskov, and they don't screw up. We'll trust Tanner unless he proves that we can't."

"It's really true?" Maria whispered. "It's not a trick?"

"Not as far as I know." But Lara was afraid to tell her anything more than that. They had both been disappointed before. "If it's a trick, it wasn't one of Volkov's. Tanner killed one of Volkov's men. That's good enough for me to take this chance. I just don't know why Kaskov would interfere."

"I might be able to guess. I'd watch his face when you were playing. At times there was something…" She paused and then said quietly, "It's too good to be true, you know. I'm afraid to believe it."

"Believe it," Lara said. "All I need is an opportunity, I'll take it from there." She added quickly, "Do what this Nash tells you to do until we meet in Stockholm. After that we'll talk and make decisions for ourselves. Okay?"

"It will have to be," Maria said. "I'm just having a little trouble with remembering about decisions. I haven't had the opportunity to do that for a long time. Take care, Lara." She ended the call.

"Content?" Tanner asked as he took his phone.

"No, I want you to call that Nash back and make sure he treats her very carefully. She didn't really know what was happening. It worried her."

"I don't have to call him back. He had his

instructions and I'm sure she told you she was treated very courteously. She'll have no complaints when she meets you in Stockholm." He smiled. "We don't generally harass mothers or children. And a bit of worry wouldn't have been a criminal offense."

"It depends on the person. Maria is tough, but you don't know what my mother has gone through in her life. It might have brought back memories I don't want her to have to ever think about again."

"I can't be responsible for memories," he said. "Not hers, not yours. You'll have to handle those yourselves. I can only guarantee that I'll inflict as little insult or pain as possible." His lips lifted in a lopsided smile. "Which you weren't being too careful to do yourself. 'Errand boy'? Neither word accurately describes me."

"It served its purpose." She shrugged. "Though I admit I don't like that you've been in control of my life since the moment I saw you in that forest. It makes me feel…I don't like it."

"So you decided to sting me."

"I'm sure it didn't bother you."

"No, it amused me. Still, quite a change from that moment when you were tearing up with gratitude."

"I didn't tear up. I don't cry. I meant what I said, but it's all mixed up because I'm afraid that you've been lying to me." She lifted her chin. "And I won't forgive you if you are. I'll find a way to punish you."

"I'm sure you could," he murmured. "But it's wise of you to wait until you're sure, so that you won't have to exert unnecessary energy if you're wrong." His gaze was raking her face. "You look very tired. You were out there in the forest for three nights?"

"I'm not tired." She kept her back very straight in the seat as she added sarcastically, "How could I be, when you so kindly saw that I was unconscious for the past few hours?"

"I'd bet that you were fighting exhaustion before you took that little nap. I doubt if it did you any good." He tilted his head. "But you're not going to admit it, and you'll resent it if I suggest you stop worrying and relax. You'd probably suspect my wicked motives and be all the more on edge." He got to his feet. "You never did get that coffee I promised you. I imagine you'll accept, because the caffeine will keep you alert enough to detect any of my foul plans." He smiled. "So I'll make certain that the coffee is very black and strong, and I'll send it back with Mallory to avoid you having to contend with me for a while." He was moving down the aisle toward the cockpit. "You'll have a lot in common with Mallory. He spends a good deal of his time giving me a hard time, too…"

———◆———

"Has she calmed down?" Mallory turned in the copilot's seat and gazed at Tanner as he opened the door. "Nash said her mother was pretty cool after he convinced her that nothing bad was going to happen to Lara. She was principally just confused."

Tanner nodded at Jordan who was flying the plane before he turned back to Mallory. "Calm?" he repeated thoughtfully. "I don't think she knows the meaning of the word. She's like a beautifully balanced dagger ready to strike at the first hint of an attack. And I don't think it's because she's feeling threatened by the situation. I have an idea she's like that all the time."

"One can hardly blame her," Mallory said, "considering how she grew up. The attack must have always been right around the corner." He snapped his fingers. "But that's right, you were too busy to read that file Kaskov left for you. That's okay, you'd probably have found it boring anyway. But it might help you to control her since we have to get her settled."

"Really? I hardly think so. She has a particular dislike of being controlled."

"And you have a passion for being in control," Mallory said. "My, my. What a conundrum. What are we going to do?"

"I don't have to do anything." Tanner grinned. "I can leave it up to you. You read the file. Deal with her. Reassure her, so that she won't choose the parachute option." He jerked his thumb toward the door. "But take a pot of strong coffee with you and watch your back."

"What a challenge." Mallory got to his feet. "But I will persevere. I'm always better with people than you are. You're far too impatient."

"Are we back to those dealers again?"

"Why should I let you forget them? You caused me a full two hours of smoothing their egos and then coaxing them to stay." He passed Tanner and opened the door. "If you need something to do while you're sitting up here as I do your job, her file is in my bag beside the chair."

"So?"

"Just thought I'd tell you. You're fighting it, but you're curious as hell. You're always like that when you have a hand you don't quite know how to play. Shall I give you a teaser?" He didn't wait for an answer. "The bastards called them the Trials. They'd get together and choose a task to give Lara to accomplish in a certain amount of time, usually six months or less. Usually something dangerous, almost always illegal. Nothing easy, nothing familiar. Then Volkov would bet a certain amount against her, and her father would choose if he wanted to accept it. He always did. Then her father would give her as much tutoring as he thought she'd need and then she'd have to do the Trial. She did the first one when she came back from Moscow after the competition. I think she was about eleven. She lost that Trial and ended up in the hospital with a broken leg and a concussion. Is that intriguing enough for you?"

He left the cockpit before Tanner could answer.

Crafty bastard, Tanner thought. He knew damn well he'd be intrigued and pissed off at that "teaser." Yet the last thing he wanted was to feel pity or protectiveness toward Lara Balkon. Mallory was right, he did know how to handle people better than Tanner—except when he applied himself. He'd always been tough when necessary, but he genuinely liked most people and was interested in what made them tick. It had taken Tanner a long time before he'd learned to accept Mallory's intrusion into his own privacy. He might never have done it if they hadn't been in the service together. He was too guarded to let anyone that close.

But Mallory was right about Tanner's curiosity. It sometimes overcame his instinct to keep the world at a distance. He was definitely curious about Lara Balkon. Probably natural enough considering how they'd come together. He'd been feeling a wild mixture of feelings toward her since she'd turned and attacked him in the forest: wariness, respect, impatience, and, yes, even attraction. She was beautiful and fiery and so complex he couldn't deny he'd had to smother moments of intense arousal.

Or it might be the music. He was having trouble looking at her without remembering the sound of that Rachmaninoff concerto she'd been playing on the disk that night Kaskov had pulled him into this. That was weird in itself. It was all strange and complicated, and the only thing he was sure about was that he didn't like this responsibility that Kaskov had wished on him.

So give in to the curiosity. Read the notes. The fascination would disappear once there was no longer mystery.

He went forward and reached for Mallory's bag, then sat down in the copilot's seat as he took out the file.

CHAPTER

3

Hello, I'm Mallory. I'm supposed to provide you with coffee and reassurance."

Lara looked up to see a tall, good-looking, sandy-haired man coming down the aisle toward her. He was carrying a tray with a pot of coffee and cups, and his smile lit his face with warmth. She warily braced herself. "I'll take the coffee. I don't need your reassurance. Why should I trust anything you say? I don't know either you or Tanner."

He shrugged. "Because it's easier and anyone can see what a magnificent human being I am?" He was pouring coffee in a cup. "But I don't imagine that would go very far with you, considering your background. Particularly since your first encounter was with Tanner. He has many phenomenal qualities, but sometimes he doesn't play well with others. He's often too quiet, and he's always watching and trying to see beyond what you want him to see. You have to accept that, along with the knowledge that he's brilliant and will usually be several steps ahead of you, which can be very frustrating." He handed her the cup. "But it's balanced by the fact that once he accepts you, he'll never desert you and you couldn't be safer."

"Did he tell you to say that?" she asked cynically.

"No, that's personal experience." He grinned as he poured himself a cup of coffee. "I thought I'd throw it in for good measure. Since your meeting was fraught with violence, I knew you'd need a more neutral view of him."

"You're hardly neutral. It's clear you're good friends."

"Yes, but I pride myself on never letting that cloud my judgment. You have to do that with friends." He sat down beside her. "I suppose you've found that, too?"

"No, I've never had that many friends. Just my mother and Maxim." She took a sip of coffee. "And I'd think that it would be terrible to have to judge your friends."

"That's not what I said. The whole point is not to judge them, but to keep them from dominating your life." He looked down at his coffee. "Maxim?"

"Maxim Petrov. He lived in the village near the compound. He taught me to play the piano." She frowned. "Though I guess you couldn't call him a friend. He yelled at me a lot in the beginning, and once he slapped me. But that didn't matter. He was right, I wasn't playing it the way it should be played. It was important that I didn't make mistakes. I had to serve the music."

"No, I wouldn't say that fits the description of a friend. Did he make you unhappy?"

"Of course not. Are you a fool? He was wonderful. He...filled me with melody." Her face was suddenly luminous. "And he taught me to listen for the music and then how to let it flow out of me. Much better than any friend."

"I can see that." His gaze was narrowed on her face. "How long did he teach you?"

"Maria started to take me to his house in the village when I was three. My last lesson was after I came back from Moscow after the competition. They'd delivered the piano they'd given me as a prize, and he came to tune it. He told me I had to be worthy of such a fine instrument or he would no longer be proud of me. He went away the next day. Maria told me he'd left the village." She added quietly, "But I thought it might happen someday, and I was ready. I knew that I just had to keep doing everything that Maxim had taught me, and the music would still be there for me."

Mallory cleared his throat. "Very good thinking. And you still had your mother."

She nodded. "Maria was always there." She suddenly frowned. "But you took me away from my piano. If it's as fine an instrument as Maxim said, it might be too expensive for me to replace. Though that doesn't really matter, it's still part of me." So much a part, she thought. She'd started and ended every day at that piano. Just the thought of being without it was throwing her into a panic. "You said Tanner is brilliant. Do you think that he can find a way to get me my piano?"

"I wouldn't be surprised, or one that's comparable. But that's not important. First, we have to get you settled."

"It *is* important. If he can't get it for me, I'll have to find a way to do it myself. And I'll get myself settled after I make sure Maria is safe. Just getting me free is probably all that Kaskov wanted from you."

"That wasn't the deal," Mallory said. "And Tanner always keeps his word. I'm afraid he'll insist that we keep to the original arrangement."

She shook her head. "No. What difference does it make to you if I want to be on my own? Just because I've lived in a small town in Russia all my life doesn't mean I can't take care of myself. I've had to go places and do things that would surprise you. I won't be stupid enough to get killed and mess up Tanner's deal."

"I'm very aware you can take care of yourself," he said gently. "Kaskov didn't let us go into this blind. But why not accept a little help?"

"I'm safer on my own." Then when Mallory didn't speak, she said stiltedly, "Look, Volkov is going to be coming after me as soon as he figures out that I'm on the run. What if Kaskov changes his mind and makes a deal with him to turn me over to him? Or what if Tanner decides to make a deal with Volkov? I'll be better off if I don't depend on anyone but myself. You can tell that to Tanner."

"You'd do better to tell him yourself." He was refilling her cup. "He doesn't take bad news at all well, and I try to keep him in a good humor as much as possible. Except when I manage to strike on a subject that's just too enjoyable to miss the fireworks."

"I'll talk to him," she said curtly. "I just thought you—"

"Were more approachable," he finished. "Yes, I am. Which is why he sent me to you. That reassurance thing…" He grinned. "See, you've already told me about Maxim and the piano and the fact that you're going to run out on us at the soonest possible moment."

Yes, she had done that, she realized. She was usually more wary, but there was something about Mallory that was appealing and unassuming. Perhaps because he had not tried to hide anything about himself or Tanner. Even now he was being open and frank. "Nothing I told you was important. Nothing I would have tried to hide. You just didn't matter."

"Oh, that hurt." He flinched. "Cut to the quick."

She found herself smiling reluctantly. "I don't think so."

"Maybe not. You've obviously begun to see right through me." He got to his feet. "But you might not want to chat with me anymore at the moment since I've made you a little wary. So I'll leave you to rest, and I'll go find Tanner and do what you ordered me to do and see if he can think of a way to get your piano to wing its way to you. However, pianos are a bit bulky to do that." He picked up the blanket from the chair where she'd been lying when she woke and draped it across her shoulders. "I'll be sure to report back to you."

"I don't want to rest. And I certainly don't need this blanket." But she was a little chilly and the blanket felt good. "I'm not wary of you. I believe you're harmless."

"Another blow." He was walking up the aisle. "But I'm definitely harmless to you, Lara. Remember that."

She didn't answer. She was tired and in spite of those two cups of coffee she was a little drowsy and didn't want to be on guard right now. Mallory was probably more dangerous than she thought. When she was around any of Volkov's men, she was aware of exactly who and what they were; absolutely she was wary. But neither Mallory nor Tanner gave off those ugly vibes. She felt almost comfortable with Mallory, though there was no question Tanner was one of the most dangerous men she'd ever run across. There was a sleek-panther aura about him, a watchfulness that was mesmerizing. Yet she hadn't felt threatened— more excitement and a kind of eagerness. So she'd give herself this moment to catch her breath and try to relax before she started to think of the challenge that lay before her. She mustn't be afraid. She must think of this as another Trial. She had to handle this opportunity and these new people who had come into her life very carefully.

Or she might not get another chance.

Tanner was sitting just outside the cockpit as he watched Mallory stride toward him down the aisle. "Mission accomplished?"

"You tell me." He dropped down in the seat next to him. "How long have you been sitting there eavesdropping? Is there anything I can still fill you in on?"

"I wasn't eavesdropping. I just wanted to get out of the cockpit."

"And away from her file while you had Jordan next to you seeing how it affected you. Not pleasant reading, was it? How angry did it make you?" He was scanning Tanner's expression. "Ah, the great poker face. That much, huh?"

"Stop trying to get a reaction," he said coolly. "She's a job that I have to do and I'll do it. I have to know everything I might contend with. Kaskov probably gave me that file for a reason, and I won't let him manipulate me. He used Sandrino to tip the balance, and I'm going to hold him to it no matter what else he throws at me."

"Of course you are," Mallory said. "I don't doubt that for a minute. But I'm glad you read the file. I don't want to be the only one who feels the need to kill both those bastards." He got to his feet. "Well, I'll go back to the cockpit and keep Jordan company. I wouldn't want him to feel insulted because we both deserted him."

"By all means," Tanner said dryly. "You're pushing it, Mallory."

"I feel like pushing it." He glanced back to where Lara was sitting. "When you were eavesdropping, did you hear her talking about Maxim, her piano teacher?"

"I wasn't eavesdropping," Tanner said. Then he met Mallory's eyes. "Yes, I heard it."

"Good. Since I trust your acumen and ability to read both situations and odds better than anyone else on the planet, I have a question to ask you: What do you think happened to Maxim?"

"I don't have all the facts."

"What happened to Maxim?"

Tanner shrugged. "Either her father or Volkov killed him after he left her that day. Her mother covered it to shelter Lara as much as she could."

"Anything else?"

"Lara probably knows it happened, but she doesn't want to admit it to herself. Sometimes you can take only so much pain."

"Damn," Mallory said. "That's not what I wanted you to say. I was trying to be an optimist."

"Then you shouldn't have asked me. And you shouldn't have given me that file to read." He shrugged. "Serves you right."

"It was worth it. I didn't want to be alone in this." He made a face. "I didn't want *her* to be alone. Now I've thrown it into your court and I feel much better about it." He opened the cockpit door. "Though I do feel bad about Maxim."

"Then make up your own story about him. Maybe I'm wrong."

Mallory sighed. "That hardly ever happens."

He closed the cockpit door.

Tanner didn't move for a few moments. Then he got to his feet and moved down the aisle. He should never have read that file. He needed to keep his distance from everything to do with this job of Kaskov's. And he shouldn't be going down this aisle and making contact with Lara at this moment. It was too soon after he'd been immersed in those years when she'd been fighting the world just to stay alive. Yet he was irresistibly drawn to see her as she was now, to make the connection between her and the child she had been. Stupid. Grossly sentimental. A mistake.

Lara was leaning back in her seat, her eyes closed. Dozing?

No. Her eyes were opening and she was suddenly alert and looking at him. She scrambled to an upright position. "What are you doing? Is something wrong?"

He shook his head. "I just wanted to tell you that we'll be in Stockholm in another couple of hours. We're landing at a private airport, and Nash should be delivering your mother shortly before we get in. She'll be waiting for you."

"She's still okay?"

"Nash would have told me if there was a problem. Is there anything else you want to know?"

"No. Yes." She hesitated. "Did Mallory ask you about my piano?"

"I understood there was a discussion. We'll have to work around it."

"So it's no. You should have just said it. I'll find a way to get it myself."

"I didn't say no. Don't put words in my mouth. And you'll not think about getting it yourself until I say it's not going to screw up my plans." He drew a deep breath. "You'll get your damn piano, but it will be on my terms."

She was just looking at him.

He muttered a curse. "Never mind. I'll send Mallory to talk to you. He seems to be on your wavelength."

She was frowning. "You're…different. Why?"

"I'm not different. How would you know? Different from what? You don't know anything about me."

"That's true. We don't know anything about each other."

But he *did* know her. He felt as if he could read her better than he did Mallory. Every word, every defensive posture, the stubbornness, the independence, the wariness, that passionate protectiveness for her mother because she was the only one on earth who gave a damn for her. And he could trace it all back to those blasted files.

She tilted her head, studying him. "I think you were trying to be kind to me. You were going to give me the piano, but I couldn't be sure why, and I said things that made you angry. I didn't mean to do it. I just had to make certain that you knew I didn't expect it. No one has to give me anything. I'll get it for myself."

"I'll be sure that I remember that." He thought for a minute before he added, "But from now on, it might be wise if you remember that I'm being paid for every-thing I do for you. No favors. So just ask. If you want or need anything, you come to me and tell me."

"But wouldn't that be a favor from Kaskov?"

He wasn't getting through to her, he thought in exasperation. "That shouldn't count. I'm willing to bet that Kaskov needs to chalk up quite a few favors on the good side to balance against his murky past."

"I see." She nodded solemnly. "Then you think I should write a thank-you card to Kaskov for my piano?"

"Not until I manage to—" He stopped. "You're joking. You set me up." He added softly, "Where did that come from?"

She smiled faintly. "You were treating me as if I were a half-wit child. How could I resist?"

"Evidently you couldn't. I didn't expect a sense of humor."

"But even when you were trying to be kind, you were still trying to control who I am and how I should behave." She was gazing thoughtfully at him. "Maybe I shouldn't blame you. Mallory didn't try to control me, but he said something about Kaskov not letting either of you go into this blind. Which probably meant that Kaskov knew all about the Trials and told you about them." She added wearily, "I didn't think that he did, but I shouldn't be surprised. Even though he didn't visit my father's or Volkov's compounds very often, I could tell they were intimidated by him. Maybe they even let him into the gambling." Her smile was suddenly reckless. "And perhaps the reason you showed up in that forest was that he had some twisted idea how he could cheat both of them and win the bet. You *did* kill Razov."

"Yes, I did. But he wouldn't have done that," Tanner said firmly. "Kaskov's not one of my favorite people, but I'd bet that wasn't why he hired me to get you out of Russia."

"You'd bet?" she repeated bitterly. "But that's always what it's about, isn't it? With my father, with Volkov, with all those gorillas who'd lay their bets on whether or not I'd fail. I did fail sometimes, you know."

"I know you did," he said quietly. "But I would have liked to have been there to see those failures."

She frowned. "What?"

"Because I believe that there would have been more to learn from them than from anyone else's successes."

She blinked. "I wasn't expecting you to know that," she said slowly. "When I first started with the Trials, most of the time I had to teach myself how to do them. It was so *hard*. They deliberately chose things I knew nothing about. But then I realized that it was like playing a new piece on the piano. I had to just keep on and learn from every mistake until I had it perfect." She moistened her lips. "How did you know?"

"I could see the progression as you moved from Trial to Trial, and what you brought to them from what you'd learned in the past. I have a talent for that kind of thing."

She frowned. "I don't know if I like that."

He smiled wryly. "Practically no one in my circle does. But I promise I won't use it against you." He added deliberately, "And you can bet on it."

"No bets for me," she said curtly. "Not ever."

"Your choice. Perfectly understandable. But there are bets, and then there are bets. It's all how you play the game."

"I don't play it at all."

"Pity. You might be very good at it." He smiled. "But we'll discuss that some other time. Right now, I want to convince you that no matter what Kaskov might have in mind as a long-range goal, he would never have involved me if it had anything to do with your archnemesis, Volkov. Kaskov researched me very thoroughly, and he'd know that I wouldn't go along with it. He wouldn't waste his time."

She frowned doubtfully. "Maybe." She bit her lower lip. "But Volkov might know about Gregor and Razov by now. And the first thing he'll do is to check whether Maria is still at home. He'd know I wouldn't do anything without her. When he finds out she's not there, he'll start hunting. I have to get to her before he does."

"A few hours…"

"If you're telling the truth. *If* she's really going to meet us in Stockholm. Perhaps you're just telling me that to keep me from causing you trouble."

"A few hours," he repeated. "They don't know yet. I have someone watching and reporting from the forest. I'll let you know when I hear that they do know." He bent down and took her chin between his thumb and forefinger and looked into her eyes. "I promise. It would be very stupid of me to lie to you at this early point in our relationship because it would cause me boundless problems later when I'll have to count on you trusting me. I want this job to go smoothly."

She gazed at him searchingly. "Then you'll probably be disappointed. Maybe you should have asked for more money from Kaskov. Volkov isn't going to give me up easily. At first, the Trials were a way of getting revenge and punishing me, but lately they've become more intricate and I can feel him building toward something. He's not going to be satisfied until he finishes whatever his master plan is for me."

"Revenge?" His eyes were narrowed. "I thought it was just a case of two sadistic lowlifes using a kid in their games. You couldn't have been more than twelve when this started."

"Oh, that was my father. It was more than that to Volkov." She smiled sardonically. "Evidently Kaskov either didn't know it all or didn't want to share it with you. Well, neither do I." She leaned back in her seat. "You said that you had someone watching the forest. Will you let me know what's happening?"

He nodded. "As soon as I get a report."

"Thank you."

"You're welcome," he said mockingly. "Always glad to oblige."

"You're making fun of me." She gazed at him soberly. "But I realize you could be making this more difficult for me if you chose. I'm grateful that you aren't doing that."

His smile faded as he looked at her. "I figure you've had enough problems to contend with since I met you." Then he added dryly as he turned away, "Besides, I've noticed you're very good at karate. I wouldn't want to get on your bad side."

* * *

AVGAR FOREST

"What do you mean, she's gone?" Volkov asked harshly. "Didn't you tell her she was to stay here until we picked her up and could verify the kills?"

"Of course I did," Balkon said. "She couldn't have misunderstood." He looked down at Razov. "And she wouldn't have been afraid since she'd managed to get rid of both of them. You saw how she took care of Gregor. There wouldn't have been any reason for her to run away." He frowned. "But she wouldn't have run anyway. She's very careful about what effect her actions have on Maria."

Volkov was on his knees examining Razov. "If she did manage to kill them both..." He began to swear. "But she didn't kill Razov. Whoever killed him took him from behind and broke his neck. Lara would have been too small and wouldn't have had the strength for a move like that."

"She might have been able to do it." Balkon added suspiciously, "Are you sure you're not trying to get out of paying me?"

"Call Maria," Volkov ordered. "Stop arguing. Someone else did that kill. You fool, something's *wrong*. Who would have tried to help Lara? Was she sleeping with one of your men?"

Balkon quickly shook his head. "They know she's off limits. She doesn't see anyone." He reached for his phone. "All she does is practice for the next Trial and play that damn piano." He was punching in the number. He listened and then looked up. "It's out of service."

"Of course it is." Volkov got to his feet. "Lara's managed to get her away. She's probably been planning this move ever since she tried to run the last time." He was motioning to two of his men on the path ahead. "I told you to make certain that she wouldn't try that again. You weren't hard enough on her. You should have left it to me."

"I handled it right. I had to go through Maria. It's the only thing that works with Lara."

"And look what's happened. She had to have found a way to get someone to help her. She wouldn't have been able to do it on her own."

"No one in Avgar would dare to get in the way of the Trials." Balkon moistened his lips. "They're too afraid of you." He smiled weakly. "And me. We make a wonderful team."

"You're nothing to me or to anyone else in either of our families," Volkov snarled. "I would have gotten rid of you years ago if I hadn't needed you. I can't believe that now when I've almost finished with the bitch's final lessons, you screw it up. I won't stand for it. You're going to find Lara and whoever took her. We're both going to send our men all over Russia and you're going to deliver her to me. Do you understand?"

"I understand," Balkon said eagerly. "You know I have contacts everywhere. Trust me. I'll do it even if I have to go to Moscow to find her."

"You'll find her if you have to go to the ends of the earth," Volkov said coldly. "Use Maria, use anyone else you have to, but bring her to me. Now get moving!"

"We're landing." Lara was looking out the window as Tanner came down the aisle. "Is that the airport? The scenery looked beautiful as we flew in, but the airport is out in the middle of nowhere."

"Which is the best place for us to be since we have no documents, and my friend who owns this facility doesn't appreciate attention from the authorities." He leaned over and fastened her seat belt. "It's a small world and there are always people who want to make it even smaller by selling information." He sat down beside her and fastened his seat belt. "We won't be here long. I just wanted to rendezvous with your Maria and pick up some equipment before we took off again for somewhere safer."

She stiffened. "Where?"

"I'm weighing our options. I'm making a few calls and I'll have a decision for you by tonight."

"What if I don't accept your decision?"

"Then we might have problems," Tanner said. "But we won't borrow trouble until we have to." He smiled wryly. "Though I haven't allowed myself much time to persuade you that I'm almost always right, since I want to get you out of here as soon as possible. I have an idea that might be as much a difficulty as it proved in Avgar Forest."

"You didn't find it that difficult," she said quietly. "We both know that. But it was only because I wasn't prepared. I'd make sure it wouldn't happen like that again."

"I'm quite certain you would. So I'd better change the subject to keep you from deciding you should try to prove yourself," he said. "I got a report from the man I left in Avgar Forest. Volkov and your endearing father found the bodies of Gregor and Razov, and they weren't pleased. There was a minor explosion between them when they found Razov. Volkov knew you hadn't taken him down."

"Of course he did," she said between set teeth. "I wouldn't have been able to kill him from behind with a hold like that. I don't have the height or the strength. I'd even considered it, and then I discarded it. Volkov has studied everything about me and would realize that. That's why I was so frantic when I woke up and found out you'd done it. If you wanted Kaskov's money that bad, you should have just waited and let me kill Razov. It might have given us more time."

"I humbly apologize. You'll have to forgive me if I didn't want to waste the time waiting around to watch you dispose of a man I thought was probably a dangerous killer. Particularly when I wasn't sure that you were capable of doing it."

"Then you should have known. Mallory said Kaskov hadn't let you go into it blind. Research is everything. I found that out during my first year doing the Trials. You have to know what to expect."

"The first year…" He tilted his head. "That was when they sent you out in that speedboat to distract a smuggler who was trying to interfere with Volkov's heroin traffic. It was one of your failures." His expression hardened. "A broken leg and a concussion. I suppose you deserved that?"

"It doesn't matter what I deserved. You have to accept whatever happens if you don't do whatever you must to succeed. I was too scared, and I hadn't researched that speedboat to find out what it would do if I pushed it too hard. I got too close to Dimitri and he swung a boat hook at me. I didn't know anything about boats. I'd never been out of the village except for that trip to Moscow. My father had just given me a few lessons before they sent me out there in the ocean with my orders." She smiled bitterly. "I had to go on a few other trips after that and I failed one more, but then I started doing my research and I learned how to win. Volkov didn't like that, so they switched me to something that would be more challenging. I wasn't being entertaining enough."

"Not enough broken bones or concussions?"

"I got the broken bone from that smuggler, Dimitri. But the concussion was from my father. He doesn't like to lose." She smiled crookedly. "Volkov wasn't pleased, he said my father was lucky that I hadn't been permanently damaged and then what would they have done?"

"Yes, there's always that to consider. No kid to beat up on? No wonder Volkov was upset."

"I didn't tell you that to make you feel sorry for me. I don't want your pity. But it was important that I learned the value of research." She frowned. "Which you should have done."

He nodded slowly. "You're probably right. I believe in research. I use it in my business constantly. There were just a few things about this job that made me more careless than usual about applying it. I'd already had to move too quickly, and I wanted to get you out of there."

She gazed at him. "You're apologizing?"

"I'm explaining. There's a difference."

"But you said I was right." She smiled. "So there's not much difference."

He held up his hands. "I surrender."

Her smile faded. "But it's not because you were feeling sorry for me? I don't need that."

"Would I dare?" He shook his head. "No one needs pity less than you, Lara." He paused. "But I should tell you that your father and Volkov were in a rage. Volkov appeared particularly angry about losing his favorite punching bag. They tried to get hold of your mother, and that's when they realized that you'd done a flit. Volkov sent off your father with orders to bring you back."

"That's all right as long as they can't get hold of Maria." Her gaze flew to his face. "You told me the truth? She'll be there when we land?"

"I told you the truth. Not everyone lies, Lara."

"Most people I know do." She rubbed her temple. "And I'm confused, and I don't know why Kaskov would do this when I've hardly said more than a few sentences to him all the times he visited me. It bothers me. I don't want to trade a Volkov for a Kaskov."

"That won't happen. Kaskov's in a different league. That doesn't mean he's less dangerous, but he operates out of his own playbook. He didn't confide in me why he wanted you out of Russia except that he didn't want you killed in that forest." He met her eyes. "And he knows how I operate, and he realized when I took the job that I'd be in complete control. So it doesn't matter what he wants from now on. The only one you have to worry about is me. I'll call all the shots."

"Complete control," she repeated. "I don't think so, Tanner."

"Then you'll have to argue with me later," he said coolly. "But haven't I removed Kaskov from your current list of those you need to worry about? I can only eliminate so many threats at one time." He tapped his chest. "Better the devil you know."

Her searching gaze had not left his own. "Are you a devil, Tanner?"

"It depends on who you ask. I've been called worse. I like my own way and I don't stop until I get it. That doesn't make me popular." He smiled crookedly. "Certainly not with you, Lara. The only thing I can promise you is that I'm nothing like the devils you've been accustomed to all your life. Completely different breed."

She didn't speak for a moment. "That might be enough," she said slowly. "You can't be worse. I'll just have to research you to know how to get what I want from you."

He chuckled. "You really shouldn't be so frank about your intentions. Deception is the way to go when you're dealing with an adversary. You'll never win the game that way."

"I told you, I don't play games. You said I had to deal with the devil I know. But I don't know you well enough. I can't win unless I research you and find your faults and strengths." She nodded. "So that's what I'll do." She added, "But I've already found that you don't like lies or deceptions. Whenever we speak, you keep digging and probing until everything is clear and on the table between us. So that advice you just gave me was exactly how not to get what I want. You'd only fight me."

"Very true. But wouldn't it be easier to just let me run the show? It will be much more comfortable for you."

"No, it wouldn't." They'd reached the ground and the plane was bumping down a runway. Maria. In a moment she was going to see Maria and find out if all of this had been truth or only a cruel elaborate trick by Volkov to raise her hopes and then dash them. She unbuckled her seat belt. "But I can't talk to you any- more right now, Tanner. I have to get off this plane. I have to *see* her."

"Yes, you do." He undid his seat belt and was heading for the door. "And you will. I do play games, but not that kind." He motioned to Mallory, who had come out of the cockpit. "Okay?"

Mallory nodded. "They're opening the door and

putting down the steps." He grabbed a suitcase from the coat closet by the door. "Better take this. Tanner thought you might need it." He tossed a Sherpa jacket over Lara's shoulders. "Wear it. It's colder out there."

She put it on impatiently as she heard sounds on the other side of the door. Then the door was sliding open and she was flying down the steps!

"Lara!" Maria was running toward her. "I was afraid to hope. It was like a miracle…"

Then Lara was in her arms, holding her tight. "I know. I know. Me, too. But maybe it's not." She pushed her back and looked at her. "They treated you well? You weren't lying about Nash?"

Maria shook her head. "I just didn't understand. I was afraid Volkov was playing a trick to hurt you." She tenderly cupped Lara's face in her two hands. "You really got away from them?"

"*We* got away from them." She was trying to keep the tears from falling as she went back into her mother's arms. "And we're never going back. You're not going to have to worry about them ever again. I'll find a safe place for you."

"Shh, now isn't the time to talk about that." She looked beyond Lara to Tanner standing a few yards away. "You brought Lara to me? You must be the Logan Tanner that Nash was telling me about." She was studying him. "I believe we all have a lot to talk about. Can you find a place where we can do that?"

"That's not on a plane," Lara added quickly. "Not yet."

"Right. I'm very glad to meet you, Madam Balkon," Tanner said. "From what I've heard about you from your daughter, you must be an extraordinary woman."

"Maria." She was still looking at Lara. "Call me Maria."

"Whatever." He smiled and waved his hand toward the building across the tarmac. "Maria, I thought we might need a bite to eat and a little neutral ground, so I asked Oliver Radkork, the manager of the airport, to let us use his office facilities and his apartment for the rest of the day. If you'll take Lara over there and get settled, I'll see if I can get Oliver to recommend something good from a restaurant in town to deliver." He smiled. "If that's all right with you?"

"It's fine. Thank you." She looked at Lara. "Thank you for everything." Then she slipped her arm around Lara's waist and led her away. "Come on. Let's get inside out of this chill. You need a shower and I need a hot cup of tea and a lot of information from you. Nash kept telling me I'd have to ask Tanner every question I asked him, which did me no good at all. I hope to hell you had better luck getting something from Tanner."

"He wasn't hesitant about talking to me if that's what you mean. Whether it's true or not…" She glanced back at Tanner, who was still talking to Mallory. "He brought you to me, that was the truth. That's all that's important now. We'll decide the rest later."

CHAPTER

4

I'm very impressed by Mama Bear," Mallory murmured to Tanner. "She's not what I expected. Lara was so protective of her that I thought she'd be more…helpless. And that photo Kaskov gave you didn't do her justice. She's very attractive, almost as stunning as her daughter." He looked critically at Maria's dark hair swept back in a plain chignon and her features that were almost classic though without even a hint of makeup. "When Kaskov visited Lara and had her play for him, maybe he was really after the mother. What do you think?"

"I think you're way off base about Kaskov. But I agree that Maria is unexpected. She's very strong. So it's a puzzle why she could let her daughter take the punishment she has." He was watching as the two women disappeared into the airport office. "Exceptional affection and protectiveness on both sides. Understandable. Very natural that the closeness would be that extreme considering what they've shared through the years."

"You're taking her apart, piece by piece." Mallory smiled. "I assume you have a reason other than my idle query?"

"Your queries are seldom idle," Tanner said. "They almost always have an objective. And I'm taking her apart because I just realized that I have to understand her as well as I do Lara. As you say, she's strong. She'll fight me if she believes I'm doing something that isn't in the best interest of the team."

"Team?"

"That's how I'll have to think of them until I get Maria on my side." He grimaced. "I'm going to have to call Kaskov and ask him a few questions."

"About Maria?"

"And several other subjects."

"Sandrino?"

"Definitely Sandrino." He turned away. "Why don't you see about setting up a decent dinner. A mellow atmosphere will ease my way this evening. I don't know how long this call will take."

To his surprise he was able to get past a secretary to Nikolai in under thirty minutes and then was instantly put through to Kaskov. "All is going well, I assume?" Kaskov asked. "Lara Balkon is out of Russia and not injured?"

"We're outside Stockholm and I've brought Lara together with her mother. They're both safe, and I'm getting ready to make final transfer plans. What about Sandrino?"

"I'm making progress," Kaskov said. "I'm sure I won't disappoint you."

"Progress isn't good enough. I want facts. How far have you gotten?"

"I know Sandrino was in Moscow about the time you told me you'd tracked him down to Kazan."

"That's all?"

"That's more than you've found out from anyone else. Patience, Tanner."

"Are you playing me, Kaskov?" Tanner asked softly.

"A good question. But you're much better at that than I am. And you're too valuable for me to break faith with you when I might need your services in the future. I should be able to give you what you need by the time you finish my job." He paused. "But I understand Volkov and Balkon are already in a fury trying to find her. Balkon is asking a lot of questions, and he'll eventually get answers if he pays enough. That final transfer had better be made quickly, and be far away from Stockholm. It's definitely too close for me. Where are you taking her?"

"Perhaps I'll tell you...when the job is finished."

Kaskov chuckled. "Tit for tat? Just so you don't make the mistake of using her against me. That's not permitted. I haven't made my final arrangements for her yet."

"I imagine she might have a few objections to you doing that," he said dryly. "It's clear you don't know her that well."

"And it's clear you think you do. No, I admit I wasn't really interested in anything about Lara but her music." He paused. "Did you play the DVD I sent with you?"

Tanner was tempted to lie, but that would be an admission that the answer mattered to him. "Yes."

"How many times?"

The son of a bitch. "She's very good." He changed the subject. "But she's also exceptionally difficult. I might have trouble with her. And Maria Balkon was a surprise to me. They're close and might present a united front that will make it necessary to separate them to avoid problems."

"Separate them…" Kaskov repeated. "From what I've observed in my time with them, that might be a challenge. Actually, the idea is amusing. I'm glad that you're the one that's going to do it. Do tell me how it works out."

"I'll be sure to do that." He kept his temper. "But I'd like to avoid a radical step like that if I can. So I want you to tell me everything you know about Maria Balkon and I'll see if I can use persuasion. I hope you paid more attention to Maria than you did Lara."

"Only her attitude toward Lara, but naturally she was part of the picture when I made the decision. You're right, Maria Balkon is an interesting problem…"

———◆———

"You've told me everything, Lara?" Maria asked. "All Tanner wants is to take us away somewhere safe until Kaskov finishes making his arrangements? What arrangements?"

"I have no idea." Lara held up her hand as Maria opened her lips. "And Tanner didn't ask. He made it clear this is just a job and as soon as it's finished, he's gone. But not until then. He has some kind of code where his work is concerned." She frowned. "He's probably going to get in my way."

"A code isn't bad." Maria's lips twisted bitterly. "Though very rare. I can't remember either one of us running across anyone else who has one in all these years."

"Maxim," Lara said quietly. "He had one about the music and he taught it to me."

Maria nodded. "I'd forgotten. Of course he had a code." She quickly changed the subject. "So how is Tanner going to get in your way?"

"We don't know anything about him, so there's no way we can really trust him. I have to find a secure place for you that only you and I know about. That's the only way I can be certain you'll be safe."

"And then you'll go and lead Volkov and Anton away from me?" Maria was shaking her head. "No, Lara. That's not the way it's going to be."

"That's the way it has to be. If I have you safe, then I'll be able to go wherever I need to so that I'll be free, too."

"While you're looking over your shoulder and waiting for him to find you? He *will* find you eventually, Lara. The only value Anton ever had for Volkov was that he could use him to get to you. First with the Trials, and then with the fact that Anton's family has contacts with cartels all over the world that he can tap for information. That's how he found us before."

"But we never managed to get out of Russia that time, only to the Ukraine border. It will be different now. I'll make sure of it."

"You'll try," Maria said softly. "And if you don't succeed, it will only be you that suffers. That's been your philosophy all these years, but it's going to stop. You're right, we do have more of a chance now. But we're not going to waste it with you trying to persuade me to hide away while you go on the run and enjoy that nonexistent freedom you're telling me about. So we'll come up with a way that makes sense to me. One that won't involve either of us hiding away and still being a victim." Her lips were trembling as she tried to smile. "We've had enough of that, haven't we?"

Lara flew across the room and into her arms. "Yes," she whispered. "But none of it was your fault. You should let me do this."

"Let you lose all the joy and the music?" She held her closer and then let her go. "Because that's what it might mean, and I couldn't bear it, Lara. So you'll let me have my way in this. Say it."

She was silent. "I'll let you have your way if I can. But only if I can see another path that will keep you safe."

"Then we'd better start exploring," Maria said. "And one of the paths might be Tanner. We might not have to trust him as long as we can come to terms with him. I got Nash to talk about him a little on the way here. He respects him. And it wasn't like the fear of Volkov's men. What do you know about him?"

"Not much. He's intelligent. He's really good at karate. He took down Razov better than I could have. He's not afraid of Kaskov even though he knows him better than Volkov does. Mallory says he's always watching and trying to see beyond what you're seeing, which usually puts him a step ahead. I believe that's true. And when he promised me that he'd tell me something, he kept his word. He likes control." She frowned. "I think that's all."

"Really?" Maria raised her brows. "I'd say that's quite a bit for one plane ride. I believe it would be worthwhile to probe a little deeper and see if he can be of use."

Lara shook her head. "He likes control."

"Then we'll give it to him. But that doesn't mean we can't shape the way we want him to use it." She put her cup down on the coffee table.

"I want to talk to him. I'm certain that you're right about everything you've said about him, but I need to make my own judgments. So why don't you go and take that shower and wash your hair while I give Tanner a cup of tea and we size each other up. I'm sure he's curious about me, too."

"You're trying to get rid of me."

"Absolutely." She smiled. "Don't be so wary. He's only another man, and you know I'll have no problem."

"Yes." She slowly got to her feet. "If that's what you want. But be careful, he's…different." She picked up the suitcase and started back toward the bedroom. "He might surprise you."

"I doubt that. It's more likely that I'll surprise him," Maria said. "But either way, we'll both know where we stand." She paused. "And he'll understand that you're not alone in this. And so will you, Lara."

"I've never thought I was alone. You were always there for me."

"Was I? It didn't seem that way to me." She grimaced. "But this is a new day. We both have another chance." She made a shooing gesture. "Now jump in that shower. I don't want you to get in my way."

Tanner smiled at Maria when he came into the office fifteen minutes later. "Dinner is on the way." His gaze wandered around the room. "Lara?"

"She decided she couldn't do without that shower

you mentioned. She should be out soon." Maria went to the bar. "But I've made another pot of tea and I thought we could have a cup and get to know each other. I wanted to thank you for taking such good care of Lara."

"She was my responsibility." He took the cup she handed him. "I couldn't do anything else." He took a sip. "Very good. But of course you're a tea drinker. You're English, aren't you?"

"Kaskov told you?"

"He merely mentioned it in passing. He was centered on Lara." He went to a leather easy chair and sat down. "I didn't know anything about you until I called him back after I left you today and asked him for more details."

She stiffened. "Kaskov and I hardly knew each other. He rarely said more than a few words to me when he came to the house to listen to Lara. She plays the piano, you know."

"Yes, I know very well. Kaskov made sure I did." He tilted his head. "But Kaskov is a great fan of research. He knew much more about you than you would have thought." His glance went to the bedroom. "Lara will feel much better after she has that shower. Did I give the two of you enough time to catch up?"

"It didn't take long. We're so close we almost speak shorthand." She followed him and sat down in the chair across from him. "She means everything to me."

"I could see she does. Which is why I thought I'd better see if it was going to cause me any trouble." He smiled. "I detest trouble. Are you going to be a problem?"

"I might be." She looked down into her tea. "I hope

not. I don't want to be. It depends on what you decide to do. What did Kaskov tell you?"

"It was very cut-and-dried. Only a brief description of what must have been a terrible time for you," he said quietly. "I have no intention of using it to hurt you in any way. I wasn't looking for anything like this. I just wanted to find a way to handle you. I don't think I could hurt you if I wanted to. I can see you've put it behind you, and it's only made you stronger."

"Yes, it has." She smiled bitterly. "No one can use that nightmare against me ever again. Even though I'm still living through the aftereffects from Volkov." She lifted her cup to her lips. "Cut-and-dried," she repeated. "It wasn't cut-and-dried to me. And you might not want to use this to hurt me, but you're still trying to manipulate me or you wouldn't have brought it up. You'd have politely ignored that you knew about my deep, dark past."

"Very true. Though your past isn't dark, it's very deep, and it's created a woman who could still throw my plans into a hellish mess. I have to know you. And the reason I wasn't discreetly polite is that I thought you could take anything I threw at you. But I still have to find a way to know exactly how you think, and I thought this would break the ice."

She looked at him and started to laugh. "That's one way of putting it. You're...unusual, Tanner. I don't believe I've ever met anyone like you." She took a sip of her tea and then leaned back in her chair. She said bluntly, "I need to know you, too. You might be important to Lara. So let's put all the cards on the table. I'll go first, and it won't be cut-and-dried. I was born in London. My parents were poor and hardworking and did their best to give me a good life, send me to church on Sunday, and teach me all the things decent parents teach their kids. But by the time I was eighteen, I thought I knew everything and only wanted to have a good time. Well, one night I was out at a club and the boy I was with slipped me a mickey. The next morning I woke up chained in a cellar with a dozen other girls and found out that boy was a supplier for sex traffickers. I was raped every night while I was there, but then they decided I was special and sent me to one of their cribs in Istanbul for special training. They turned me over to Madam Alya. She told me I had great potential and if I applied myself, I would not be hurt. Since they kept me drugged most of the time, I was a very willing student. I learned to perform so well I can't tell you how much in demand I was. Everyone wanted Maria." She took another drink of tea. "Are you bored yet?"

"Not in the least," he said quietly.

"Neither was I. As long as they kept me drugged, I did fine. But unfortunately one of the house's clients was Anton Balkon, who visited the house whenever he was in Istanbul. They gave me to him whenever he was in town. I didn't care—he was just another client, and I did what I was told to do. But I did it too well. He went a little crazy about me. Of course, he was on drugs, too. He decided he wanted his own private whore back at his compound in Russia, so he bought me from Madam Alya for a very pretty penny." She shrugged. "The idiot even married me. He told me that the mafia family respected marriage and that it would keep other men away from me. He told the madam to get me off the drugs and he'd be back to get me in a couple of weeks." She shook her head. "Big mistake. If he'd left me on the drugs, I would have done anything he wanted. He'd have been much happier. But by the time he got back I was starting to get off them, and when I got to Avgar I was almost clean...and beginning to think. That was fatal for me. I began fighting every time he touched me, and he started beating me. I tried to run away, and the beatings got worse. It was a very bad time. And I didn't think it could, but it got worse. I found out I was pregnant. That made Anton even angrier. All he'd wanted was a sex toy; he had no use for children. Madam Alya had even told him they'd operated on me when I'd arrived in Istanbul before they'd started my training and he wouldn't have to worry that I'd breed. He was furious that they'd lied to him. He started to grumble about having the child aborted and then having me fixed himself. I didn't care, I was almost numb by that time and heaven knows I didn't want to have his child. I thought it would have to be a monster. But he went away on a smuggling job, and while he was gone the numbness went away." Her hand touched her stomach. "And I felt the baby move."

"And it wasn't a monster to you any longer?" Tanner asked gently.

She shook her head. "I didn't know what it was, but I knew I couldn't kill it. Maybe it was the way I was brought up. Maybe I thought that out of all this misery there should be something that wasn't completely ugly, that if I protected it, perhaps I'd feel...cleaner. There was no way I was going to keep it. I'd just have the baby and then find someone to take it and give it a home. Providing I could even convince Anton to let me do it. I knew I'd have trouble getting him to let the baby live. I'd have to fight him until I gave birth and could get rid of it."

"But you did it?"

"I fought him in the only way I knew would work. The only thing he'd ever wanted from me. I went back to what I'd learned in Istanbul. It was much harder without the drugs, but I kept telling myself once I was rid of the baby, I'd find a way to leave him. All I had to do was hold on." Her lips curved ruefully.

"But then one night the child was born. It was a girl, and somehow, I had never thought of it being a girl. Anton stormed out of the house and I delivered her myself. She was crying and I thought I might have done something wrong. I stared down at her and she stopped crying and gazed up at me with those huge eyes. She looked like me; there was nothing of Anton in her. I know babies aren't supposed to smile, but I swear she was smiling at me and I didn't feel alone any longer. There was something special about Lara even then, and I knew there had to have been a reason she'd been given to me to care for. It was literally love at first sight. Very bad. I hadn't wanted to love her, because I knew what that would mean for me. I'd have to struggle just to keep her alive and protect her until I found a way to take her away."

She added curtly, "And I did it. But then when she could barely toddle, she discovered the old piano that had belonged to the previous owners of the house. She started to play it, and it was…magical. First, the melodies of the lullabies and songs I'd sung to her since she'd been born. Then she started making up melodies of her own. I couldn't get her away from the piano." She took another sip of her tea. "And I knew that it was going to be much longer than I thought before I could run and hide both of us away in some dark cave somewhere. How could I hide all that beauty and genius in a cave until Anton got tired of looking for me? He considered me property; that might never happen." Her lips twisted bitterly.

"So I changed plans and thought I'd delay for a few years longer until I could find a way to break free. But that turned out to be a disaster. Volkov appeared on the scene." She pushed her cup away from her. "I'm not going to tell you about that particular mistake. That's another episode in the story, and it belongs to Lara. You've heard enough about me to judge whether you can manipulate me." She lifted her chin challengingly. "What do you think, Tanner?"

"I think you're a remarkable woman," he said quietly. "And I'd like to hire you to work for me if you could see your way clear after we get Lara settled."

She looked at him in surprise. "Doing what?"

"Management. I have several enterprises that need a deft hand."

"And you think that my sexual training in that crib in Istanbul would be a dynamite qualification?" she asked sarcastically. "I don't have any other job experience. Just what kind of enterprises do you run, Tanner?"

"I don't deal in sex trafficking." His lips were tight. "Never, Maria. I detest the idea of preying on helplessness. Life is rough enough without stacking the decks against someone. I enjoy a battle, but that takes the kick out of it for me. But I have quite a few flourishing businesses in several cities around the world and an office on Wall Street where you might find a good fit." He smiled. "I can see you as a wheeler-dealer. You're decisive, and you'd do anything necessary to get your own way. But you won't need me once you get on your feet. You'll be able to hold your own. You know that."

"Yes, I do." Her eyes narrowed. "Are you bribing me?"

"No, you can't be bribed. But I'm giving you an opportunity to consider once I get you away from Volkov and your dear husband. Kaskov seems to think that he's going to be able to find you both a safe haven somewhere. But why not New York? It would only take a few adjustments. I'm good at adjustments."

"You're very confident." Maria shook her head. "I can't remember when I was that sure of anything. And I never allowed myself to think of a life after Volkov and Anton. I could only take one day at a time."

"Then it's time you started."

"Anton's family has contacts all over the world. Volkov snaps his fingers and Anton produces. Why do you think you can keep us safe?"

"I'm exceptionally good. Ask Kaskov."

"I don't want to get near Kaskov. That's a recipe for disaster." She was looking at him searchingly. "But he's clever and he does trust you. I'm on the edge of trusting you, too." She was silent a moment. "I might have trouble convincing Lara. She wants to take care of everything herself, and the first thing she'd do is find a hideout for me and then leave me."

"I got that impression. But she doesn't trust me. That's why I'm going to have to work through you." He paused. "And I don't want to use force."

"No, you don't," she said dryly. "Neither of us would tolerate it. So you'll have to find a way to get around that, because you might be worth trusting." She shrugged. "At any rate, I can't let her take off without me."

He nodded. "I can see that."

Maria was gazing at him. "I believe you can," she murmured. "Tell me how."

"You're afraid that when she leaves you, she'll go back and try to kill Volkov. Not your husband. She told me that you both had learned to survive him. She thinks that Volkov is the main threat— the one who has to be eliminated to keep both of you safe."

She nodded. "Amazingly perceptive. I can't let her do it. He's surrounded by his men all the time. She could be killed herself or might be arrested for murder. Her music is everything to her, and I won't let it be destroyed to protect me."

"Then if I promise you that won't happen, will you let me do my job?"

She was silent. Then she nodded. "I'll let her know that I won't get in your way, but you'll have to deal with persuading her yourself. It would only make Lara more stubborn if she felt you'd pressured me." She added with sudden harshness, "And I won't forgive you if you break that promise. I'll find a way to punish you."

"I know you will. That's why it won't happen," he said. "Among other reasons."

"What other reasons?"

"I usually try to perform my work without emotion, because coolness is more efficient and productive when everyone around me is ready to explode. But I'm having difficulty this time." He smiled. "I find myself experiencing barbaric impulses where Volkov is concerned. They've been growing since that night in the forest when I saw how alone your daughter seemed against those jackals. Not that she didn't acquit herself extraordinarily well. Still, I can't seem to shake them off, so I may have to act on them."

"What does that mean?"

"I've no idea, but I'm sure it will come to me." He reached for his phone. "Suppose you go tell Lara that she should get out of the shower before she drowns. I'll call Mallory and let him know we're ready for that dinner."

"Not just yet." She didn't move. "You've gotten what you wanted from me, but you haven't reciprocated. All I've actually found out about you is that you have no use for whoremongers and you hate cheats." She smiled crookedly. "And you probably only let me know that because you knew that it would influence me to give you what you wanted. I want more."

"I've given you more than that. I've been honest with you. I've been very open for me. That's not my usual custom." He tilted his head. "Think about it. What have you learned about me?"

She frowned. "You see too much. Lara said that about you, and I believe she's right. I think you may be the most intuitive person I've ever run across. Everything I said today, you were weighing and evaluating and answering before I even finished. You have a strong work ethic even if you don't like what you have to do to exercise it. Kaskov doesn't own you, but you respect his intelligence." She thought for a moment. "And there's something about Lara..." Her eyes suddenly narrowed. "Yes, there's definitely something about Lara, but you didn't even let me get close to it. I wonder if that should bother me."

"That's up to you. You respect your own opinion."

He smiled. "But I'll tell you a little more about my background if you'll answer one more unpleasant question for me afterward. Deal?"

She shrugged. "It couldn't be more unpleasant than what I've already told you about myself."

"Don't be too sure. It's always the unexpected that trips us." He took a sip of his tea. "I'll start at the beginning as you did. I never knew my parents. They evidently didn't like the idea of having a kid and left me behind in an apartment in Brooklyn when they were evicted. I was two then, and I spent the next few years in a series of foster homes until I lost the cute factor. Then I was tossed in an orphanage, which I much preferred because I could get my hands on books—for me the Holy Grail. It also gave me time to explore ways to trade what I had to offer to get what I wanted from the world."

"What you had to offer?"

"I had a talent for numbers. I had to learn how to use it on the streets and then in the boardrooms in ways that wouldn't get me beaten up or dead." He smiled. "And I did. The rest is history. Satisfied? Even Mallory doesn't know about the Brooklyn days."

She shook her head. "Too brief. But I guess you kept your promise. What's your question?"

He was silent a moment. "Maxim, the piano teacher: Did you know he was going to be killed that day? And if you did, why didn't you try to stop it?"

She stiffened in shock. "You knew about Maxim? How?"

"We got the base story from Lara. The rest was just clearing away the lies and working out the truth. But I need the entire truth, Maria. It might be important."

"The hell it would. So that you could tell Lara?

She doesn't have to know, dammit. It would only hurt her."

"No, I won't mention anything about Maxim to Lara. I just want to be prepared for an answer if she ever admits to herself that there was something wrong about the story she was told."

"She wouldn't go to you. She'd come to me."

"Not if she thought it would hurt you." He paused. "It might not be a problem, but it's the only thing I think might get in my way."

"Heaven forbid that the job might not go as smoothly as you'd like," she said bitterly.

"I promise that she won't be told unless I don't have a choice," he said. "But I won't lie to her. It means too much to her. I have to know the truth."

"The truth?" She looked away from him. "I didn't know it was going to happen. But everything was so bad that day that I was afraid, and I went to Anton and tried to get answers. It took me a little while, but he finally got impatient and told me to be quiet about it. He said by now Volkov would have already taken care of Maxim. I ran to the village, but it was too late. Volkov had already killed him and was disposing of the body. He saw me and he smiled. He told me not to be upset, that he'd see that Lara would have no use for a piano teacher from now on." She looked back at Tanner and added bitterly, "Was I supposed to tell her that?"

He shook his head. "Of course not. You did what you had to do." He got to his feet. "Now I think I'd better go outside to make that call to Mallory. You might need a little time to curse me for an interfering son of a bitch. After that you'll be back to your usual self and remember I made you a promise." He moved toward the door.

"I'm almost back to myself already," she said. "Just a little shaky. You're right, the unexpected kicked my butt." She added fiercely, "But you'd better keep that promise."

"Absolutely." He looked back over his shoulder and grinned. "I haven't forgotten you threatened to punish me. I'm definitely taking it seriously."

———◆———

"You look much better. Not like you've been wrestling with monsters in the forest," Maria said brusquely as she came into the bedroom where Lara was blow-drying her hair. "Which of course you have, but I'm trying to forget. Now, get dressed while I duck into the bathroom and freshen up. Tanner said that he was telling Mallory to serve dinner right away. I'm hungry, aren't you?"

"I don't know. I guess I am. I haven't been paying attention." She brushed her hair out of her eyes. "You can't just come in here and start talking about having dinner. What happened with Tanner?"

"We had a talk. I told you I would. He's…interesting." She took the brush away from Lara and began to brush her hair. "I haven't done this for a long time. You were too grown up. You didn't want to bother me. Too damn grown up…You should never have had to grow up that soon."

"Life is life." Lara smiled at her. "But we made it through the bad times. Now we're going to have a chance to see what we can make of the good ones." Then her smile faded as she saw Maria's expression. It made her uneasy. Her entire demeanor since she had come in that door had been different from what Lara had expected. "Or are we? You're being very peculiar. You're almost in tears over my damn hair. Why?"

Maria chuckled and brushed her lips over the top of Lara's head. "I've always loved your 'damn' hair. It's like silk. And maybe seeing you all tousled brought back memories of when you were a kid and I used to put it up in a ponytail."

"Or maybe your talk with Tanner had some sort of weird effect on you." Her gaze was narrowed on Maria's face. "What did you talk about?"

"Not about your hair, I assure you." She turned and was heading for the bathroom. "We hardly spoke of you at all. We were just trying to get to know each other and attempting to find common ground."

"And did you?"

"No. We're very different and anything common was defined with very broad strokes. That doesn't mean that I didn't find him fascinating and worth the time I was spending exploring." She paused. "But I did learn one thing. You said he kept his promises. I think I'd agree with you in most cases." She added wryly, "And he does like to be in control. You'll have to be careful in the way you handle him."

"I will?" She was gazing at her in bewilderment. "What do you mean? I've told you what I want to do. Once we find a way of losing Tanner, he won't matter to us."

"Except I haven't made it clear enough to you that I have no intention of going along with your plan," she said gently. "We're going to stay together until we find some way to make that permanent. You're not hiding me away; you're not ever putting yourself into a position where you'll have to face Volkov again. Do you understand?"

"No," she said sharply. "There's only one way, Maria. Can't you see that?"

"No, I can't." She gave her daughter a cool glance. "Because I have no crystal ball that's telling me we can't have it all. So you'd better turn yours in for a newer model and figure out how I can have my way."

"Did Tanner have anything to do with this?" Lara asked through set teeth. "I'd bet he did. I told you he was persuasive."

"No, I told him that you were in charge, and you are. You're the one whose life is on the line." She smiled. "Except for this one small item that I won't back down on."

"Maria…" She wanted to shake her. "You're wrong."

"I'm right. I've never been more right." She was suddenly smiling. "I'll go along with anything you want to do. Pretend it's that concerto you play when you want to get ready for a difficult Trial. Just concentrate and come up with something that you can live with. Literally." She opened the bathroom door. "Now get dressed. I'll only be a few minutes."

Lara's hands clenched as she saw the door close behind Maria. Damn. Damn. Damn. She knew that tone; she had no chance of budging her mother. Not unless she could persuade her that there was nothing else she could do to save them. And it might come to that, she thought in despair. This moment of hope could disappear in a heartbeat if she didn't reach out and grab it before it slipped away. She hadn't let Maria know how close Volkov had come during the last two Trials to taking her down. She'd been aware of an increase in his levels of recklessness and viciousness, but what would have been the use of worrying Maria? Still, this weird escape that Kaskov had brought about would have sent Volkov into a fury. He would never stop, and there was every chance he would try to hurt her by using Maria.

That must not happen. Okay, she'd do what Maria suggested. Concentrate. Try to get what she wanted without resorting to what she knew was the most efficient way of handling it. How?

Tanner. She was sure he'd had something to do with Maria's sudden determination. And she hadn't seemed to want to talk about him when she'd first come back. If he'd had something to do with Maria's decision, he might also be able to reverse it. Even if he hadn't made an overt attempt at persuasion, Lara had been exposed to that deep, subtle probing during the flight here. He'd always been one step ahead…

But she couldn't let him be one step ahead from now on. He held all the power in her world right now. She had to *know* him. If anyone was going to do any further probing, it had to be her. He had to be in control. So be it. But only in the beginning. She knew how to research and work to get what she wanted. She had learned it in all those hellish Trials. Find the right key and then turn it. Tanner was no different.

She only had to find the right key.

CHAPTER

5

The table was set with fine linens and Mallory was putting out covered dishes when Lara came out of the bedroom. He glanced at her white slacks and red jacket. "Very nice. I was wondering if it would fit."

"Everything in that suitcase fits. Your doing?"

"No. Tanner told me the approximate size. Kaskov gave him your DVD and he watched it a couple of times. He was sure that it would be right."

"I imagine he's usually sure of that," she said dryly. She looked around the room. "Where is he?"

"Outside. He had some calls to make." He gestured to the table. "I ordered a few Swedish specialties. I hope you enjoy them."

She sniffed. "*Köttbullar.* Probably with brown sauce. Lingonberries. Definitely cinnamon rolls."

"Very good." His brows rose. "I thought you'd never been to Sweden."

"I haven't. That doesn't mean that I'm not familiar with Swedish cuisine. I had to learn how to cook it during one of my Trials in Paris."

"Paris?"

"Hans Nilssen." Tanner was leaning against the doorjamb, smiling at her. "Born and raised in a small town in Sweden but became a rich and famous art collector and married a French artist who refused to leave Paris. He owned a Rembrandt that he'd 'liberated' from the collection of a Nazi general. It disappeared from his Parisian apartment several years ago and was presumed stolen." He added softly, "It was one of your successes."

"I didn't think so." She tilted her head. "Kaskov gave you all those details?"

"No, just the bare bones. But I'm rarely satisfied with half a story, so I spent a little time on the plane checking and filling out what needed verifying."

She shook her head in amazement. "You did that with all those Trials?"

"Most of them. A couple came up blanks."

"Well, you didn't share them with me." Mallory had finished setting the table and gone to the bar to get a bottle of wine. "But then I'm not as inquisitive as you. I believe in privacy."

"No, you don't. Only when it suits you," Tanner said absently. "Why wasn't it a success, Lara?"

"I liked Nilssen. I liked his entire family. They were good to me. I worked as an au pair for his two daughters, and I'd sometimes cook lunch for the entire family. Nilssen never really became accustomed to French cuisine." She paused. "That Rembrandt painting was a part of their life as a family."

"They must have liked you, too," Tanner said.

"You weren't mentioned in the investigation when the painting was stolen. Yet Nilssen must have suspected you."

She shrugged. "I did him a favor once. I guess he was grateful."

"Why?"

"I dove into the sea and pulled his youngest daughter out when she fell overboard." She smiled. "Colette was always a wild child. We had to watch her all the time."

"It was lucky you knew how to swim."

"I didn't, until Anton and Volkov sent me out in that speedboat to get those drugs from Dimitri." She met his eyes. "But I learned from that mistake. I built on it. That's what you have to do. Take what you're given and make it work for you."

"Or for Colette?"

She nodded. "I liked her. I used to play for her and Gina before they went to sleep at night." She turned away. "It wasn't a success, Tanner."

"Then we might have to make it into a success. I'll have to think about it." The bedroom door had opened, and Maria was coming into the room. "I was wondering where she was. Did you have a falling-out?"

"No, we never have falling-outs. She's always been everything to me. We sometimes have misunderstandings." She added coldly, "And I don't appreciate you inserting opinions to try to influence her."

"As if she'd give a damn about my opinions. You know that as well as I do. She's going to do whatever she thinks is best for you. You're just annoyed because you're going to have to come up with something else since you're not getting your own way." He started across the room toward Maria. "So let's eat dinner and then we'll go out for a walk and discuss our options. By the way, your mother is looking beautiful tonight."

He was right, Lara thought. That was odd. Maria usually wore dark, understated clothes aimed to make her fade into the background, but tonight she was wearing a cream-colored sweater with her pale olive jeans, and the contrast was striking with her dark hair. "She's always beautiful. Inside and out." She smiled at Maria, and Maria smiled back. "No matter what happens, she never changes." She added fiercely as she started to follow him, "And it's going to stay that way. Do you hear me, Tanner?"

He nodded. "But she's already changing. You can't alter that. You might not want to once you get used to the idea." He'd reached Maria and held out his hand. "Come and have a drink before dinner. I want you to get to know Mallory. You'll find him pleasant enough. I'm going to whisk your daughter away for a while after dinner to talk, and I'd like you to keep each other company so she won't want to run back right away. Is that okay?"

Maria's gaze shifted to Lara. "I believe it might be very much okay," she said slowly. "You'll both have to see, won't you?"

———◆———

"Where the hell are you taking me?" Lara asked impatiently as she quickened her pace to keep up with him as he strode across the icy tarmac. "You said a walk. This is more like a run."

"Stop whining." He smiled at her. "You're tough, you can keep up." He nodded at the hangar just ahead. "They've fueled up the jet and it's ready to go. It will be warm enough so that you'll be comfortable for the time you'll be here." He opened the hangar and nodded at the plane steps. "I told them to have a thermos of coffee ready. I noticed you didn't drink any wine at dinner. Why don't you get a cup?" He was strolling toward Jordan, who was sitting at a desk across the hangar. "I need to check with Jordan to make sure he's taken care of our arrival arrangements. I don't want any surprises. I'll be with you in a minute."

It appeared she had no choice, she thought ruefully as she ran up the steps and entered the dimly lit plane. She found the thermos and cups and settled in a seat to wait for him. She should be glad that she had this break to consider the "options" they were supposed to be talking about. She had an idea they wouldn't be inviting.

Then he was dropping down into the seat next to her. "All in order," he said as he took the thermos from her. "I just don't like being this close to Mother Russia. I would never have stopped here if I hadn't needed to pick up your mother." He poured his coffee. "Kaskov made it clear you wouldn't leave without her."

"He was right," she said coolly. "Though I suppose you could have taken me anyway. I was already on this plane and halfway here when I woke up."

"But then it would have been kidnapping and not extraction," he said lightly. "Not that I wouldn't consider it if the price was right, but I prefer a willing extraction."

"Then you must be disappointed. I'm not willing. If Kaskov was going to be generous enough to get us out of Russia, he should have let me do it my way."

"I'm not disappointed. Kaskov is paying me in information, not in cash. I'll still get the information because I've already gotten you safely away from your father and Volkov. All I have to do is keep you safe until he finds a way to do so himself."

"Why should he even want to do that?" she asked in exasperation. "I know what he is. Even Volkov was nervous around him. Why should he help me?"

"A whim? Because he chooses to?" He paused. "Because he likes the way you play the piano? Who knows?"

"And you don't care?"

"Not as long as it doesn't affect how I do my job or my agreement with him." He added slowly, "Though he was very sure that I'm the right man for this job, but he might have been wrong."

Her eyes widened. "Why?"

"I'm having problems with it." His gaze was suddenly on her face. "Sex, of course. That's always to be expected with a beautiful woman around." He frowned as he reached out and his index finger touched her lower lip. "But that's not all. I wish to hell it was. I keep thinking of those damn Trials. It's pissing me off. I don't want to think about them. I don't want to think of the kid in that speedboat."

"Pity?" She threw his hand away from her lip. "I don't need pity, Tanner. Why should I? That was all in the past. I learned from it."

"I know you did. And I can see I'm making you angry just mentioning it. But I thought I'd get it out right now along with the rest of the problems we're going to have to come to terms with before we leave in the morning."

"In the morning?"

"At four. It was going to be tonight. But my reports don't show Volkov heading in this direction yet. And you and Maria are on edge; I thought you should get some solid sleep."

"How kind of you." She added in exasperation, "Damn you, Tanner."

"I told you that I have to get you out of here. Since your mother isn't going to go along with your plans for her, I'm your best bet and you know it." He smiled. "So here's how it's going to be. I'm taking the two of you to my place in Connecticut. I have contacts all over the Northeast, and I should have no trouble moving you around if needed."

"Connecticut?" She frowned. "That's the U.S."

"Is that far enough away from Volkov for you?"

"I've never been to the U.S. Neither has Maria. It will be...strange."

"I'll make sure it won't be too strange. I was born in New York, which is very close." He smiled. "Leave it to me. Just part of the service."

"I don't want to leave it to you. I don't want to do this," she said. "It shouldn't be this way. I've always had a way to prepare for anything strange or difficult I had to do. I was in charge, and if I worked hard enough, I could make it happen."

"Can you look on it as a kind of vacation? I know you don't trust me, but I'm very good at what I do. I promise I'll keep you safe from Volkov and Anton." He paused. "I'll even keep you safe from Kaskov. If you don't like his plans for you, then I'll help you make new ones. The only one you'll have to worry about is me. Since I'm a known quantity, that shouldn't be too much for you to handle."

"I'm not sure about that," she said slowly. "I've never known anyone like you. Sometimes I don't know what you're thinking. It makes me uneasy."

"I wouldn't want that. Suppose I promise to concentrate on thinking about you as that kid in the speedboat, and on not remembering what I'd like to do with you sexually."

"With me?" She stared at him blankly. "What has that to do—" She started to laugh. "Sex? You were talking about me? I thought you were talking about Maria."

"Maria?" He shook his head. "Though I'm beginning to realize why you were being so fierce back at the office. You were protecting her? You thought I was making a move on her."

She nodded. "Of course I did. It's always about Maria. She's beautiful. It's natural you'd want her." She shrugged. "And you're probably like all the others. You don't know or care how good she is. All you can think about is getting her into bed. She's worth so much more than that."

"I'm sure she is." He was studying her expression. "And how long have you been defending her with such ferocity from us predatory males?"

"As soon as I realized how you all treated her. There was no love, no gentleness. There was only pain. I had to protect her. We took care of each other."

"And she protected you, too?"

"Whenever she could." She made an impatient gesture. "That didn't matter."

"Well, this time she's trying to protect you," he said quietly. "And it matters quite a bit to her. So if you'll go along and try to trust me, I'll see that you both come out of this with a better life."

She gazed at him uncertainly.

"Look, I don't want to have relations with your very gorgeous mother. I admire her, and I think that I could like her. But you're the one I'm having trouble keeping my hands off." He reached out and his finger traced the line of her cheek. "But I'm not into pain or force, so you don't have to worry about S and M. I'll try to keep away from you, but if it doesn't work out, feel free to give me a karate chop." He smiled slightly. "I promise I won't return it."

She couldn't look away from him. Her cheek felt warm, almost hot, beneath that light touch. "You're very good at karate, but so am I. As I told you, last time you caught me off guard." She added absently, "And I don't worry about pain. I know how to take care of that."

He went still, and then his hand fell away from her cheek. "You do? Someday you must tell me how you learned that particular skill. You're a constant surprise to me." He got to his feet. "But not right now. I'm feeling a bit volatile at the moment. I think it's time you went back to the office and told Maria that we've come to an agreement." He pulled her to her feet and tucked the fleece collar of her jacket closer to her throat. "Jordan is going to escort you back. I'm expecting a very special delivery and I have to be here to receive it." He was nudging her toward the door.

"I don't remember coming to any agreement," she said impatiently. "You were the one doing all the talking and planning." They'd reached the door and she felt as if she was being tossed out. "And you're being ridiculous. I don't have to have anyone go with me."

"From now on, neither of you goes anywhere without an escort. And you didn't actually refuse me, so that's enough of an agreement." He paused. "Do you remember how grateful you were when I first told you that I was taking you and Maria away from

Volkov and Anton? I was touched, even though you diluted a lot of the gratitude with suspicion and lack of trust. But now since I'm going to give you everything you could possibly want in an extraction, I'll be magnanimous and forgive you for not being equally generous." He opened the door, and icy air blew into the cabin. He motioned to Jordan below. "Have a good night, Lara."

"Good night." She was halfway down the steps before she looked back. He was still standing there. He was not smiling. But there was that same intentness about his expression that he'd had in those last minutes.

"Don't worry, it's going to be okay," he said gently. "I'll take care of you." Then he turned and went back into the plane.

She stood there for a minute longer. Why should those few words have filled her with such a glowing sense of warmth and security? If anything, she should have resented them. She probably would if she thought about it. But she didn't want to think about it. She wanted to keep this feeling of warmth a little longer before she had to face the coldness again.

◆

Mallory was on the phone when Jordan opened the door of the office for her ten minutes later. He nodded to Lara and then hung up. He turned to Jordan. "You go back to the plane and get some sleep, since you'll be doing most of the flying tomorrow." He turned to Maria. "You'll have to put up with me for a while longer. I have orders to camp out on the couch in here. Do you need anything?"

Maria turned to Lara. "Do I need anything?"

"According to Tanner, a good night's sleep," Lara said, shaking her head. "Though he's not giving us much time for it. We take off at four in the morning." She nodded at Jordan as he left the room before turning to Mallory. "I don't need you. I tried to tell Tanner. He wasn't listening."

"He's like that," Mallory said. "You just have to give him his way. It's much easier." He turned to Maria and inclined his head. "It was a pleasure. Have a good night."

She smiled. "Much better than I've had for the past three." She took hold of Lara's arm and pushed her toward the bedroom. "Come along. We need to talk." She barely waited until she'd shut the door before she leaned back against it, staring at Lara. "You agreed to do this?"

"Tanner says I did," she said wryly. "I think he may be right. Though he was using everything from the urgency of getting us as far from Russia as soon as possible, to making me promises that he probably can't keep."

"But you believed those promises?"

"While he said them. But words are cheap. Yes, he made me believe them. He made me *want* to believe them." She shook her head. "What else can I do? He's right, we have to get you somewhere safe right away. You won't let me do it myself, so I'll have to use Tanner. It might not be a bad idea. He keeps telling me he's an expert; now let's see if he can keep his promises."

"So we get on that plane tomorrow morning?"

Lara nodded. "If that's all right with you."

"I told you it was up to you."

She shook her head. "It's your life, too."

"I always survive." Maria took a step forward and gently enfolded her in her arms. "And it makes sense to me, Lara. We've got to trust someone sometime." She kissed her on the forehead. "I liked Mallory. I think he might be a good man. And if he works for Tanner, that's a recommendation, isn't it?"

Lara chuckled. "I guess so. I think maybe we're both being a little optimistic." She hugged her close for a minute before she let her go. "But I'm ready for a little optimism. It will be gone by tomorrow anyway." She turned toward the bed and started to take off her clothes. "Let's get some sleep. You didn't ask where we were going." She yawned. "It's a place called Connecticut. It's in America. Have you ever heard of it? It's supposed to be near New York where Tanner…"

⬥

"Right on time." Tanner met Lara and Maria as they came up the plane steps. His gaze raked Lara's face. "And you look rested. That's good. It's a long flight and you might need it." He turned to Maria. "It's the best thing to do. Did you tell her so?"

"I said it made sense…at the moment," she said. "The rest is up to you. You'll have to perform well to please her. She can be very demanding."

"I'll keep that in mind." He turned away and headed toward the cockpit. "Mallory, take care of them. Get them something to eat. I want them to have had their breakfast by the time we reach maximum altitude. I'll have to go do the takeoff checklist with Jordan. We've got to get out of here."

"You heard the man." Mallory gestured to two seats

on the left side of the plane. "I've been chosen to play flight attendant and keep you from fading away."

"He's in a big hurry." Lara was suddenly tense. "Is there a reason?"

"Probably. He likes efficiency, though I don't remember him demanding anyone having to be fed by a certain time. I'll find out later. Settle, while I see what I can find you to eat." He strolled back toward the galley.

Maria was dropping into the window seat. "Stop fretting," she said quietly. "It might be nothing. Fasten your seat belt."

"I should be fretting. Maybe I should go talk to Tanner. What if something's wrong? I'm the one who talked you into this."

"Not true. And you can't try to take over. You have to let Tanner handle it."

Lara opened her lips to protest. Then she closed them and fastened her seat belt. "But I'll talk to him later if I can't get an answer from Mallory."

"You do that." She leaned back in her seat as the plane's engines started and the aircraft started to taxi. "And we'll see how far you get and that will tell us something, too." She opened her computer. "In the meantime, I'll look up this Connecticut and see where he's taking us…"

<hr>

"Your after-breakfast tea," Mallory said as he set the cups on their trays. "Can I get you anything else?"

"No, but you can go and ask Tanner if there's a problem," Lara said. "He hasn't stuck his head out of the cockpit since we took off."

He held up his hand. "I'm ahead of you. I called him from the galley. There's no real problem, but he heard from Sorens, one of the men we left to keep an eye on what Volkov was doing. Anton is moving fast and asking lots of questions. They knew you left in a helicopter and they found the heliport we leased it from. It will take them longer to trace it to the private airport where we boarded this jet, but they'll get there. We just have to hope they don't do it before we get to Connecticut and can tuck the jet in a hangar."

"How long will that be?"

"About eleven hours. But they'll have to trace it first to Stockholm, and that will give us more time." He added gently, "Tanner knows what he's doing. He's done it many times before, and he's never lost an extraction. He won't lose you, Lara."

"Is she giving you a hard time?" Tanner was coming down the aisle toward them. "I thought she might. I'm surprised that she didn't have you bounding into the cockpit to grill me."

"I was planning on doing it myself," she said. "You could have given me a report on what was happening. You should have known that I'd suspect something was off kilter when you were orchestrating a simple breakfast with such military precision."

"Heaven forbid you just assume I'd tell you if there was anything really to worry about." He paused. "Or that perhaps I had something else in mind." He turned and headed for the back of the plane. "Come along. Let's get this over. I want to make sure I haven't screwed this up."

"What?" She didn't move. "Screwed what up?"

He looked over his shoulder. "I made you a promise,

didn't I?" He suddenly smiled teasingly. "Come and see if I kept it."

She got to her feet. "I will." She glanced at Maria. "I'll be right back."

"She can follow us if she likes." Tanner was already halfway down the aisle. "Maybe she can protect me from your wrath if I didn't do it right." He stopped and gestured to the four seats opposite the galley opening. "But I did the best I could considering the time constraints."

"What on earth are you talking—" She inhaled sharply as she looked down at the black rectangular object lying across the two seats in front of her. "A keyboard? You got me a keyboard?" She was looking dazedly down at the keys. She gingerly reached out and touched one of the keys. The sound, the beautiful sound… The feel of the key beneath her finger. The music waiting…

"It's a Yamaha," Tanner said. "I talked to a musician at a club in Stockholm and asked him to buy me the best quality he could find. He managed to get me the same kind of instrument that Samer Bou Khazaa uses. I thought that might be okay until I can replace your own piano. Since there's a good chance we might be on the run, it had to be portable and battery-driven and yet be as close in quality to your full-size piano as I could make it." He grimaced. "I'll worry about getting you the real thing later. My chances of getting back to Russia anytime soon aren't the greatest." He was trying to read her expression. "You're disappointed?" He shrugged. "I know it's probably going to fall short of what you're accustomed to, but you'll have to make do until—"

"Be quiet." She whirled on him and could feel

the heat flushing her cheeks as excitement zinged through her. "It's *wonderful*. How could it not be wonderful? I'll have the music." She frowned; her gaze drawn irresistibly back to those keys. "Though I don't know much about keyboards. I've only played one once in my life, when they let me try out some of the other instruments at the Moscow competition. It felt strange, but sort of…exotic. Lots of bells and whistles that sometimes got in the way of the purity of the melody." Her fingers reached out once more to stroke those magical keys that were beckoning, waiting. "But it will be fine once we get to know each other." Her heart was pounding, the exhilaration was building, the eagerness becoming sharper. Her gaze flew back to Tanner. "When can I play it?"

"Let's see, I'll have to consider it." He was staring in bemusement at her luminous expression. "Another five minutes?" He pointed to the two seats he'd arranged facing opposite the keyboard. "I tried to make the setup as comfortable as possible for you. I had the musician who sold me the keyboard set it up when he delivered it last night, but I'm at your service if you want me to try to adjust it."

"No, I'll want to do it myself." Then something he said hit home. "Deliver? This was your very special delivery last night?"

"I assure you it was very special for him," he said dryly. "For a musician, he became quite the entrepreneur when he found out I needed it fast and wasn't going to argue price."

"It's very special for me, too," she said. "Thank you."

He shrugged. "It was a promise. And it's really only half done, but I'm glad it pleased you."

"It pleased me." She looked beyond him to Maria and gave her a brilliant smile. "Isn't it splendid?"

"Yes, completely splendid," Maria agreed. "It's also splendid you had a good breakfast, because we're not going to get you to eat for a long time, are we?" She glanced at Tanner. "Good planning. You do know that she's going to be playing that instrument all the way to your Connecticut? I hope you like music."

"I don't expect to have a problem. I've heard she's a passable artist." His eyes were suddenly twinkling at Lara. "I have some business calls to make, and I could probably use some soothing background music."

"I don't know how to do that," Lara said. "But I'm really grateful, so I could try if that's what you really want." She tilted her head. "But I don't think it is."

"Neither do I," he said softly. "So go ahead. Blow me away if you can."

It was a challenge. He'd been a challenge since the moment she met him, but she had felt too vulnerable not to be wary. Yet now she was so filled with elation that she wanted to reach out and meet it. "I will." She turned toward the keyboard. "But first I have to see what kind of help I can get from this new friend. Both of you go away and let me work." Then she suddenly turned back to Tanner. "I don't care if you only kept half the promise. Thank you for doing it. It means a good deal to me."

"I thought it would. Sometimes a half promise can win the day."

"It certainly did this time," Maria said soberly. "Excellent move. Very clever, Tanner."

"Lara appears happy about it." He smiled. "Or will be when we get out of here and let her work." He nudged her down the aisle. "And now I can turn my attention to you. What's it going to take to keep you from getting bored or edgy on this very long trip?"

Lara stared after them for a minute. Maria was smiling, amused, but Tanner wasn't going to be able to manipulate her unless she chose. Yet he had managed to turn Lara's own life and attitude around today. Maybe he could do the same with Maria? She had an instant of wariness but shrugged it off. She didn't want to worry today. She was going to have the music again after being all these days without it.

Then she was going to meet that challenge Tanner had thrown down.

And she was going to blow him away.

———◆———

SEVEN HOURS LATER

"She's got you," Maria said softly. "What about all those calls you were going to make, Tanner?"

He opened his eyes and gazed at her across the aisle. "I made a few of them."

"Before she really got started," she jeered. "She had to learn the instrument first. Admit it. She blew you away. And she'd still be doing it if I'd been able to resist saying *I told you so*."

"Point taken. What can I say? She's absolutely magnificent and I do appreciate music."

"I could see that. You might have more in common with Kaskov than a business arrangement. He used to have the same expression on his face as you did today while you were listening. It's good to know."

"Is it?" He tilted his head. "But you went to the trouble of disturbing me and letting me know you were aware of it. You didn't act on impulse. You're not a person who does anything without considering it first. Were you probing for a possible weakness?"

She nodded. "You're one very cool customer. I thought I might catch you off guard. Giving Lara that keyboard was a masterstroke. You went to a lot of trouble when you were busy balancing a lot of other problems. But it was exactly the right way to help Lara start to trust you." She looked him in the eyes. "It made me uneasy. Lara is no fool. She's gone through too much hell, but anything connected to her music might tip the scales. I had to see if you'd spotted that vulnerability and were exploiting it."

"And if I had recognized it, would it have been a crime to give her a gift that she'd enjoy even if it might make things smoother for me? Surely that would have dual benefits."

"It might, and it would be something I'd expect of you." She paused. "But you're very, very deep, Tanner. I doubt if anyone can read you except maybe Mallory. However, I have a duty to attempt since I have Lara to consider. I have to know the purpose of that gift and what you're after in return."

His brows rose. "What do you think I'm after?"

"It could be as simple as what you said." She shrugged. "Or it could be even simpler. Sex."

"Indeed? Did it occur to you that sex would only get in my way? It could be a complication."

She nodded. "And you wouldn't like that. Too bad. Because, like it or not, that 'complication' is sending out signals loud and clear whenever you're around Lara. I'm an expert at sex in all its many and perverse forms, and I picked up on it right away. What I want to know is if you're going to do anything about it?"

"No," he said curtly. "The keyboard wasn't a bribe to get her into bed. She seemed to need it. She's just a kid, and she's lost everything else. This was important to her. It wasn't that much trouble for me, so why shouldn't I have seen that she had it?"

"Good question." She was studying his expression. "Do I detect a touch of softness? I liked that answer, though we both know she's no 'kid.' You're thinking about that file Kaskov gave you? She might not have the same experience as the women you're accustomed to inviting for joyrides in this magic carpet you call a plane, but she's learned to survive any situation. Not only that, but she hasn't let it twist her or take away the joy she can feel. Though that's because she had the music."

He frowned. "What?"

She lifted one shoulder in a half shrug. "At least, that's what I think. After all the rough, dirty things those bastards have put her through, she should be rock-hard by now, but it hasn't happened." She jerked her head toward the back of the plane where Lara was still playing. "Personally, I believe it's because she immerses herself in her music whenever she gets the chance, and it softens and clears everything harsh and ugly away." She smiled mockingly. "Weird, huh? But that's my story and I'm sticking to it." Her smile faded. "And I thank God for it every single day."

"Maybe not so weird," he said slowly. "I can see living with the kind of music she's been playing today could be something of a catharsis. It was almost mesmerizing." He made a face. "At any rate, I'm glad she had something to hold on to during those years."

"Hmm, that sounded sincere." She tilted her head. "So perhaps I'll accept that you don't intend to do any damage to her if you can help it. But that doesn't mean I won't keep an eye on you. Good intentions don't mean a damn where sex is concerned."

"That doesn't surprise me considering where it's coming from." He smiled crookedly. "And I couldn't agree with you more. By all means, watch me like a hawk. It will take a lot of pressure off me."

"You mean that." She paused before she added, "You might even be a good guy. Though I don't remember the last time I met one. But I can't afford to take chances with Lara. It would be very dangerous for her to learn to trust you and then have you turn out to be the usual son of a bitch." She lifted her chin. "So you can bet I'll be watching you for even one misstep."

"And then you'll jerk her away and lecture her on how wicked I am? As you said, she's not a child."

"She doesn't need lectures." She added cynically, "Hell, I'd even like her to believe that not all men in the world are just wanting to hurt or screw her. I want her to be healthy—even what people call normal. But she's learned too much from the life she's had to live with me. Maybe after we've had time to heal, we'll go for normal."

"If it even exists. I've always thought normal was what you make it." He added quietly, "And I believe you were probably a very good mother, Maria."

She shook her head. "You don't know what you're talking about. There were hundreds of ways I failed her." She leaned back in her chair. "But I'll be quiet now and let you go back to listening to Lara. I've got what I wanted from you."

"But I haven't got what I wanted from you," he said softly. "You can't just interrogate me and then run away until you need to know something else. You know that's not how the game is played. I have to get my turn."

"Do you?" she asked warily. "What do you want to know? I couldn't have been more frank with you before."

"And what you told me was raw and painful and should have been enough for me? What kind of beast would ask anything more of you? Except I could see that you'd already put it all behind you, and you were strong enough to keep it there." He smiled. "And that's where I want you to keep it. I know about the struggle; now I want to know about how you fought back." He nodded at the computer on the seat beside her. "When I was making my phone calls before Lara blew me away, I took the time to notice how absorbed you were in your computer. Your fingers were flying over the keys, and you were very intense. What were you working on?"

She gave him an innocent stare. "Solitaire?"

He shook his head. "Close. Though I bet it did have something to do with gambling. What did you find out about me?"

She looked at him for a moment. "Not much. It's difficult to access information when a person doesn't want his background known. Your public persona is evidently as inscrutable as your personality. I found out about your time in the service, but nothing about you being an extractor. You now own at least three casinos, perhaps more. But if you do, they're not in the name of Tanner. I checked on this plane and it once belonged to a Claude Starbarth, a billionaire corporate giant, but it's now registered in the name of Tanner Industries." She smiled. "That's as far as I got today."

"Pretty good. I'm impressed. You'd probably have

done even better if you'd had more sophisticated equipment. That computer looks fairly basic."

"Anything else would have been too expensive, and Anton wasn't going to buy it for me." Her lips tightened. "But I couldn't do without a computer, so I 'persuaded' him to buy the first one years ago. I've been homeschooling Lara all her life, which means I've been teaching myself, too. I taught myself all kinds of skills to get ready for the time when I'd find us a way to escape." She reached out and touched the computer. "We've gone through a lot of computers in that time. But I had to make sure they all looked the same so Anton wouldn't realize that Lara would occasionally bring home a new one when they sent her out on one of those damn Trials."

"She stole them?"

Maria stiffened. "How do you think she'd get them? And you should be impressed. You have no idea how difficult it was for her to figure out a way to get a computer I needed when she was in the middle of concentrating on a Trial."

"Or how you hated to ask her to do it?" He held up his hand. "I wasn't criticizing. I'm lost in admiration for both of you."

"Sarcasm?"

"No way." He added simply, "Truth." He got to his feet. "And now I think I'll go back and watch Lara play for a while. I've always liked to *see* the passion of an artist, as well as hear it. Why don't you go back to your computer and discover more about me? I'll let you know if you're right before we get off the plane in Connecticut."

"I might do that." She gazed at him consideringly. "See the passion of an artist you admire? Or is that only an excuse? Never mind, maybe you don't know yet." She paused. "But since I did so well, I think I deserve you to answer one question for me."

"Ask it."

"This fantastic plane. It's like something from a movie set. I was curious and dug deep to find out how much this plane probably cost. It was enormous. Did that billionaire, Starbarth, give it to you in exchange for a job you did for him?"

He chuckled. "You're wondering what amount Kaskov might have had to cough up for my services? No, the Gulfstream was the stakes in the last hand of a very enjoyable poker game I played with Starbarth and several others a couple of years ago in Lima, Peru. It wasn't quite as enjoyable for them as for me, but that's the luck of the draw. Actually, I don't use the plane enough to make it worthwhile, but I haven't been able to bring myself to get rid of it. Satisfied?"

She nodded. "You told me what I needed to know. You're a gambler. Big time. You've dropped a comment now and then, but I couldn't be sure. Not like Anton or Volkov, but maybe even more dangerous. I don't like gamblers, and Lara hates them." She smiled. "Which means I won't have to worry about you, Tanner." She turned back to her computer. "That's a huge relief to me."

"Is it? I'm so glad." He smiled back at her as he started down the aisle. "But I should let you know that's exactly what Starbarth said to me just before I took away his Gulfstream."

CHAPTER

6

Y ou can stop now. I'm meekly surrendering. You blew me away."

It was Tanner, Lara realized vaguely. But didn't he realize how ridiculous he was being? She couldn't stop. It wasn't about that silly challenge. It was the music.

"Now." Tanner was suddenly beside her, his hand on her shoulder. "I'll let you come back to it later, but it's time you had a break. It's been over six hours. You'll realize you're exhausted after you've had a chance to lose a little of that adrenaline. You're not stupid. I'm sure you've learned to pace yourself. The music will still be there."

"I don't want to—" She stopped as she saw his expression. He didn't understand. She had to fight him. She wasn't tired. She could go on and on and on…

"Later. My plane. My rules." He took her hands off the keyboard. "Get up. Go to the bathroom and then get something to drink before you start yelling at me."

He pulled her to her feet. "I promise I'm not going to toss the keyboard out the plane while you're gone."

She nodded jerkily. "But I'm not tired. Stop ordering me around. I should be the one in control of this." Still, she headed for the bathroom and relieved herself before washing up and taking a deep breath. She was feeling a little light-headed, and she took a cup of water from the dispenser and drained it. It wasn't enough; she drained another one. Then she started back down the aisle, where Tanner was standing beside the keyboard drinking a cup of coffee. "You could have been right. Maybe I was a little tired, but I'm fine now."

"Good." He nodded at the tray on the window seat on which he'd set a sandwich and salad. "Sit down, have a bite to eat, and then I won't object to you playing for a little while longer." He looked at his watch. "Maybe another two hours before we put this keyboard away. We'll be landing soon after that."

"Object? I told you that I'm in control where my music is concerned." She dropped down on the seat and started to eat the salad. "You were correct, I know how to pace myself."

"Except this time you were suffering from withdrawal and exhaustion besides a heady exhilaration that might have made the pacing a little off kilter." He sat down beside her. "Not to mention that you were under severe pressure to blow me away."

She made a rude sound. "That was no pressure. I knew I could do it once I became accustomed to the instrument. Piece of cake."

"That's what Maria told me." He made a face. "I'm sorry that neither of you considered me a worthy challenge."

She grinned. "You didn't stand a chance." Her smile

faded. "Because it wasn't me, it was the music. I knew it would take you to another place."

"The music and you," Tanner said softly. "I'd say you had a little to do with it."

"Of course I did. I'm part of it." She took another bite of salad. "I'm meant to be part of it. I've always known that." She glanced down the aisle. "Is Maria all right? We should get her something to eat."

"She's fine. I called the cockpit and told Mallory to take care of her. When I left her, she was busy on her computer." He added dryly, "I gave her a project."

She gave him a wary glance. "What kind of project?"

"One that I'm sure you'll approve of." He took a drink of coffee. "Since she's the one who initiated it. Ever since I met your mother, we've been exchanging information in order to reach a harmonious agreement regarding my proposed participation in getting you both to safety. It's been very interesting. Particularly since she doesn't trust me any more than you do."

"Why should she?" she said fiercely. "You don't know what she—"

"But I do know, she told me," he interrupted. "And that's why I've felt she had every right to be suspicious of anyone who crossed her path. I'm a very private person. I've been much more open with her than I usually am with anyone. I want you to know I respect her, or I wouldn't even consider letting her know anything more. I'd put a stop to it."

She stiffened. "That sounds like a threat."

He sighed. "And there we have you defending her. Not necessary. It's just the opposite. Before this plane sets down, I want to give you both a chance to make you feel you know me. Maybe I'll even answer questions."

"Why would you do that?"

"To make the rest of this trip easier and not risk having you take off." He paused. "Maria decided to go digging in her computer to bare all my secrets she could find. She didn't find much, but she'll keep trying. I encouraged it."

"Why?"

"She wants to protect you. She won't be satisfied until she's sure she knows everything that could harm you. Once she reaches that point, she'll feel more comfortable." He smiled. "And that brings up what she did find out today that you should know about. I'm sure she'll tell you herself, but I prefer to make a pre-emptive strike. I've not done any extractions for a long time. I decided to go into more lucrative businesses some time ago. I own eight casinos in the U.S. and Europe. I have an office on Wall Street, and I do very well with stocks, too. It's all a question of numbers, and that's where I excel. In short, I'm a gambler. Maria was very comforted when she dug that up, because she realized you hated my profession so much that I'd have no possible influence on you."

"You wouldn't have any influence on me anyway," she said flatly. "And I wouldn't have had to look you up in a computer to know that you gambled. You've made comments about betting since the moment I woke up. You didn't exactly try to keep it a secret."

"But I didn't spell it out for you, either," he said quietly. "I let it slide by. I didn't want to deceive you, but knowing your background, I thought it might add to the stress."

"And make it harder to control me."

He grinned. "Right. And heaven knows I didn't need that."

"No, you didn't." She finished her sandwich. "Because I can't let anyone do that. Did she find out anything else I should know about?"

He shook his head. "That was the big one. I'm sure she'll fill you in on the rest. I thought that you'd be more upset."

She met his eyes. "As long as I don't trust you too much, it doesn't matter what you do for a living. But men who gamble don't care who gets hurt. It's just a game. All it means is that I'll have to watch you in case you might decide it's me you want to hurt."

His lips tightened. "Will it make a difference if I promise you that will never happen? There's no way I'd ever hurt you. That's not how I play the game. It never has been. I play by the rules. I like to win, but it's too damn easy for me. And if I cheat, it's not a win at all. In the end I'm only cheating myself. I found that out a long time ago."

She studied his face. "That's…peculiar. That's not how my father and Volkov feel. Winning is everything. I don't know if it would make a difference or not," she said slowly. "So far you've kept your promises, but you could be tricking me. Could I ever be sure?" She added wearily, "And why would it make a difference to you if I believed you anyway? I've already told you that we'd go with you until you finished Kaskov's job. That should be all that matters to you."

He muttered an oath. "I don't know why the hell it makes a difference, but it does." He finished his coffee and got to his feet. "So what the hell?" He was smiling recklessly down at her. "And since it does matter, I'll just have to look on you as a game I have to win. Oh, not like the games you've had to play before. What do you want to bet that before this is over, I'll get you to admit that I've never broken a promise to you and that you actually trust me?"

"I told you that I never bet."

"You don't have to. I'll win either way." He took her plate from her and tossed it in the trash disposal in the galley. "Now you can go back to playing. Two hours…as promised. Make the most of it." He turned and strode up the aisle away from her.

Lara sat there looking after him. For an instant she had thought that she might have hurt him, but that was ridiculous. Tanner was tough; nothing she said would have bothered him. Though he'd obviously expected her to be upset to know that he was a gambler, and it had probably annoyed him that she had compared him to Volkov.

No one was less like Volkov than Tanner. Volkov was a nightmare of ugliness and cruelty. Tanner wasn't like anyone else she had ever met. Pantherlike sleekness, strength, intelligence, the way he'd watch with narrowed gray-blue eyes as she spoke, seeing far too much. That smile so rare, you found yourself waiting for it. Yet she felt that he understood and accepted her words in a way no one else could. And he had understood how much the keyboard would mean to her and gone to the trouble to get it for her.

The keyboard.

Why was she staring after Tanner, she thought impatiently. He was an enigma and too fond of hurling out challenges. She could deal with him later. She only had another two hours of the music before she'd have to give it up for a little while.

She flexed her hands, leaned forward, and started to play.

"Time's up," Mallory told Lara gently. "Tanner told me to pack up the keyboard and ask you to go up and sit with Maria and buckle up. We'll be landing in fifteen minutes."

"That soon?" She got to her feet and shook her head to clear it. "Tanner left it to the last minute, didn't he? He said he'd only give me two more hours."

"He was probably enjoying himself." Mallory grinned. "As were we all. It was quite a concert."

"A very long one." Lara made a face. "I was being completely selfish. It was good that Tanner set me up at the back of the plane. I hope I didn't disturb you."

"No way. It was a pleasure." He made a shooing gesture. "But I've got to get this keyboard ready to go in the trunk of the Land Rover. It can't be left behind. Tanner told me it had go in first. Go buckle up."

She was already making her way toward the seat next to Maria.

"Was it good?" Maria asked as Lara dropped down in the seat. "Or at least enough to hold you?"

Lara nodded. "Both." She watched Maria put her computer in its case. "I hear you were doing a little work yourself."

"I thought he'd tell you. It was the clever thing to do. How much?"

"Only the part that was the most damaging to him. You can tell me the rest later."

"And by telling you himself, it served to dilute the poison. He realized what I was doing, and he didn't try to stop me. He even told me to go on with it." She paused. "He's very dangerous, Lara."

"I knew that in Avgar Forest. But he's not Volkov,

and he's not my father. He swore that he doesn't play the game the same way." She smiled crookedly. "And as he told me, he's the devil we know. That may have to be enough. We'll have to watch and see if he's telling the truth. Between us, we can find a way to handle him if he isn't."

"Besides, he gave you that keyboard that's made you so happy," Maria said dryly. "You seem to be the one being handled. Just because it's not the same game doesn't mean that he doesn't intend to win. He as much as warned me that he does."

"And he gave me the same warning, but isn't that more honest than threatening? It depends on how you look at it."

Maria shook her head. "It's that damn keyboard. Everything's rose-colored because you've been playing all day." She reached over and took her hand. "It's okay," she said gently. "I love to see you this mellow and full of hope. Relax. Lord knows you deserve not to worry every minute. Enjoy it. Just don't enjoy Tanner too much." She squeezed her hand. "Let me do the worrying for a change. It will be good not to feel as helpless about you as I usually do."

"You're never helpless." Lara's hand tightened on hers. "And you always help me. Every day. Every way."

"Not every way. We've been limited. But that may be still ahead for us." She looked out the window. "We're landing. Lots of trees... This Connecticut looks very... green. Green for hope? Green for opportunity? We'll have to see, won't we?"

"Welcome to the U.S.," Tanner said as he came out of the cockpit after the plane had taxied to a stop. "Land of the free…sometimes. At least, most of the time you have a chance if you work hard or have a gift." He grinned down at them. "And it can be a great place to lose yourself. Let's go and I'll show you." He headed for the door where Mallory was giving orders to a group of men as he orchestrated the removal of the keyboard. "It's a private airport, and I use it more than any other when I come back to the U.S. I have contacts here that are very susceptible to bribery, which is necessary…particularly since you have no passport or other papers. You'll have no problem here. It accommodates the Gulfstream and several helicopters, and I like the people in the neighboring town." He was running down the steps. "They're typical New Englanders: They don't talk much, and they mind their own business."

"I can see how that would appeal to you," Maria said as she and Lara followed him down the stairs. She looked around the airport. "Very clean and neat and quiet…and boring."

"I'm glad you like it." His lips were twitching. "I take it you didn't find out anything else about my iniquitous past?"

"You know I didn't. But I'll never give up."

"She won't, you know," Lara said absently as she watched Mallory slide the keyboard into the back of a tan Land Rover parked beside a small building across the tarmac. "She's very stubborn."

"I realize that. I'm looking forward to it. I've been thinking about helping her along." Tanner handed Lara a key ring. "Why don't you get in the car and guard that keyboard you can't keep your eyes off? Though I assure you that Mallory made sure it survived the trip from the plane to the Land Rover. I've got to go in and check on a few things with Pete Sherman, my airport manager."

She looked speculatively down at the keys in her palm. "Trusting. I could take the car and go back to my initial plan. What's to stop me?"

"Good judgment? You're a stranger in a strange land. No documents? And you know I'd just go after you." He added, "Plus if you were going to bolt, you'd first do your research and set up a plan. Right?"

"Unless there wasn't any other way."

"But there is another way. Try me and see."

"And where are we supposed to be going?"

"I have a place in the mountains that I've used occasionally. It's beautiful country, and it should be very safe until we find somewhere more permanent for you." He headed for the office building. "I'll be right back."

She watched until he disappeared inside before she started across the tarmac. "Let's go."

Maria fell into step with her. "He was very sure of himself."

"He should have been. He made sense."

"And he's beginning to know you very well." She looked back at the office. "He's put all the pieces he has together, but he's still on the alert for any new ones that might drop into his puzzle."

"But then we're getting to know him, too." Lara grinned as she unlocked the Land Rover. "He doesn't seem to mind answering my questions, and you're discovering all his deepest, darkest secrets with your computer."

"I doubt it. But I might learn enough to feel more

comfortable. We'll have to see." She got into the back-seat and opened her laptop. "You enjoy the scenery. I'd rather see if I can find out more about Tanner by connecting him to this place."

Lara shrugged as she got into the front passenger seat. "By all means, but I think he's considering it a game. He doesn't seem to care."

"He told me he was a very private person, so he does care. There might come a time when it's necessary that we do know everything about him." She started typing. "Like he told me, information can be a weapon, too…"

───◆───

Tanner didn't come out of the office for another thirty minutes. When he did, he was talking on the phone, and his expression…He wasn't frowning, it was more of an intense absence of expression.

Lara tensed. "I think something's wrong." She sat up straight in the seat, her gaze on Tanner's face. "I don't like the way—" She opened the door and jumped out of the Land Rover. "I've got to find out." She was moving toward him. "I'll be right back…"

The next moment she was standing in front of Tanner, glaring up at him. "What's happened? Why do you look like that? What can I do to help?"

"Maybe nothing." He hung up the phone. "Why do you think—"

"What's happened?" she interrupted. "Don't lie to me. I can *see* it. Don't shut me out. I might be able to help."

He was studying her intense expression. "You're…

different. I've never seen you like this. Almost as
fierce as you were in Avgar Forest...I don't know if
I'd dare shut you out. Providing there's any problem
to solve."

"There's a problem. What is it?"

He was still staring at her with narrowed eyes as
he murmured, "Very different." Then he said with
sudden abruptness, "I can't get in touch with Nash and
his crew. I tried to contact him from the cockpit an
hour before we landed, but I only got static. I decided
to try again using the equipment in Sherman's office.
It's much more sophisticated, and there shouldn't have
been any trouble."

"But there was?"

"Same result."

"Your friend who runs the airport in Stockholm?"

"No answer."

"Damn," she whispered. "Not good. What orders
did you give Nash?"

"He had a slight engine malfunction. It shouldn't
have taken any more than a few hours to fix. I told him
to do the repair and get out of Stockholm ASAP. He
was supposed to head back to the base in England."

"Not back to Russia?"

"I'm not an idiot, Lara."

"I don't know what you are," she said curtly. "I
just know that I don't like this. You said you knew
the Gulfstream had not been seen or tracked. What
about the helicopter that picked up Maria and brought
her here?"

"Nash is very competent. He set down the helicopter
in the middle of the woods, miles from Anton's house,
and they hiked to the house. After they secured Maria,
they took her back to the helicopter, making sure they

weren't seen." He added quietly, "He was careful. There shouldn't have been any slip-ups, Lara."

"You're right." She felt sick. She closed her eyes for a moment as she fought the chill. She could almost see the way it had happened. "There shouldn't have been, but there were." Her lids flipped open. "Because the one and only time Maria and I escaped Volkov and my father, he swore it wouldn't happen again. Even if Nash checked the security in and around the house, they wouldn't have caught all the cameras scattered around the woods. It might have taken my father a little while to access the right one where he could get the helicopter information and facial IDs, but he'd be able to do it."

"Son of a *bitch*." Tanner was swearing softly and vehemently. "I told Nash to check for security around the trees bordering the woods, but I didn't tell him to send a search team deep into the woods. Dammit, why didn't Kaskov tell me? He knew I only had a couple of days to do the recon."

"He probably didn't know. Even Maria didn't know," she said shakily. "It was just between my father and me. He took me deep into the woods and beat me with a whip after he showed me the cameras. Then he said if I tried to run again, he'd tie Maria to one of those trees and leave her there for a week and beat her every day. He said he could hardly wait to see the photos. He loved those cameras." Her lips twisted. "He liked to film her in pain. It was the only way he could make me do what he wanted."

"My God." He involuntarily reached out and took her by the shoulders.

She quickly stepped back away from him. "So it wasn't your fault or Kaskov's fault. It was *my* fault.

You told me she was safe, and I just accepted it. I should have remembered the cameras. I was just so glad to know she was safe I forgot everything else. It was a mistake. I shouldn't have done that. Now tell me what harm I've caused."

"Maybe none. I won't know until I find out what happened to Nash." He added roughly, "And regardless, it wouldn't have been your fault. I was in charge. It was my responsibility."

"Don't tell me that," she said fiercely. "I was the one who decided to come with you, didn't I? I could have said no. That means we're in this together. What's bad for you is bad for Maria and me. That means I'm just as much responsible for whatever happens to you or your men as you are for me. Now how do we find out what happened to Nash?"

"Sherman is already trying to do that. He's reaching out to some of the contacts in Stockholm I've used before to go and check out the airport. I should know something soon."

"Then can we climb in that Land Rover and get out of here?" she asked jerkily. "Can't Sherman call us while we're on the road?"

"It may not be an emergency situation, Lara," he said quietly. "We should have time."

"What if we don't? What if they're on their way? I don't want to take a chance. We're free now, I want to stay that way." Her hands clenched into fists at her side. "I can't let them get their hands on Maria."

"I won't let that happen. I promised I'd take care of both of you."

"But what if you can't do it? You don't know them. I'm the only one who can protect her." She added through set teeth, "Can we please *leave*."

He nodded slowly. "Get in the car. I have to go back into the office and talk to Sherman. We'll be on the road in five minutes." He turned on his heel and headed back into the office.

She whirled and strode back to the Land Rover.

"I was about to come and get you. You looked like you were pretty upset," Maria said as Lara got into the car. "Did Tanner screw something up?"

"No, I did," Lara said. "I forgot something I should have remembered."

"You don't forget anything," Maria said. "Sometimes I wish you would."

"I did this time." She paused. "Tanner can't get hold of Nash. Maybe something's gone wrong."

"Or maybe it hasn't," Maria said. "Nash seemed very smart while I was with him." She glanced at Tanner, who had just left the office and was coming toward them. "But he doesn't look too happy."

"Sherman hasn't been able to contact anyone in Stockholm yet," Tanner said as he opened the driver's door and got into the vehicle. "But I've set everything in place here, if there proves to be a problem." He took the leather box he was carrying and handed it to Maria in the backseat. "Still, it's just as well I had to go back to Sherman. I almost forget this."

Maria was looking at it, puzzled. "What is it?"

"I hate inefficiency. It was beginning to annoy me to see you using that computer that wasn't worthy of you. So I called ahead and asked Sherman to make certain he contacted my New York office and had them send down one of mine with all the bells and whistles when we arrived here." He started the car. "It's a very special computer that I won from one of Silicon Valley's geniuses, Herb Cramer. I've always thought technology gives an edge in any business, and I set up the stakes deliberately when I heard about the new computer he was developing. He wouldn't put anything but the prototypes into the pot anyway, but that was all I wanted. Most technology is out of date in a couple of years."

"What's so special about it?" Maria asked.

"It's a laptop equipped with the next-gen CPU that won't be available to the public for a few years."

"What will that mean to me?" she asked.

"That CPU is capable of millions of more calculations per second than anything else out there. That, combined with the state-of-the-art decryption software package also provided, will give you the ability to crack into private files and business records of almost anyone you choose. It will give you power you would never have had otherwise." He grinned. "And it will offer you at least a shot at discovering all my deepest mysteries. My only request is that you reserve it for personal use only and not let anyone else have access to it. I promised Cramer that when I won it from him."

Maria gazed blankly at him. "Why would you give me this? You're defeating your purpose."

"Because he'd think it wasn't fair," Lara said suddenly. "It wouldn't be fun for him."

Tanner smiled at her. "Along with a few other obscure reasons. I believe we may be getting to know each other, Lara." He glanced back at Maria. "And it's an extremely complicated piece of technology. It will give you something to do putting it together and discovering all the search engines and such." He was pulling out onto the road and gestured at Mallory, who was waiting at the side of the road at the wheel of a Toyota truck. "Lara will just have to be bored. She's had her treat for the day. I'm not going to have Mallory set up her keyboard. We'd be crowded for space."

"Whatever," Maria said absently. She was already digging into the box and pulling out leaflets.

Lara's gaze was on Mallory. "He's going with us?"

He nodded. "I decided I might want to have Mallory and a few other men to patrol the woods near the house."

"How many men?"

"Four." He looked at her inquiringly. "I hope that's okay?"

"Don't make fun of me. I just want to know what to expect. I've learned that surprises usually aren't pleasant."

"I'm sure you have. I wasn't making fun of you." He thought about it. "Or maybe I was. You're being very solemn. I might even be hoping to make you smile."

She shook her head. "I made a mistake. There's nothing funny about that. Were you thinking about bringing Mallory with us before you knew about Nash?"

"No. I was going to send him to check out the next stop on our itinerary. I wasn't planning on staying at the house for more than a couple of days."

"But you changed your mind. So you must have thought that there was reason to."

"I often err on the side of caution."

"I don't think you do. I believe you study the situation and then go over all the possible implications and ramifications before you make your moves. There's probably instinct involved, too, but like Mallory said, you're usually a step ahead." Her gaze was narrowed on his face. "And that step led you to bring Mallory and those other men along."

He snapped his fingers. "My, my, you have me all figured out. We'll have to tell Maria she doesn't need to bother with any more research. Would you like to continue? I'm fascinated."

"No, you're not. You're probably angry or at least on guard. You're very wary about anyone invading your space. That's too bad. It's not as if I wanted to do it. I've been trying to keep you at a distance because you scared me. But you can't keep me out now. It's too dangerous for us."

He didn't speak for a moment. "I'm not angry or on guard. You got that wrong, though you were close on the rest. I am curious about how long you've been concentrating on doing that rather interesting psycho-analysis on me?"

"Concentrating?" She shook her head. "That's something *you'd* do. I just let it come to me. Like a piece of difficult music that I had to learn. Then I went a little bit farther and threw in what I'd do if I were you in the same situation."

"Pure instinct. Intriguing," he murmured. "I suppose the skill was forced on you to survive those life-or-death Trials." He tilted his head. "At least you judged me to be difficult instead of simple. It's a pity you're so averse to gambling. I'd really like to see you in a poker game."

"You never will." She moistened her lips. "Though it was probably rude of me to—" She stopped.

"Invade my space," he finished. "The experience was worth the intrusion. But I doubt if you were really scared of me. I've never seen any signs of it."

"Of course I was scared. You've been the most

important person in my world since I woke up on that plane. I had to be careful not to make stupid choices and do the wrong thing." She made an impatient gesture. "But I can't sit back and let you make stupid choices, either. I have to know what you're doing so I can help you. When should you be receiving a call from this Sherman about Stockholm?"

"Very soon. It depends on how quickly he can get someone out to that airport to ask questions. I'd say within the hour."

"Not before that?"

He shook his head. "I doubt it." He smiled crookedly. "I promise you'll be the first to know."

"Okay." She leaned back in the seat. "I guess I can't do better than that. Unless you can call Sherman back and make him—"

"Aren't we done, Lara?" Maria asked dryly from the backseat. "I've been sitting here listening to you gnaw at the problem, and I'd like to get back to setting up this computer to work. I agree Nash might be trouble, but you don't know anything yet. Let Tanner worry about him. You said we could use him. Now don't get in his way. He signed on with Kaskov to get the job done. Let him do it."

"You heard your mother," Tanner said. "Let me worry about it…"

<hr />

The call came from Sherman thirty-five minutes later. Tanner put the call on speaker. "Answers?"

"You're not going to like it." Sherman's voice had a twang, but his words were clipped. "Oliver Radkork, the manager of the airport, is in the hospital with injuries." He paused. "All three of Nash's men are dead. Shot with automatic weapons. Nash himself may die eventually. He was still alive when he was found, but he's in bad shape. He was tortured for a long time and was almost cut to pieces." He paused before he added hoarsely, "He said to tell you he was sorry. That must mean he told them what they wanted to know. Radkork said there was a lot of screaming."

"Bastards." Tanner's lips tightened. "Tell them to get him the best care possible and let me know if he makes it. What else do you know? Who did it?"

"Radkork said several hours after you left a Boeing Chinook helicopter landed and fifteen or twenty thugs poured out of it. Nash was still working on his copter in the hangar, but they were all over the airport in seconds. They knew what they were doing, and Nash and his guys didn't have a chance."

"IDs?"

"The one who was giving the orders was Balkon. The son of a bitch was laughing when he was interrogating Nash."

Lara inhaled sharply.

Tanner reached out and covered her hand with his own. "What else? Did they get back on the Chinook or take another aircraft?"

"They got back on the Chinook."

"Good. It's not as fast as some other aircraft. That will buy us time, though probably not much. Tell Les to get the Gulfstream the hell out of there and take it to Toronto. You and your crew take care of moving the helicopters. Then call your friend Abner Clark, in the sheriff's office and tell them to be on the lookout for some neo-Nazis who have been making threats against the airport."

"That might be entertaining. The only people Abner hates worse than neo-Nazis are the Ku Klux Klan. Maybe I'll stay around and help him round them up."

"No, you get out of there now. I want that airport deserted in the next thirty minutes. Do you hear me?"

"I hear you." He sighed. "Les is almost ready to go. I had him gas up when you told me to do it before you left."

"Then get him out of there. I don't want a repeat of Stockholm."

"There won't be. I'll be in touch." He cut the connection.

"Neo-Nazis?" Maria asked.

"I knew it would make Sherman's friend move faster. The townspeople up here like their peace and order and can't stand vigilantes of any sort. I wanted them to be prepared for any violence they ran into, but I didn't have time for explanations." He glanced at Lara, who was sitting frozen beside him. "You're too quiet. Are you okay?"

"No," she whispered. "A lot of people died or were terribly hurt and they didn't have to be."

"And you're blaming yourself," he said roughly. "Stop it. It's my job, and I'm responsible for every single thing that happened, bad or good. So stop whining and tell me why Volkov wasn't in Stockholm with your father. Do I have to worry about an attack from a different quarter?"

Whining? She felt a ripple of anger. Then she realized he'd probably said it deliberately to jar her out of the shock she was experiencing. She shook her head to clear it. "Probably not. It's not unusual for Volkov to send Anton to run errands for him. I can see him ordering my father to find me and bring me back. Volkov was always the stronger. He held all the power. If he wasn't in Stockholm, then that's probably what happened." She moistened her lips. "My father would only call on Volkov for help if there was no other way. He wouldn't want him to know he failed."

He glanced at Maria. "You agree?"

She nodded. "Anton liked to play the big man, but he was thoroughly under Volkov's thumb." She added bitterly, "Unfortunately, Lara is more familiar with the dynamics of their interaction, but I can vouch for that."

"Why did you say we might have some time?" Lara asked. "You obviously thought he might be on his way here."

"Nash knew about this airport. He knew that's where we were heading. Under torture I don't have the slightest doubt he would have told your father." He paused. "But they took the Chinook when they left Stockholm. There's a chance that they might have changed to a faster aircraft somewhere along the way, but I'd bet they'll use the Chinook to come directly here and try to catch us off guard. So it will give us a little time to get out of here."

"And where are we going?" Lara asked.

"I haven't changed our destination. No one knows about the mountain house. It will still be safe."

"Until it's not," Lara said. "I don't like the idea of hiding out anywhere close to an airport where you're expecting an attack. This is a big country. Maybe we should move on."

"We will," he said quietly. "But not yet. We'll bury ourselves in the mountains for a couple of days while I gather information, look over the situation, and make a few decisions. I didn't expect to be on the run quite so soon." His lips twisted. "And Nash would have told your father everything he knows about me along with where I was taking you. It makes me a bit vulnerable. I don't like that. It's nothing I can't handle, but I have to consider possible consequences."

"I can see how you wouldn't like to feel vulnerable," Lara said sarcastically. "What a shame. Maria and I wouldn't know what that feels like."

"Point taken," he said. "But it doesn't change anything except it adds to my empathy, and I didn't need that." He stepped on the accelerator. "We're still going to the mountains. You can argue with me when we get there."

CHAPTER

7

I can see why you thought this place would be safe,"
Lara said dryly as she held on to her seat belt while
Tanner made another sharp turn through the tall
jungle-like thornbush at the sides of the dirt road they
were traveling. It had been a nightmare of those twists
and turns since they'd left the main road a full twenty
minutes ago. And that thornbush...She shivered. "I've
never seen banks of thorn plants like those. Very in-
timidating. And there's no way I could find my way
here even if I knew where I was going. Are you sure
you do?"

"I'm sure." He made another sharp turn. "I covered
all this ground on foot many times before I was allowed to put a foot inside a car. I was a city boy, and I
can't tell you how many times I got lost. That tends to
engrave every turn into one's memory."

She looked at him in surprise. "You learned to drive
here? This is your home?"

"Something like that. More than any other place, I suppose. We're almost there. The gates are just beyond the next bend." He pressed a button on his key ring as he made the turn. "I've let Sam Rennell know we're coming, and he'll probably meet us. Don't be startled if he's not what you'd call friendly. He was one of the hotshot, idealistic police officers injured when the South Tower came down on Nine Eleven. When he finally recovered, he had trouble...adjusting. He's still one of the best security people on the planet, but there's nothing young or idealistic about him."

"He works here?" Maria asked.

"This is his home, too. I doubt if he could live anywhere else now. He's the caretaker and wears a dozen other hats. But he's happy here, and this is where he'll stay." He glanced at Lara. "So if you have trouble, you'll have to be the ones to adapt."

She shrugged. "We'll only be here for a couple of days. Less if I get my way. If he's not violent, there shouldn't be trouble."

"He's not usually violent, but no promises." They were approaching a twelve-foot stone fence, and the metal gates were swinging slowly open. "If he is, it's usually aimed at me. That shouldn't bother you." They'd reached the gates, and Lara saw a huge SAN-DRINO PLACE engraved on the post. He drove through the gates, and a massive stone house came into view at the end of the driveway.

She gave a low whistle. "It's a mansion. That I wasn't expecting. It's like fighting our way through Sleeping Beauty's thorny forest to get to her castle." Her gaze ran over the glittering deep-set mullioned windows. The house was in perfect repair and the gardens and floral bushes surrounding it were well kept, the lawns perfectly barbered. "It's beautiful. Does it belong to you?"

"In a way. I sort of act as guardian." He pulled up to the front door. "But I guarantee there will be no Sleeping Beauty lolling around to get in your way. No laziness permitted on the property. Rennell makes sure that the interior is as perfect as the gardens. In his eyes we all have our duties to perform."

"In a way. *Guardian*," Maria repeated his words thoughtfully. "Yet you seem to be in charge." She suddenly smiled. "Maybe we should have asked if you won it in a poker game like you did the Gulfstream."

"Not exactly. And I didn't win Rennell, either. I guarantee they're both more of a burden than a treasure." He gestured to a tall, powerful man with blunt impassive features who was coming down the path toward the Land Rover. He was dressed in jeans and a blue chambray shirt; a sleek Doberman at his heels looked as powerful and menacing as the man himself. "And here he comes." Tanner got out of the car and waited for the man to reach him. "Give me a minute and I'll introduce you. He'll only be interested in one thing to start out."

He smiled at Rennell and held out his hand. "You look well. How have you been, Rennell?"

Rennell ignored his hand. "Sandrino?"

Tanner shook his head. "Not yet. I'm working on it."

"It's been too long," he said bluntly. "You said you'd do it. You made a promise."

"And I'll keep it." He reached down and stroked the Doberman at Rennell's side. "How is Kembro doing?"

"Well enough," Rennell said curtly. "When will you keep it?"

"Soon." He nodded at Lara. "I'm working on it right now. So leave me alone, Rennell. I want it as bad as you do." He gestured. "Maria and Lara. They're very nice, and you should treat them as Sandrino would wish you to. I've brought Mallory and a few other men, too. They should be arriving any minute to do sentry duty. It was necessary."

"I won't let them ruin my flowers if they're clumsy."

"Mallory knows the rules. I don't believe you'll have any trouble."

"I never have trouble. *They* might have trouble." He turned away. "You can tell Mallory he can set them up in the coach house." He glanced over his shoulder at Lara. "You'll need the guards for her?"

"Possible. It's just a precaution. Food?"

"I made a stew after you contacted me. How long will I have to put up with you all?"

"A few days. Mallory and his men will be keeping watch, but I'd like it if you'd also do it. Compared with you, they'll be blind out here at Sandrino Place. You're the one who taught me how to see."

Rennell nodded. "Yes, I did." He added grudgingly, "And you weren't terrible. You never bitched when I left you out there in the wilds all night."

"Because I knew if I did, the next time it would be for two or three nights instead of one," Tanner said dryly. "You were nothing if not consistent."

"I had to make sure it had sunk in. You were a city boy who thought you knew everything. Sandrino told me I should make sure that you realized there was more to learn before someone killed you. I always did what Sandrino said." He was striding away. "You're not dead yet, are you?"

Tanner turned back to Lara and Maria. "And now

you've met Sam Rennell. I'm sure you'll agree he's one of a kind." He was going up the steps and throwing open the front door. "You might as well go in and choose one of the suites and start settling in. It doesn't matter which one. They'll all be spotless and in fantastic shape. Rennell makes sure that the entire property is always as ready as if Sandrino is going to walk through that door in the next ten minutes." He was reaching for his phone and dialing. "I'll call Mallory and remind him that he has to smooth Rennell's way with the men. It's been a while since he's been around Rennell, and he might have forgotten that when annoyed he takes no prisoners."

"Wait," Lara said. "Who is this Sandrino? Is that who owns this place? And why in the hell did you give Rennell the idea that I have something to do with him?"

"Because you do. And I'm aware that I have explanations to make, but I'm not in the mood right now. I'm feeling a bit raw at the moment. Maybe later." He turned and walked away as Mallory answered.

"Maybe?" Lara repeated.

Maria nudged her arm. "You know you'll get it out of him, you're just impatient. It's been a bad day for all of us." She was gently pushing her into the house. "Distraction. I've never been told to make myself at home in a mansion before. So that's what I'm going to do. Actually, I like the idea of being able to give you the chance of doing it, too. I've always hated not being able to give you anything better than that house on the compound. Then I'm going to have a shower, and after that I suggest we dive into that stew Rennell was talking about." She was leading her toward the grand staircase. "But as usual you'll do what you want to do. Which will be fine with me as long as it doesn't involve tracking Tanner down and interrogating him when he's this close to exploding."

"He isn't going to explode. He'll just withdraw and go inside himself." Lara shrugged. "Which would mean I won't get what I wanted anyway. So I'll leave him alone."

"He's right," Maria said softly. "You are getting to know him. That might not be good."

"I *have* to know him." Lara stopped at the bottom of the stairs and then whirled and headed for the front door. "And I don't feel like going up there and picking out some fancy suite. I want to look over the grounds, and then I'm going to take another glance at that thorn-jungle we drove through to get here."

"Why?"

"I don't like that Tanner was stressing how difficult he found it. Maybe it was a warning. And I should know how to get out of here if we need to. If I study it, it might not be that hard."

"And then it might. It would be humiliating if I had to ask Tanner to go rescue you. You'd hate it."

Lara smiled. "Which is why I wouldn't let it get to that point. I'd be certain I could do it before I made an attempt. And I'd have to have a good reason." She opened the door. "I'll be fine. I'm just taking a look around. I'll see you later."

"See that you do. And not much later."

"Right." Lara closed the door and looked around her. Beautiful blossoms, perfect order, lush greenery…but that wasn't what she was looking for. She wanted to see what was beneath all that perfection. She headed for the tall stone wall in the distance…

———————

"Are you going to jump down on the other side? Or are you going to make me climb up on that wall and get you?"

Lara looked down from where she was sitting on the top of the stone wall to see Tanner in the garden below her. He didn't look pleased, and she automatically braced herself. Then she forced herself to relax her muscles. "You don't have to come up, I was finished here. I just wanted to take another look around." She started to climb down the wall. "I wasn't going anywhere. I would have taken Maria with me if I'd decided to do that."

"That's what I told Rennell, but he thought that if you were at all important, I might want to keep you from tearing yourself up on those bushes." He lifted her down the last few feet to the ground. "Next time I won't follow his advice."

"Rennell?" She looked around and spotted him leaning against a maple tree about a hundred yards away. "I didn't see him following me."

"Because he didn't want you to see him. He watched you for a while and then got nervous when you climbed the wall."

"I wouldn't have cared if I'd known," she said. "I just wanted to know if I'd have as hard a time as you did on foot down there."

"And you decided you would?"

"There's a good chance. Those thorns look nasty. What kind of bushes are they?"

"A special variety of pyracantha. Extra large, and the leaves are poisonous. Commonly known as firethorn. Needle-sharp spikes all over those stems, and the growing tips are four-inch-long hypodermics. Nasty enough for you?"

She nodded. "I thought it might be something like that. But I had to know."

He smiled crookedly. "Just in case?"

"Just in case." She started back toward the mansion. "I realized how little I knew about you, and suddenly I was in an isolated place that might be difficult for me to get away from. Worse. It might be almost impossible for me to get Maria away even if I could find a way out for myself."

"So it was my fault you perched yourself on the top of that wall?"

"It was your fault," she said flatly. "You don't say 'maybe' to me when I need answers. That sends me to look for them myself." She turned to him as they reached the front door. "That's a nightmare stretch of thornbushes before I could get through those woods. But they only climb ten to fifteen feet high into the trees. Once I got into the higher branches, I'd be safe from them. But, as I said, getting Maria out would have been almost impossible without getting her cut to ribbons. I can't allow that to happen, so get your shit together and let me know what the hell is going on." She opened the front door. "And it better be very soon, Tanner." She slammed the door behind her.

* * *

Tanner swore beneath his breath as he whirled away from the door.

"She was angry that you stopped her from getting away?" Rennell asked.

Tanner turned to see him now standing a few

feet away. "No, I told you that wasn't what she was doing," he said curtly. "She said that she had no intention of trying to get away; she was only looking at the possibilities if she decided she couldn't trust me."

"Really?" A flicker of interest lit Rennell's face. "And I suppose those possibilities discouraged her?"

"No, she thought she could make it to the main road, but it wouldn't be without damage, and she'd need to use the trees to get her away from the thorns."

Rennell's gaze went to the wall. "And would she be able to do that?"

"Probably. She once told me she'd spent six months training herself to be able to survive in the forest. When I first met her, she'd just spent three days on the run from two hit men in Avgar Forest and had already taken down one of them." He grimaced. "Yeah, she would have had to use the trees there, if only to hide at night."

Rennell nodded. "And we both know that someone not familiar with this property would have to use the trees in order to escape. It would be the only way to avoid being torn to pieces by the thornbushes." He paused. "She must be much more clever than you, Tanner. You never even made an attempt to use them. You just waited for me to hunt you down. I wondered about that the first couple of times."

"Only the first couple?"

"Before I figured it out. I thought surely you'd use the trees because I knew how much Sandrino respected you. But then I realized that you never wanted to escape; you wanted me to bring you back. It was part of the game you and Sandrino played."

"Then you were playing it, too," Tanner said

quietly. "Because you've never mentioned to me that
you knew. Why not?"

"He didn't want me to know. It was always between the two of you. I had my place in his life, you
had yours."

"Then what's different now?"

"You promised you'd bring Sandrino back." He
gazed directly into Tanner's eyes. "You didn't keep
your promise. That changes everything."

"No, it doesn't. It just means I need more time."

"You're going to use the woman? How? Are we
going to trade her for Sandrino?"

"No—well, maybe in a way. But she knows nothing about Sandrino. However, Sergai Kaskov tells me
he does, and I have to keep her safe until I get the
information I need from him."

"Kaskov," Rennell repeated. Then he shook his
head. "It all sounds too clumsy and involved to me.
And definitely not soon enough. It doesn't matter if
she's safe. Trade her now and find him." He paused.
"Or I will, Tanner."

"No, you won't," Tanner said softly. "Stay out of it,
Rennell. Help me or disappear. Either way, I'm going
to find Sandrino, and I'll use Lara Balkon to do it. But
I'm not going to let you get her killed because you're
too impatient and don't give a damn. We've waited this
long, and we'll wait a little longer. Understand?"

"I understand that I might give you a little more
time." His gaze never left Tanner's. "Or I might not.
Until I make up my mind, she won't leave here. Make
sure she knows that. If she goes over that wall, you're
not going to get her back."

"She's not going to try to get away," Tanner said.
"I'll work it out." He turned and started down the

path toward the coach house where Mallory and his crew were unloading equipment in the garages. "But it would help if you'd stay away from both of them until I do. Give me some space."

"Why should I?" Rennell called after him. "When you didn't keep your promise."

———◆———

MUSIC ROOM
9:40 P.M.

"Maria told me you were in here," Tanner said as he strolled toward the chair where Lara was sitting before the keyboard. "I see Mallory got you set up." He looked around the tiled floors, the beautifully crafted amber windows and arched ceiling. "Your keyboard looks like a poor relation in here. I don't blame you for just sitting there and not playing. This room deserves a grand piano, but Sandrino never got around to finding one and left it up to me." His lips twisted. "I got busy and disappointed him as I did you. Life has a habit of getting in the way. But I'll still keep my word to you. Did you and Maria have something to eat?"

"Rennell's stew," she said curtly. "It was excellent." She got up from her chair. Then she braced herself and turned to face him. "And I don't give a damn about this fancy music room. Once I start playing, I don't notice anything else. And the reason I'm not playing right now is that I didn't want to become distracted before I got answers. Are you ready to give them to me?"

"It's why I'm here," he said simply. "Rennell brought it to my attention that I had no choice. You were making him very edgy. Which meant you were obviously going to cause me too much trouble unless I got you on my side." He shook his head. "Correction. I wouldn't expect you to go quite that far. Ask your questions, Lara."

"I'll start with the most important one. Have you heard from your friend Sherman about any attacks happening at the airport yet?"

"Not a word. I would have told you right away. You'll know everything as soon as I do." He paused. "But it's probably only a matter of time."

"I know that. It's always only been a matter of time with my father and Volkov," she said bitterly. "But this was different, I had a chance. I could give Maria a chance. I won't give that up. Second question. Why did you bring me here?" She took a step closer to him. "Who is this Sandrino? And what do I have to do with him? You nodded at me when you were talking to Rennell about him. Does Sandrino have anything to do with Kaskov?"

"That's a lot of questions. I'll take them one at a time. I brought you here for the reason I told you: I can keep you safe here. It's totally private, and you have to admit that it wouldn't be easy for anyone to storm this house." He paused. "Who is Sandrino? He's a bit harder to explain." He pulled out his phone to show her the photo of a silver-haired man in his late fifties or early sixties who was smiling sardonically up at her. "This is Antonio Sandrino. I met him in Hell's Kitchen when I was fourteen. I was playing cards in the back room of a bar and doing damn well for myself. Of course, I got beat up pretty frequently when one of the other players thought I was doing too well. Not that I cheated. I learned very early that if I was good enough, I wouldn't have to cheat. Sandrino owned several restaurants in New York and had money to burn, but he was better known for the games he ran. He was the best poker player in the country, maybe the world. He was always jetting to Europe or South America to some game or other. Everyone wanted a chance to play Sandrino. He was in the big leagues. I was flattered he'd drop into the bar every now and then and watch us play. He wouldn't say anything, he'd just watch the game. I thought he was weird, but I kind of liked him. Then one night I ended up in the alley outside the bar with my pockets picked and a very bad concussion. I woke up in a bedroom here a few weeks later with Sandrino staring down at me. I got very nervous. I was afraid he was even weirder than I thought." He grinned. "It turned out he was, but not in that way. He told me that he and Rennell had wasted a lot of time taking care of me, and he made it a habit of never making an investment without demanding a return. So he'd decided to keep me here and teach me until he was sure that I wasn't going to end up in a morgue instead of an alley next time." He shrugged. "And that was the start of my relationship with Sandrino. He became my mentor, my friend, and many other things I'd never known before."

"Which has nothing to do with me," she said in exasperation. "Why did you let Rennell think it did?"

"Because it has a good deal to do with you," he said quietly. "Sandrino disappeared eighteen months ago on one of his trips overseas, and I've been trying to track him down ever since. I got as far as St. Petersburg, Russia, before the trail ran out." He smiled wryly. "But last week Kaskov paid me a visit and told me he'd use all his connections to find him for me if I'd do him a small favor."

"Me?"

He nodded. "Not so small, as it turned out. But I needed that information about Sandrino. I was at a dead end."

"And that was why you agreed to get Maria and me out of Russia?" she asked slowly. "He could have been lying to you."

"I didn't think he was. I was willing to take a chance." He made a face. "Though not with any degree of eagerness. I didn't like the idea of doing Kaskov's errands." He looked her in the eye. "But I didn't think this one was meant to hurt you. One of the last things he did to convince me to take the job was to hand me a DVD of you playing Rachmaninoff. He said I should see what they were trying to kill. It was a good move on his part."

"Together with the Sandrino info," she said quietly.

He nodded. "He had me." He added, "But I made you a promise about protecting you from Volkov and your father—and if you remember, that also included Kaskov. I intend to keep that promise. That hasn't changed."

"Except that they're coming closer now than I thought they'd be." Then she made an impatient gesture. "And I know that's my fault, but it scared me. And when I realized this place would be as hard to get out of as a prison, it just made it worse."

"It's not your fault. I told you I always run any job I take on." He smiled faintly. "But I agree this place can be a prison until it becomes a haven. It was both to me. Along with being a school and sometimes a therapy workshop. Sandrino grew up on the streets, and life was as rough for him as it was for me. Once he'd made it big time, one of the first things he built was this place, where he could always be safe in case life crashed down around him."

"He certainly did that," she said dryly. "Those thorns are a huge deterrent."

"Not one you can't conquer. Rennell was impressed." He added, "Which is another reason we're having this talk. Since I had to let him know that you're important for me getting information about Sandrino, he's a little nervous about you deciding you might want to leave us. Could you please not hang out on the top of that wall again?"

She suddenly chuckled. "I can't imagine him nervous. He's totally without expression—he reminds me of the giant in the fairy tale Maria used to read me when I was little. I might want to do it again just to see it for myself."

He flinched. "That would make it extremely difficult for me. Rennell and I have had our disagreements over the years, but I'd prefer not to be at odds with him. Sandrino had an unwritten rule to that effect, and neither of us disputed it because Sandrino had saved both of us."

"How did he save Rennell? You said he was a cop."

"One of the best, totally devoted. But his captain sent him undercover with the Gardellas, one of the deadliest crime families in New York. In order to get evidence, he had to stay undercover for over six years. That meant he had to become one of them. Rennell never did anything halfway. By the time he got his evidence, he was the most valuable 'made' man in the family. He'd become a killer, a thief, anything required by the mob. He'd begun to like it. It was questionable that he'd even turn over that evidence after he'd gathered it. But Nine Eleven happened and he left the family and ran to help his old unit at the tower. He was the only one of them who survived when the tower fell. He ended up in a psych ward in bad shape for six months. Sandrino was working with the survivors and he decided to take him home with him." He paused. "He was totally loyal to Sandrino, but don't make the mistake of thinking that he's lost any of his lethal capabilities. One of his jobs was to act as Sandrino's bodyguard."

"Why would you believe I've any intention of making that kind of mistake?"

He shook his head. "Because you're enjoying this a little too much. I really appreciate those flashes of humor, but not when they're aimed at me."

Her smile widened. "And that's when I enjoy it most."

"And I'll accept it, because it's worth it to me. We were on our way toward a peaceful coexistence before you panicked like a deer in headlights. I can understand why, and that's the reason I'm here baring my soul. But I want that status back. Is it enough for you? If it's not, then tell me what else I can do."

Her smile ebbed as she stared at him. His expression was slightly mocking, but this hadn't been easy for him. She had learned enough about him to realize that he wasn't given to either explanations or confidences— and he had just given her both with amazing generosity. She should try to be equally generous. "It's enough," she said haltingly. "It was that I didn't know what was going on. I felt...helpless. I hate to feel helpless. I...strike back."

"I've noticed." A warm smile lit his face. "But

now you do know what's going on. Welcome to my world. If there's anything else you want to know, just ask me."

"That would be an intrusion. You'd be right to resent it."

"Then we could trade information. No intrusion involved."

"You'd be cheated. You already know everything about me," she said ruefully. "Thanks to Kaskov."

"I know the bare bones, and that's not nearly enough. I had to guess the rest. I want to hear it all from you."

"Why?"

"How the hell do I know?" he asked with sudden harshness. "Curiosity? I want to have a reason to hate your father and Volkov even more than I do now? Maybe I feel like I have an investment in you like Sandrino did in me? For some reason it matters to me."

She shook her head. "You're not making sense."

He nodded. "Okay. I'll back off. You're allowing me closer than I expected. But I'm persistent, and someday I bet you'll let me take that last step."

"I don't know why you're so curious," she said wearily. "But I'm beginning to believe that whatever is going on with you, you won't hurt us. So I'll not make this any harder than it has to be, Tanner. I want this over as much as you do. And if you think that I can trust Kaskov, I might even give you a chance to turn me over to him."

His brows rose. "Really?"

"Might," she repeated. "Don't let it go to your head."

"Too late. I believe that could actually be trust looming on the horizon."

"Don't count on it." She turned and sat back at the

keyboard. "Now go away. I want to play. You've taken too much of my time."

"You're tossing me away? Do you mind if I stay around and listen? You're proving to be habit forming."

She shrugged. "Why should I mind? I won't know you're here." She looked back at him over her shoulder. "I never know——" She forgot what she was going to say as she met his eyes. Intensity. Heat. Electricity. She couldn't breathe and her breasts were swelling. The response was totally unexpected. And dammit, she could tell he knew it. She quickly looked away. "No, I don't mind. Sit down over there on the couch and be quiet."

She heard him moving behind her to the couch. "I promise you won't even know I'm here," he said softly. "The last thing I want to do is disturb you…"

CHAPTER

8

2:35 A.M.

Lara!"
 There was a dim shape in the darkness...
Coming toward her.

"Wake up!" Tanner was sitting her up in bed. "You said you wanted to know everything. I promised you, dammit." Then the lamp on the bedside table was lit, and Lara was wide awake.

His expression was grim, she thought as she shook her head to clear it. His lips were tight and his light eyes gleaming with ferocity. "What?"

"I got the call from Sherman." He grabbed her navy bathrobe from the bottom of the bed and draped it around her shoulders over her nightshirt. "The Connecticut airport was hit earlier tonight. It wasn't good." He was swearing beneath his breath. "I told him not to fight them, but he wasn't listening. He and his buddy in the sheriff's office decided they wanted to take at least one prisoner to interrogate." He took her wrist and was leading her from the bedroom. "Idiots."

She had to hurry to keep pace with him. "Where are you taking me?"

"To the library. I need a drink." He was pulling her down the staircase. "This isn't going to be easy for me."

She pulled her arm away from his grasp as they reached the bottom of the stairs. "Just tell me. Sherman was hurt?"

"No, but his friend Abner was killed." He threw open the door and strode past her into the library to the bar against the far wall. "And your father's men set fire to the remaining aircraft left in the hangars. Everything but the office was burned to the ground, and the only reason that was spared is that they wanted to send a message." He was pouring himself a whiskey. "Sherman was in the woods trying to stop Abner from bleeding to death or he would have probably been killed, too. They hit hard and fast and were in and out of the airport in forty minutes. After Abner died, Sherman made his way back through the airport to the office to see why they hadn't touched it." He handed Lara his phone. "Anton came prepared. You told me he liked cameras. Evidently, he had this photo enlarged and brought it with him. He tacked it on the door of the office."

She slowly took the phone. She didn't have to look at it to know what she was going to see.

Maria.

Half naked, her hands bound above her head. Her upper body was crisscrossed with whip marks. The only mark of brutality Lara hadn't seen before was a gaping red mark that had been drawn across Maria's throat. One word had been scrawled in Russian beneath the photo. COME.

She vaguely heard Tanner cursing as she blindly thrust the phone back at him. "He did that to her a long time ago." Her voice was shaking. "I could usually keep it from happening. But he always kept the photos. Sometimes he'd show them to me when he needed to threaten me." She was talking fast, and her voice was getting hoarser. She could feel the tears sting her eyes. "It usually didn't take much. It was better than having him touch her. She'd never cry out because she knew how much it hurt me. No matter what—"

"Shut up." He'd pulled her into his arms and was rocking her. "You're killing me. I didn't want to show the damn thing to you, but I'd promised." He took out his handkerchief and was dabbing at her wet cheeks. "It won't happen to her. I won't let it."

She nodded. "No, it won't. I'm sorry, I let it all come back to me just as he intended it to." She took a step back. "It was clever of him. The threat and then the demand that I do what he wants. It's been ingrained for years. I can't let him do that to me this time." She had to stop shaking. She wrapped her arms tightly over her chest. "But I have to be sure that what you've told me about her being safe here is the truth. There's no way they can track us here? I'll have a little chance to think what's best for me to do?"

"No way will they find you. I told you, this was Sandrino's safe house. No one knows about it, and I have you secure. Nothing can happen to you while you're here." He was pouring another shot of whiskey into a glass. He took her elbow and half nudged, half pushed her across the library toward the couch. "Now sit down and drink this whiskey." He pulled her down beside him and put the glass in her hand. "You look like you're going to shatter any minute. It's driving me crazy."

"I don't drink."

"You do now." He watched her take a swallow and then make a face. "Though it doesn't surprise me. You're probably afraid to let your guard down."

"I won't shatter." She took another tentative drink and shook her head. "It tastes terrible. Sometimes I had wine when I was in Paris. Everybody drinks wine there. That was much better."

"But it doesn't have quite the healing power. And I'm all for healing right now." He pulled her closer. "Don't stiffen. Just relax. It's all part of the therapy. For both of us. I'm not in such good shape myself. I hate like hell seeing you like this. It makes me homicidal and frustrated at the same time. I don't like feeling that helpless. Let me *do* something."

He *was* doing something. She just didn't know what it was. How could she relax? She could feel his heartbeat under her ear and the strength he was trying to give her. It felt…good. Some of the shock and pain was going away. She didn't move for a moment. "You don't have…to do anything. I know it always has to be me."

He was swearing beneath his breath again. He pulled her head back to look down into her face. "There you go again. Look, I want to help you. I *need* to help you. It drives me crazy to know what Volkov and that monster you call a father have done to you and Maria. Okay, maybe I'm not as empathetic as Mallory, but it still bothers me." His lips twisted. "So you should take advantage of my weakness, because it definitely gives your position additional strength."

She tilted her head. "Are you pitying me?"

"Would I dare? No, I'm just angry as hell because you weren't given a fair break. Nothing I hate more than a dirty game."

"Yes, you've told me that." She stared at him curiously. "But I didn't think it would upset you this much. Maybe you're right, perhaps it's a weakness that I should take advantage of. But I don't think I can, because no one has ever told me anything like that before. It would feel very strange to use it…" She pushed away from him. "At any rate, I think you're being kind, so thank you." She glanced absently down at the glass of whiskey still in her hand. She swallowed the rest of it and then set the glass on the end table beside the couch. "I don't want Maria to see that photo. We'll just tell her there was a raid. She doesn't have to know how close they came tonight."

"And you want to protect her. Just as she wants to protect you." He smiled crookedly. "It's rather touching."

"Of course," she said simply. "That's how it has to be. You're making fun of us?"

"No, actually I was being sincere." He took a sip of his whiskey. "I might even envy you."

"Don't you have anyone that you have to protect?"

"I had Sandrino. But I evidently screwed that up." He thought about it. "And I protect Mallory sometimes." He lifted his glass to her. "And now I have you to protect. So evidently my horizons are beginning to expand."

"I don't want you to have to protect me. I need this to be over." She shivered. "Anton is going to be upset. This was the second time he missed getting us. He'll be on his phone to Volkov making excuses and asking for help." She nibbled on her lower lip. "Volkov will be furious."

"And will he come running to help your bastard of a father?"

She nodded. "He'll start to get worried. He won't want to lose me, so he'll come after me. I'd have a chance of my father giving up, but not Volkov, he'll never give up. He's not finished with me."

"Why?" Tanner asked suddenly. "Finished? Why do you say that? Talk to me."

"Revenge. He hates me. He's always hated me. He always will. I think he believed this last Trial might be the end, but it didn't turn out that way, and that will only make him more bitter." She was talking too much, she thought. And she was a little dizzy. She shook her head to clear it, but that made her even dizzier. "I don't think I should have had that whiskey. I told you that I don't drink."

"And I probably should have paid attention to you." His eyes were narrowed on her face. "I could see the pain and I just wanted it to go away. I wanted to make you stronger, not weaker. And now I've changed my mind, I don't want you to tell me anything. It might not be fair."

"You think liquor would do that?" She shook her head. "Not to me. And I don't think you'd use it just to get me to confide in you. You'd regard it the same way you would a crooked game. Besides, you couldn't be that curious."

"Yes, I could. And I'm an opportunist who wants very badly to know everything possible about you and Volkov. So don't trust me. I've always found information to be a weapon, and I have an idea that before this is over I might need a weapon or two to use against Volkov." He leaned forward, and his voice was suddenly velvet soft and persuasive. "But I've promised to keep you and Maria safe, and I'll do it. You don't have to pay me by letting me know anything about what you went through with Volkov."

He wasn't touching her now, but that persuasiveness mixed with total honesty was strangely overwhelming. And it was true he had committed himself to helping them, and she believed he would do it. She looked away from him. "I don't like to think about it. It was...ugly."

"Then forget it." He went still. "If it had anything to do with Volkov, I'm sure it was," he said quietly. "But the ugliness only had to do with Volkov. Not with you. Whatever he did to you, it didn't touch who you are."

Her gaze flew back to his face. "You think he raped me?"

"I wasn't sure...He didn't?"

She shook her head. "He didn't hurt me that day. I hurt him. But it was still ugly and horrible." She shuddered. "I was only eleven years old and it was the day I was supposed to go to Moscow for the competition. I was scared and excited and I was just praying I wouldn't do anything that would disappoint Maria. She'd arranged to have Maxim take me to Moscow that day. My father never let Maria and me go anywhere alone together. I was to have my usual lesson with Maxim, but it was to be in the village at his house instead of ours. She said I was supposed to go directly to Moscow instead of coming home afterward. I didn't know why Maria had made the change, but I never asked questions. I knew Anton was out of town, but I thought he might have come back. Maria tried to make sure that I was never around when he came to her. She'd send me to my room or out into the woods and tell me not to come back until she came for me. But after my lesson with Maxim I found I'd not brought a piece of sheet music I needed to take to Moscow, so I had to go home to get it. I thought I could go in the back door and straight to my room and get the music and then slip out again." She drew a deep breath. "But it didn't work out like that. When I got to the house, I saw Volkov's car in the driveway. Volkov had just moved into the area from St. Petersburg, but I didn't really think anything about him being there. He'd been dropping in and playing cards with my father for the last few months. I thought my father must have come home and that Volkov was just visiting. So I went in the back way as I'd planned, grabbed the music, and started back down the hall." She swallowed. "But then I heard Maria cry out and Volkov laughing. He kept telling her to scream for him. I ran toward her bedroom. He had her naked on the floor and he was inside her, doing what my father always did to her. But he had a candle and he was burning her breasts. She saw me in the doorway, and she started to shake her head and tried to tell me to go away. But how could I do that? I ran to the fireplace and grabbed a poker and then I flew back across the room and I hit him with all my strength, and I hit him, and I hit him, and I hit him again. I took him completely by surprise. He was cursing me as he scrambled to get away from the poker instead of coming after me. But then I struck him on the head, and he collapsed, unconscious."

"You're lucky to be alive," Tanner murmured.

"I couldn't think about that. He was *hurting* her. I thought I'd killed him. I *wanted* to kill him. But then

Maria was there, holding and rocking me and telling me that he wasn't dead and everything would be okay. That it wasn't my fault, and she'd find a way to fix it. All I could do was cry and clutch her as hard as I could. But even then, I couldn't see how she'd ever be able to fix what had happened in that room. But Maria promised she'd do it, and then call me later to tell me how. My part was to leave the house right then and run back to Maxim and let him take me to that competition. I was to stop crying and not let him see that anything was wrong." Her lips twisted. "And I was to play as I'd never played before, and let the music take me to another place. Because that was the only thing she'd ever wanted for me, the only thing I could give her."

He shook his head. "And you won that competition when you must have been falling apart inside."

"I couldn't do anything else. It was the only thing I could give her. She gave me everything. Life, sacrifice, love, music. You don't realize what she went through all those years."

"I believe I'm beginning to. But unless I'm guessing wrong, I think that you probably ended up an equal contributor. How did she keep Volkov from killing you?"

"She's very clever. She had to learn a lot about the Russian mafia families' customs and beliefs just to survive those years with Anton after I was born. She had to make bargains, use sex, learn trickery—anything she could do to keep us both safe. She'd always tried to keep me insulated, but after what I did, she knew that was at an end. So she told me the truth. One of the prime rules in mafia families is that bosses' wives and their children are off limits. It's a matter of respect and isn't violated. But Volkov thought he was so powerful that if he was careful, he could do anything he wanted. He wanted Maria. So he tried to find a way that wouldn't cause an intramob war. And the way to do that was to make sure it was Maria who would take the risk and do anything he wanted until he was tired of her. He can be diabolically clever, and it wasn't long before he found the way to do it. Everyone knew that Anton had no use for me, and Maria was always trying to keep me from being punished. So the next week that Anton went out of town on one of his business trips, Volkov went to Maria and told her that he enjoyed playing with little girls, but if she could keep him entertained, he'd not bother with me." She added bitterly, "She kept him entertained all that week. Until that day I tried to kill him."

"And rightly so. Brava. But you haven't told me how she managed to save you."

"The cameras. Maria was frantically trying to think of something to do until she remembered the cameras. Anton always kept them running in the bedroom because he liked to play back all their sexual activities. He'd even taught her how to process the films and alter them whenever it amused him. She'd hated it, but it had come in handy when she'd had to erase the last week of footage with Volkov. And now she realized what she'd learned might save both of us."

"What was that?"

"Humiliation. Maria had a few minutes of footage of a naked Volkov being attacked by me with that poker and trying desperately to escape it before finally being knocked out. It was clear I was only a child, and it would have been embarrassing for Volkov— who is very proud of his machismo—if any of his men had seen it. He would have been a laughingstock. She erased her own image out of it, and it would have looked like Volkov was being beaten up by a little girl."

Tanner gave a low whistle. "Wicked. You're right, very clever if she could manage to pull it off."

"It wasn't easy, but she did it. She stashed copies of the film in a cave in the woods but kept the original to blackmail Volkov. But it still might not have worked if I hadn't hit Volkov so hard with that poker. He had a severe concussion, and for a while she was afraid he'd die. She was wondering desperately how she could deal with that. But he woke up a few days later." She smiled grimly. "And then she gave him an even bigger headache. She showed him the film and told him she'd sent copies to one of her old friends in Moscow. She'd asked him to circulate them to every mafia boss in Russia if she didn't check in with him every few months. Which she promised she'd do as long as Volkov didn't hurt us." She paused. "It was a giant bluff. If Volkov hadn't been new to the neighborhood, he would have known Anton had made sure she had no friends or even acquaintances outside the village."

"I'm surprised he still didn't torture her to try to get his hands on them."

"I guess he wouldn't have taken the chance. He had his own copy right in front of him, and there was no way he would have done anything that might give anyone else a chance of seeing those photos. As I said, he was sick with humiliation. Maria said he seemed helpless and furious and she thought she'd won. He threw on his clothes and was stomping out of the room, but he looked back at her and said, 'You think this is over? I haven't even started. You've forgotten

I can still use Anton. There are all kinds of ways I can hurt you and that bitch girl. And believe me, I will.'" Lara shrugged. "And he was telling the truth. He never touched Maria again, but after Anton came back from his trip, he acted as if he was his best friend. They were constantly playing cards or at the racetrack. Anton was flattered that a man as powerful with the other mafia families as Volkov would want to hang out with him. He agreed with everything Volkov said, and his influence grew by leaps and bounds."

"And how did he treat you after you came back from the competition?"

"I tried to stay out of his way, and Volkov ignored me at first. Then he was suddenly coming around to the house all the time. He started to make remarks to Anton about what a pity it was that I was such an undisciplined girl, and how he should be careful not to let any of his men show him disrespect because of it. He kept on and on about it. He said it was bad enough that Maria hadn't given him a son that he could be proud of. As boss of his family it was Anton's duty to not display weakness of any kind, and I was definitely a weakness." She added bitterly, "A few weeks later they took me aside and told me what was in store for me. Volkov just sat back in his chair smiling like a Cheshire cat while Anton went over what was going to be expected of me from now on. I was to be taught how to do something besides play the piano so that I'd be useful to him and the family. He kept looking at Volkov for approval, and I knew it had to be his plan. He didn't actually mention the Trials until later."

"Maria couldn't help?"

"I knew she'd try, but I didn't want to ask her. She'd managed to keep us both alive. If she'd tried to interfere with Anton, Volkov would have found a way to make him punish her. Every day she spent with Anton was already a punishment. I was scared, but I thought if I worked hard enough, I'd be able to do what they wanted. I was the one who had hurt Volkov, I was the one who should pay the price." She drew a deep breath and lifted her chin as she looked at Tanner. "So that's how it started. And you want to know how he plans to finish it? He told me once. He wants total possession of me. He wants to be able to treat me as he did Maria that day when I hit him with the poker. He said that I'd no longer be permitted to play my piano no matter how I begged him. Never again. He wants to break me and make me a slave. I told you it was ugly. Is your curiosity satisfied?"

"More than ugly. And the only thing that I found satisfying was that my targets are now very well defined." He added quietly, "And you can't designate it as curiosity any longer—it's kind of an obsession. I need to know everything about those bad years you went through so I can try to absorb the pain and take it from you. Pretty weird?"

"Completely," she said blankly.

"I think so, too. It's never happened to me before." He took her hand and raised it to his lips. "But I think it's been growing on me. It doesn't feel new." He turned her hand over and kissed her palm. Heat. Tingling. Shock. His tongue moved gently upward, and she felt the tingling move to her wrist. "But you've got to watch me, because it keeps changing. It did just now, and at the moment it's purely selfish and sexy as hell. It might not be a bad idea if you went back up to your room. I'd prefer not to take advantage of an emotional moment and then feel guilty later." He grimaced as he lifted his head. "Though heaven knows I want to."

"You mean you want to have sex with me? You mentioned that before." Her wrist was still tingling, and her heart was pounding. Such a small thing to make her feel like this. She wanted to reach out and touch him. She moistened her lips. "And I'm not going through an emotional moment. I've lived with those memories too long to be hurt by them. They're just ugly, and I don't dwell on them. Maria taught me that you have to let them go and block them out. The only time you bring them out is if you can use them."

"Wise woman."

"Always." She reached out and tentatively touched his lips. The pad of her index finger was throbbing as it moved slowly back and forth over that smooth, sensuous warmth. Just touching him was igniting that electric heat again. Not only in her hand and lower arm but in her breasts, which were swelling, tightening. There was a tingling, a clenching, in her lower body. "I...liked the feel of you. I think I want you to do it again. If you do want...to have sex with me I think it would be all right. But you might not enjoy it. I'm a virgin and I don't know how to please you. Though I know some men even like rape. Volkov's men kept talking about it. But I don't think you would." She felt his muscles stiffen, but she was too absorbed with tracing the texture of his upper lip to pay attention to it. "Maria said she'd teach me whenever I needed to learn." Her gaze flew up to meet his eyes. "Would you like me to ask her? She told me she's very, very good at it."

"I'm sure she is," he said harshly as he took her hand away from his mouth and put it aside. "But no, I don't like rape. Never. And I don't want Maria to give you lessons." He muttered a curse between set teeth. "I'm an idiot. I knew how you grew up and how you had to fight to survive. I suppose I just didn't want to admit that your layer of toughness might not translate to experience, because it would keep me from getting what I wanted." He got to his feet and took her arm. "Those bastards have already robbed you of enough. I've no desire to take anything else from you. Shit. That's a bitchin' lie, but I'm not going to do it." He was pulling her toward the door. "So go back to bed and I'll see you in the morning."

She went out the door and started up the stairs. Then she looked back down at him. "You're a strange man, Tanner." She was gazing down at her hand. "It's still...tingling. Maria told me that sex can sometimes be very pleasant, if it's done right. I think I would have liked it with you."

"If you don't get out of my sight in the next few minutes, you might find out. I'll chalk this up to that whiskey I gave you, but I can only take so much, Lara. That dips into the category of teasing."

"It wasn't the whiskey. And I'm not teasing. I don't know how." She suddenly smiled. "But maybe I should learn. I'll have to think about it. I'll see you in the morning, Tanner." She turned and ran up the stairs.

She hesitated at Maria's door before she continued down the hall toward her own room. She had to tell her what had happened at the airport tonight, but it could wait until morning since Tanner had assured her that they were still safe. Although that had obviously been the most important thing that had occurred since Tanner had dragged her out of her room tonight. But it had not been the only thing.

She had moved closer to him than she thought she could. She had told him things she'd told no one else simply because he had asked. No, it had also been because trust had been there, the trust that she had been fighting from that moment in the forest. Trust and something else she had never experienced. She had allowed that intense sexual magnetism she'd been guarding against since she had woken on the Gulfstream to overcome the caution of years. The impulse had probably been too bold and foolish, and she shouldn't give in to it again. But the boldness had been natural to her, and learning new things was never foolish. Those minutes had been exciting and made her come alive in a very different way than she had ever known.

Repeat it? That thought was exciting, too. Particularly since Tanner was being so difficult about such a simple thing when she'd offered to make it as pleasant as possible for him. It might be…a challenge. Why not? she thought recklessly. After all the Trials she'd been forced to do over the years, it could be interesting to do one of her own choice that might bring her pleasure. As she'd told him, she'd have to think about it.

Because it had definitely not been the whiskey.

———◆———

He was going to have to call Volkov, Anton thought gloomily. He'd been putting it off since Stockholm in the hope that he'd have something positive to report after they got to Connecticut. But that damn bitch, Lara, had slipped through his fingers again, and Volkov was going to be furious. Not that it wasn't

Volkov's fault, too, he thought sourly. It was his men who had been so inept that they hadn't been able to bring Lara down during those first two nights.

Stop putting it off. The longer he stalled, the worse it was going to be when he reached Volkov. He placed the call. "There's been a problem."

"Which you've solved?" Volkov's tone was dangerously low. "Don't tell me you've failed again, Anton."

"The situation was awkward," Anton said. "I told you that the trail led me out of Stockholm. Once we reached Connecticut, we found they'd already closed down the airport and scattered. I was equipped for an initial attack, but I'm going to need more firepower and men to hunt them down. This is the U.S., and we'll have to worry about the authorities. I've already had to kill one law enforcement official. I'm going to go to ground for a while until you can send me what I need."

Volkov was swearing viciously. "And in the meantime Lara and Maria will find a place to go to ground, too. It will take months to dig them out while you're sitting there waiting for me to save your ass."

"I won't be twiddling my thumbs, I'll be busy," Anton said quickly. "I told you that I'd found out who helped them get to Stockholm. It was Logan Tanner, who does an occasional extraction if the money is right. That was all I could find out from the informant in Stockholm, and I didn't want to waste time when I was afraid we might miss them. I'll find out more about Tanner, and we'll track Lara through him."

Silence. "Tanner?" Volkov asked. "You're sure the name was Tanner?"

"I'm sure. Why? Do you recognize it?"

"I think I've heard of him."

"That's all I know so far, but now that I have the name, I'll know more about him soon."

"You'll find out *everything* about him," Volkov said harshly. "It's your fault that you didn't even realize they were making contact with someone who could just whisk them out of Russia. Where the hell did they get the money for an extractor?"

"We'll find out. I'll find out everything, just like you said." He paused. "But you might have to be patient. The last time we tracked them down very quickly, but it was because they were totally on their own and they didn't even make it out of Russia before we caught up with them. This is another country, and we don't know what resources this Tanner has."

"Are you saying that she might actually be able to get away?" Volkov asked with soft venom. "Don't even think about it. That's not going to happen. Word has already gotten around to my other men about Gregor and Razov. They all knew about that Trial, and I won't be made the fool if everyone finds out that Lara took both of them down and then just flitted away."

"I didn't think you would. I just wanted to warn you there would be problems." Anton hesitated. "If I don't have help."

Volkov was cursing again. "You'll have help. Get me all the information you can gather and set up a camp. I have business here in Avgar, but I should be ready to leave within a few days. If you manage to get her before then, let me know. No excuses, Anton."

"After all we've been through together? We'll get through this patch, too." He added eagerly, "And I'll make it up to you, Volkov. Whatever you want."

"Exactly," Volkov said harshly. "I'll see that you do. Whatever I want. I'll carve it in your flesh."

Tanner had one more whiskey before he reached for his phone and called Kaskov. This time he was put immediately through to Nikolai. "Get me Kaskov," he bit out. "Now, Nikolai. I don't care what he's doing."

"Certainly, Mr. Tanner. He's left word he'll always be available to you until further notice. I trust all is well?"

"Everything is not well. Everything is bullshit at the moment. Put me through to him."

"Regrettable." The next minute Nikolai had made the connection.

"You've upset Nikolai," Kaskov said when he came on the line. "I trust you're not going to do the same to me. I'm not known to be nearly as patient." He paused. "Lara Balkon is still alive?"

"Yes, and difficult as hell."

"That's your problem. You took the job. We have an agreement."

"And I'll keep it. But I'm having losses in both personnel and equipment, and I want a progress report from you to make sure I'm not spinning my wheels for nothing. Sandrino. What have you found out?"

"I don't have to give you any reports until I take over possession of Lara and Maria."

"Which you're being very slow about. I want action, Kaskov." He paused. "Or I might decide to take over their disposal myself."

Kaskov was silent. "That wasn't in the agreement," he said softly. "What are you trying to pull, Tanner? I'd hate to think I was mistaken in you. It would seriously damage my ego, as well as several of your body parts of which you might be fond."

"Cut the crap. I extracted Lara Balkon and Maria as I promised. But since you haven't given me any sign that you're going to keep your word, I don't see why I should turn them over to you." He paused. "Particularly since I told Lara that I thought she'd be safe with you, and you haven't given me any assurance about that, either. I don't like to be used. I'd rather get her settled somewhere safe myself than trust you not to sell her and Maria back to Volkov and her father if you took the notion."

Kaskov was silent again. "You're a bit upset about this," he said slowly. "And I can't determine whether it's about Sandrino or your distrust of my intentions toward Lara Balkon. I find it very interesting, particularly when I had such a difficult time convincing you to take the job."

"But I took it," Tanner said curtly. "I've almost completed it. Now do your part. Were you just stalling when you said you'd made progress?"

"I never stall. I regard it as beneath me. It was difficult locating Sandrino—and then he disappeared again, and I had to discover what had happened to him again." His voice was mocking. "I knew you wouldn't regard our deal as complete unless you had the complete story."

"And do you have the complete story?"

"Not yet. I have background. I have history. I have location." He paused. "I'm not sure about the name."

"Name." He pounced on the word. "What the hell are you talking about? I gave you the name. Sandrino."

"But he was the victim," Kaskov said quietly. "Not the killer. You asked me what happened to him. You're a very intelligent man. You must know that your friend may no longer be alive." He added thoughtfully, "Or is it that you don't want to admit it to yourself?"

"Of course I knew that was a possibility." But the bastard was right: His instinct had been to deny the possibility, because it was too painful. "But Sandrino was extraordinary, and he wouldn't have been easy to kill. There might be a chance that he walked away from an attack. Or he could be a prisoner somewhere. I was looking for any explanation."

"It wasn't an explanation you wanted." Kaskov's voice was suddenly weary. "I've been there myself a few times. But you'll get what I promised, even if it's not what you want. You'll know what happened to him."

Tanner had to go deeper. "But you already know he might have been murdered? You just don't have a name. That's not good enough. I want more, Kaskov."

"You won't get it. Not until I'm ready. But I'll tell you one thing that might interest you. Though Sandrino was definitely in Russia, he wasn't killed here. He took the bait and moved on."

"To where?"

"I've no desire for you to take the same bait when I prefer you to remain occupied with Lara Balkon. Now that I've decided my judgment of you wasn't in error and I won't have to remove you, I'm still satisfied in our arrangement." He added before Tanner could speak, "Be patient. It may only be a day or two. I told you once you were perfect for this job, and I'm even more convinced now. You'll have either your friend or your revenge, and I'll tuck Lara away somewhere she'll be safe and happier than she's ever dreamed of being. I just have to put up safeguards to make sure that everything flows together. It's all in the package."

"And I'm supposed to believe you?"

"It does sound a bit bizarre. Yet I've been known to have a few moments of whimsy now and then. This is definitely one of them. So take advantage of it and you'll get to know what happened to Sandrino." He paused. "Now, is there anything else?"

"The name of the person responsible for him disappearing. You might not be sure, but you have a damn good idea."

"Very good. But you won't know it until I'm quite sure that I'm right. It might be a delicate situation." He chuckled as Tanner cursed. "But I will tell you that you're at least on the right continent. Good night, Tanner." He cut the connection.

Bastard. Kaskov had enjoyed that a little too much. He jammed the phone into his pocket and poured himself another whiskey. Then he opened the French doors and went out on the veranda. The air was cool and fragrant with the scent of the lilac bushes that Sandrino had Rennell plant along the edge of the veranda. He took a deep breath. How often had he sat out here with Sandrino and laughed and talked and played a hand or two of cards with him before he went up to bed…

Shit!

The memories had brought back all the raw pain he'd felt when Kaskov had casually mentioned the possibility of Sandrino's death. Why had it hit him so hard when Kaskov had only stated what Tanner had already known had to be true? He'd accepted it long ago. But there had been the barest chance that somehow Sandrino had pulled a trick out of his hat and would be somewhere in the world for him to find. There was still that hope, but Kaskov had made him realize how slim it was.

"Mallory just assigned extra guards to the perimeter. Why?"

Tanner turned to see Sam Rennell coming down the path toward the house. That was all he needed right now, he thought impatiently as he automatically braced himself. "It was just a cautionary move. Probably not needed. I just got a bit of disturbing news and I thought it best."

Rennell's gaze went to the upper windows of the bedroom suites. "About the woman?"

"In a way." Rennell wasn't going to let him get away without knowing more. Why should he? Tanner would have felt the same way. "There was an attack at the Connecticut airport. I have to be sure that she's still safe here."

"You know she's safe. We've always been safe here. It's not like you to worry." His gaze was searching Tanner's face. "It's something else. You're upset. Talk to me. It's about Sandrino?"

"Isn't it always?" He lifted his glass. "That's the only thing we've had in common since the day Sandrino dumped me into your life. Yes, it's about Lara Balkon, and it's about Sandrino. I made a deal to get the information I needed if I protected her. So you'll have to excuse me if I take an extra step to keep her alive." He took a sip of whiskey. "And I'm upset because I might get her killed for no good reason. We both know that Sandrino is probably dead."

"More than likely." His voice was hard. "But we have to be absolutely sure. We owe him that. We belong to a very special club, and I won't let you walk away. I might need you." His lips twisted. "Because Sandrino always said you were very lethal. He made sure of that when he made you join the army when all you wanted to do was trail around with him instead. He told me once that you were too good with the numbers, even better than him, and there would always be someone who would target you."

"No one was better than him." Tanner frowned. "And he didn't tell me that."

"Because he was jealous. What he felt for you was complicated. You were the closest thing to a son that he'd ever known, so he cared about you. But no one was more competitive than Sandrino. When he ran across you in that bar and found out how good you were, he had to make a few mental adjustments. You were lucky his generosity was stronger than his ego." He paused. "And that you were so starstruck, you deliberately blinded yourself to the fact that you could have beaten him whenever you wished."

"He was brilliant. You don't know what you're talking about."

"He was human. I was glad that you didn't get it in your head to hurt his ego. I would have had to punish you. And though I would have enjoyed that quite a few times during those years, I couldn't risk Sandrino losing whatever he had going with you. It made him happier. He deserved to be happy."

"Because you cared about him, too. I suppose I always knew that, but I never understood how much. You weren't about to let anyone close enough to see that deep." He was silent for an instant and then added abruptly, "Okay, I knew after a month here that I could take him down. But I was never even tempted to show Sandrino that he was less than he thought himself to be." He grimaced. "Though it was difficult as hell. It was too much like cheating, and it would have been easy to slip back. But it got easier after a while and I just kind of coasted when we were playing. I suppose I wasn't as good as I thought I was."

"I wouldn't say that. You were good enough to not let him realize anything that would blow apart what you had together. As far as I was concerned, that was the only important thing. I think he was lonely sometimes. He liked having you here. He was always restless when you weren't around." Rennell took a step closer and stared him in the eye. "Now tell me why you're out here drinking whiskey and talking about Sandrino being dead when you usually go out of your way not to mention even the possibility."

"Maybe because it's more than a possibility." Tanner's lips twisted. "And I thought it was time for me to admit it."

"Why?"

"Because I just got off the phone with Kaskov and he seemed very sure that I was a fool for thinking that Sandrino could still be alive. And he can be very convincing. Though he told me he had no idea yet who had killed him."

Rennell went still. "Shit," he said between set teeth. "How can we squeeze it out of the son of a bitch?"

"We can't. I believed him. We have to wait until he's ready. He said it would only be a couple of days." He smiled crookedly. "He did throw me a bone. He said I was on the right continent to find out what happened to him."

"Not enough. We could use the woman."

"Forget it," he said sharply. "I told you to leave her alone."

"I might. You've haven't been shutting me out, so you have a chance." He added coolly, "But we're in this together. The only time we've ever cooperated was when Sandrino wanted us to. That has to end. We're going to find whoever killed Sandrino and we're working together. You understand, Tanner?"

"I'm not arguing with you." He turned to go back into the house. "Who knows? Maybe Sandrino wants it that way. We'll see how it works out."

"I want to know the minute you get another call from Kaskov."

"Reasonable."

"And I'm still keeping an eye on Lara Balkon."

"As long as that's as far as it goes. Otherwise, you'll have to deal with her mother, Maria. She has her own opinions where Lara is concerned." He looked back over his shoulder. "I still don't want to believe it, Rennell," he said hoarsely. "It hurts too damn much. I *won't* believe it. Not yet. He shouldn't have taken off like that by himself. Why didn't he take me with him?"

"You know the answer. Not only was he a law unto himself, but he knew how independent you are. He encouraged it from the minute he brought you here. Like to like." He paused. "It was the same with me. I asked no questions when he drove out the gate that last day. But I'm asking them now, Tanner. And you're the only one left I can ask. Find me someone else who knows more, and I won't bother you again." He turned on his heel and strode down the path.

Tanner stared after him for a moment before he finished his whiskey and turned toward the French doors. He had learned more about Rennell tonight than he had all the years he'd known him. Considering how wary they both were, it was no surprise. But evidently it was going to change, he thought wearily. And why not? Maybe it was time. After all, they had Sandrino in common.

It had been one hell of a night and it wasn't over yet. Volkov and Balkon had his name, and that made him vulnerable. He'd have to contact his casinos and put his supervisors on alert to protect his assets. He'd already lost men in Stockholm and one here tonight because he'd taken on this extraction. He didn't want there to be any other deaths or complications before this was over.

He glanced up at the windows of the suites on the second floor.

Don't think about her. Out of bounds.

Hell, easy to say. He could still feel the touch of her finger on the curve of his lip as she explored…

Get to work. Don't think about it.

CHAPTER

9

"Why didn't you wake me?" Maria asked when Lara had finished telling her about the attack on the airport. "Why wait until this morning to tell me? You must have been frightened."

"I was at first. But then I thought this morning would do as well. Why disturb you? Tanner told me that we were still safe here. That was all that was important."

"And you believed him?"

She nodded. "He told me right away. He kept his promise. Hell, he pulled me out of bed to tell me. Yes, I believed him." She paused. "He doesn't want to hurt us, Maria. I told you about his friend Sandrino."

"Which means he has a stronger reason than cash to bargain with Kaskov." Maria's gaze was searching her face. "You've taken that into consideration?"

"Of course. But it won't hurt to give him the benefit of the doubt. Most of the time he makes things…easier." She shrugged wearily. "And I do get so tired of not trusting anyone. I guess it's because this place seems like a different world. It would be nice to at least pretend that's different, too." She got up from where she was sitting on the edge of Maria's bed and headed for the bedroom door. "I'm going to get a bowl of cereal in the kitchen before I start practicing. What are you going to do today?"

"Work with that new computer. It's magic. It opens all kinds of new doors for me." She made a face. "A gift that makes my life easier and is fascinating. Another reason Tanner is at least temporarily invaluable. He chooses wisely." She added, "Then perhaps I'll go and see if I can find Sam Rennell. Mallory might be able to help me. It might not be a bad idea to get to know him if he has influence with Tanner."

"I don't know if anyone has influence with Tanner. Except Sandrino, Sandrino mattered to him." She stopped at the door and looked back at Maria. "Why Rennell? Why would you want to look up anyone here? You made sure that you kept me away from all of Anton's men at the compound."

"Because I knew exactly what kind of predators they were. But if this is a different world, the people and the rules are different, too. We have to weigh them and see which ones we can use and which ones we have to avoid." She met Lara's eyes. "I should be the one to decide which people are best to cultivate. I believe you're showing signs that your judgment might be a bit impaired."

Lara went still. "What are you saying?"

"I'm saying that I'm noticing a change between last night, when I sent Tanner into the music room to see you, and this morning when you walked into my room." She asked gently, "Did you sleep with him?"

Lara's eyes widened in shock. "No." She moistened her lips before she admitted, "But I thought about it." She should have known Maria would sense even the subtlest change in her demeanor, particularly if it was triggered by sex. Because Maria herself had been forced to study and learn every facet of sex over the years. And they were so damn close. "I wanted to. He touched me and I felt…" She shook her head. "He kept talking about feeling guilty. I think it was the virgin thing. Even when I told him you'd teach me. But I probably said all the wrong things."

"Maybe. How do I know anything about relationships?" Maria shook her head. "I've always just played everything by ear that wasn't connected to sex. I knew all about that, and it went a long way toward surviving. Sex is everything to most men." She paused. "But it doesn't sound like Tanner was being a bastard about it. That was the only thing I worried about when I saw where he was heading." She frowned. "No, I also worried that you'd think that sex was love and might get hurt. That would have been bad. I would have had to do something to him if he'd not been honest with you." She suddenly crossed the room and took Lara in her arms. "But I think it will be okay if you want to go to bed with him. You might like it. It's time you had sex. I was worried that living with me would ruin the thought of it for you. I don't want you robbed of anything. Sex is fine as long as you remain the one in control. I can teach you how to do that." She shook her head. "Not that there have been any choices I'd approve. I thought you might find someone yourself while you were away on one of those damn

Trials. But I guess you were always too absorbed in completing them to think about anything else." Her brow wrinkled thoughtfully. "I don't believe Tanner will hurt you, and if he does, it will only be once. I'd take care of it."

Lara shook her head dazedly. "Stop right there. I didn't ask your permission, Maria. It was a complete surprise to me when you asked that question, and my answer just tumbled out. He might not even want to go to bed with me. He turned me down flat. Maybe it was an excuse. It's natural he'd like women with more experience."

"You can get him over that. It's hardly your fault. I'll show you. It won't take any time at all." She turned away. "We can manage it."

Maria was going too fast, and Lara suddenly felt panicky. "Back up. That was last night. He was kind and I was a little shaken. I'd never felt like that before. I might have changed my mind since then. On second thought, I'm almost certain that I have." She opened the door. "I'll see you later, Maria."

"It's okay, Lara," Maria called softly after her. "Whatever you want. I didn't mean to push you either way. It's just that I've never had a chance to be a real mother to you all these years. You always had too much responsibility, and we were more like prisoners in the same cell than mother and daughter. I've wanted to do things for you, and with you, like a normal mother. It's probably a little twisted, but I thought this might be a way to let you know that I'm here for you."

Lara looked back at her and was suddenly filled with warmth as she saw Maria's expression. "You're crazy," she said huskily. "No one could have been a better mother than you. Do you think I don't know that?"

She closed the door quickly behind her. She drew a deep breath as she hesitated outside the door. It was one thing to toy with the possibility of having sex with Logan Tanner. That had been almost dreamlike and vaguely exciting. But her interchange with Maria just now had been unexpected and brought that possibility into stark reality because that was what all sex was to Maria: carnal intimacy, technique, and control. Yet somehow the acceptance of that reality had made Lara's excitement deepen and come alive. Even her body felt…different.

Ridiculous. Forget it.

She started downstairs. She'd have breakfast and then get to work. Music always took her mind away from everything else, and she obviously needed that where Tanner was concerned. By the time she saw Tanner again, she would be in full control and—

"Do you want an omelet or just oatmeal?" Tanner was coming toward her across the foyer. "I'll give you one or the other, but if you want anything fancier, you'll have to fend for yourself. I figured you'd probably want something light to start your day anyway."

She stopped short in surprise. "I do." She recovered immediately. "What are you doing here this early?"

"Trying to intercept you before you started to work and managed to rebuild all your defenses against me. I didn't want to have to go back to square one after I'd worked so hard to establish minimum trust. I knew it was going to be an uphill battle no matter how you decided to play it." He grimaced. "Last night was a mistake on so many levels that I was pretty dizzy before I threw you out." His lips suddenly curved in a rare smile. "But some of them were yours, and I don't think I should take total blame. Your reaction was…unexpected. You caught me off guard. But that was probably my fault, too. In my profession I have to be able to read the other players or lose my shirt. I thought I was beginning to be able to gauge your responses." He made an impatient gesture. "Anyway, that's my elaborate explanation that was at least a half apology. Now may I fix you breakfast, give you a cup of coffee, and mend fences?" He added coaxingly, "I talked to Kaskov and Rennell last night after you went upstairs. I'll share it with you."

He was being completely honest, and as usual it disarmed her. "This isn't necessary. I *was* partly to blame. I'm sorry if I made you feel awkward. We'll forget about it." She slowly came down the final few steps. "And you shouldn't feel bad for not being able to read me. These days I have trouble doing that myself. Everything is…new to me." She frowned. "No, that sounds like an excuse. It's not as if I was sheltered or anything. Maria tried to shelter me, but once I was in a Trial, I was on my own. I had to make whatever adjustments were necessary to get it done. I suppose Maria is right, and I couldn't behave normally with the people around me even if I'd wanted to." She shrugged. "So I guess you could say I sheltered myself."

"And your Maria is displaying her usual perceptiveness." His eyes narrowed on her face. "When did she utter those particular words of wisdom?"

"This morning when I went in to wake her to tell her about what happened at the airport. Why?"

"If she's awake, then I should invite her to breakfast. I never want to get in her bad books. Will you come to breakfast if she chaperones you?"

She wasn't at all sure that was why he had asked that question. He always saw too much, and she had an idea he had gone that one step ahead again. But she wasn't going to challenge him—there was no real reason why she shouldn't have breakfast with him and listen to what he had to say. They needed to be on the same page, and it was better that last night's foolishness fade away. She shook her head. "I asked her if she wanted to have breakfast with me, but she turned me down." She started across the foyer toward the hall leading to the kitchen. "I want an omelet and some of the strawberries I saw in the refrigerator yesterday. Does Rennell grow them?"

He nodded as he followed her. "He has gardens galore at the back of the property. Sandrino told me that working in the earth relaxes him. When he's not target shooting or painting in his studio."

"Painting?" Her eyes widened. "I wouldn't think...it's a surprise. Is he good?"

"I have no idea. He's very private where his paintings are concerned. He's never let me see one. I don't believe even Sandrino was permitted into his studio." They were in the kitchen now, and he was at the refrigerator taking out eggs. "I know Sandrino would never have asked if Rennell didn't offer. He respected his independence just as he did mine." He nodded at the peacock-blue granite kitchen bar. "Sit down while I whip up that omelet. Or you can put on the coffee if you like."

She headed for the coffeemaker on the cabinet. "I'll do my part. Since you said that even omelets were difficult for you."

"Not difficult. Just boring. I learned to cook in a dozen restaurants in Hell's Kitchen when I was growing up. That was enough for me. As soon as I could afford it, I started hiring other, more talented cooks to do it." He was beating the eggs. "Except here. Sandrino liked my cooking, even the fast food. So I'd spend a couple of evenings a week doing my duty." He shrugged. "I owed him, and it was kind of fun. Rennell put in his kitchen duty, too, but he was much more high cuisine." He put some butter in a frying pan. "But I like butter, and you won't find anything high cuisine about what I put before you." He glanced over his shoulder. "Not like those Swedish meals you had to prepare when you were doing the Trial with that family in Paris."

"Those weren't high cuisine, either. I told you, Nilssen wanted comfort food that reminded him of home. Once I learned how to do that, they were happy."

"And you were happy, too?"

"Until the end."

"The Rembrandt." He turned back and poured the whipped eggs into the pan. "I imagine that was rare, wasn't it?"

"Yes. Though there were a few other times that weren't so bad, because I was able to learn something. That made all the difference."

"Such as?"

"Well, I learned to ride horses for a Trial at a horse farm in Austria."

"What?" He glanced at her. "I didn't see anything mentioned in Kaskov's notes on you about horses."

She chuckled at his surprise. "I made sure that not many people knew about that Trial. I was supposed to work in the stables exercising the horses so that I could get information when they were moving Montara, a prize racehorse, to another stable so they could steal him. Volkov wanted him because his stud fees were enormous, and he planned on either ransoming him or selling him outright." She made a face. "I didn't know anything about riding horses. I'm sure that was the point of the Trial. Because they never made it easy for me. They took me to a stable outside Moscow, hired two stallions for me, and told me they'd give me three months to teach myself what I needed to know."

"Son of a *bitch*. You could have been killed."

"That's what I thought for the first three days. I couldn't stay on the damn horses. But then I watched the other riders at the stable and studied everything they did and didn't do. And I saw the expressions on their faces... The next week I started to learn. Soon I managed to stay on the stallion's back, and I let him free to run."

Tanner's gaze was fastened on her face. "And how did it feel?"

"How?" She was suddenly no longer in the kitchen but back to that day in Moscow with the stallion streaking around the track and the wind tearing at her hair. "It was wonderful. And frightening. Like nothing I'd ever felt before. It was almost like the thunder of the music in a Tchaikovsky concerto."

"And nothing could be any better than that," he said softly. "I can see it in your face."

"Can you?" She shook her head and smiled. "I'd never felt anything like that before, and it made me want to reach out and see what else was out there that I'd never experienced. That was a good day, and the time working in Austria was good, too."

"But only until the end?"

She shook her head. "I couldn't let that Trial end like the others. I was afraid the racehorse would be hurt, and I'd be responsible. So I did everything exactly as Anton told me to do. It all went well, and they managed to steal the racehorse. But a few weeks later the police received a tip and raided the stable where he was being kept by two of Volkov's hired henchmen while they waited for the ransom to be paid."

"No one realized it was you?"

"Why should they? When I'd been so meek during the other Trials? They knew how terrified I always am about Maria. Besides, I was very careful." She suddenly chuckled as she looked down at the smoking pan. "More careful than you. You've burned my omelet!"

He swore beneath his breath and jerked the pan off the flames. "I'll make you another one." She couldn't stop laughing as he reached for another pan. He grinned back at her. "And it was worth it to hear about how you got the better of those bastards. Just the look on your face was enough. I like that story much better than the ones I read about in your file." He cracked another egg into the saucer. "Like you, I appreciate a happy ending. I don't imagine that there are many more like that tucked away in your memory."

Her smile faded. "No, but sometimes I learned things even from the bad ones." She turned and opened the cabinet to get down cups. "And I had the music. Maria is smart and kind and she went through so much, and she had nothing." She looked at him over her shoulder. "But she loves the computer you gave her. She mentioned it again this morning."

"Then we'll have to see what else we can come up with to keep her entertained." He added quietly, "But she had you, Lara. She might have thought that was enough."

She shook her head. "You don't understand. I know

she loves me. But I've always been trouble for her, and a chain that kept her bound to a place she hated. Even the love she felt for me was another shackle."

"Bullshit. I've never seen two people as close as you. And you're both free now, and you'll find a way to give her whatever she needs."

"If she doesn't decide she still has to take care of me." She added soberly, "We're not free of them yet."

"The hell you're not." He frowned. "It's just a question of time. You're not going to go through all this for nothing." He slid the fresh omelet onto a plate. "Now sit down and let me tell you how eager Kaskov was to take me out when I hinted I might want to interfere with his plans for you."

"And Kaskov said it would be over soon?" Lara gazed thoughtfully down into the coffee in her cup. "What if he was lying?"

"That might be a possibility, but I don't think so," Tanner said. "He doesn't have that reputation. I'm not saying he's honorable, but he keeps his word. He thinks it's good business." He grinned. "We made a deal about Sandrino. I told him I expected him to keep it or I'd keep the merchandise."

"Merchandise?" she repeated dryly. "I assume that's me and Maria?"

"I'm glad you're smiling. Well, I didn't use that word. But this was a business negotiation and I wanted to make sure he got the point. I think it came across loud and clear." He smiled crookedly. "He was getting pissed off enough to make a few subtle threats. Look, I was upset last night, and no one can say I'm the most selfless person in the world. I wanted to get the information I needed about Sandrino and get out of the box I was finding myself in. I used you to try to get it. But you should be pleased that he didn't like the idea of me trying to take over. He even sounded a bit possessive." He added bitterly, "That might have been why he was so blunt about Sandrino almost certainly being dead. He wanted to punish me for questioning the great Kaskov. It's definitely not a common practice in his circle."

"And it did hurt you," Lara said quietly. "You care about him. I'm sorry. He could be wrong."

"Yes, he could. It's only been eighteen months. He doesn't realize how smart Sandrino is. But it's unlikely." He took a swallow of his coffee and leaned back in his chair. "I'll know everything soon. Kaskov knew a hell of a lot that he wasn't telling me, but he made it clear that if Sandrino was killed, it didn't have to be the end of…there was something about bait. He told me he thought it would only be one or two days. That's all I'll give him before I follow up."

She smiled. "And then what will you do? Threaten to get rid of the 'merchandise' if he doesn't give you the information?"

He grimaced. "No, it only took him a couple of minutes to see through that bluff. I'm still working on alternative plans." He pushed his cup aside. "But I thought you might want to know what Kaskov said about making sure the place where he settles you and Maria would make you very happy."

"If he told you the truth. He made a deal with you about Sandrino. He had no deal with us."

"You know I'll check it over before I let you go," he said curtly. "I gave you my word."

"And I think you'll try to keep it," she said. "But things happen, and in the end I'm the one responsible. You got us this far and I'm grateful." She forced a smile as she pushed her chair back. "And I'm very grateful for my breakfast. Now I must get to work." She tilted her head curiously. "What are you going to do today?"

"Check on my properties. Do a bit of dealing in the market. I'm going to need to recoup funds for the losses in Stockholm. Phone Sherman and see how the local police are handling the killing of one of their own and the destruction at the airport. I called the hospital in Stockholm last night and it looks like Nash is going to make it, so I have to make arrangements for his rehabilitation." His lips tightened. "It's going to take a while. Your bastard of a father nearly tore him apart."

"He likes to hurt people." She shivered. "It's something he and Volkov have in common. Though I think he's gotten worse since Volkov came into his life. Volkov gives the orders and he obeys." She shook her head wearily. "But I'm glad that Nash is going to live. I still feel terrible about not remembering those cameras in the woods."

"I've told you before. My job, my responsibility. I hired him and I'll take care of him. I'll just add it to my score against Anton and Volkov." He carried her plate and the cups over to the dishwasher. "It continues to grow and grow…"

"And all for Sandrino," she murmured. "He must have been an extraordinary man."

"I thought so. Other people had different opinions. He was tough and took no prisoners. He saved my neck—and besides, I could see myself in him. Since

I have more than my share of ego, I was bound to find him appealing. I'd never run across anyone else like him."

"And that was enough for you?"

"He was my friend," he said simply. "I'd never had one before. Yeah, that was enough." He glanced over his shoulder. "Why do you ask?"

"Don't I have a right to be curious about him? You're always asking me questions. I wouldn't even be here now if it wasn't for Sandrino."

"That's true. That would probably amuse him. I believe he'd find you very interesting."

"Would he?" She was standing and staring at him. She didn't want to turn and leave. She wanted to ask him more about Sandrino and the bond that had drawn them together. She wanted to ask him about all the years before he had come here. It was different from that moment last night so charged with sexual tension. It was warmer and deeper and held a kind of yearning for closeness that was almost irresistible.

And yet she somehow realized it was far more dangerous.

She whirled on her heel. "Then I have a perfect right to be curious. Thanks again for breakfast, Tanner. I'll see you later." The next moment she was out of the kitchen and almost running toward the music room. It wasn't as if she was trying to escape, she thought. She was just going to the music, where she belonged.

She wasn't trying to escape.

Maria heard the sound of the Rachmaninoff concerto as she left her room five minutes later. She'd expected to hear it much earlier since she'd known that their conversation had upset Lara. It was standard operating procedure for Lara to seek comfort in the one safe harbor that was always there for her. But evidently, she'd been distracted, and Maria realized by whom when she saw Tanner going out the front door as she started down the stairs.

Problems? Well, Maria had done enough direct meddling in Lara's intimate business for one day. She had only meant to help, but because Lara's life had been balanced precariously between the brutality of the Trials and whatever protection Maria had been able to offer her, she'd only managed to confuse her. In the end she knew that Lara had to make her own mistakes; she could only stand watch to make certain that they didn't hurt her too badly. But that didn't mean she couldn't position herself to be ready to jump into the fray if that happened.

Her phone was ringing as she reached the bottom of the stairs. It was Mallory, and his tone was not pleased. "I'm on my way. I should be there in a couple of minutes. But I just ran into Tanner and he told me to guard the main house and keep everyone happy. I don't believe he'd include what you have in mind on his list of acceptable amusements."

"But you didn't tell him I'd called you?"

"No, because I thought you'd find another way of doing it. Tanner has enough problems right now." He chuckled. "And there's a certain amount of amusement value potential that I need right now. So I called the coach house and ordered another guard to watch over Lara."

Maria had opened the front door and saw Mallory coming down the path toward her. She cut the connection as she walked toward him. "Amusement value? I got the distinct impression that Rennell wasn't a man to play games with."

"He's not. But he's interesting, and I've always thought the tensions and interplay between him and Tanner were worth watching." He glanced at Maria as she fell into step with him. "So it didn't surprise me that you might have recognized that, too. I just didn't realize that you were going to involve me in the exploration." He wrinkled his nose. "Which might catch me between them."

"You could have told Tanner."

He nodded. "But then you would have felt you couldn't trust me, and Tanner has gone out of his way to show you that you have nothing to fear from us. Tanner and I don't always operate on the same wavelength, but most of the time we agree on principle." He smiled. "So I'll take you to Rennell and see that he doesn't do anything too traumatic, even if I have to put my scarred, beaten body between the two of you."

"I wouldn't let it get that far. I'd save you." She glanced around her. They'd left the mansion behind and were going through a barricade of bushes. "So where are we going? Tanner said that he and Rennell both have their own private apartments on the grounds. Should I be grateful that these bushes don't have thorns?"

"Rennell's place is just around the next bend. Neither Tanner nor Rennell is that far from the central mansion. Tanner could be back there in a couple minutes using the shortcut. He told me he always liked to be close to Sandrino in case he needed him. But Sandrino was almost paranoid about giving everyone privacy. I just didn't want to run into Tanner with you in tow. It would require…explanations." They were around the bend now, and Maria saw the glittering windows of a brick one-story structure that looked like a luxurious summerhouse. "There it is. I'm not sure Rennell is inside. He's probably out back on the target range. I heard shots when I started for the mansion."

"Then let's go there and see." She smiled recklessly as she started on a path leading around the house. "I don't hear any shots now. Maybe he needs a target to aim at."

"No, I don't." Rennell stepped around the corner of the house. His expression was grim, and there was an automatic weapon in his right hand. "I've had a target since you came around the bend." His glance swung to Mallory. "What's she doing here, Mallory? Tanner was telling me I should stay away from both the women."

"And since when have you paid attention to Tanner?" Mallory took a step forward so that he was between the weapon and Maria. "And evidently neither does this lady. You've met Maria Balkon? She insisted on me bringing her to see you." He held up his hand. "And Tanner doesn't know or approve. I didn't think it would make any difference to you."

"It doesn't." His gaze was back on Maria. "You're just the mother. You're not important to me. Take her back, Mallory."

She took a step forward. "Yes, I'm Lara's mother." She looked him in the eye. "And Mallory isn't going to take me back until I get what I want from you. And I *could* be important to you, if I decided it was worth my while, you chauvinistic bastard. So put that huge toy gun you're playing with away and give me what I want. I've been abused by experts and you're not even close to making me afraid."

"Maria," Mallory murmured.

She ignored him and took another step closer to Rennell. "You want to get rid of me? Tell me what I want to know."

Rennell's expression was enigmatic. "And what do you want me to tell you?"

"You threatened my daughter. I want to know if you meant it or if you were using the threat to strike out at Tanner. I don't know anything about the two of you, but Lara is not going to be caught because of this Sandrino. She's been a pawn too long. Which is it?"

"Why should I tell you?"

"Because I'll do everything I can to help you, if you answer the way I want you to. If you tell me you'd willingly hurt her, I'll find a way to kill you."

His brows rose. "I'm the one holding the gun."

"But Mallory is here and there's always next time."

He suddenly smiled faintly. "That's true. I'm beginning to believe you might be formidable. Except you won't know if I'm lying to you."

"Yes, I will. I've had experience with liars all my life. I can tell the difference. But you'll be very difficult. That's why I want you to let me stay with you for a little while this morning. Show me your target range. Let me see your house. *Talk* to me."

"And why should I go to that bother?"

"Because I mean what I say. Because if you convince me, I can convince Lara to help you. Because you might actually be a decent man. You evidently cared for Sandrino."

"Yes, I did." He was silent. His expression still enigmatic. Then he shrugged and turned away. "I have a few hours to spare, and there might be a few things I can learn about you and your daughter that would be valuable. Come out back to the range with me, and I'll show you that this gun is definitely not a toy."

"I'm going with you," Mallory quietly told Maria. "And don't push it. You got what you wanted."

"Not yet. But I'm getting there." She was following Rennell. "It's fine if you come, but stay out of my way." She added tensely, "I was telling him the truth. I need to *know* him. He could be dangerous to us."

"Really?" Mallory asked dryly. "Tell me about it…"

———◆———

2 ST. MARKS PLACE, MOSCOW
6:45 P.M.

"I've heard from Rogoff, sir," Nikolai said quietly as he came into Kaskov's study with the antique samovar. "Las Vegas was confirmed as a positive."

Kaskov leaned back in his leather chair. "Excellent. And the name checked out?"

Nikolai nodded. "Just as you thought. And Rogoff said everything is moving precisely on the schedule you thought it would. Mr. Tanner will be very pleased, won't he? Shall I get him on the phone for you?"

"I don't believe so." Kaskov lifted his coffee to his lips. "There are times when a more personal touch is required. This might be one of them. I think that you should tell Egor to get my plane ready."

Nikolai frowned. "And you'll take assistance? You shouldn't leave Moscow without an escort. I've told you that things are not good right now."

"Yes, you have, old friend." Kaskov smiled faintly.

"And I'll arrange help if I need it once I arrive in the United States. I prefer not to cause too much of a ripple among our associates here in Moscow regarding this trip." He tilted his head. "And I have you, don't I?"

"Always," Nikolai said gruffly. "But I will make sure I have everything in place to move quickly in case I'm not quite enough for this situation."

"You're always enough. You're a tiger." He chuckled. "And perhaps we can recruit Tanner if I feel overwhelmed. I understand he's also a tiger."

Nikolai shook his head. "I could not control him. I might have to kill him, and you would not like that after all your trouble. Leave the recruitment to me."

"As you like. I couldn't be happier about the way you've handled this problem so far." He got to his feet and moved across the library toward the foyer. "Let's get on the move."

Nikolai gazed at him curiously. "You don't care if there might be trouble. You're…pleased."

"I always like it when a good plan starts coming together. Sometimes seeing that happen is worth a little trouble." He glanced over his shoulder. "Call Egor, Nikolai. I want to be in New York by tomorrow."

———◆———

SANDRINO PLACE
9:40 P.M.

"What is that I smell?" Lara asked as she came into the kitchen after Maria had made her close down the music room for the night. "Spicy…"

"I have no idea," Maria said as she stirred the bubbling cheese dish. "Some recipe from India that

Rennell had in his freezer that I couldn't pronounce if I wanted to. He handed it to me and told me not to add anything to it on pain of death." She grimaced. "I think he was being sarcastic, but I wasn't sure at the time. That deadpan expression…I thought it better not to risk it. Rennell has an odd sense of humor."

Lara sat down at the bar. "And how did you come to that conclusion? I gather you followed up on your plan to find out if Rennell was going to be a problem?"

"It was necessary. He was a threat to you, and I didn't know if Tanner could control him." She tasted the mixture. "Heavenly." She put the spoon aside. "I found out that he probably could, because they have a common love for Sandrino. Otherwise, it might be a battle. Though I don't believe it would come down to sacrificing either one of us on the top of a temple. Rennell has a basic code that he tries to ignore if it gets in his way. But I don't think he's able to do it very often. That's why he gets so frustrated with Tanner. Tanner almost never uses violence to get his way, because he can usually do it with a deck of cards."

"I didn't find that true in the Avgar Forest," Lara said ruefully. "Violence was definitely on the agenda."

"Well, he wasn't going to invite you to sit down for a game of poker," Maria said. "But think about it. He used minimum violence that night."

"And Rennell told you that while you were with him today?"

"Not exactly. He just dropped puzzle pieces and I put them together. But I don't think Rennell is going to give us any trouble as long as we don't get in his way with Sandrino."

"Puzzle pieces," Lara repeated. "Did he even know what you were doing?"

"Yes. Not at first, but he got there soon enough. That's when he turned brusque and threw this dish at me before kicking me and Mallory out of his house." She grinned. "But not before we got to know each other much better than he expected." She turned and was getting two plates out of the cabinet. "Get silverware and we'll have dinner. You must be starved. You've been in the music room since this morning."

"I'm hungry." She hesitated and then said quickly, "But Tanner fixed me an omelet for breakfast before I went to work."

"I thought he might have." Maria's voice was noncommittal. "And how did that work out?"

"Fine." She put the silverware out on the bar. "Different. We agreed to start a new page. I told you that he probably thought it was a mistake." She watched her spoon the cheese dish onto the plates. "We…talked. It was nice. I liked it."

"And he did, too?"

She nodded. "But I did most of the talking. He always asks a lot of questions. I told him about the horses."

"Really? I don't think you've ever told anyone about them but me." She made a face. "Not that you have a wide circle to chat with."

"It just came up. I told you, he's always asking questions. And it was fun to share something happy."

"I'm sure he enjoyed hearing about it," Maria said gently. "I know I did."

"Maybe." She shrugged. "It was kind of weird. But then so was my life."

"But you made the best you could of it. That makes you remarkable." She took another bite. "And Rennell's dish is totally remarkable."

But they were only halfway through when Tanner strode into the kitchen.

Lara instinctively stiffened as she saw his face. His eyes were glittering, his cheeks flushed with color, everything about him vibrantly, wonderfully *alive*.

"Hello, Tanner," Maria said. "Have you had dinner? Try some of this mystery meal that Rennell concocted."

"He doesn't want anything to eat." Lara put down her fork. "Look at him. Can't you see? What is it? What's happened?"

"Maybe good news for a change." He grinned at Maria. "No, I don't want any of Rennell's exotic cuisine. I had enough of that when we were competing in the kitchen for Sandrino's approval. I could never win that battle."

"What's happened?" Lara repeated.

"I just got a call from Kaskov. He phoned from his plane. He's on his way to New York. He should be arriving tomorrow."

"And why is that good news?" Lara asked warily. "He's still an unknown factor to Maria and me. The last I heard, you weren't on such good terms with him, either."

"But I told you that I thought he'd keep his word and when he called me tonight, it was to tell me he's ready to do so." He poured a cup of coffee from the coffeemaker on the cabinet and sat down on a stool at the bar. "Which means that we'll manage to get you settled, too. It's all part of the deal. He said we'd work out all the details when we meet at the hotel tomorrow."

"Hotel?" Maria asked. "What hotel?"

"Kaskov said he was going directly to the Indian Hills Hotel Casino I own in upper New York State. He'll meet me for dinner and then we'll have the discussion. I'll take Rennell with me." He smiled. "It will be fine, Maria. I'm not going to sell you down the river. And I won't have to worry about you trying to come to terms with Rennell, who can be just as lethal as Kaskov in his own way."

She met his eyes. "I had to find out for myself. We got along quite well for the most part."

"So Mallory told me. But that didn't keep me from tearing him a new one for letting you con him into taking you." He took a swallow of his coffee. "You may not be able to trust me, but that's your problem. I'm doing the best I can. But it did make it clear that the sooner the two of you are safely settled, the better for all of us."

"We know that," Lara said. "And the sooner that you'll know about Sandrino. That's always been the first order of business for you."

"I won't deny it." He looked her in the eye. "I've never told you anything else."

"Why should you? Everyone has to take care of themselves." She pushed away from the bar. "When do we have to leave for this hotel?"

"You don't."

She stiffened. "What?"

"I'm going alone. You and Maria are going to stay here. There's no place safer, and I'm leaving Mallory in charge." He glanced at Maria. "And to make sure it's safer is the reason I'm taking Rennell with me. I owe him that."

Lara stared at him in disbelief. "You think you're just going to keep us tucked away in this bed of thorns while you go and decide with Kaskov how you're going to dispose of us? Not likely, Tanner."

"It's the practical thing to do," he said curtly. "Your father found out that I'm the one who extracted you. Now he and Volkov have a name. By now they've also had time to find out a hell of a lot more about me. Which might mean the location of most of my properties here in the U.S., including Indian Hills. But no one knows about this place. You'll be safe."

"Then change your meeting place," Lara said. "It's about time I talked to Kaskov myself about what's going to happen to us. It's our lives that are at stake. All I know is that for years he'd drop in and use me like some windup music box before he suddenly decided to hire you to do this. I have to know why, and I have to know what he plans to do next." She glared at him. "And I don't want to hear it secondhand from you, because I know damn well it might be tempered by how desperate you are to know everything there is to know about Sandrino."

"You're not being reasonable," he said through set teeth. "I won't bring Kaskov here. This was Sandrino's private place and I won't violate it by bringing a mafia boss here. And there was a reason why Kaskov chose Indian Hills. A crime boss like him can be a major target, and he realizes I'd have ample security at any of my properties."

"Good. Then you'd have no trouble arranging protection for us there." She added, "When do we leave?"

"*I* leave in two hours. You're both staying here." He looked at Maria. "Talk sense into her. I only want what's best for you."

"There's a problem…" Maria shrugged. "Lara is

accustomed to making her own decisions, and she does it very well most of the time. But I promise we'll discuss it."

"Do that." He strode out of the kitchen, and the next moment they heard the front door slam behind him.

Maria murmured, "He's having a bad day. I believe you succeeded in irritating him more than I did."

"He deserved it," Lara said jerkily. "He was entirely wrong. You know I was right. We should be involved. I *will* be involved. It's dangerous for me not to be."

Maria straightened, her expression suddenly intent. "I believe you're using the singular entirely too much," she said slowly. "I don't think I like that. By all means, let's have a discussion."

Lara drew a deep breath and sat back down on the stool. "Perhaps we'd better. Because maybe Tanner wasn't entirely wrong…"

CHAPTER

10

11:57 P.M.

Tanner was leaning against the door of the Land Rover with arms folded across his chest as he watched Lara walk down the path toward the coach house. "Get in the car," he said curtly. "I need to get on the road."

She stopped short. "You were expecting me. Maria?"

He nodded. "Though I was hoping against hope that you wouldn't show before I got her call."

She'd expected him to be angry. She wasn't disappointed. She could tell he was just barely holding on. She opened the passenger door. "I asked her not to let you know. I wanted to have a chance to explain it to you myself. I know I was a little too brief."

"Oh, she didn't need any help from you on that score," he said as he went around and got in the driver's seat. "She was very clear and completely concise. She gave me my instructions in no uncertain terms. I was to take care of you and not let anything happen to you or she'd be coming after me." His voice was tiger-soft. "I have problems with orders, Lara. Even from some-one as charming as Maria."

She reached out and stopped him from starting the car. "Wait. Don't blame her. It was my fault. I was the one she was upset with." She moistened her lips. "I told her that she wasn't going to be able to talk me out of going with you to see Kaskov. That would have been okay with her. But she didn't like it that I didn't want her to go with us. You were right about it being safer here for her. I had to be sure everything was safe. There was no reason for both of us to go."

"Or for either one of you to leave here," he added caustically. "You both trust Mallory and you even agreed that this place was the height of security. Why couldn't you just leave Kaskov up to me?" He smiled bitterly. "Why do I even ask? We both know the answer."

"Yes, we do." She added wearily, "It was just another risk, Tanner. I've trained myself to overcome most of the risks Volkov and Anton have thrown at me. That's okay, it's just my part in helping Maria and me to survive. But I don't have the right to run even the slightest risk involving Maria if I can help it. She's sacrificed too much for me." She turned to look him in the eye. "I think I can trust you to help us. I'll help you any way I can to get info from Kaskov about Sandrino. But I have to be sure that whatever he's planning is safe for Maria. I'm the one who has to judge."

He was scowling. "I don't like this. I could throw you out of the car, you know. What would you do then?"

"Wait until you were gone and then go over the wall, climb the trees to avoid the thornbushes, and make my way to the main road. From there I'd hitchhike. I had Maria look up the address for Indian Hills on her computer. It would be difficult, but I could find it."

Tanner swore. "And you'd do it."

She nodded. "I didn't think that I'd have to. I know you're smart and you'd realize it would be easier for you to just take me. I'll cooperate as long as I believe what you're doing is safe for us. But yes, I'd do it." She paused. "Wouldn't you?"

His face was suddenly wiped clean of expression. "Hell, yes." Then he reached out and started the car. "But you're damn right you'll cooperate. I'm not going to let you blow this deal for me. I've waited too long."

"I know you have." She leaned back on the seat. "But then so have Maria and I, so I can't be over-sympathetic." He was actually going to take her, she realized in relief. For a few moments, she'd thought she'd lost him. She still wasn't sure why she hadn't. "Where's Rennell? I thought you said he was going with you?"

"I sent him ahead in his own car. We might need another vehicle, and besides, I'd prefer not to have to act as referee between you for a long drive."

"I wouldn't have tried to antagonize him," she said. "And Maria seemed to get along with him. She said she thought they understood each other before she left his place."

"I don't doubt it." He was going through the gates. "But I've noticed you lack a good bit of Maria's tact and have an overabundance of stubbornness on occasion. I don't want Rennell to change his mind about working with me, or to use you to strike his own deals."

"I would have been polite," she said quietly. "I won't cause you trouble."

"You already have." He glanced sidewise at her as he took the first treacherous turn. "But you might remember your good intentions over the length of the trip."

"I don't promise not to talk to Kaskov."

"I didn't think you would."

She had a sudden thought. "After Maria called, you could have just gotten in the car and driven away. Why did you wait for me?"

"Because I knew you'd do something weird like hopping that fence. I might have cut myself to ribbons on those thorns trying to avoid taking you to the nearest hospital."

"You don't think I could have made it?"

He didn't speak for a moment. "I think you could have made it, but I didn't want you to try." He smiled crookedly. "I thought, what the hell, if you wanted it that bad why not just let you do it."

She smiled back at him as she nodded. "Yeah, what the hell?"

"But it doesn't mean I'm not irritated with you, and I'm holding you to your word." He leaned forward, his eyes narrowed on the road ahead. "Now be quiet while I negotiate these turns."

──◆──

INDIAN HILLS HOTEL CASINO
5:45 A.M.

"It looks like a country club," Lara said as she got out of the Land Rover in the parking lot of the hotel. It was enormous, and the lot was full of cars and vehicles of every description. She could see an airport in the distance. The main building was situated on a hill above a sparkling river, and Lara saw a few boats on the water. "It's beautiful. And it doesn't look like a casino."

"That was the point. There are game rooms on the first floor, but nowhere else. I've never liked the idea of having slot machines in the bathrooms or other meeting rooms. Enough is enough."

"Volkov and my father wouldn't share your dislike. Whenever they went to a casino, they could never get enough. They loved every minute of it. Every chance they got, they'd go to whatever casino was nearest and stay for at least a few days. I thought all gamblers were like them."

"Gamblers are just people. Unless they're addicts. That's an entirely different animal."

"You should know about that. I'm sure they must be your best customers."

"Sure, I know all about them." His smile was twisted. "I can spot most of them in the first five minutes from across the room. I've taught my pit bosses to recognize them, too." He shrugged. "Don't look now but your distaste is showing."

"I told you, I don't like gamblers."

"That's your privilege. You're in the minority. Gambling has been around from the time of the Neanderthal."

"And you love it like Volkov."

He flinched. "Please don't compare me to that bastard. Everyone has their own way of dealing with their passions, and I'm sure I wouldn't appreciate his methods. We're nothing alike."

She shook her head. "I don't believe he'd have any problem dealing with addicts, either. He'd enjoy it."

"Then that should prove we're nothing alike. I don't deal with them at all. I don't allow them in my casinos."

She frowned. "What?"

"Addicts are sick. That's not how I run my business. I told you once I don't cheat. It's no fun for me. Dealing with addiction is a form of cheating. If someone wants to feed that addiction, I won't help them."

"I . . . see."

"Do you? I'm sure that proved a disappointment to you."

"No." They had reached the front door and a doorman was opening the glass door for Tanner with an ingratiating grin. Tanner nodded and then ushered her into the palatial lobby. "It . . . just surprised me. Why should it disappoint me? I like to know that not everyone is like Volkov." She looked around the lobby. "This is beautiful, too. The paintings are wonderful. Fields and mountains and seascapes . . . Everything soothing and yet colorful."

"I didn't choose them. They were here when I bought the place. I only had the good taste to insist they stay. I bought the property from an Indian family who wanted to retire and go out and see the world. Most of the paintings were done by the owner's grandson." He punched the elevator button. "The ones in my penthouse are just as good. You'll like those, too." He pressed the PENTHOUSE button. "You'll stay in my guest room tonight. I need to keep an eye on you." He glanced at her. "Okay?"

"Why not?" she asked. "When do you expect Kaskov?"

"Later this afternoon." He nudged her out of the elevator as the doors opened. He led her across the foyer and down the hall, then unlocked a door and handed her the key. "Take a nap. You didn't sleep on the way here. If you need anything, don't call room service. It should be safe, but don't take the chance. Let me know and I'll get it for you." He put her suitcase inside the door. "I'll see you later. I'll let you know when I hear from Kaskov."

"I'm sure you will."

He turned to go and then abruptly turned back. "It will be all right, Lara. I'll make certain that Kaskov walks a straight line." Then he was gone.

She felt a rush of warmth at that reassuring last comment after the chilliness that had gone before. It shouldn't have mattered to her, but she needed comfort from any direction at the moment.

She gazed around the bedroom. The colors were blue and beige and the furniture was luxurious but not ostentatious. It was a guest room, but it was not a room meant to impress. But then neither was Tanner. He was a man of silences and intensity. That was why she was always intrigued and fascinated when he did speak.

Which he hadn't done on the trip from Sandrino, she thought ruefully. Very noncommunicative. She was surprised he'd noticed that she hadn't slept on the way here. That bed looked good to her right now.

But not before she called Maria to let her know she'd arrived, she thought as she reached for her phone. Maria hadn't been at all pleased with her when she'd left her last night, and Lara always hated being at odds with her.

"Are you all right?" Maria asked when she picked up the phone. "It took you longer than I thought it would."

"I'm fine. Not a pleasant trip. Tanner really didn't want me to go with him."

"I could tell," Maria said dryly. "And neither did I. It's a mistake, Lara. You should have let me go along."

"I told you why I didn't. You're better off with Mallory."

"We should face Kaskov together."

"Tanner doesn't think we have anything to worry about."

"Then why was he going to leave both of us here while he went to have his chat with Kaskov? You wouldn't have given me such a bad time if you hadn't been afraid things would blow up and we might have to go on the run."

"I just didn't know."

"Exactly. Which is why I should be there with you. Does the hotel have good security?"

"As far as I can tell. It seems to have the best of everything. But I haven't had a chance to check it out. All I saw was the lobby before he took me up to the guest suite at the penthouse. I'll go look around later after I take a nap. I need it."

"You sound a bit on edge. I'm not surprised."

"I'll feel better once I get a chance to look around." She paused. "I just wanted to let you know I'm all right…and that I'm sorry I upset you."

"You're not forgiven, but I might change my mind if you call me the minute you finish talking to Kaskov." She added, "And take care when you're wandering around that place. I'm not only worrying about Kaskov. Tanner's right about Anton and Volkov being able to zero in on his location now."

"I know he is. I'll be careful. Goodbye, Maria." She cut the connection.

Not too bad. Maria was still upset, but Lara couldn't blame her; she would've felt the same. Still, she could only do what she thought best. She got to her feet. Now to shower, take that nap, and then see if she could get a look around the property before it was time to meet with Kaskov.

The sun was going down.

Lara knew she'd been here too long, but she'd wanted to check out the river walk before she went back to the hotel. She turned away and quickened her pace as she started down the hill.

"Enjoy your walk?" Tanner was standing at the bottom of the hill. "I'm glad you decided to come back and join me. It's almost time to dress for dinner. Kaskov just checked into the hotel, and you wouldn't want to miss the fireworks."

"I hope there won't be fireworks. And I thought you'd phone me when you didn't find me in the suite." She went past him and continued down the hill. "Or you could have just told one of those security men who have been following me around since I left the hotel to come and let me know."

"I needed a stroll anyway." He fell into step with her. "When did you notice they were tailing you?"

"About ten minutes after I left the hotel. They were very casual and blended in with the crowds. I might not have noticed them if I hadn't been on the lookout for someone following me."

"Like Volkov?"

"It was my first thought. But they wouldn't have just followed me. They would have been on the attack. So

I figured you'd told them to follow me." She glanced at him. "You didn't have to do that. I wasn't going to cause any trouble. I told you I'd cooperate."

"You did cause trouble. Besides, I can never tell what you're going to do next. You might have decided to steal one of the boats and taken it for a joyride."

"Don't be ridiculous. I came here to see Kaskov. What about Rennell? Is he going to join us for dinner?"

He shook his head. "Not his style. He said he intended to run his own show while he was here. He'll probably join us later."

She was frowning as she remembered something he'd said. "Dress for dinner? Why would I have to do that? I thought we'd just talk in your apartment."

"And we might. But when I told Kaskov I'd brought you along, he insisted on dining in the hotel's formal dining room. Didn't you notice? He likes to live the good life when he's not attending to company business."

"How could I notice?" She shrugged. "The only time I saw him was when he dropped by to hear me play. And then he spoke mainly to Maria, barely to me."

"Then perhaps he wants to get to know you. He was most insistent. I thought it wouldn't hurt. The discussion might get a little tense later."

"Then he'll have to get to know me in my usual slacks and shirt," she said bluntly. "That's all I brought with me. Hell, that's all I have. I'm not like him. I don't know anything about the good life."

"The good life is generally what you make it. But it wouldn't hurt to expose you to what Kaskov considers to be his version. I dropped by one of the hotel shops before I went after you and told them to send up an outfit for you." He punched the elevator button. "I have a few things to attend to. I'll see you later. Dinner is in an hour."

"Wait. How would they know my sizes?"

"I did okay before. I've got a good eye." He smiled as he turned away. "And I'm very good with numbers."

———◆———

The gown was simple, cream-colored, with a neck that was square and deeply cut. When she slipped it on, it reminded Lara of a picture she'd seen of a Renaissance noblewoman in a history book. She looked...nice. But not like herself at all. And there was nothing she could do with her hair, so she gave it a good brushing and let it flow loose down her back.

She didn't have time for anything else because Tanner was knocking on the door. She swung it open to see him dressed in a tuxedo and looking very elegant. "I did the best I could. But I don't look like myself. It isn't important anyway. Why should I care how I look for Kaskov?"

He looked her up and down. "Very nice. Exceptional, really. Everything fit?"

She nodded. "Even the shoes. You do have a good eye. I'm glad they're flats." She turned toward the door. "I'm not sure I could handle heels."

"You can handle anything." He put out his hand and stopped her. "Stand still for just a minute." He took his phone out of his pocket. "I want to take your photo."

She frowned. "Why?"

"Stop frowning. You don't have to smile, but don't look as if I'm beating you."

"What?"

He took the photo. "That was almost a smile. Now I'll just send this…"

"Where are you sending it?"

He opened the door. "To Maria. Considering the life the two of you have led, I thought there was a good chance she'd never seen you looking like a princess. I thought she'd like it. I've heard mothers get soppy over stuff like that."

I've wanted to do things for you, and with you, like a normal mother. Maria's words suddenly came back to her.

And this must be exactly what Maria had meant when she'd told her that. How had Tanner realized that about Maria?

"I've heard that, too," she said huskily. "Thank you for thinking of her."

"Necessary. I had to show her that I was obeying her instructions. That appears to be my role in life tonight." He was whisking her out the door. "Now let's go and get this dinner over with so that we can get down to business."

The first thing Lara heard as they crossed the foyer toward the open doors of the formal dining room was the sound of a piano, soft, melodious, playing the strains of "Impossible Dream."

Then they were through the doors and being bombarded by the sensory overload of gleaming tile floors, chattering guests, and black-clad waiters moving swiftly among the tables. The dining room was as faultlessly elegant as the rest of the hotel, and the tables were packed with equally elegantly dressed patrons. She saw the young man who was playing show tunes on a beautiful Yamaha piano at the opposite end of the long room.

Kaskov smiled as he rose to his feet when they came toward the table. He inclined his head as he took her hand. "I'm delighted to see you, Lara. You look quite lovely. And these surroundings suit you much better than Anton's place. But then I always knew they would."

"Hello, Mr. Kaskov." She pulled her hand away. "I hope I'm going to be happy to see you. Right now I'm a little confused."

"And very frank." His smile deepened. "I find it refreshing. You hardly said a word to me when I visited you at Anton's."

"You weren't interested in anything I had to say. I had only one use for you. So why should I have talked to you?"

He chuckled. "All quite true. So I'll excuse your bluntness." He turned to Tanner. "This is a nice enough restaurant, but that pianist leaves something to be desired. I would have thought you'd be more selective."

"It's music to accompany dinner, Kaskov. He's good enough." Tanner was seating Lara as he spoke. "Most patrons don't require concert-quality entertainment to get through a meal. It might even interfere with digestion. Are we going to order dinner?"

"Of course." Kaskov picked up the menu as Tanner lifted his hand for the waiter. He glanced at Lara. "What do you think about the pianist?"

"I feel sorry for him," she said simply.

"Really?" He tilted his head. "Why?"

"He doesn't realize everything he's missing. All he'd have to do is reach deeper, and he doesn't know it."

"Interesting."

"Are you ready to order?" Tanner asked.

He nodded. "Though it doesn't really matter. I'm certain everything on the menu is excellent. You wouldn't make two such glaring mistakes."

That was a direct barb and Tanner was ignoring it, Lara noticed. Which only showed how eager he was to get this dinner over. No more than she was, she thought bitterly. She had the impression that Kaskov was playing cat and mouse and enjoying it enormously.

Thank heavens the service was quick and the dinner delicious so that Kaskov had nothing to complain about. She barely tasted it. She wanted this dinner *over*. She was vaguely aware that Tanner was no longer allowing Kaskov to have the conversation all his own way. But she was only glad that she was not involved except for answering Kaskov's occasional question.

Then it *was* over.

Kaskov tilted his head. "Dessert?" He smiled teasingly at her. "No, I don't believe you want dessert."

"No, thank you," she said through set teeth. "Can we go up to Tanner's suite and talk now?"

"Yes, we can." Tanner was already signing the check. "Let's go, Kaskov."

"I'd think that would be a perfect ending for the evening," Kaskov said. Then he sighed and shook his head. "But I'm still not quite satisfied. I need one more thing. That mediocre pianist has almost spoiled my dinner. I need to be soothed." He turned to Lara. "And no one could do that better than you. Would you be so kind?"

"No!" Tanner said sharply. "You don't have to do that, Lara."

"Of course not," Kaskov said. "Only if she wishes to please me."

That catlike smile again. She had probably annoyed him before, and he was not going to allow her to get away with it. "I don't want to please you, but I want answers. I'll give you what you want." She got to her feet and started to cross to the piano.

Tanner was right beside her. "You don't have to do it."

"And I didn't have to insist on coming with you." She was looking straight ahead. "But I did it. And I didn't bow down to him like I suppose he wanted. But now if he wants his pound of flesh, I'll give it to him." Her lips tightened. "No, I'll give him more than that. Because it's the only way I can win. Because no matter what he thinks he's taking from me, it's nothing to what I'm getting."

Tanner was swearing as he tapped the pianist on the shoulder and nodded for him to leave.

Then Lara was slipping onto the stool and flexing her hands. She closed her eyes for a moment and let the music start to flow through her. Tchaikovsky. Kaskov always requested Tchaikovsky.

Make it sing.

Not for him.

For the beauty and the wonder and the genius of the composer who had created it.

Show Kaskov that he was nothing and the music was everything.

Show him…

She started to play.

And then she was lost…

"Lara." Tanner's hand was on her shoulder. "Enough," he said gently. It was never enough, she thought dazedly. Didn't he realize that?

His hand tightened. "Kaskov."

She shook her head to clear it. Then she took a deep breath. "How long was I playing? Was it really enough?"

"About forty minutes." He helped her to her feet. "And judging by Kaskov's expression it was more than enough. But I thought you needed to get paid for that performance." He added quietly, "It was magnificent, Lara."

"The music is always magnificent. But it doesn't belong to anyone unless it's given. He was trying to take it." She walked straight toward Kaskov and stopped before him. "Did you get what you wanted?"

"Yes." He got to his feet. "I got exactly what I wanted. We can leave now." There was no hint of the sly catlike expression that had been there previously. He was all cool business. "I not only thoroughly enjoyed myself, but I gave Nikolai the time he needed to check out Tanner's suite and the grounds."

"I told you the security was good," Tanner said impatiently.

Kaskov shrugged. "Nikolai had been insisting lately that we be extra careful."

"And you had Lara perform just so that you could have that extra time," Tanner said with dangerous softness. "You son of a bitch."

"I thought it necessary. And since you're the one who's been pushing me for answers, I'd say the ball was in my court."

"It is," Lara said. "What difference does it make, Tanner? He's going to give us what we want. Let's get out of here." She was striding toward the door. "Now, dammit!"

CHAPTER

11

The first person Lara saw when she got off the elevator was Rennell. He was leaning casually against the stone of the fireplace in the large living room. He nodded at her. "I hear Maria isn't here with you. She must not like that."

"She doesn't. Hello, Rennell. I'm jealous that you managed to dodge dinner. Tanner said it wasn't your style. It wasn't mine, either." She glanced at Kaskov. "Have you met Rennell?"

"No, but Tanner told me about him." He nodded coolly at Rennell. "But I'm most interested in what you did with my friend Nikolai. Where is he? I gave orders that he be here…alone."

"In the kitchen making coffee. I offered to help, but he said that with him it was an art form."

"Quite true. But he never changes schedules without letting me know."

"But I'm such a harmless soul." Rennell smiled

wryly. "I introduced myself to him. I gave him a chance to check me out. Then I spent the evening helping him check out your hotel, Tanner."

"And that was enough?" Tanner asked. He snapped his fingers. "Of course it was. Kindred spirits."

"Not really. But we have a basic understanding and respect for each other. That's enough."

"It may not be enough for me," Kaskov said grimly. "He broke a rule."

"Yes, I did," Nikolai said as he wheeled in the coffee tray. "It was a judgment call, sir. You gave me permission to recruit and I decided Rennell would do very well. He has all the qualifications I need, and he will not be volatile like Tanner. He will just do the job and keep on going until there's no one left."

Kaskov turned to Rennell. "Is that true?"

Rennell's gaze was ice-cold as he met Kaskov's. "Absolutely. No one left at all. If I choose to do it. And I'll be glad to help out occasionally if Nikolai decides he needs me. But that's not why I'm here, as Tanner must have told you."

"Pity."

"You might not say that when it's over." He began to help Nikolai serve the coffee. "It will depend on your point of view, and that's what I'm here to find out."

"And you will," Kaskov said as he turned to Lara, who had dropped into a chair in front of the fire. "But I believe I'd better deal with Lara first. She's on edge and Tanner is becoming very protective. Not that I object—that's one of the reasons why I involved him." He dropped down in the chair next to her. "But I admit I haven't given you the courtesy you deserve, so let me rectify that."

"I don't give a damn about courtesy. I want

information about why you decided to hire Tanner to move Maria and me around like pieces in a chess set." She paused. "And I want to know what you intend to do about us going forward."

"I imagine that you're more interested in the future than the past," he said. "However, I still feel bound to explain why I put you through that very boring dinner tonight. I knew you were eager to cut to the chase." He smiled. "But I'd been looking forward to having my own way in this, and I was selfish enough to ignore what you wanted."

"Why does that not surprise me?" Tanner asked caustically.

"It shouldn't," Kaskov said. "I never pretend to be anything but what I am." He turned back to Lara. "I wanted to see you how you should be seen. I wasn't going to give that up after all the trouble I'd gone through to arrange it. You walked into that room tonight in that gown and it was almost enough. But not quite. So I pushed it a little more and made you play." He smiled. "And that was perfect. I could see you at a concert hall playing with all that fire and passion. It really annoyed me when I'd drop in at Anton's and see you sitting there in jeans pounding on that piano."

She frowned. "Clothes don't make a difference."

"But a waste of talent does, and once I'd made a decision, I thought that the entire package should be perfect."

"What decision?" she asked.

"To save you from Volkov and Anton, free all that beauty stored inside you, and get you out of Russia. Of course to do that, I had to adjust my plans to include it on another transaction I was working on."

"You're saying you did it out of the goodness of your heart?"

"Partly. But nothing with me is ever that uncomplicated." He added, "Once I've finished completing my business with Tanner, though, I can assure you that you'll be happy with my arrangements. I do want you to keep playing. That's surprisingly important to me. I've even arranged to send you to an excellent music school to get a little extra polish. But once you're settled, you'll no longer have to deal with me. I'd be an albatross, and I want you and Maria to have decent lives."

"Free from Anton and Volkov?"

He smiled again. "Definitely free from them. Satisfied?"

"I'm not sure. It seems very generous. It's too good to be true." Her gaze was searching his face. "And you don't have the reputation of being particularly noble."

"Yet every word I've said is true. I've just not elaborated."

She was going over everything he'd said. "You said after you'd finished your business with Tanner, I'd be happy with the arrangements. Isn't he finished now? What does he have to do with it?"

"Yes, that's a good question," Tanner said softly. "What do I have to do with it, Kaskov?"

"Well, as I said, I was working on another transaction when I became fascinated with the idea of getting Lara and Maria away from Russia." Kaskov took a sip of his coffee. "So I decided to combine the two. I'd already done extensive research on my 'project,' and I only had to do a little more to make it all come together."

"What kind of research?" Tanner asked. "From what we discussed, you were only involved in one area of research. Mine."

Kaskov smiled. "It seems one thing led to another. Only I might not have been totally honest about the order in which they came. You see, I've been having a good deal of trouble with other mafia families who were a bit jealous of my power and influence and thought they could handle my affairs better than I could." His glance shifted to Lara. "One of them is Volkov."

She stiffened. "What?"

"He's been getting closer and closer. That's why I've been making trips to the south so frequently lately. I had to see if Anton was going to throw in his lot with Volkov if he made a move." He shook his head. "Volkov doesn't want to share the territory with anyone when he takes over. He regards Anton as disposable."

"I could have told you that," Lara said bitterly.

"No one needs to tell me anything about Volkov," Kaskov said. "There's no one who one knows him better than I do these days."

"Why?" Tanner asked harshly. "Why are we talking about Volkov?"

"I think you know." Kaskov's gaze was narrowed on his face. "You're putting it all together."

"Why?" Tanner repeated.

"Sandrino," Kaskov said. "You asked for a name. The name is Volkov."

"Volkov killed him?" Tanner said hoarsely. "You're sure?"

"What!" Rennell was suddenly across the room next to Tanner. "Is it true?"

"Back off. I'm trying to find out." His gaze was on Kaskov. "How do you know?"

"I told you, I know everything about him. For instance, he has a passion for gambling. Everyone in Russia knows that, and he's very good at it. Almost as good as your friend Sandrino. Anton was a small fry compared with Volkov; he often trailed behind him but never made the big games. I found out that Volkov was in a game with Sandrino the week he was in Ukraine and Sandrino beat him." He shrugged. "Evidently a very humiliating defeat. Volkov tried to get him to play him again but he refused. The stakes weren't big enough. So a few months later Volkov managed to set up a big game in Las Vegas with some very high stakes and invited Sandrino. He took the bait. The game was played the night he arrived in Las Vegas. Sandrino beat Volkov again. There was something of an uproar and he walked out of the game. Sandrino was due to leave that same night, but he disappeared."

"Where in Las Vegas?" Tanner's hands were knotted into fists. "I should have heard about it if there was a big game."

"Maybe Volkov kept the game quiet on purpose. He was very angry with Sandrino. Maybe he had something on his mind besides poker."

"Maybe. What else? No one knows Volkov killed him? He got away with it?"

"As far as I know. I've no real proof that he was killed. Only the supposition. I've sent a man to Las Vegas to ask questions and I did get some answers. I have a few reports about where the game happened, and where Sandrino might be found whether he's dead or alive. But yes, almost certainly Volkov had something to do with his disappearance."

"You set me up," he said roughly. "You came to me and conned me into taking Lara when you knew it would send him after me. You wanted me to kill him."

"Yes, but I also made a deal with you to give you what you wanted in return. I just delivered him to you. You were smart enough to figure the odds."

"I'm not complaining. But I'm curious. I can't see why you'd be shy about going after Volkov yourself."

"Ordinarily, I'm not. But all Russia is a tinderbox right now. And I seem to be the prime target. Besides, I didn't want all the families to be warring among ourselves. It's bad for business. If I'd made the first move, that's what it would have come down to. It would be much cleaner to let an outsider do it."

"So you supplied me with a reason to go after him for you."

"I just supplied you with a name and location. You'd been searching for Sandrino for a long time. Are you going to stop now?"

"Hell, no."

"I didn't think so. I'll give you all the information I have. If you find it getting a little too hot for you, let me know and I'll get you help."

"He won't need help," Rennell said coldly. "Just let me know where to find this Volkov."

"The general direction will be easy enough. Nikolai told me he left Moscow for New York shortly before we did. I rather imagine he was heading somewhere in Connecticut or this area to join Anton." He added, "If you were helping Nikolai scout out the grounds this evening, you might have stumbled across him then. Nikolai had orders to keep an eye out for him."

"You thought he could be here?"

"He had Tanner's name." He looked at Lara. "And she was going to be here. Though he might not have known that, it still increased the possibility."

"You were going to use me as bait," Lara said slowly. "That's why you paid Tanner to extract me."

"The idea did occur to me. But I decided to let Tanner make the call. Though it would have been the most practical thing to do."

Her lips creased bitterly. "Much too good to be true."

"I got you out," Kaskov said quietly. "And the bait concept came as an afterthought. I didn't find out that Volkov had set up a Trial that might kill you until that Friday night. I had to move fast."

"Still, it was a brilliant idea."

"That I'm not going to use," Tanner said curtly. "I told you that if Kaskov set you up with a comfortable situation, I was out of your life."

"Yes, you did." She got to her feet. "But maybe you'd better make sure that Kaskov is going to follow through with his promise to us before you desert us. He's very wily, and I'm not sure I can trust him. I'll have to think about it." She started toward the door. "I'm going to my room. I have a lot to think about. I'll leave you to squeeze Kaskov for all that information you need from him."

"I never allow myself to be squeezed," Kaskov said. "It's so undignified. But I might graciously allow myself to dispense whatever wisdom they need." He tilted his head. "Good night, Lara. It's been a difficult time for you. I *am* wily, but all the trickery concerning you is at an end. Now you're the one who has to make the decisions." He took another sip of his coffee. "Which isn't going to be that difficult considering your options."

"I'll come by later and tell you what arrangements I've made for you," Tanner said in a low tone as she passed him. "I'll make certain that you'll be safe."

She nodded and the next moment she was closing her bedroom door behind her.

Silence.

She needed the silence and the darkness in this moment. She'd been bombarded by emotions and sensations tonight and she wanted to take them apart so that she could think and come to some decision.

Because there was a decision to be made. Tanner was all set to tell her what she had to do again. He would try to fit her into his busy schedule and then talk her into what was best for her.

Bullshit. She had to clear her mind and think.

———◆———

She still had the lights out when Tanner knocked on her door two hours later.

She was across the room in seconds and threw open the door. "Come in." She stepped aside. "You were a long time. Did Kaskov give you everything you need to know?"

"Everything he knows." He turned on the lights and she saw he'd taken off his tuxedo jacket and unbuttoned the top buttons of his white shirt. He had a bottle of beer and handed her a Coke. "Which was considerable since he was digging deep for facts about events eighteen months back. There are some things Rennell and I will have to find out for ourselves on the spot."

"You're going to Las Vegas?"

"It's the next step. Kaskov couldn't tell me absolutely

that Sandrino is dead. I have to be sure. I have to know what happened in Las Vegas. Then, if that leads me to Volkov, I'll go on the hunt."

Her gaze was searching his face. "You still hope he might be alive."

"Hell, yes." His lips twisted. "Sandrino performed magic for me and Rennell, and I can't help hoping he might have pulled one more magic trick out of his sleeve for himself. But I know how slim that chance is." He looked at her sleep shirt. "You took off the white gown. Pity. I liked it."

She made a face. "It wasn't me."

"Kaskov wanted it to be you. He went to a lot of trouble to turn you into the prima pianist of the century. He's still working on it." He dropped down on the couch and took a drink of his beer. "But you're not going to have any trouble with Kaskov wanting to harm you. He's a genuine music lover, and he'll fight to keep that talent alive. You can cross that off your list of things to worry about."

"I figured that might be true. Maria said that she'd watched him while I was playing, and he was…feeling…it. You think that I can trust him and accept favors until I get on my feet?"

He frowned. "I said he's not a danger. Accepting favors is different. I don't want you owing him. Come to me if you have a problem." He was thinking about it. "And you shouldn't be around him, if you can help it. Even he said that wasn't a good idea. He has too many enemies."

"Is there anything else?" She sat down across from him. "I'll have to memorize all the things I *can't* do with Kaskov."

He grinned. "Not a bad idea."

"Yes, it is." She put her Coke on the coffee table. "I don't mind suggestions, but I don't like orders."

"Faux pas? Sorry. It's just that Kaskov could be a threat and I didn't want you to do anything that might put you into a bad spot."

"You wanted to take care of me." She nodded. "Very kind, Tanner, but it gets a little old."

His expression was suddenly wary. "That's not about Kaskov. What are you trying to say?"

"You dropped by to tell me what you've arranged for me. What did you decide?"

"Things aren't going to be safe for the next few days, but I want you to be as secure as possible. Kaskov was a possibility, but I've already told you the problems I have with that. I decided that the safest place would be for me to send you back to Sandrino Place to be with Maria. I'll leave Mallory there to take care of both of you until I get back and can make other plans." He tilted his head. "Sound good?"

"Excellent. But it's not going to happen."

He tensed. "Why not?"

"Because I'm going to be in Las Vegas with you." She held up her hand as he opened his lips to protest. "Don't argue. I thought it over, and that's what I'm going to do. I told you once that it wouldn't be a one-way street, and if you helped me that I'd do anything I could to help you with Sandrino."

"Hell, I'm not asking you to do that. Sandrino is my business. I don't *want* you to do it."

"That doesn't matter. It's not only about Sandrino now. You said it was only the first step. You're going after Volkov and Anton. I told you that's what I intended to do from the moment I woke on your plane." She was speaking fast, trying to make him understand. "Don't you see? As long as they're alive and free, Maria and I will never be safe. I'm sorry I can't care as much about your friend Sandrino, but it's pure self-preservation for me to go after Volkov."

"Dammit, it's not *necessary*." He was on his feet, grabbing her by the shoulders and pulling her up to face him. "*I'll* do it for you. Rennell will do it." He shook her. "It doesn't make sense. We know what we're doing. We've both been trained."

"That doesn't mean something can't go wrong. He kills people. He probably killed Sandrino." She looked him in the eye. "He wants to kill me, and if he gets a chance, he'll do it. I'm not going to sit in that nice, safe mansion and wait to see who he kills next."

"I don't need your help. You'd get in my way."

"Then teach me how not to get in your way. I learn fast. Make this another Trial for me." She glared at him. "And you *do* need me. Kaskov was speculating what great bait I could be. He was right and you know it."

"That doesn't mean I want you to—" He stopped. "You're not listening to me." His teeth were clenched. "Why won't you listen to me?"

"Because you're wrong. You know it's smart to take me with you. If you don't do it, I'll find a way to follow you. I want to be free. I *will* be free. You're just being—" She searched for a word. "What are you being, Tanner?"

"Scared shitless." He let her go. "Okay, you'll go with me. But you obey orders and you let me take the lead."

She drew a deep breath. "That sounds reasonable."

"And you're not committing yourself."

"I'm not stupid. I won't be careless."

"I know you won't." For an instant, his fingers gently touched the hair at her temple. Then he turned away. "We'll leave first thing in the morning. We've already been here for too long. I phoned Sherman and told him to have Jordan fly the Gulfstream to the airport here and pick up me and Rennell. Do me a favor, call Maria and tell her what you've talked me into? Maybe she'll be able to talk you out of it. She's the only one who has a chance of convincing you of anything."

"I'll have to call and tell her everything that happened tonight anyway." She hesitated and then smiled shakily. "It really is the right thing to do, Tanner. I've known that since I was eleven years old and hit the bastard with a poker."

"I just hope you'll let me be the one to hit him this time," he said grimly. "I promise he wouldn't get up." The door closed behind him.

Lara took a deep breath and tried to relax. It had been quite a battle, and she was still shaking. She'd hated fighting with Tanner, but it was a battle she couldn't afford to lose. She sat back down in the chair and pulled out her phone. Time to call Maria and hope that there wouldn't be another battle.

Evidently it was too much to hope for. Maria listened quietly as she told her about the events of the evening. It was only when she'd reached the end, when she'd told her about her plan to go to Las Vegas with Tanner, that she spoke one succinct word. "Bullshit."

"I'll be fine," Lara said quickly. "Tanner won't let anything happen to me. He's being ridiculously protective."

"Good. But that doesn't mean that you'll allow him to be as protective as I'd like. You can be impulsive. Who knows that better than me."

"I won't this time. It can't happen. I have to be slow and deliberate." She paused. "I know you've told me not to do this, but it's the only way I can be certain that we'll both be safe." She added quickly, "And then there's Tanner and Rennell. I can't let anyone else be killed."

Maria was silent. "No, I don't like the idea at all. It scares me. We've almost gotten free of them, Lara. I want to tuck you away and not let you out of my sight." She paused. "And I particularly don't like the idea of you trying to keep me stuffed out here at Sandrino Place. I won't be a prisoner here. I'll follow you. If you're going, I'm going with you. At least, I'll be able to keep an eye on you."

Panic raced through Lara. *I'll follow you.* They were almost the same words she'd used with Tanner. "Don't do that to me, Maria. I have to keep you safe. You're my Achilles' heel."

"Then you'd better get this over very quickly, because when you look over your shoulder, I'll be there. Call Tanner and let him know he's going to have another passenger and make arrangements to get me there." She cut the connection.

"Dammit!" Lara should have known that she wouldn't be able to get Maria to stay at Sandrino Place after she'd had so much trouble with her when she'd come here to Indian Hills. Perhaps she *had* known, but wouldn't admit it to herself, she thought. They'd fought Volkov and Anton together all her life, and now Maria wouldn't want to be left out of the final battle. Lara could understand it, but it terrified her. She was remembering the ugly photograph of a tortured Maria that he'd posted on the door of the office at the Connecticut airport. The threat and command had been clear. *Come.*

Well, she was obeying that command, she thought bitterly, but so was Maria. And because she was, it doubled the stakes and they had to somehow find a way to turn that demand against Anton and Volkov.

Come on, you bastards. Follow us. We'll be waiting.

She picked up her phone and started to dial Tanner.

◆

ATLANTIC CITY, NEW JERSEY
3:20 A.M.

Volkov was not looking pleased, Anton thought as he watched him come through the ornate casino door and stride toward him across the foyer. Well, screw him, he'd done everything he could do without the funds Volkov had promised. Nevertheless, he pasted a smile on his face and got to his feet. "You made good time. I reserved you a suite in case you wanted to rest. It's a first-class hotel, and the casino is up to your standards if you want to play. Evidently, Tanner does well for himself even when he's not doing an extraction."

"Are you an idiot? I don't want to play. I want you to tell me that you've been able to locate Lara." He glanced impatiently around the luxurious lobby. "Or tell me why you've dragged me here. Have you been able to contact Tanner? Can we negotiate with him?"

"I haven't been able to reach him. He owns this casino, Indian Hills in New York State, one in Miami, and another in Dallas, Texas. He owns several others around the world, but he delivered Lara and Maria to Connecticut, so I'd bet they're still in the U.S."

"Brilliant," Volkov said sarcastically. "But you can't locate them for me."

"I'm sending a team to Indian Hills and I've questioned his people here at Atlantic City." Anton paused. "I've hired an investigator to give me a dossier on Tanner. I know you said you'd heard of him, but I hadn't." His brow wrinkled as he shook his head. "He has money to burn. He hasn't done an extraction in years. Why would he decide to make Lara an exception?"

"How do I know?" Volkov asked harshly. "Find out. Someone had to have paid him. You kept saying you never let them have contact with anyone, so they couldn't have arranged it even if they'd had the money."

"I'm only saying it's strange," Anton said. "I didn't say I wouldn't be able to find him for you. You said you'd heard of him before. Did you hear anything about him that would help me locate the bastard?"

"No." Volkov was silent a moment. "The only thing I heard someone say is that he's one hell of a poker player."

"That won't help. He owns casinos, for Pete's sake."

"Then don't ask me stupid questions," he said. "I don't like this. It has to be over quickly. See that the word gets out that Tanner has merchandise that I want and I'm willing to pay premium for immediate delivery."

"I promised you I'd get her back. You're not going to wait?"

He shook his head. "You've made me uneasy. I don't like it that Tanner's in the picture and no one knows why. I'm going to get that bitch back so that I can ask her myself."

INDIAN HILLS AIRPORT
6:40 A.M.

Maria was waiting inside the door of the Gulfstream when Lara, Tanner, and Rennell got out of the hotel courtesy car and started up the stairs. "You were very efficient, Tanner," she said. "Mallory had me out of the house and delivered to the Gulfstream before daybreak."

"Good." Tanner nodded, then strode directly up the aisle toward the cockpit. Maria glanced at Rennell, who had come in behind him. "We keep running into each other. Sorry. I know it must be annoying for you."

"No." He shut the door and tossed his duffel in a closet. "I've no problem with it. Tanner says we may be able to use Lara as bait." He smiled cheerfully. "Maybe you, too? I have to accept the bad with the good."

"We can always count on you to be pleasant." Maria looked at Lara. "She didn't mention that to me. But then she's much more valuable to Volkov than I am. I'm sure she didn't want me to worry."

"It probably won't happen." Rennell shrugged. "We'll take care of it if it does."

"That's comforting." She hugged Lara. "Come to the galley and have a cup of tea with me. I need to get away from all the sunshine and rainbows that Rennell is throwing at me."

"He was joking...I think."

"Tea," Maria repeated firmly.

"We should probably wait until we take off," Lara said. "That's why Tanner went directly to the cockpit. He didn't like it that we've stayed here this long. He wants to get on the move."

"Whatever." Maria was heading down the aisle.

She dropped into a seat and started to buckle up. "We're already taxiing back down the runway. He *is* in a hurry."

But Tanner was running out of the cockpit. "Get down!" Then he was talking on the phone as he waved Rennell back to the door. "Get it open. Nikolai's calling from the lobby of the hotel. We're going to have company." He glanced out the window. "They're already on the field. Black Suburban Chevy. One of them has a rifle. He'll be aiming at the tires. Stop him. Not final."

It was already happening. Lara saw a man with a red cap looking down the scope of a rifle as the Chevy drove alongside the Gulfstream taxiing down the runway.

A shot!

But it pinged as it struck the tarmac instead of a tire. The shooter aimed again.

Rennell was at the open door, and he'd drawn his automatic. "Sorry," he murmured. "No second chances allowed." He aimed at the rifle. His shot hit the barrel and caused the rifle to skew to one side and fall off the vehicle to the tarmac.

Another rattle of bullets from Rennell's automatic. The Suburban's tires exploded one by one.

The vehicle cartwheeled across the tarmac and rammed against the fence!

"Done," Rennell said. "Now help me get this damn door closed."

Tanner was already beside him, struggling to close the door. They finally secured it, and Rennell leaned back against the wall. "At least you got that right."

"I was on the phone talking to Nikolai and giving

you moral support," Tanner said, deadpan. "I didn't want to get in your way."

"You didn't." The plane was lifting off now and Rennell dropped into a chair. "Do we know who they were?"

"Not specifically. All Nikolai could tell was that they were asking the reception clerk a lot of questions about me, and they tore out very quickly when they got answers."

Lara was making her way back to them. "Will that crash cause us any problems?"

Rennell shook his head. "I was careful. Tanner said not final. If anyone is hurt in that crash, it's not because they were shot."

Tanner shrugged. "And they were shooting at us first. They won't be filing any reports."

She frowned. "You asked Nikolai to come down to the lobby and watch for any problems?"

He nodded. "No one is any better at it. It's always wise to cover your ass."

"I can see that. I'll remember from now on." She started toward the galley. "But I think I'll get that cup of tea for Maria that she wanted before all this began. She might need it more now."

Rennell shook his head. "I doubt it. She's tough. Just give her time and she'll snap back."

"I'm sure she'll appreciate your opinion." She smiled at him over her shoulder. "But I'll still get her that tea."

CHAPTER

12

Maria looked up as Lara handed her the cup of tea before sitting down beside her. "That was interesting. It appears that Volkov and Anton have been busy." She took a sip of her tea. "It was close."

"Perhaps not that close," Lara said. "Neither Tanner nor Rennell seemed to be worried about it. They took it as a matter of course."

"I'm glad they did. It gave me a feeling of comfort." She made a wry face. "As far as it went. Watching bullets flying isn't my favorite entertainment."

"Rennell said it wouldn't bother you." Lara grinned. "He said you'd snap right back. It seems you've impressed him."

"Because I talked back to him and didn't give him his own way." She shivered. "Maybe I wouldn't have been that bold if I'd seen him take down a truckload of gunmen before I decided to go visiting."

"Yes, you would. You've faced down Anton all

these years. Rennell might be dangerous, but I haven't noticed cruelty." She smiled. "And he and Tanner seem to have an understanding these days. They're very different, but perhaps the chance of going after Sandrino's killer has developed a bond they never had before. I guess people change as situations change."

"Well, I've noticed Rennell has a wicked sense of humor occasionally." She looked down into the amber depths of her tea. "But I've only had to do what I had to do with Anton. It was my contribution to making sure that we'd survive. It was nothing like what they put you through with those damn Trials. I couldn't stop them, and I couldn't help you." She lifted her gaze to Lara's face. "But that's over now. That's why I'm refusing to sit this one out. You told Tanner that you'd look at it as another Trial. Well, so will I, Lara. But it's one that I won't let you face without me. So don't try to sideline me or protect me. We're in this together."

"That's going to be hard." Lara's voice was shaking. "You mean too much to me."

Maria's lips turned up in a wry smile. "Your Achilles' heel? I hope I'll be of more active help. I'll work at it." She finished her tea and put the cup in the holder. "And now it's time for me to access that great computer and see what I can learn about Las Vegas before we touch down. Run back to Tanner and see what we're going to be facing."

She hesitated. "You don't want to go with me?"

Maria shook her head. "I want to be part of the action, but I'm not going to try to take over."

Lara grimaced. "And I'm probably going to have to face just holding my own. I wasn't welcomed to the party." She got to her feet. "But we're still in this together, just like we've always been." She leaned down and brushed a kiss on her cheek. "I promise, Maria."

Then she turned and went up the aisle toward where Tanner and Rennell were sitting in the aisle in front of the cockpit. She dropped down across the aisle from them. "You talked to Kaskov a long time last night, Tanner. What did you find out? Don't try to leave me out of it."

"As if I'd stand a chance," Tanner said wryly. "Kaskov did do his research but there were blanks about Volkov's personality and you might be able to fill them in for me. You probably know him better than anyone."

"Only one side." Her lips twisted. "And it's not a pretty side."

"I doubt he's multidimensional. You probably know more than you think you do."

"What do you need to know about him?"

"His strengths, his weakness, his vanities, his tells."

"Tells?"

"In a poker game, it's a change in a player's demeanor or behavior that can give clues to his hand. In real-life situations, it can be the ultimate character betrayal that will let you take him down. You study him until you find it."

Her gaze narrowed on his face. His silences, the way he watched, the way he was always one step ahead. "Is that what you do?"

"Sometimes."

"All the time," Rennell said. He got to his feet. "And he has since the time he ended up at Sandrino Place when he was fourteen. It can be exhausting trying to keep up with that. The only one who really liked it was Sandrino—it fascinated him."

"But not you?"

"Hell no, it was an intrusion."

"It wasn't intentional," Tanner said quietly. "It was a coping mechanism from the time I was a kid."

"I knew that, but it didn't help." He smiled crookedly at Lara. "Like I said, it didn't bother Sandrino. Maybe it won't bother you. But a little goes a long way. The only thing that's good about it is that it works." He started down the aisle. "I need a cup of coffee."

Tanner glanced ruefully at Lara. "You don't have to worry about it. I don't know what you're going to do two-thirds of the time."

"I think you do. But I don't really care. Most of the time it's not worthwhile trying to hide what you are. I'm not that complicated."

He shook his head. "Wow. What an enormous fib. Or maybe you just don't know." He leaned back in his seat. "Tell me about Volkov."

"He's cruel, egotistical, narcissistic. But he's not stupid, he can be very cunning, and he always has to be seen as the smartest and the most admired man in the room. He's rich and influential and he loves gambling and has a passion for collecting rare cars." Her mouth twisted. "And he's very proud of his macho image and has a horror of being laughed at. Which is how Maria managed to keep him from killing me that day." She paused. "But believe me, he always gets his revenge. He has a long memory and never forgets. He can get very elaborate in the execution." She shrugged. "The reason he's so determined to get hold of me now is that he's enraged. He'd almost reached his grand finale, and then I skipped out."

"I believe we'll move away from how he treated you." His lips had tightened. "It's beginning to make me angry and disturbing my clarity. Let's go to women. Is there any woman he uses frequently?"

She shook her head. "He enjoys S and M. I told you how much he likes torture. But he usually uses whores. When he's at his property, he likes to use the workers from the marijuana fields. I think it gives him a feeling of dominance. Master of all he surveys. He's done that for years." She added bitterly, "I know he'd like to do that with me. He convinced my father that he should do the same with his workers. Anton almost always goes along with whatever Volkov suggests." She paused. "Do you mind if I don't say any more? This...upsets me."

Tanner nodded. "It upsets me, too. The son of a bitch."

"Yes. Do you want to know anything else? I don't think I can help you about those vanities or strengths or tells you mentioned. Most of the time when I'm looking at him, I try not to really see him. I don't want to know what's there; it always frightens me." Then she added quickly, "But I'm getting better all the time. I'll be fine for whatever I have to do."

"I'm sure you will," he said gently. "And you've told me all I need to know. I can put the rest together when I see him face-to-face." He added, "Tell me about the gambling. Kaskov said it was a big part of his life. It was definitely a part of his interaction with Sandrino. What do you know about that?"

She made a face. "Not much. I told you I didn't like it. I saw Anton and Volkov at the casinos sometimes, and I know he played poker with Anton some evenings when he couldn't get anyone else to play with him. He thought Anton was a terrible player and not worthy of him. He was very proud of his reputation as a great poker player. He was always bragging to Anton. I guess he was pretty good. I know he traveled all over the world to play cards." She frowned. "And he'd get furious when he lost. He was always claiming someone must have cheated him or he would have won." She shook her head. "That's all I know, Tanner."

"And it gives me a good background for what Kaskov told me about his card game with Sandrino in Ukraine." He put up his hand. "He lost to Sandrino, which would mean anger, rejection, and desire for revenge. Then he lost again and that would have triggered the same response. Then he decided to try one more time, but not where his friends could see his humiliation if he lost again. He set up the game in Las Vegas." He added, "And set it up in a place where there weren't any major players so the word wouldn't get around about the game. I was wondering why I hadn't heard of it."

"Everyone knows about Las Vegas."

"But not if the game took place an hour outside Las Vegas near the Muddy Mountains. Kaskov said it was held at an old saloon-casino that closed down in the 'fifties and was only offered as an occasional rental property after that time. Volkov rented it for the game."

"Muddy Mountains," she repeated distastefully. "Not exactly an appealing name to lure someone to a location."

He smiled with amusement. "Gamblers generally don't give a damn about what a place is called or where it's located. The only thing important is the game, the stakes, or who's playing. I played one of my most profitable games at a shack near a diamond mine in South Africa." He added, "But the Muddy

Mountains aren't as drab as they sound. They're part of a wilderness preserve that has good hiking and great, sometimes exotic views like the Bowl of Fire." His smile faded. "And Sandrino was different from most gamblers. He'd been at the top so long that he got bored easily. He'd spent a lot more time at home that year and only occasionally was tempted to take off for Europe or Asia for a game. Yeah, he might have been attracted by something else other than a chance to beat Volkov again."

"How did Kaskov know that Volkov had found that place in the Muddy Mountains?"

"Money, contacts. You can find anything if you want it bad enough."

"He said he couldn't be sure Volkov killed Sandrino."

"No, but he had the man who set up the game for Volkov interrogated. Lenny Walker. His statement was definitely incriminating, but he was too scared to say anything definite. He skittered away before he could be interrogated in depth. Kaskov said that I'd have to question him again when I got to Las Vegas." He added grimly, "He'll talk to me."

"And then?"

"We get Volkov back to Las Vegas to tell me all about that visit eighteen months ago. Once he knows that Walker is talking, we may not have any trouble bringing him back there. If he's as proud as you say about his reputation as a gambler, he's not going to want anyone to know that he might have killed Sandrino when he was in a rage because he'd lost to him again. Not the thing to do among his gambling brethren. He'd be ostracized. It kind of discourages anyone from wanting to play cards with you."

"What if you can't find Walker?"

"Then we wait for Volkov to zero in on us. His men saw us at the airport, and this Gulfstream is rather showy. He won't have trouble tracing it if we park it in a spot at one of the Vegas airports that's equally showy. I don't want to make it too difficult for him."

"That's two." She shook her head. "I hate to ask you to go for three."

"Then don't. I'd have to think, and I'd much rather go for the obvious." He stared her in the eye. "But I'd do it if I had to. Because I can't stop now. We're going to do this, Lara."

"I know we are. I'm just a little overcome at the moment." She forced a smile. "But I'll get with the program. I've just been a little intimidated by being pushed to the side while you and Rennell take over the action. Usually that's not the way it is."

"Do you think I don't know that?" he said roughly. "Well, I like it that way. Give me a break. It's not going to last forever." Then he sighed. "Sorry. I'm a bit on edge. Can I make it up to you by making you and Maria an omelet?"

She smiled. "What? Another omelet? That's a supreme sacrifice. You said you don't like to cook."

"Well, maybe I'll con Rennell into doing it. He doesn't mind." He got to his feet. "Or maybe I'll do it myself so that you'll realize I'm a true penitent." He reached down and pulled her to her feet. "I just don't like the idea of bringing you into this brouhaha. I didn't care for those bullets flying around you today."

"They were mostly Rennell's bullets, and they weren't around me."

"Don't quibble. It was the concept that counts."

"It most certainly does not." She was studying him.

As usual, she couldn't read him. There were elements of hardness and recklessness and yet something else that was deeper, twisted, and hurtful. "What does count, Tanner? Why are you talking such nonsense?"

He looked away from her. "I don't like the idea of what might have happened to Sandrino. And I don't like what I might be dragging you into, when your whole life has been shit. And I know I'm going to do it anyway." He glanced back at her with a bitter smile. "So I'll make you a damn omelet to make up for it. Because that's the kind of wonderful guy I am."

"Bullshit." She pulled away from him. "It's my choice, so shut up about it. It's an insult for you to think that it has anything to do with you. Maybe I didn't have such a great life, so what? You didn't, either. At least I had Maria. And I'm trying my best to make it better, and you're trying to help me. I'm no victim. I won't be anyone's victim. I've already done that."

He was staring at her, stunned. Then he slowly smiled. "Anything else?"

"Yeah, make me and Maria that omelet and it better be good. I deserve it."

"It will be magnificent." He took her elbow again. "You'll never have a better omelet. I'll even make one for Rennell, and you can't imagine the abuse I'll have to take from him."

Her lips were curving a little. "Yes, I can." The smile became catlike. "And how I'll enjoy it."

———◆———

"I've just had word about Tanner," Anton said eagerly as he strode into Volkov's suite. "The team I sent to Indian Hills located him, and he took off in the same Gulfstream he was reported to have left Stockholm in."

"Took off?" Volkov couldn't believe what the idiot was saying. "Are you telling me he got away from you again?"

"We just missed him," Anton said quickly. "But the receptionist at the hotel said that he was with a woman of Lara's description so she's still with him. And that Gulfstream won't be hard to trace, it's almost one of a kind. I'll get right on it."

"You bet you will," Volkov said grimly as he leaned back in his chair "Tanner has made a fool of both of us. I won't tolerate this, Anton."

"He hasn't exactly made a fool of us," Anton said. "If anyone did that, it was that bitch Lara. All he did was take a job she offered him and run with it. As soon as I can contact him, I'll try to negotiate to get her back." He paused. "You are willing to pay top dollar?"

"I told you I would." He added slowly, "If that's what he wants. I'm not sure it is."

"What else could he want?" Anton said, puzzled. "No matter how much money anyone has, if you offer them enough, they'll take it. He'll just tip his hat and walk away."

But that bastard, Sandrino, hadn't thought Tanner would walk away, Volkov thought bitterly. He could remember Sandrino lying there, propped against the wall, yet still taunting him. *You think you're going to get away with this? You always were a fool. Tanner won't give up. Tanner never gives up. I've told you about him. He'll just keep coming.* He was actually smiling. *"You're a loser, Volkov. And you'll lose to him, too."*

But he wasn't a loser, he thought furiously. He had beaten that scornful son of a bitch, and that made him a winner. He had been the one who had walked away, and he would walk away from anyone else who thought he was less than he was. He had been so clever that no one had known what happened that night.

Yet suddenly Tanner had appeared in his life and had taken Lara. Coincidence? Or a connection?

Tanner never gives up.

Either way he'd have to take care of him. "I'll pay whatever I have to pay. Just find him for me. I want Lara back."

"As I said, the Gulfstream should be easy enough to locate," Anton said. "I'll put out the word. Check with the civilian air authorities. I'll start calling different cities around the country and inquiring."

"That sounds like a good enough plan." Then Volkov added thoughtfully, "But why don't you begin with Las Vegas?"

DURANGO AIRPORT, LAS VEGAS, NEVADA
5:40 P.M.

"This is where we part ways." Tanner turned away from the rental car desk and handed Rennell a set of keys. "Find us a safe place to hang out for the next few days while I see if I can dig Walker out of the hole he's dug for himself." He turned to Lara. "The two of you go with Rennell. He'll take care of you."

"And when did I sign up for that job?" Rennell said dryly. "I can't quite remember."

"Would you rather I took care of you?" Maria

asked. "There's more to caretaking than shooting off big guns and yelling at everyone."

"Is there?" He suddenly grinned. "That's the only kind I know."

"Where are you going?" Lara asked Tanner. "Kaskov told you Walker was hiding out. Wouldn't he have left town?"

He shook his head. "The Strip. Kaskov said Walker has lived here in Vegas for the last thirty years. It has to be home to him. And he's a gambler. He'll have friends."

"And probably told them not to tell anyone anything."

"Anything that wasn't safe. But everyone always has a different idea of what's safe, depending on how big the bet is. I'll just cruise along until I find the right friend and the right bet. It shouldn't take me that long. I've got a list of his friends and acquaintances and the casinos they frequent."

"I don't see how that would work." She frowned. "There's such a thing as loyalty."

"It will work," Rennell said. "I've seen him do it. It used to amuse Sandrino."

"Why?"

"I think he was always hoping that Tanner would fall on his face. He said everything was always too easy for him."

Tanner shook his head. "He was always rooting for me. He was like you, Lara: He didn't like the idea that loyalty could be compromised. He thought that anyone who allowed it deserved what happened to them."

"And what about you?"

"I'm a cynic. I play the game." He shrugged. "Sometimes I get bored with it. But I won't this time." He started to walk away. "Give me a call and let me know where I should come once you settle in, Rennell."

"Will do." He glanced at Lara and Maria. "Are you ready to—"

"No." Lara was suddenly striding after Tanner. "I want to go with you. I want to see you do it. It must be harder than you say. Do you mind?"

He smiled. "Not as long as you're the audience and not a participant. You might get in my way."

"Whatever." Lara glanced over her shoulder at Maria. "You'll be all right?"

"Perfectly. I've no desire to run around casinos and watch Tanner perform his rather dubious magic. I've had enough of having to stare at Volkov and Anton salivating at the card tables over the years. I'm surprised you haven't." She glanced at Rennell. "Besides, Rennell may need my help finding a suitable safe house. I wouldn't want anything sleazy. I've grown accustomed to Sandrino Place."

"Then you should have stayed there," Rennell murmured. "I'm not sleazy by any stretch of the imagination. We only needed one hostage. You might just be trouble."

Lara drew a breath of relief. No problem there. Maria could handle anything Rennell threw at her. "Then I'll see you later." She caught up with Tanner at the taxi stand outside as he was opening the door. "Where do we go first?"

"Bellagio. It's glossy, beautiful, and touristy, and will be busy enough to be interesting at this time of day." He closed the door and ran around the other side of the cab. "Why did you want to go along?" he asked as he got in. "You hate gambling as much as your mother. You should be as sick of it as her."

"I'm curious." She leaned back in the seat. "I've seen photos of Las Vegas, and it looked like a wonderful fairy-tale land. I wanted to see what you see in it. You own casinos. Do you own one here?"

He shook his head. "Though I spent a lot of time here when I was a kid trying to prove I was the best in the business. Everyone has to do Vegas at one time or another. It's magical and addictive and there's no other place like it. But when I started to create a career, I didn't want magic. I wanted something solid that I could build on, and the only thing magical would be the way I handled the cards and the respect I received from everyone around me."

"And you wanted that respect?"

"I didn't before Sandrino picked me up in that alley. But yeah, he was not only the best, he was a class act. Everyone knew it. I was better than he was in many ways, but he left me behind when it came to class."

"I don't know anything about class, but I think maybe you have to grow into it." She frowned. "Like Maria did. Things have to happen to you. Sometimes not good things. And just getting over them makes you this class act. Maybe that's how Sandrino got there."

"You could be right." He smiled. "Because Maria is certainly on her way."

She shook her head. "She's *there*. You don't know..."

"I guess I don't." The taxi had pulled up in front of the fountains of the Bellagio, and he got out of the vehicle. "But here's the way we handle this. We go into the gaming room and I'll get you chips to play with while I start drifting around the room looking for prey."

"I don't need chips. I don't want to play."

"But you do need them. I don't want you to stand

out too much. Just go for the slot machines." They
were going through the casino front door, and he
smiled at her. "Relax. Enjoy yourself. It's wonderland.
And after this we'll go to another wonderland where
everything glitters and the music plays and promises
you the world. You know about music and promises,
don't you? It might even make good on a portion of
that promise. We'll have to see..."

WYNN RESORT AND CASINO
9:30 P.M.

Tanner was coming at last, Lara saw with relief as she
watched him weave his way through the crowds of
the game room. She slipped off her stool and walked
toward him. "What's the story? I knew it wasn't going
to be as easy as you told me."

Tanner smiled. "Oh, ye of little faith. But you're
right, I did find one of Walker's buddies here and he
was very interesting. But he didn't know anything that
could help us."

"So where do we go from here?"

He was studying her face. "That depends. You look
a little tired. Are you?"

"I'm fine," she said quickly. "After all, I'm the one
who asked to go with you. It was interesting watching
you when you were talking to those men at the tables.
They...responded to you."

He shrugged. "You just have to study each one of
them for a few minutes and then start the conversation
to strike the right note."

"But it didn't get you anywhere you wanted to go."

She held up her hand. "We've been to five casinos. The Bellagio, the Mandalay, the Venetian, Caesars Palace, now Wynn Las Vegas. Still, no answer. Are you sure this was worthwhile?"

"I'm sure." He smiled. "But you're getting tired, and the dazzle is wearing off, so we can leave now."

"The dazzle?"

"I wanted you to feel what I felt, but without the lure of the tables you couldn't quite get there. You came close, though, didn't you? For a little while it was wonderland."

Her memory was going back over those hours as she'd experienced all the glitter and magical wonder he'd been talking about. Her gaze met his. "I think I came close."

"And it was good for you? Something new and different that you'd never experienced. A little like the horses?"

She nodded and said softly, "It was good for me."

"Great, that's what I wanted." He took her elbow. "We can leave now." He was pulling her toward the front entrance. "Call Maria and see if they've found us a place to lay our heads. If not, we'll go to a diner and have a bite to eat. That's a Las Vegas experience, too."

"But you're not finished. Are you going to just quit?"

"No, I got the information I needed when we were at the Venetian. But you were so fascinated by all that ambience and the boats that I thought we should take in a couple more casinos while the dazzle was still there. We hadn't gone to Caesars Palace yet, and Wynn's is completely different."

"What?" she said, shocked. "You didn't tell me because of the dazzle?"

"Dazzle can be important. Particularly when you've been deprived of it. I didn't want you to miss it." He grimaced. "And don't look so stern. If it had required an urgent follow-through, I would have cut it short. Walker wasn't giving out his address to anyone, but I did talk his friend Lou Delks into giving me his current phone number, which he used only two days ago. I'll call Walker tonight and see if I can get the address from the man himself. I promise I'll let you listen in."

She shook her head dazedly. "And all because dazzle is important?"

"Only in certain cases." He reached for his phone. "I'll call Rennell and ask him about the safe house. You might think you had to explain to Maria." He turned away and spoke into his phone. "Do we have a house?" After listening for a bit, he turned back to Lara. "No dinner. Rennell and Maria managed to agree on a house. Judging from Rennell's tone, I believe it was more Maria than Rennell."

"Maria approved of Sandrino's house," she said absently. "I think for my sake. She might have nudged him in a more luxurious direction."

"For the love of Lara," Tanner said mockingly. "Then she'd certainly approve of the dazzle." He was heading for a taxi. "Even if you don't."

"I didn't say I didn't approve," she said as she got into the taxi. "I was just surprised. It didn't seem...practical." She paused and then said awkwardly, "I think you might have been trying to be kind. I don't really need that from you, but I thank you anyway. The dazzle was...different."

"And that's good enough for me." He leaned forward to give the driver the address, then leaned back. "I'll work on the rest later."

She frowned. "The rest?"

He smiled and said again, "Later."

———————◆———————

TAJ SAFE HOUSE, LAS VEGAS

Lara closed the library door and crossed to the massive desk where Tanner was sitting. "Are you ready for me yet? You said only an hour." She paused. "Or have you changed your mind about me listening?"

"I'm ready for you." He gestured to the desk chair. "Sit down. Did you get something to eat?"

She nodded. "Maria made me a grilled cheese sandwich while she interrogated me about everything I did today." She smiled. "She approved when I told her about the dazzle. She said I needed it, and wished she'd been there with me. I told her that when we're both safe, I'll take her. Particularly to the Venetian. She'd laugh at some of the theatrics, but she'd still enjoy it."

"I think she would, too. Then I'm still in her good graces?"

"She wouldn't commit herself, but as I said, she liked the dazzle." She smiled as she looked around the luxurious library. "Of course she'd indulged in it a little herself today. The house looks like something from the Arabian nights. She was calling it the Taj. She said it was on lease from some Saudi sheik who only showed up once or twice a year. I think she only insisted on it because Rennell was telling her how impractical it was. She does like to goad him."

Tanner nodded. "That sheik must have needed pretty heavy protection, because Rennell okayed the gates and the security arrangements. So maybe they both got what they wanted. I'll have to ask Mallory when he gets here tomorrow morning."

Lara tensed as she watched him start to punch in the number on his phone. "It's late. Will Walker even answer the phone?"

"It's Vegas. People like Walker never go to bed early, if they even sleep in Vegas."

"You talk as if they're vampires."

"Sometimes it comes close." He held up a finger as Walker answered. "Walker, you don't know me, but if you hang up, you'll be very sorry. You could be in deep trouble and I might be the only one who can save you."

Silence.

"I know you're hiding out, Walker. I don't blame you. You thought you were safe these years and suddenly it's right in your face. It wasn't your fault, was it? That's what you said. You just wanted to disappear and hide away so that no one would find you. But I've found you, and if I choose, I'll let Volkov find you."

She heard Walker's breathing suddenly sharpen.

Tanner heard it, too, and immediately pounced. "But I won't do it, if you can convince me that you weren't to blame for Sandrino's death."

Silence, but the breathing was very heavy now. Finally, a hoarse voice. "Who is this?"

"Logan Tanner. You might not have heard of me."

"I've heard of you. Sandrino talked about you a lot. He was always bragging about you. Sometimes I heard him taunting Volkov about how much better a poker player you were than him." The words were suddenly tumbling out. "I think Sandrino hated the son of a bitch, and the only reason he agreed to the game was the chance to beat him again. I hoped he'd do it." He was silent again. "None of this was my fault. All I did was rent the casino, set up the game, and pick up Sandrino at the airport. The last time I saw him was the night Volkov lost to him again and told me to get out and keep my mouth shut."

"And Sandrino was alive then?"

"He was alive." He was suddenly cursing. "But I didn't go back and pick him up to take him to the airport as we'd agreed. Volkov called and told me he was already gone. I didn't like the way that sounded. So I took off for Yuma and told my buddies to tell me when Volkov left Vegas."

"But none of this was your fault," Tanner repeated sarcastically.

"You don't understand, Volkov was really *mean*." His voice was frantic. "He paid good, so I set up games for him whenever he came to Vegas, but I've seen how nasty he could be when he lost or someone talked back to him. He liked to *hurt* people. I heard stories about him. I didn't want to be the one on his bad side." Another pause. "And I didn't really know what happened to Sandrino. I guess I didn't want to know. I told myself that Volkov could have been telling the truth. Then about two months later I got a postcard in my post office box from Sandrino from Santa Rosa, some town in Bolivia. It was the type of picture postcard that bars make on the spot and sell to their tourist customers. He was sitting at a bar and smiling. I was relieved. The date stamp proved he was okay. Right? Since Volkov had never come back to Vegas after that night, I thought I'd gotten off lucky." His voice turned bitter. "Until that other Russian tracked me down and started asking questions. I knew then that I was in trouble. He wouldn't listen. He beat me up and almost broke my nose. I only got away when he took me to the hospital."

"You're lucky he took you to the hospital. Next time I wouldn't count on it. He probably didn't want you to die before he got the information he needed."

"Why do you think I'm hiding out? Whoever that guy was, he was asking questions zeroed in on Volkov. I started to think maybe that postcard was a phony. But it looked real. I didn't want to be caught between the two of them. I've had my fill of those Russians." He stopped. "I'm talking too much. You sound as if you know them. I was hoping that you could get me away from them."

"No, I've no love for either Volkov or the man who was looking for him. And I might be able to help if you can give me more information." His voice was suddenly harsh. "But I'm a hell of a lot more dangerous to you than they are, if I don't get what I want. Sandrino was my friend and I want to know exactly what happened to him. I want to take Volkov down, and I want your cooperation to do it. Otherwise I'll turn my attention to you, and you don't want that to happen."

Walker's voice was shaking. "Hold on. Haven't I done everything I can to help?"

"You haven't even started. I want to see that post-card. I want a map of where that casino is located. I want you to tell me what Sandrino was doing and where he went all the time he was there. I want to know the same thing about Volkov. I want to have time with you face-to-face so that I can tell if you're lying to me. And you know what will happen if I think you are."

"What the hell!" Walker added defiantly, "What's to stop me from just hanging up and taking off again."

"I'd find you. I've gotten this close. Don't you think that I'll get the rest of the way? But maybe I'd bring some of my friends along. I know a few Russians myself." He lowered his voice menacingly. "Though I'd rather handle you on my own. I have motivation to get the information I want from you and I have similar talents. You did mention that Sandrino had spoken of me."

"Yeah, he did." Another silence. "Maybe we could work together. If you promise to get me away before Volkov shows up." Another silence. "Look, I'll send you the map and the other stuff you wanted but I'm not going to trust you for any face-to-face meeting yet. Why should I? I might end up in the hospital again. I'm better off not trusting anyone. I'll get that info off to you tomorrow. You can pick it up at the front desk of the Aria hotel after two P.M. If you like what you see, you can get back to me about a deal to protect me."

Tanner didn't speak. "It sounds reasonable. Unless you're trying to scoot away from me. I wouldn't recommend that, Walker."

"I'm not a fool. I listened to too many of Sandrino's stories about you. He said you were a badass, but he never said you broke your word. I've just got to make you see I'm valuable enough to be worth a deal. I'm scared, Tanner. I've been scared for a long time. I'm not about to run if there's any other way."

"Then we'll see how it goes," Tanner said slowly. "I'll get back to you after I look over what you send me. It had better be what I want, or I guarantee you'll be much more scared."

"You won't be sorry. I didn't want to get into any

of this. All I wanted was the money for setting up the damn game." He cut the connection.

"There it is." Tanner stared down at the phone for an instant before he lifted his gaze to Lara. "I might have been an idiot. Maybe he *will* take off. What do you think?"

"I don't know. Fifty-fifty?" she said thoughtfully. "You'd know better than me. You're familiar with his background and able to intimidate him." She made a face. "You intimidated *me*. If that's what you wanted, then you accomplished it."

"Nah, I don't believe you. You don't intimidate easily." He rubbed the back of his neck. "But it wouldn't have taken much to scare him. He was already pretty much there. I just added icing on the cake. It depends if it lasts. We'll have to see when we go to the Aria tomorrow. I might have blown it."

"What would you do if you did?"

"Start over. But it would be harder. I'd have to talk to people I don't want to deal with who could give me answers, but might demand payment I wouldn't want to give." He shrugged wearily. "Well, what will be, will be. I might have screwed up. I was concentrating too much on what he was saying about Sandrino when I should have had my mind on the game."

"But this wasn't a game."

He smiled recklessly. "Everything's a game. And I might have lost this one." He got to his feet. "Or maybe not. I had an ace in the hole in play and that might come through for me if I did let Walker con me." He was heading for the French doors. "But right now I'm going to take a walk in that Taj Mahal garden and forget about it. Care to come with me?" He didn't wait for an answer but was opening the doors. "Another exotic experience that will give a little more dazzle to the evening."

She hesitated and then slowly followed him. For some reason she didn't want him to be alone right now. Foolish. When no one was more capable of handling every possible emotion, from the exotic and dazzling to the tense, dangerous negotiations he had just been going through with Walker.

Everything's a game.

Only maybe, for a little while tonight, it had not been a game.

"You're very quiet." He looked quizzically down at her as he gestured to the rectangular mirrored lake leading to an ornate Arabic-style summer house. "The Taj Mahal setting getting to you? You've been exposed to quite a bit of wonderland in all its forms today. This one's not my fault. It's a little too Disney and dramatic even for me."

She shook her head. "I'd think you'd like it. If it's all a game, shouldn't you have drama?"

"Was that a jab?"

"No, I think you've had enough of that for one evening," she said quietly. "It hurt you to have Walker talking about Sandrino. It reminded you of too many things." How was she supposed to say this? *Just say it.* "I'm sorry for your pain. I wish I could help you. What can I do?"

"Nothing. Walker probably thinks Volkov killed Sandrino. But he received that postcard and it might have been authentic. It depends if Sandrino had taken a liking to him when he was here. It's a little too pat, but either it is or it isn't. That may be the end of it, and I'll just have to get over it." He added curtly, "Do you want me to cry on your shoulder? Forget it."

"Okay, I'll try." She turned away. "I don't know if I can. You were nice to me tonight. I think you meant to sort of give me a gift. I wanted to give one back to you, but I didn't know how." She started back toward the house. "I just messed it up and I—"

"Hush." His arms enfolded her from behind. "I'm the one who's great at messing things up," he said gruffly. "I've never known how to accept sympathy. It ruffles me. I have to either laugh it off or strike out. Either way it ends up hurting someone." He suddenly inhaled sharply. "Or it ends up like it's doing right now with me aching and trying to keep from pulling you down in the grass. Any way you look at it, it's bad news."

She could feel his lower body hard and warm against her buttocks. She was having trouble breathing, and she unconsciously melted back against him. "I think we decided this was a mistake. But I can't remember why right now."

"I remember why." His hands moved across her breasts and then dropped away as he stepped back. "You might think it's okay to do a little experimenting, but I don't want the responsibility. It's even worse now because I *like* you. I enjoyed the hell out of taking you to see the dazzle tonight. There's so much glitter and dazzle in the world, and it would be a pleasure to show it all to you. But you've got your music, and after all this is over Maria can find you someone wholesome and clean-cut who will never hurt you. That's the plan we should follow."

She tilted her head. "You like me?" She thought about it. "I like you, too, Tanner. Why else did I feel so sad for you? I think that maybe you have this all wrong."

"And I think perhaps you don't have enough experience to judge."

"Experience. Hmm."

"Are you laughing at me?"

"I think I am, but it's better than when I was feeling sad." She smiled. "And I like it that you're not feeling sad right now. It's clear all I'd have to do to make you feel better is let you lecture me. Even when you're not being reasonable." She reached out and gently touched his cheek. "I believe that Walker will leave the notes he promised you tomorrow. Because you're clever and can read people very well. Maybe that postcard will even be the real thing. In fact, I feel everything is going to go exceptionally well for us." She started back toward the house. "Now I'll go and tell Maria the same thing."

"Anything else you want to share?"

"Yes, I liked touching you as much as I did the last time," she said solemnly. "But I won't do it again until I get your permission."

She was laughing as she heard him start to swear while she ran into the house. She was still laughing when she ran into Maria's room a few minutes later and plopped down on the chair beside the bed.

"Well, you look happy." Maria set her computer on the bed beside her. "I gather the call to Walker went well?"

"Not really. It was scary and a little sad, but Tanner might have gotten a promise that Walker will work with him. He handled him very well. Though he thought he might have screwed up. We're supposed to pick up some information tomorrow."

"Then why are you looking so happy?"

"It was a good day." She smiled. "Wonderland and

glitter, and then I was able to help Tanner a little later with Walker. He's a man who doesn't ask for help often. Neither do I. On a Trial, I always had to do everything alone. It felt…warm to be working together. Sort of like being one with the music, only…different."

"I'd think so," Maria said dryly. "No one would compare Tanner to a concerto."

"Oh, I don't know." Lara was grinning again. "Complicated. A multitude of varied shadings of darkness and light. He could come close." She got to her feet. "But I'd have to decide to which one." She leaned down and brushed a kiss on Maria's cheek. "And now I'll let you get back to that beloved computer. We got a little nearer to the end today. Tomorrow could be even better. Good night, Maria."

"Good night." She reached for her computer again, but her gaze was still on Lara's face. "I'm glad you had a good day," she said softly. "We have to make sure there are many more on the horizon."

CHAPTER

13

The Gulfstream is hangared at Durango Airport in Las Vegas," Anton said as he strode into Volkov's suite. "I told you I'd find him!"

"And I told you where to find him," Volkov said sarcastically. "I had an idea Tanner would have a reason to show up there. What else did you learn from the airport personnel? Were Lara and Maria there, too?"

Anton nodded. "Two women of their description. Plus the pilot, and one more man who accompanied them to the car rental counter. He was designated as a driver..." He checked his notes. "Rennell."

"Of course it was," Volkov murmured. "No Las Vegas address given?"

Anton shook his head. "But I had two of my men on a flight to Las Vegas an hour ago with orders to monitor the airport. They'll stop Tanner if he tries to board the plane again."

Volkov muttered a curse. "Useless. I don't think he'll fly out of there until he finishes what he came for."

"Finishes?" Anton repeated. His eyes narrowed. "How did you know Tanner was heading for Las Vegas? Why should he take Lara there?"

"Because somehow he must have found out that I'd been there." His lips tightened. "Shit, he probably knows a hell of a lot more than that. Or maybe he's trying to dig it all out now or use Lara to get it."

"You've been to Las Vegas?" Anton frowned. "You've never told me that. When?"

"Several times. And why should I have let you know? It was none of your business. It's not as if I have to account to you. We really only have one thing in common and that's the Trials." He added harshly, "You would never have appreciated Las Vegas. You're a terrible gambler, and you're lucky I've let you tag along to Moscow the few times I have."

Anton flushed. "I'm not that bad. And you wouldn't have had the Trials if it hadn't been for me. I let you run the show, but I had control of Lara through Maria. You only got mad when she started winning more than losing." He smirked. "You didn't like it that I won those bets, did you?"

"I like it less that you're talking back to me like this," Volkov said coldly. "I believe you're forgetting how much you owe me, how many favors I've done for you, how many women I've sent to your bed. It's time you came to an understanding that you'll treat me with the respect I deserve."

Anton immediately wilted and smiled weakly. "Just joking. We've been friends too long to have disagreements."

"Have we? Perhaps. From now on you won't

disagree, you'll just obey me." He got to his feet. "And the first thing you'll do is tell the pilot to get ready to transport your men to Las Vegas tomorrow. Set up camp outside the city. I'll join you there tomorrow night. The second thing is for you to locate a local gambler, Lenny Walker. I definitely have to reach that bastard. I've an idea he might have been talking to someone. I've tried to call him, but his phone's been disconnected." He was heading for the closet to begin packing. "If you have trouble, I have some other contacts that I can use to reach him, but it's been over a few years since I used them."

TAJ SAFE HOUSE
7 A.M.

Rennell opened the ornate gates of the Taj for Mallory and his team to drive onto the grounds. Mallory saw Lara and Maria standing on the balcony watching and waved to her. "Hi! Here I am to the rescue. But Rennell's going to be a little picky about me getting my men settled in that glorified bunkhouse first. He's still got that police discipline thing going. I lost that the first month after I left the service. I'll be right there!"

"Okay." Lara watched him, puzzled, as he followed Rennell's hand motions toward the huge lodge. She glanced at Maria. "Rescue? What's he talking about?"

Maria shrugged. "Maybe something about Rennell shooting up that Chevy at the airport? Who knows? Men can be competitive." She pulled Lara off the balcony toward the staircase. "But the only thing I'd feel competitive about at the moment would be a cup of tea. Let's go down and get one."

But they'd had two cups of tea before Mallory came through the front door. "Here I am, as promised." He grinned at them and glanced longingly at the tea. "That reminds me, I haven't had coffee yet." Then he shook his head. "No, I'll suffer without coffee until I do my duty. Where do you want the keyboard?"

"Keyboard?" Lara repeated. "You brought my keyboard?"

"Tanner told me that it was on the A-list. I didn't have time to get it to the Gulfstream when I brought Maria, but I knew I'd better get it on the helicopter when I followed with the team." He grimaced. "And it was the first thing Tanner asked about when I called him last night to tell him we'd be arriving early this morning. He said to get it to you ASAP. That you needed it."

Lara felt a ripple of shock. "That's what he said?"

"Sure, but I already knew that." Mallory nodded. "So where do you want it?"

"I'm not sure. I wasn't expecting it. He didn't tell me." She still felt stunned. "Give me a minute."

"That grand ballroom would probably be good," Maria said quietly as she took a protective step closer to Lara. "High ceilings. Okay?"

Lara nodded numbly. "I guess so."

Maria turned to Mallory. "Down the hall and to the right."

He nodded. "I'll go get it out of the truck."

"You do that."

She waited until he was out of the room to turn back to Lara. "What's wrong?"

"Nothing. It was very considerate, wasn't it?" She took another sip of her tea. "He put it on the A-list."

"Don't say nothing. What the hell is wrong?"

"He talked to Mallory late last night. He told him it was urgent. That I needed this keyboard."

"And you do."

"Of course I do," she said shakily. "I'm just being stupid. He said he liked me. That made me feel…close to him. Because I didn't expect anything else, but it would have been nice for us to like each other. And when he started lecturing me and telling me how bad he'd be for me, I laughed at him. I thought that I could make it okay. But I was wrong. Because when he talked to Mallory later, he told him how desperately I needed that damn keyboard."

"It's a very nice keyboard," Maria said quietly.

"But is there any reason why I can't have more? I want the whole world, Maria. I believe if I had it, I could put it into the music. I think he was starting to show it to me."

"Not one reason," Maria whispered as she took Lara in her arms. "And we'll get there. But you might have to work your way through a few idiots and people who get in your way. At least this one has your interests at heart."

"He made sure I had that keyboard because he thought it would totally absorb me. He wanted to put me back in a box and keep me there where I'd be safe. That way he could walk away and live his life the way he wanted and not worry about me. It never occurred to him that I've never really been safe, and I've survived it."

"Maybe it did occur to him, and that was the problem." She pushed her away and looked into her eyes. "All I know is that you were happy last night, and I liked it. I want it back. You're smart and you can figure out how to make that happen. You want it all? Go and take it."

Lara drew a shaky breath and nodded. She gave Maria a hug. "You're right, of course. There's nothing I can't do. I told you I was being stupid. I'll handle it." She stepped back. "And the first thing I'll do is go and play for a while, so that Tanner will hear it and be sure that he got his way." She headed for the door. "Will you give Mallory his cup of coffee? He deserves it…"

◆

TAJ SAFE HOUSE
1:05 P.M.

Tanner was coming out of the library as Lara came down the stairs.

She smiled. "Are you ready? I am."

He stopped warily. "I was going to take Mallory. I thought you were busy."

"I know you did. You made certain that I would be. But I run my life, you don't. Thank you for arranging with Mallory for me to have my keyboard. I practiced all morning, and it was wonderful. It's always wonderful." She came toward him. "But right now it's not my entire life. That's not why I'm in Las Vegas. You know that, Tanner." She stopped before him. "But it seems I scared you by letting you think I might want to have a life outside that keyboard. I thought that we were on the same page yesterday—maybe you were even a little ahead of me. I *liked* the dazzle, Tanner. I might decide to go searching for a little on my own."

"You're pissed off with me," he said quietly. "Are you going to let me explain?"

"I'm not pissed off, I'm disappointed. You said you liked me, and I thought I had a friend who might guide me down some new paths." She shrugged. "But I'll have to find my own way just as I usually do."

"Which is a lot safer for you." His hands closed on her shoulders. "New paths? Shit. Look, I can get obsessive and then I can't let go. I guess it comes from being a street kid. That's why I'm trying like hell to keep my distance. You don't need that."

She shrugged away from him. His hands felt too good, and she was trying to be cool and collected. "I'm the one who decides what I need or don't need. And right now I need to go to that hotel with you to pick up those papers. And then I need to go over them and see if they'll be useful, and if we need to do anything with them."

He gazed at her in frustration for a moment and then muttered a curse. He turned on his heel and headed for the front door. "Do you drive?"

She was right behind him. "I drive very well."

"Of course you do. A necessity for one of your Trials, I presume." He handed her the keys to the black Mercedes parked in front. "You'll drive me to the hotel and let me out, so that I can case the area to make sure that Walker didn't lay a trap for me. If it's okay, I'll go in the back way and retrieve the envelope at the desk. I want to avoid any video cameras. You can wait in the parking lot until I come out. Okay?"

"Yes." She was already in the driver's seat. "Give me directions. You won't want me to use GPS if you're going to have to possibly move around the area."

"Right." He raised his brows inquiringly.

"Drug pickups," she answered. "Directions?"

He smiled and started to rattle off the directions. When he finished, he reached in his pocket and pulled out a small leather wallet. "Your documents came in. Driver's license, one credit card, and a Social Security card. All made out to Mary Wayne. All phony, of course, but not bad quality considering I didn't have time to go to the best."

She looked down in shock. "Why?"

"Because you need them." He grinned. "And because I trust you not to grab Maria and run off now. Even if I'd been able to do it, I would have stalled when you first arrived at the airport in Connecticut."

"And you should have. Maria?"

"They're in the desk in the library. You can give them to her when you get back. But I wanted you to have yours in case you get stopped by a cop."

"I won't." She started the car. "I told you, I'm good."

It took Lara forty minutes to get to the general area of the Aria hotel. She glanced sideways at him when she was a block away. "Instructions?"

"I'll get out here." He was opening the passenger door. "Go five blocks, make a U-turn, and cruise back in this direction. That should give me enough time. If you don't see me, park at the hotel." Then he was out of the car and disappearing among the crowd of tourists strolling on the street.

Lara drew a deep breath and then pressed the accelerator. Not too fast. Give him plenty of time. Don't get nervous. This was just another Trial.

Ten minutes later she was on her way back toward the hotel.

No Tanner.

She parked on the hotel lot and waited, her gaze on the front entrance.

"Let's go!" Tanner slipped into the passenger seat from the street side. "Straight home." He smiled. "And I'll bet I don't have to give you directions going back. You probably remember every twist and turn."

She nodded absently as she left the lot. "It was part of the job." She looked at him. "Did he leave the envelope?"

Tanner patted his jacket. "But I don't know what's in it. We'll have to see, won't we?" He leaned back, watching her. "It was interesting seeing you do our particular drug pickup. You're very good. Volkov did an exceptional job training you."

"It was Anton, not Volkov," she said curtly. "It was too easy, and not enough risk. The only time Volkov bothered with any of the training was when there was a chance I might break something, and he'd get to see it."

"That's right, what was I thinking? I must remember that when we run across Volkov."

"Shouldn't we pull over and go through the envelope?"

"And spoil the suspense?"

She just looked at him.

He grimaced. "Ouch. That hurt. I asked for a map. I'd rather wait to get back to the library where I can check out visual references. Is that okay?"

She nodded. "I'm impatient."

"Walker might have sent us the location of the casino where Sandrino died," he said quietly. "I'm a little impatient myself."

She nodded jerkily. "We'll wait."

"And I think Rennell should be with us when we go through it. It might mean a lot to him."

She hadn't thought of that. But Tanner had, in spite of the tension that was often between them. "I think he would, too."

"Thank you." He was looking out the window. "You did a great job, Lara. I couldn't have asked for anyone better."

He was sincere, and she felt a sudden rush of warmth. "Not even Mallory?" she asked lightly.

"Absolutely not. I don't think he ever made a drug pickup in his entire career." He looked back at her. "And I wish you hadn't." He quickly held up his hand. "But I'll take advantage of any other skills you show me. And I'll try to watch my tongue."

"I only drove you. You're the one who has the damn envelope." She paused. "And I'm wondering if Rennell was right about you being able to persuade anyone to do anything. Did you just play me?"

He smiled. "Not this time. I promise. Though I do admit I was upset with you being angry with me. What can I do to make it right?"

"Promise me that you'll never play me."

His smile ebbed and then vanished. "I promise."

She chuckled. "Swear on your gorgeous Gulf-stream?"

He shook his head. "On Sandrino," he said quietly. "Will that do?"

Her smile disappeared. "Oh, yes, that will do."

LIBRARY, TAJ SAFE HOUSE

"I'll make the coffee," Lara said as she followed Tanner into the library. "You call Rennell and get him here."

"Yes, ma'am," he said solemnly.

"Stop that." She made a face at him as she headed for the entertainment bar on the other side of the library. "I just want to get this going. I'll call Maria, too, and see if I can get her down here. I told her last night that we might be getting closer, and I want to prove it to her."

"I'll get her." Tanner was already on the phone, and within five minutes Rennell was striding into the library with Maria in tow. While he'd been waiting, Tanner had opened the envelope and taken out four or five yellow scratch sheets of paper covered with scrawled, ink-stained notes and diagrams. He spread them out on the large coffee table. "They're not exactly things of beauty. Walker was no artist. But let's see if he gave us anything that we can use..." He reached deeper into the manila envelope and pulled out a smaller plastic envelope. "But this is what I want to look at first." He slid a postcard out of the envelope and examined it. "Shit, if it's a phony, it's a damn good one." The postcard itself looked a little weathered, and the Bolivian postmark appeared totally authentic. He turned it over and the photo of a smiling Sandrino sitting on a stool at a rattan bar jumped out at them. He was in a white suit, and his shirt was a colorful silky print. It was the first time Lara had seen anything but the photo from Tanner's phone, and she leaned closer. "Is it him?"

"It could be." His lips twisted. "Or it could be a

very expensive and beautifully crafted phony. I'd bet the postmark and stamp are genuine. We both know Volkov has the money and the contacts to have this made on the spot in that Bolivian town. We'll have to send someone down there to Santa Rosa to make certain." Yet his fingers were lingering on that photo of Sandrino. "I'd like to take off and go myself, but I can't let it distract me right now. We're getting too close. I'll get Kaskov to send one of his people to do it."

"It's a wonderful smile," Lara said softly. "He looks happy."

"Yeah, which can be easier than the postcard to counterfeit if you already have a photo to work with."

"He's right." Rennell met Tanner's eyes. "Because people always want to believe in the smile of someone they love. Don't send one of Kaskov's errand boys. We'll check it out ourselves after we tie this up." He turned away and bent over the coffee table, flipping through the scratch sheets. "This one looks like it might be a diagram of the interior of the casino." He went to another sheet. "This one could be a trail and a lake. Lots of rocks? Or is it a mountain? I can't really tell."

"I can tell what's written on the other side." Lara had come to stand in front of Rennell and was looking at the opposite side of the scratch sheet. She turned it over. "Sandrino." She looked at Tanner. "You told Walker you wanted to know where he went, anything he did. He gave it to you."

"If I can interpret it." Tanner had picked up another sheet. It was a panel of pointed jags and something that could have been trees. There was a huge letter V in the center of the jags. "Mountains? I believe the V is self-explanatory."

"But which mountains?" Maria asked quietly from where she was sitting a few feet away. "Sheep Mountain, the Spring Mountains, the Muddy Mountains, Sunrise Mountain? I could go on. I've been researching on my computer ever since we got here. The Muddy Mountains might be where that casino is located, but what about that last sketch of Walker's? The *V* has to be Volkov, and it might not be in the same mountain group."

"You didn't tell me you were researching the area," Lara said.

Maria smiled. "But why wouldn't I? I have that fantastic computer at my disposal just waiting for me to unlock the secrets of the universe. I told you I'd be watching your back. I didn't tell you that was all I was going to do."

Lara nodded. "I should have known."

"You've been busy." Maria's gaze went back to Walker's notes. "What else?"

Tanner had picked up the last one. "I hope it's the map that should lead us from Las Vegas to that casino. It looks like there's a Highway Fifteen on it, which is north of Las Vegas." He made a face. "Again, it's not that clear. I'm beginning to think Walker sent us a teaser to tempt me into making a deal to save his neck."

"Then go after the bastard and get what we need," Rennell said harshly. "Or let me do it. We're almost *there*."

"Stay away from him. I don't want him taking off in a panic. We agreed to a division of labor and so far, it's working. He gave us a part of what we needed; all I have to do is push him the rest of the way." He looked through the scratch sheets again. "If we had the time, we might even be able to figure it out from these."

"We don't have the time. We've already wasted more than eighteen months."

"Do you think I don't know that? Back off, Rennell. I'll move as fast as I can. Leave Walker to me. You concentrate on maintaining security and keeping Volkov from pouncing before we're ready for him."

"I'm ready for him right now."

"I'm not. I want the whole story before I cut the son of a bitch's throat. Even Walker doesn't know what happened to Sandrino. There's still a chance that postcard is legitimate, and Sandrino is down there in South America winning another fortune from all those unlucky billionaires." He added fiercely, "I want to know everything. Tell me that you don't."

Rennell gazed at him for a moment, fists clenched. Then he muttered a curse and turned on his heel. "It had better come soon. Let me know when you squeeze more out of Walker." He slammed the door behind him.

Maria gazed thoughtfully after him. "He's furious. Can you keep him away from Walker?"

"If I move fast enough. I empathize, I know exactly how he's feeling." He picked up the sheet with the highway indicator. "And I think I'd better study this map and see if I can make heads or tails of it before I talk to Walker. I'll give him until later this evening to sweat a little before I contact him."

"Are we going to make a deal with him?" Lara asked. "I'm upset he didn't give us exactly what we wanted, but he was only bargaining for his life. He didn't ask for anything else."

"That may be in the second negotiation," he said dryly. "But we'll see what he comes up with."

Maria got to her feet. "Would you like me to make copies of all these notes?" she asked. "Even if they're not exactly what you need, perhaps you can work with them if Walker gets stubborn."

Tanner nodded. "If you would." He smiled wryly. "But we all have to hope that he doesn't get stubborn. Rennell isn't going to be patient for long."

"That was patient?" Lara asked.

"Definitely." Maria finished gathering the notes and was heading for the door. "He didn't pull a gun, did he?"

<hr />

11:10 P.M.

The first words that Tanner spoke when he called Walker that night were, "Was it supposed to be a joke, you son of a bitch? I wasn't amused."

"I kept to my word," Walker said quickly. "I gave you everything you asked for. If I'd been there with you, I could have pointed it all out in detail. I just hedged a little on the descriptions. You couldn't expect me to do anything else. If I showed you the whole picture, you wouldn't have any reason to get me out of this mess I'm in."

"I still don't," Tanner said flatly. "Give me one."

He was silent. "I didn't quite tell you the truth. After I came back from Yuma, I waited a couple of days to make sure Volkov was gone for good, and then I went searching at his place up in the mountains."

Tanner tensed. "And?"

"And I found some dog tags in the brush. I'd seen Sandrino wearing them once when he'd been playing cards with Volkov. I remarked on it and he laughed and said you'd given them to him. He said you'd told him that since he'd been the one who'd talked you into joining the service, he might as well have them because you had no intention of going back." He paused. "There was a trace of blood on them."

Tanner swore, long and vehemently.

"I've still got them," Walker said. "Do you want them?"

"Yeah," Tanner said hoarsely. "Yeah, I want them." He was silent. "Anything else?"

"I don't think so. You already know about the postcard. I didn't look hard. I wanted out of there. And after I received the postcard, I thought maybe the dog tags weren't important." He hesitated. "But the bastard will be coming back, won't he? And he'll be coming after me. You've got to get me out of here. Sandrino trusted you. You'll find a way to keep me safe until I can come home to Vegas." He was silent again and then said shakily, "Look, I liked Sandrino. I thought he was kind of funny. I wouldn't have done anything to hurt him."

"You didn't do anything to save him."

"No. I was scared. I was out of my league. I told myself that Sandrino could take care of himself."

"Most of the time he could," Tanner said wearily. "And maybe this time he did, too. I'll have to investigate that postcard from Santa Rosa."

"I'll still have to hedge my bet. Volkov is mean, but he's smart, too," Walker said. "That's why I have to get away from here. Will you take me somewhere safe?"

"Yes. But no more tricks. I'll pick you up tomorrow

morning and we'll go over those notes. Then I'll put you in the custody of someone I trust who will take you out of Vegas and keep you safe until it's secure enough for you to come back here. Is that good enough?"

"That's great, thanks," Walker said eagerly. He rattled off an address. "I'll be packed and ready to go by nine."

"See that you are."

"And I'll dig up those dog tags and have them ready to give to you. Thanks again, Tanner."

"No problem." He cut the connection.

"Is there really no problem?" Lara asked from the chair where she was sitting. "You seemed upset."

"A little." He turned to her. "He hit me where it hurt." He smiled sardonically. "But on the other side of the deck, he didn't ask me for money. Your faith was restored."

"Sometimes money doesn't help, it gets in the way." She met his eyes. "Are you going to let me go with you tomorrow morning?"

He nodded. "I've given up that battle. I know you'd only find a way to go by yourself. At least, I can keep track of you if you're with me."

"And it's where I should be."

"Which is debatable."

"Yes, but I'm right, and you're wrong. End of debate." She got to her feet and crossed to the desk. "Now be still for just a minute." She took his hands and held them tight. "Look at you, stiffening up. Go ahead. This isn't any more than I'd do for Maria if I felt she needed someone to reach out to her. I swore I wasn't going to touch you again. I was very angry with you. I was even insulted. But it doesn't seem to make a difference. For some reason I don't like to see you hurting. It would be easier if you didn't some-times have that black cloud hovering over you. I know you're tough. I know you don't need comfort. But for some reason I need to give it." Her grip tightened for an instant in a caress that wasn't really a caress. Then she pushed him away. "And now it's done. And neither one of us was hurt by it."

"I'm not so sure," he said quietly.

"Then do what Maria told me to do," she said. "Figure it out the best you can. Even though I didn't do so well this afternoon. I guess every step prepares you for the next one." She was heading for the door. "I'll see you tomorrow morning, Tanner."

"Do you want me to drive?" Lara asked as she walked toward the car the next morning. "I checked that ad-dress and it's about forty minutes from here. Though you probably haven't got any reason to have me do it today."

"On the contrary, I'd like you to drive." He got in the passenger seat. "I need to check out the grounds before I go in and get Walker to go over these notes with me. We might have to move fast if he has visitors."

"Wouldn't he have contacted us if there had been trouble?"

"Hopefully. But I've never liked to take chances. As you saw at the hotel yesterday. The apartment address is Three Eighty-Six Sunrise Place. Use GPS. I can't give you directions. I've never been there. Just try to stop the block before you get there and let me get out."

"Right." She took off, listening carefully to the GPS.

The directions were taking her to a poorer side of town. Shops. 7-Elevens. Grocery stores. Gas stations. She stopped. "Get out here. That should be it on the right." She pointed to a gray three-story building with chipped paint and a wide porch with a broken swing. "It's supposed to be on the second floor. Apartment Twelve-G. Where do you want me?"

"A hundred miles from here," he murmured. His gaze was on the parking lot in front of the apartment. "I don't like that tan Subaru rental car in front of the entrance. Most of the other vehicles in the lot are pretty beat up and old, but that Subaru is sticking out. Just as ours would be if we parked over there. I'm going to check out the rest of the grounds and circle back around. Park at the curb over there."

"How long?"

"Probably not more than fifteen minutes." He was out of the car and disappearing into the backyard of the house to their left.

She started to count the minutes.

He'd said only fifteen…

But he was back in ten. And he looked very tense. She asked, "Trouble?"

"Not on the surface. No other vehicles in the parking lots or on the streets in the next three blocks that appeared suspicious."

"But you never pay attention to surface. Tell me."

"I don't like that Subaru. I think it's time I called Walker."

He was already dialing. "If he answers and sounds weird, I'm in trouble. If he doesn't answer, I'm still in trouble." He listened. "He's not answering. I'm going over the roof and down the back fire escape to get to him."

"Why don't I call the police?"

"Because if he's still alive, I want to keep him that way. Nothing like police dropping in to cause a ruckus." He was out of the car again. "Stay put."

Her hands clenched on the steering wheel. She felt angry and helpless and wanted to hit someone. Stay put?

She stayed in the car for another few minutes, her eyes straining to see what was going on at the apartment house.

Nothing.

She grabbed a flashlight out of the glove box and jumped out of the car. The next moment she was crossing the street toward the Sunrise Apartments. How was she going to get to that second-floor apartment? Tanner had said he was going to go in the back way down the fire escape. Then stay out of his way and go in the front. She went past the Subaru and straight to the front entrance. She opened the screen door and went silently up the steps.

She heard a child crying on the first floor.

Nothing from the second floor yet.

She was almost to 12G. Still no sound.

Then the door to 12G exploded open and a dark man in a hoodie was catapulted out into the hall!

He saw her in front of him. "Shit!" He went on the attack. His fist plowed into her stomach. She lost her breath. She instinctively lifted the flashlight and brought it down on his head. When he staggered, her other hand came down in a karate chop on the back of his neck. She followed it with another blow to his throat and the man was lying unconscious on the floor at Lara's feet.

"Out of the way, Lara." It was Tanner following

the attacker through the doorway. He looked down at the unconscious man on the floor and then shrugged. "Or not." He gave her a quick look. "Okay?"

She nodded. "He...surprised me. I didn't expect him to come through the door like he was blown from a cannon." She added defensively, "Otherwise I would have been able to put him down sooner. Or if I'd had a gun. I should have had a gun."

"Why? When you had that handy-dandy flashlight? I told you to stay put."

"And then you walked away. I've told you I didn't like that."

"So you did. I'll pay more attention next time." He was dragging the man in the hoodie back into the apartment. "Come in and shut the door. We don't want anyone tripping over bodies in the hall."

"Bodies? Then she saw another man crumpled on the floor a few feet in front of an open doorway. "There were two of them?"

He nodded. "But he came in the bedroom when I was jumping in the window from the fire escape. I broke his neck, but the guy in the hoodie heard us and went after me."

"And he was the one you tossed through the door?" She was looking around the apartment. "Where's Walker?" She stopped, her gaze flying to the man lying in the doorway. "Was one of them—"

"No, Walker was supposed to be in his fifties." His glance followed hers to the doorway. "I think he's the man lying on the bed in the other room. I didn't have time to examine him, but I don't think he's going to be telling us anything."

She stiffened. "Dead?"

"I'll go check in a minute." He was taking off the man's belt. "I need to tie this one up before he comes to."

She watched him for an instant. "But what if Walker's not dead? He might need help." She was already through the open doorway. "Maybe we should take him to—" She stopped as she saw Walker's face. His mouth was wide open in a silent scream. His eyes were glaring into nothingness. His shirt was covered with blood.

"You couldn't wait, could you?" Tanner was standing behind her. "I didn't want you to see it. It only took a glance for me to see that they'd decided to play with him before they'd killed him."

"Why?" she whispered. "Why would they do that?"

"Probably for the same reason that they'd come after him in the beginning. Orders. Volkov probably thought that I'd somehow learned about Sandrino's game here and went to the most logical source. Those guys look like the usual hoods for hire you see at casinos around the world. Volkov probably sent them to find Walker and keep him quiet or punish him for squealing on him."

"Then it's our fault. We should have gotten him out last night."

"If we'd seen it in our magic ball. He was well hidden. Volkov probably went to the Albanians, who have no trouble getting any information they want as long as you don't mind that they might kill a few bystanders along the way."

"He was so scared, Tanner. He knew what a monster Volkov is."

"And so do you. That's one of the reasons you're this upset."

"I've got to stop him. He hates me, Tanner. He'll hurt anyone I love. He'll hurt Maria."

He pushed her gently toward the door. "Come on. We've got to get out of here. But first I've got to search those guys and see if they found anything on Walker that we can use." He was already swiftly going through their pockets. "Here's something…" He pulled out a yellow sheet like ones they'd been examining yesterday and glanced at it. "May help. May not." He took out their phones. "And I'll check their phone history before we leave and see if they've made any calls that might strike a familiar note. After that I'll turn them off and let their boss come look for them."

She watched him check their phone history and write down a couple of numbers. "Definitely the Albanians. Which means Anton and Volkov are either here or on their way. Okay, that's it." He got to his feet. "Let me go first and see if there's anyone around."

"No. I'll go with you." Then she had a sudden thought. "I forgot something. I'll be right back…" She heard Tanner cursing behind her as she ran into Walker's bedroom. She shivered as she went over to the bed. "I'm sorry," she whispered. "We were going to try to get you away. I promise that we'll punish Volkov." She was searching all around the bed and the floor. "Just this one more thing…" She found it and ran back to Tanner. "We can go now."

Tanner called Rennell on the way back to the safe house. "I need you to go to Walker's ASAP. Don't be seen. There's a back fire escape you can take to the second floor. The room is Twelve-G."

"I thought you were on your way there this morning." He paused. "Did you kill him?"

"No, but there's a cleanup to be done. He had visitors when we got there. Gangster affiliations. The Albanians. Walker is dead and the two men who did it are still there. One dead, the other tied up and gagged awaiting your services. Lara and I might have been seen so we need them all to be removed as discreetly as possible from the premises to another location. Preferably somewhere on the Strip so that you can use Walker as the victim he was and frame the other two goons so that the police or their bosses, the Albanians, will think they fouled up the job."

"You have it all thought out," Rennell said sarcastically. "Am I allowed to change it to suit myself?"

"By all means, use your ingenuity. Only a suggestion." He asked quietly, "Do you need any help?"

"They'd only get in my way. You didn't get to talk to Walker?"

"No, but I'll make sure it won't matter. I did find another piece of the puzzle that the Albanians stole from him."

"Yes, you will, if you're going to make me take on the Albanians."

"As I said, use your ingenuity. If you need help, call me."

"You'd *really* get in my way." Rennell hung up.

"Will he be able to do that?" Lara asked.

"I wouldn't have called him if he couldn't. He's totally experienced and he's very innovative. Sandrino used to tell me stories about him." He grimaced. "And I was involved in a few of them myself when I first came to live with Sandrino." He glanced at her. "Don't worry, neither the police nor the Albanians will be after us."

"And what about Volkov?"

"Why should I promise you that? You've been telling me that I can't keep you away from him." He added grimly, "And you demonstrated it today, didn't you?"

"Do you think he's here in Vegas yet?"

"If he is, he hasn't brought his entire crew or he wouldn't have gone to the Albanians for outside help." He paused. "But I think he'll be here soon. So we'd better see what we can do to get ready for him. As soon as we get back to the safe house, we'd better start going over those scribbles Walker sent us and see if we can make anything of them."

"I suppose I should have seen if there was anything else in his bedroom when I ran back that second time."

"This last note I took from the Albanians was probably the only thing of any value. I can't see Walker leaving anything valuable lying around when he had the entire casino area memorized. But I'll call Rennell again and tell him to take a look when he's there." He looked at her. "I didn't ask you why you went back."

"Because you were pissed off that I wasn't doing what you wanted. I forgot something." She slipped her hand in her jacket pocket. "This." She pulled the object out of her pocket and handed it to him. "I was afraid that I wouldn't be able to find it, but he'd dropped it on the floor."

"The dog tags." Tanner looked down at the metal in his palm. "You went back for this?"

"You told him you wanted them. They belong to you. There are probably memories. You should have them." She moistened her lips. "There's no blood on them. Walker must have wiped them clean."

"Yeah." He seemed to be having trouble looking away from the dog tags. "Only memories…" His gaze lifted to her face. His eyes were glittering, though his lips were taut. "I think you've done it now," he said hoarsely. "I was doing pretty well. I was holding on, but you've blown it."

She shook her head. "I did the right thing. They belong to you."

"And I told you I could be very possessive about things that belong to me. That's why I'm careful about that obsessive streak I mentioned. I never give up."

She frowned. "What are you saying?"

"I'm saying more than I should." He suddenly smiled recklessly. "I'm telling you all bets are off, and you take care of yourself because I'm done with it. From now on you're on your own."

"I always have been."

"And a remark like that would have immediately sent me reeling but not now. I won't let it." He looked away from her. "We'll do what we both came here for, and we'll come out of it on top. You'll get what you want. I'll definitely get what I want because I make a habit of winning." She was driving through the gates. He looked over at her, smiling again. "But I'll make sure you win, too, Lara. You won't be sorry."

"I'm not exactly sure what you're talking about, and I don't know if I like it." She parked in front of the house and looked down at the dog tags in his palm. "And all of this was because I ran back and got your damn dog tags?"

"Small actions can trigger earthquakes." His smile had deepened. "I felt the need to give you fair warning."

He opened his passenger door. "I feel more relieved than I have since you first woke up on the Gulfstream. Now let's go inside and check out the last note I took from that Albanian and see if it's going to help us."

———◆———

"You've got the midnight oil burning bright," Rennell said as he walked into the library that night. "And all to welcome me back from the wars?"

"Among other things," Tanner said dryly. "And was it a war?"

"I exaggerated a bit. It was more a piece of cake after I got them out of the apartment. But they're all safely ensconced in a neighborhood not too far from the Strip in appropriate murderous positions that would put their Albanian bosses in a rage against his inept goons. I'll place a call to the police in an hour or so and let them know that a gang war has obviously erupted in their completely sin-free city."

"Sounds like an excellent job. I'll give Kaskov a call and tell him to use his influence to smooth out any problems with the Albanians."

"Couldn't hurt." He paused. "So what have you been doing while I've been busy saving your asses? Did that note you snagged at Walker's pay any dividends?"

"It might have." He handed him the note. "It's much better crafted than the others; it was probably done last night after I'd agreed to protect Walker. It's the Volkov mountain sketch, this time in detail. It even indicates a waterfall. He must have been feeling generous because he'd told me that he'd found those old dog tags I gave Sandrino in the brush near there. He probably knew I was going to ask him to take me there."

Rennell was studying the sketch. "Interior and exterior. He did do a good job. Anything else?"

Tanner shook his head. "We've just been going over the other sketches again. Maria's been comparing the lines and features in the sketches to the possible actual natural geographic features in the areas she found doing research on her computer. She was able to line up quite a few possibilities."

"Sharp lady."

"We're all in agreement there," Tanner said. "But we'll still have to do on-the-ground visuals to find out how accurate she was." He picked up the map sheet. "We can go only so far with this one before we run into areas where Walker indicated practically no features. After I leave the road, it looks like I'll be on my own."

"What about the casino?"

"When I get there, it will be pretty much the same. No friendly warnings of booby traps on the horizon."

"Any word of Volkov showing up yet?"

"Mallory has one of his men monitoring the Gulfstream at the airport to see who comes knocking on their door. He said there was a report of someone asking questions at the rental car desk shortly after we landed. I'll bet that they're here in full force now and know we are, too. Which means we've got to get moving so they don't zero in on us." He tilted his head. "Or maybe make an advance move to stir the pot a little while we're doing it. That may be a way to take the initiative. I don't like the idea of the sitting around meekly waiting for an attack."

"When did you ever do that?" Rennell asked dryly. "You were always raising hell if you couldn't find any other way to get one of your games started. Sandrino used to laugh about it."

"But I have to be more careful this time. Maybe just a few phone calls to my casinos in the east will light the bottle rocket. You complained I wasn't moving fast enough; that should please you."

"It will please me if you let me go after Volkov." He added as he turned to go, "I can see you might be on the way now. Go ahead. Just don't be too subtle."

"I'll try to obey your instructions," Tanner said sarcastically as he reached for his phone. "Heaven forbid I don't let Volkov know exactly what's waiting for him."

CHAPTER

14

W hat are you doing?" Lara asked Tanner as she came into the library thirty minutes later. He was on the floor, sitting cross-legged, leaning back against the couch.

"I'm just relaxing after a busy day and trying to follow Rennell's advice to go for the bottle rocket and not be too subtle." He reached up and pulled her down to sit beside him on the floor. "I placed a call and I'm waiting for a return."

"I don't know what you're talking about. I saw Rennell come down the driveway. Did everything go well?"

Tanner nodded. "He'd be insulted that you even asked. Are you and Maria finished for the night?"

"Until we can go out to the mountains and draw comparisons. It's strange sitting here on the floor. I feel like a little kid."

"That's not bad. It's back to basics. I spent a lot of

time when I was a kid in back alleys shooting craps or playing cards. When I graduated to the bars, I thought I was big time." He smiled. "I've always liked sitting on the floor. Sometimes I can think better. I can see how you might not be comfortable. You were probably sitting on a piano bench most of the time when you were a kid."

She nodded. "When I wasn't doing a Trial. But I'm getting used to this now. It's just…strange." She leaned back against the couch. "I can imagine you in those alleys. I bet you were really good at poker even then."

"Damn straight. It was my job, and every poker hand made me a little bit better. Until I was the best. But there's always someone else who wants to be the best." He paused. "Sandrino was the best until I came along. I tried to keep him from realizing that, but I think he knew I could beat him."

"If he did, then he was probably proud of you. You cared about each other. He sounds like he was very generous. He would want the best for you."

"Maybe. Every game was a competition. We both wanted to be the very best."

"What's wrong with that? Every time I sit down at my piano, I try to be my very best. How could you serve the music if you weren't the very best you could be? I think you're being foolish."

"Do you? Then you must be right, because you manage to pull magic out of that piano. I'll accept your opinion." He lifted her hand and pressed his lips to her palm. She inhaled sharply. Warmth. Tingling intimacy. Electricity. "And probably anything else you'd care to offer." His tongue moved from the center of her palm to her wrist. "Though I should try to remember you're being generous, I'm having a good a deal of trouble. I was telling the truth earlier today. I'm done with being noble. And right now the only thing I can think about is that this floor is excellent for doing a hell of a lot more than shooting craps." He was pushing her slowly down. "And if you don't think so then you're going to have to stop me. Because I'm not going—" He froze. His phone was ringing. He closed his eyes. "Shit!" His eyes flew open and he was sitting up. "Not fair." He checked the ID and then answered the phone. "Dietrich, is it done?" He listened. "Okay. Tell me about it."

Lara sat up and tried to catch her breath. Tanner was talking swiftly, and she couldn't catch the import. But the main thing was that the moment was clearly over. She pulled herself up and sat down on the couch.

Tanner was hanging up. "Sorry. If it had been any other call, I would have tossed the phone in that ornamental lake outside." He added wryly, "But I'd placed the call and I had to hear the follow-up."

"I understand. You were busy. It's not as if anything—" She got to her feet. "We'll talk later."

"No, we'll talk right now. I'm pissed off and not going to leave this hanging." He stood up. "I decided that we needed to take control of the scenario. Since we left Indian Hills, Volkov's and Anton's men have been trying to reach me. I blocked it and told my people not to give them my phone number. I just called my manager in Ocean City and told him to contact Volkov's or Anton's crew and take the bribe they offered to give them my phone number."

"Why?"

"I wanted to start moving. More, I want Volkov to

start talking. He might give away things that we need to know."

"You didn't want me to be available by phone."

"I didn't want him to tear you up," he said roughly. "Your history with him isn't that good. Let me handle him."

"He wouldn't have torn me up. I might have gotten emotional, but I can keep him from seeing it. I've done it before. You should have let him call me."

"I thought about it." He paused. "But I want the battle turned against me. Walker said Sandrino talked about me a lot. That's a head start. Volkov has to believe that it was a kidnapping rather than an extraction because I wanted to take something of his. That's another step. He's afraid I know that he might have killed Sandrino, and that's a giant step."

"I don't need all your steps," she said. "He hates me and wants to hurt me." She smiled crookedly. "I win."

"You didn't even enter the competition. We'll see how it works out after I have my shot at him."

And she knew how persuasive he could be. She had seen him at all those plush casinos, had heard him talking, coaxing all of Walker's friends. She also realized it was essential Volkov believed in the kidnapping scenario. "Yes, we'll see. When do you expect contact?"

"Probably tonight. I think Volkov will be eager. He'll be angry that I had the nerve to take you. He'll want to strike out and see if he can hurt me. He'll want to probe and see if I'm everything Sandrino said I was."

"And I'd no longer be a challenge?"

"That's right." He was suddenly grinning mischievously. "Old stuff."

She smiled grudgingly. "Damn you."

"No doubt that will happen. Go to bed, Lara."

"No way. If you believe he's going to call you, I'm going to be here." She stretched out on the couch and drew a red velvet comforter over her. "You can use one of those easy chairs. You deserve it."

He stood looking down at her. Her smile faded as she saw his expression. Then he was kneeling beside her, stroking her hair back from her face, before tucking the comforter closer about her throat with the most incredible gentleness. "I don't know if I deserve any of this." He tenderly brushed a kiss over her forehead. "But I'll take it." He got to his feet and moved across the room toward the leather easy chair. "Try to nap at least, you stubborn woman."

She didn't answer. Her eyes were closing because she wanted to remember and hold fast that last look. It had been rather like the first few notes of a Rachmaninoff that only promised the intricacy and fascination to come...

———◆———

Tanner's phone rang two hours later. Lara raised herself on one elbow, her gaze flying to Tanner. He wasn't answering! Then she realized why as he held up his index finger. It was the middle of the night and he didn't want Volkov to know he'd set up the call. He waited for it to ring another two times and then picked up the call. "Tanner."

"Boris Volkov." Volkov's voice was curt. "I'm very annoyed with you, Tanner. You have something belonging to me and I want it back. I've put the word out that I'm willing to pay top dollar and I haven't heard from you. You'd do well to take it rather than make me come and take her. Name your price."

"But I'm just becoming accustomed to having her around," Tanner said mockingly. "I don't think I can part with her yet. She tells me you didn't treat her too well. I'm sure she'd prefer to stay with me."

"It doesn't matter what she prefers," Volkov hissed. "She's property. *My* property, and I want her back. You'd be wise not to get in my way. Just take the money."

"How can I do that? That's not the way I play the game. And I've heard you're such a superb player that you should know that. Would you like to offer something else?"

Silence. "What are you up to, Tanner? Talk to me."

"I'm only trying to make the game more interesting. I've lost something I value, and I can see you're suffering a similar loss. Surely there's some way we can find a way to soothe each other's hurt."

"And what have you lost?"

"Can't you guess?"

"I don't have time or inclination to guess," he said coldly. "And I'm getting impatient with this stupidity."

"I wouldn't want that." He paused. "I lost an old friend. And I feel just as sad as you do about your missing 'property.' I'm not saying I can't be compensated, but it will take a little while for me to consider suitable compensation. Suppose you call me back in a day or so and we'll discuss it?"

He cut the connection.

He leaned back in his chair and looked at Lara. "What do you think? Was he spitting fire by the time I hung up?"

She nodded. "And ready to hang you from the nearest light post. He doesn't like to be frustrated, and he doesn't appreciate anyone controlling a conversation but him. Why did you hang up on him?"

"I wanted to let him stew for a little while. We've made our first contact, and he knows things aren't going to go well for him unless he strikes a deal that will please me." He grinned. "Or if he can find a way to cut my throat. I've also given him a more-than-broad hint that I know about Sandrino, and that might be on the negotiating table. Then I gave him time to digest all of that for the next few days before he calls me back. By that time he should be red-hot and ready to be guided in the way we want him to go."

"Hopefully. He's not patient. He's not going to wait around before he contacts you again."

"No, and that will make him even angrier when I don't pick up. In the meantime, he and Anton will be tearing around Vegas trying to string me from that lamppost. That might give us at least one day to check out the beautiful Muddy Mountains."

"Where in the mountains? We're probably not going to be able to cover both the casino and Volkov's place in one day. It looked as if they might even be different mountain areas like Maria said."

His smile faded. "I thought we'd head toward Volkov's mountain. We have the best map leading there since the Albanians stole it from Walker's body. I believe the highway map would eventually lead us to the casino anyway. It makes sense. But if Volkov has any men staked out, it would probably be in that casino area. We'd do better to avoid it right now."

"And besides, you want to see the place where Walker found those dog tags," she said quietly.

He nodded. "I want to see what else is there. But it doesn't change the fact that it's safer than the casino."

"Unless Volkov decided to go there direct from the airport." She shook her head. "Which isn't likely. He wanted to contact you too badly, and you're an unknown element. He'd assume you'd be here in Las Vegas."

"That's what I think. But there's always risk involved whichever we choose." He added with sudden roughness, "You know I don't want you to come with me. Let me take Rennell."

She shook her head. "I'm going with you. I want Rennell to stay here with Maria. Since you've made yourself Volkov's favorite target, he'll probably be tearing Las Vegas apart trying to find you. Rennell seems to know what he's doing, and I can trust him."

"Yes, you can, though he's not enthusiastic about you doing it."

"I think he's getting used to it. So it's settled? Is there anything else that I should know?"

"I can't think of anything, since you've pretty much changed everything to suit yourself." He tilted his head mockingly. "I can only hope that everything else I've done meets with your approval."

"Part of it does." She tossed the comforter aside and stood up. "I guess you handled it as well as it could be handled. I suppose I'd better go to bed and get some sleep if we're heading for the mountains. We'll probably be leaving early."

He nodded. "I believe I suggested that earlier in the evening." He watched her head for the door. "And what part didn't you think I handled well?"

She gave him a cool glance over her shoulder.

"The part when both Volkov and you were calling me 'property.'"

———————◆———————

VOLKOV'S MOUNTAIN
10:40 A.M.

They approached Volkov's property very carefully, even getting out and examining the entire area with binoculars to make sure that there were no sentries surrounding it. The entire mountain seemed deserted. No cars, and the house seemed tightly shuttered.

"It doesn't look as impressive as I'd think Volkov would like," Lara said as she got out of the Mercedes and looked up at the mountain. She'd expected something more spectacular. The two-story gray stone house appeared spacious enough, but it looked almost like a farmhouse. Still, it was nestled in a thick stand of evergreens and she could see a waterfall cascading down the mountain to the rocks below. "He made sure that his compound at Avgar attracted plenty of notice. He always has to be the center of attention."

"This is pretty much wilderness country," Tanner said as he started up the path toward the house. "There aren't that many people around to give him that attention." He stopped and looked thoughtfully down at the waterfall. "One would wonder why he even wants a house out here. The casino makes sense considering his passion for the games. But not this place. And it's some distance from the casino." He was starting up the path again. "And this had to be where Walker found the dog tags. I can't see why Sandrino would have come up here to join Volkov in a friendly drink, can you?"

"You know the answer." She hurried to catch up with him. He'd been too quiet on the way from the safe house, and she'd been aware of his tension. "Why are we here, Tanner? What do you want me to do?"

"We're here because I think a monster lives here, and I'm going to find out for sure." His eyes were glittering fiercely as he turned to face her. "And what I want you to do is to go over to that chair on the porch and sit down and wait for me, while I go inside and search until I find out the answer." She opened her lips to speak and he put his hand on her mouth. "No, that's all I want you to do. I can get into the house by myself. I know a lot about locks. I don't want you helping me break in. I know that some of your Trials involved burglaries. But I don't want you doing it for me. Never. Do you hear me?"

She tore his hand from her mouth. "I hear you. But if you think I'm going to pay any attention to that stupidity, you're mistaken, Tanner. I *know* that monster. I also know what he probably did here. Sometimes I tried to close my eyes, but I know. And I'm not doing it for you. I'm doing it for whoever else he hurt besides Maria and me." She pushed him aside and went over to the panel on the sliding glass doors. "You think you know about locks? I practiced on Volkov's and Anton's locks and security systems for seven months during that Trial. I can get you in this house in the blink of an eye." She was quickly working on the security system. "And do you think I'll have even a hint of guilt about doing it? Particularly since I told you to leave Rennell home, and I know you wouldn't have thought twice about having him do it." She snapped the lock and security system and slid open the door. "If you need me to do anything else, let me know."

He entered the house. "I'll think about it. Right now I'm feeling a bit chastened. Did I screw up?"

She nodded. "You forgot the monster rule. We're in this together. If you don't need me for anything else, I'll sit down meekly in that chair over there. I'll let you do all the searching you want. I've no desire to see Volkov's horror chambers."

"Neither do I." Tanner was going through the CD and video library by the TV. "But it's not fair to ignore them if they exist." He was checking out one of them as he was speaking. "I don't want you in here. Sit on the porch as I first asked."

She looked at the DVDs he was holding. "Bad?"

"You told me he liked to cause pain. He evidently wanted to document everything. There's no reason for you to see it."

"I'm not arguing." But she had to ask. "Sandrino?"

He shook his head. "Not yet." He jerked his thumb. "Out."

She sat down on the porch chair and closed her eyes. She had known this would probably be what the day would bring, and she'd accepted it. She'd sensed Tanner's tension on the entire long drive here. She knew what he desperately wanted, but also what he expected. She'd wanted to be with him regardless. She should probably have stayed with him, but she didn't know if that would have hurt him as much as it did her. He'd desperately wanted to protect her just from opening those damn doors. She'd stay here and try to help when he came to her.

Tanner didn't come to the porch for another three

hours. He dropped down in the chair next to her and took her hand. "Are you okay?"

"Why shouldn't I be okay?" Her hand tightened on his. "I'm not the one who was looking through that ugliness."

"I don't know. I only wanted to check," he said wearily. "It just seemed impossible that anything in the world could be okay after what I saw in there. I'm glad you are."

"Do you want to talk about it?"

"No, but you should know. It was pure torture. Sexual. S and M. Men, women, even a kid. Most of them appeared Latino. Poorly dressed, maybe immigrants? A few park rangers who had wandered his way."

"Not Sandrino?"

He shook his head. "I even went downstairs into the basement hoping that maybe there might be a cell down there. Nothing."

She drew a sigh of relief. "So we're finished here?"

He was silent. "Not yet. But there might be something else. Not in that hideous bunch, but he kept talking about the waterfall. He asked some of the victims if they thought they deserved the waterfall."

She frowned. "What?"

"Don't ask me. I can't tell you yet. But I will." He got to his feet. "I'm going to follow that waterfall all the way down to the rocks and see what I find."

"I'll go with you."

"No, you won't. Because you're okay, and I want to think of you being okay while I'm on my way down there." He leaned over and kissed her forehead. "Stay here. It may be nothing. I'll be back soon."

Then he was gone. She jumped to her feet and ran to the edge of the cliffs. She could see him moving in and out of the trees as he negotiated the falls. She lost sight of him! Her hands clenched in frustration. Then she slowly moved back to the rocks and sat down. It would be fine. It had to be fine.

It may be nothing. I'll be back soon.

———————◆———————

Lara was still sitting there on the rocks when Tanner came up the hill over two hours later. She jumped to her feet and met him as he jumped over the last rocks from the falls. His jeans were wet and so was his hair. "You're wet. What on earth—" She stopped as she caught sight of his face. It was haggard and almost as wet as his hair. "What happened?"

"Bloody hell," he said hoarsely. "Let's get out of here. It will be dark by the time we get back to the house."

"What do you mean?"

"We'll talk on the way back." He took off his shirt and was wiping his face and hair with it. "Go back inside and lock everything up tight. I don't want Volkov to know we were here, if he drops in."

She ran back to the house and locked it; a few minutes later she was running back out. Tanner was already striding down the path toward the Mercedes. She caught up with him at the car. She didn't even ask, just climbed into the driver's seat and started to back out as soon as he got into the passenger seat.

She didn't speak until she'd driven over fifteen minutes away from the house. "Are you going to tell me what happened?" she asked quietly.

"There's a cave at the bottom of the waterfall that you can't see unless you're right on top of it," he said curtly. "Volkov has made a room of it. He has several skeletons mounted there like trophies." He cleared his throat. "And Sandrino's is the prime trophy."

"Oh, dear God," she murmured. She reached out and touched his hand. "You're sure?"

"I hoped to God I wasn't. I didn't want it to be him. I stayed there a long time to be certain. He was mostly skeleton, too, but I could recognize him. His right jaw had been smashed by a racketeer in a poker game when he was a young kid on his way up. He had to have surgery to repair it, and he had two damaged molars that also had to be replaced. He used to joke about it. He told me he might not have picked me up out of that alley if his jaw hadn't been aching a little that night. It reminded him of what a rough life a kid could have on the streets." He had to stop for a moment. "Yeah, that was Sandrino." He looked away from her. "Volkov didn't get to torture him. Sandrino must have fought. He died of a gunshot wound to the chest."

She was aching with sympathy. "I'm so sorry, Tanner. What can I do?"

"You've already started. You locked up the house again for me." He leaned wearily back in the seat. "That's our first step. I'll concentrate on the rest when I'm in a little better shape. I'm having a problem thinking right now. I'll be much clearer by the time I get back to the house."

"I'm sure you will." Her hand tightened even more on Tanner's. He'd just lost his best friend in one of the most horrible ways possible. Yet she believed him when he said that he'd be himself and ready to function in only that short time.

So hold his hand and let him know that she felt his pain. It was all she could do right now.

———◆———

It was after nine when Lara pulled up before the front entrance that night. She didn't have a chance to get out of the Mercedes before Tanner had slipped out of the passenger seat and opened the front door. She ran after him as he crossed the foyer and started up the staircase. "Tanner, tell me how I can help."

"I don't need help." He tried to smile, but the effort was forced. "I only need a little time. It's not as if I didn't know he was dead. I would have heard from him otherwise. He never let me go very long without touching base. Volkov just found a particularly savage way of killing him that tore me apart. He didn't deserve that." He shook his head at her. "Stop looking at me like that. I'll be fine. There's nothing you can do at the moment. Unless you want to scrub my back. I've got to go up and shower and change. You might have noticed I was a little wet."

"I noticed. Can I get you anything? You didn't eat." She had a sudden thought. "Am I bothering you?"

He shook his head. "No. You're company, and I've felt lonely ever since I saw him. But I don't like the idea of you in agony like this. I told you that I wanted you to stay okay."

"But I can't do that unless you are. What are you going to do after your shower?"

"I'm going to go down to the library and have a couple of drinks. Then I'm going to sit and plan how I'm going to kill Volkov in the most painful and humiliating way possible."

"That sounds productive. Are you going to talk to Rennell?"

"Not tonight, maybe tomorrow."

"Would you like me to talk to him for you?"

"Lord, no! He'd have you driving him out there to see for himself. And any plans I made would be literally shot to hell." He shook his head again. "You aren't going to let this go, are you? Why don't you curl up on the couch in the library? I can meet you there in half an hour, and you can watch me either get stinking drunk or come up with a master plan." He started back up the stairs. "Or go to bed, which would work better for you."

"I'll see you in half an hour, Tanner. And I promise I won't be annoying."

He looked back over his shoulder, and that rare smile lit his face. "I know you won't."

When he came into the library later, she'd already lit the fireplace and was curled up on the couch, waiting.

He stopped inside the door. "You're a glutton for punishment."

"No, I'm not. Or I'd have gone to bed and lain there worrying about you. I'm much better off sitting quietly and listening to you if you want to talk. You did say I was company."

"In my usual complimentary fashion." He headed for the bar. "You're a hell of a lot more than that." He poured himself a drink. "I'd offer you a drink, but you'd probably take it just to be accommodating."

"Maybe. But I did make a pot of coffee, too." She held up her cup. "I wasn't sure what you'd need."

"But you wanted to supply it."

"You're hurting. I know how that feels. But I've always had Maria." She paused. "I think Sandrino was your Maria."

"So now you want to mother me?"

She shook her head. "I just don't want you to hurt anymore. That hurt me, too." She added with a sad smile, "And that was not okay."

"No, it wasn't." He poured himself another whiskey. "I don't think I could take that at the moment." He sat down in the desk chair. "So I'll take one more drink and move on to phase two."

"Volkov," she said. "You were halfway there anyway, weren't you?"

He nodded. "But I wasn't entirely sure how deep a score I'd owe him. I knew he'd have to pay for what he'd done to you. I didn't have proof about Sandrino." He finished off his drink. "And I didn't know about all those innocent people that he'd tortured and killed."

"I didn't, either. I knew that he enjoyed causing pain, but I didn't know he'd made it a hobby." She shivered. "Maybe I should have guessed."

"It's hard to guess what a monster will do. But I think we've got the full scorecard now. I've just got to decide how to return in kind." He stared thoughtfully into the fire. "And you've given me hints about how to do that by telling me all about him. Narcissism: Show him and everyone in his circle that he's nothing. Pride and egotism: Beat him at his own games. Greed: Take away all his wealth. Revenge: There's almost too much to avenge, but we'll manage. Pain: That will be no trouble at all." He gazed at her across the room. "Have I left out anything?"

She shook her head. "I don't think so."

"Well, no one should know better than you."

"One more thing." She paused. "You don't leave *me* out of it. You have a habit of doing that." She smiled shakily. "From now on that would not be okay. Maria and I have gone through too much. We're the ones who have the most to lose if Volkov manages to somehow come out of this intact. So place me prominently right in the center and let me do my part." She sat up straight. "Now tell me how we're going to take the son of a bitch down."

9:05 A.M., NEXT DAY

"No!" Maria said sharply. "Hell, no. I was wondering why you didn't wake me when you came in last night. I just assumed you hadn't found anything up there in the mountains."

"Oh, we found something," Lara said bitterly. "Though Tanner took the brunt of it. I'm not going to let him keep on doing that. I have to do my part."

"You said Rennell was joking when he was talking about holding you hostage."

"I said I thought he was. And it's not going to be like that. I just have to do my part."

"You said that. I don't want to hear it again. It scares me."

"Do you know what scares me? What Volkov did to those victims at his house in the mountains. What he did to Sandrino. What he'll try to do to us if we don't stop him." She took Maria's arms and shook her. "It's gone on too long, and he's getting worse and worse. Think of those innocent people. Think of

all the agony Tanner went through when he found
Sandrino."

"Why should I think of Tanner? You're thinking
entirely too much about him. I'm thinking about *you*.
He shouldn't let you do it."

"That's what he said until I told him he had to put
me front and center. He can't stop me." She added
quietly, "And neither can you, Maria. But you can
keep me safer if you do your best to keep yourself safe,
and don't do anything that will cause Volkov to zero
in on any weakness I might have. As he has since I
was eleven. I can't let that happen. This has to be the
last Trial."

"Your Achilles' heel." Maria gazed at her helplessly
for an instant and then suddenly enveloped her in her
arms and held her tightly. "But I'm still going to talk
to Tanner," she said gruffly.

"He said you would. He'll be expecting it."

Maria pushed her away. "What about Rennell? Has
anyone told him about Sandrino?"

"Tanner is probably doing it now. I offered, but
Tanner said that wouldn't—"

"Of course it wouldn't. He was right about that at
least. Tanner can handle the explosion." She added,
"And maybe the emotional fallout." She paused.
"When is all this supposed to start? How much time
do I have to talk you out of it?"

"Probably tonight. Tanner said he thought Volkov
would have had enough time to stew and would be
calling him back. He'll be working all day to get ready
for him. He sent Mallory out early this morning to
track down the location of Volkov's forces in the area.
And I know he called Kaskov for additional help
last night."

"Shit!"

"Don't look at it like that," Lara said coaxingly. "It's the beginning of the end. And it's a new life for us, Maria."

"I'll do my best." She added brusquely, "And isn't it time for you to go practice? You were gone all yesterday."

"What a nag. I'm going down now. I just wanted to duck in here and talk to you first." She gave her a final hug and headed for the door. "Actually, I can't wait, Maria. After yesterday I desperately *need* the music."

Maria took a deep breath, her upper teeth biting down hard on her lower lip as the door closed behind Lara.

"Shit! Shit! Shit!"

———————

Rennell's hands clenched into fists as he turned away from Tanner. "The bastard did *that* to him?" he asked hoarsely. "You should have called me right away. We can't let him live. Not even one more day. Not one more hour."

"Yes, we can. Do you think I don't know how you feel?" Tanner asked savagely. "I'm the one who found him. I saw him. It nearly *killed* me."

Rennell whirled back to him, his eyes blazing. "Then why isn't Volkov dead? You wouldn't let me do it before. But nothing should have held you back after that. I thought you cared something about him. He *loved* you from the day he dragged you up to Sandrino Place. Anyone could see it."

"You idiot, he loved both of us. God knows why." He clutched Rennell's shoulders and shook him. "The three of us were the most mismatched sons of bitches on the face of the earth, but somehow he managed to meld us together and make a family of us. I'll be damned if I let Volkov kill you, too."

"Take your hands off me before I break your neck."

"Then listen to me." His grip loosened and then fell away. "We'll go after Volkov. It's already in the works. But Volkov brought a crew with him, and they're probably as lethal as you were when you were with the Gardella crime family."

"I doubt it."

"Arrogant prick. Anyway, there's quite a few of them, they know what they're doing, and they'll have decent weapons. Anton Balkon will see to that. He's running this show for Volkov. I don't want there to be even a chance that Volkov isn't a dead man when this is over. Not only dead, but in the most painful way possible." He added grimly, "And I don't want to leave any of his men alive to tell the story or cause any future problems for Lara and Maria. Understand?"

"I understand you may be giving me what I want. Tell me how."

"I'm going to lure Volkov into a poker game. It will take place in the mountains at that casino where Walker sent us that note. Volkov will almost certainly try to set up a trap, which I'll counter. But as soon as Volkov gets angry enough, he'll send in the big guns. At that point, we'll have to turn the trap against him. You'll have to take them out, either before or after that happens."

"And he'll get angry enough? Why?"

"It's a poker game, Rennell. The reason he killed Sandrino was that he hated to lose." He added bitterly,

"And I guarantee to add considerable salt to the wound this time."

"But you're going to let me take him out."

"No promises. You'll have an opportunity." He added grimly, "But I might get there first."

"An opportunity is usually all I need. Who's checking out the site?"

"Mallory. He'll have a report today."

"He's good. But I might want to do an additional follow-up myself."

"Go ahead. But don't make the follow-up a sniper bullet into Volkov."

"I won't. You promised me extreme pain for him if I waited." He added coldly, "For that, I can be patient."

———◆———

Volkov didn't call Tanner until nearly eleven that night.

Lara tensed and then sat up straight on the couch. She looked across the room at Tanner. He nodded, waited for another ring, and then answered. "Hello, Volkov. Have you had a good day?"

"What are you trying to pull, Tanner?" Volkov broke out explosively. "Why didn't you answer my call last night? You can't play games with me. I made you an offer."

"So you did. But I told you that it wasn't going to be that easy. We have to deal with my loss before I consider your offer. I've been thinking for a long time about what I'll need to make me happy."

"I don't know what you're talking about," Volkov said warily.

"Sandrino. You might have heard we had sort

of a...relationship. Though it was definitely up and down, and we were both competitive as hell. No matter how I tried, I could never beat him. I was even a little relieved when he disappeared, and everyone knew that I was the best in the world."

"I heard you were good," Volkov said sarcastically. "No one told me you were the best. A little bloated ego, Tanner?"

"If you didn't hear it, it must be because we travel in different circles. These days players beg me for a game, just as they once did Sandrino." He paused. "Did you beg him to let you join that poker game when you were in Ukraine? Maybe you should have sat that one out. I heard it didn't go well for you."

Silence. "You know about Ukraine?"

"Of course. It was my duty to look for Sandrino when he suddenly disappeared. Everyone knew that he'd set himself up as my mentor. I had to at least pretend to show him homage. It surprised me a little that he even bothered with that unimportant game in Ukraine. But when I heard he left there for brighter horizons, I just dropped the search and went back to running my own life and building my portfolio. I thought he was through with you, too." He paused. "Until I got a text a couple of years later from an old friend of yours, Lenny Walker, asking for money and telling me if I'd come to Las Vegas he'd tell me how you'd lured Sandrino here for a big game. I ignored it. I was having financial problems with a few of my own casinos at the time, and I wasn't about to pour cash anywhere but into my own bank accounts. Besides, by that time I was very comfortable not having to share space at the top with Sandrino."

"I never heard of any Lenny Walker," Volkov said flatly.

"I believe you did. Walker seemed positive. But I never heard from him again and I forgot about him because my stocks were plummeting. It was at that point that I took another look at you, Volkov. A thorough look that involved your very fat bank account in the Caymans—and Lara Balkon, who appeared to be a possible weapon."

Volkov was swearing. "How did you know about the account in the Caymans?"

"I'm very good with numbers. Ask anyone. And I hire very sharp people to follow up when I'm interested."

"Prying into my finances could get you killed," Volkov said coldly.

"But then I'm sure that my taking your Lara has already sent me into dangerous territory. I figured that I might as well go double or nothing."

"Double or nothing? What the hell are you talking about?"

"I need to recoup my finances. I've heard you considered yourself expert enough to go up against Sandrino in Ukraine. Perhaps even here in Las Vegas. Are you willing to take me on?"

"Why should I?" he asked incredulously.

"Because you're pissed off that I took your toy." He paused. "And because when I say I need to recoup, it doesn't mean I'm broke. I'm just stretched a little thin. I've been worse off. I can match the amount you have in that Cayman account. Which is how many million? I'll transfer it to the same account, and the big winner takes the pot. We'll set it up with the bank president."

"The deal includes Lara Balkon?"

"That's the double in double or nothing." He added, "Private game. You find the casino and set it up. But I'll have my people check to make certain you don't have any of your goons hovering anywhere close."

Volkov was silent. "You're taking it for granted that I'll take you up on it."

"I'm taking for granted that you're as arrogant and egotistical as I've heard and will think you can beat me." He added, "And that you're greedy enough to want to line your pockets with my money to punish me for having the nerve to take Lara."

"I *can* beat you," Volkov said harshly. "You're nothing. You're just like Sandrino, a crook and a cheat. I had no trouble beating him once I made him stop cheating."

"Really?" Tanner's voice was impassive, but his grip tightened on the phone. "I don't remember Sandrino cheating. But I promise you won't have that problem with me." He asked, "Is it a deal? Do you want me to call my banker and order the transfer?"

Volkov was silent, and then he said slowly, "Call him."

"How soon can you set up the game? Is it going to be a problem?"

"No, I know a place. Tomorrow night."

But it had to be the right place. "It has to be *very* private, Volkov."

"I know what I'm doing, Tanner," he said, annoyed. "It's not even in town. I'll call you and give you directions after I check with the Caymans to make sure about the transfer."

"You do that."

"And bring Lara to the game, I want to take her with me the minute I win. Any problem?"

Tanner gazed at Lara across the room. "I'm certain she'll be eager to see you." He pressed the disconnect.

"So there we are," he said as he put his phone on the end table. "Will you be eager to see him, Lara?"

"Yes." She smiled wryly. "I'll be glad to see the end of him. I believe it went fairly smoothly, don't you?"

"As well as it could." He smiled bitterly. "Considering I was selling you down the river."

"But you did such a wonderful job of it."

"Not amusing. I was praying he wouldn't demand it."

She shook her head. "There wasn't even a chance. You heard him; it wasn't going to work unless he had everything his own way. I could have told you that. And you gave him what he wanted."

"The hell I did. I felt like a pimp."

"Don't be an idiot. This was my call, and I made it."

"Tell that to Maria."

She sighed. "She cornered you?"

"Twice. I did everything I could. But how can I blame her?"

"You can't. She's feeling helpless."

"And you're not?"

She shook her head. "I think we're going to be fine, Tanner. We've gone over everything. You know what you're going to do, and you keep telling me what a fantastic gambler you are."

He grimaced. "You don't even know what that means."

She smiled. "You'll show me tomorrow night."

He shook his head. "You're impossible."

"I trust you," she said simply. "It's what you wanted, don't knock it."

"Far be it from me." He got to his feet and crossed

to where she was sitting. "I won't knock it; I'll just thank my lucky stars." He brushed his hand along her cheekbone. "Go to bed. It will probably be a rough day tomorrow. And you might not be as serene as you are now."

"We'll get through it." She let him pull her to her feet and started toward the door. "And it's not exactly serenity; I just feel that it's our turn, Tanner. All the terrible things have to end sometime, and then there will be the music and the dazzle. And even if it's not quite our turn, we can make it that way. Because we deserve it. All we have to do is take it." She smiled, lifted her hand in a half farewell, and then closed the door behind her.

———◆———

Lara took a deep breath, hesitated, and then quietly opened Tanner's bedroom door. It was dark in the room, but she knew exactly where he was. She could hear him breathing and saw him sitting in the chair by the balcony doors. She took another deep breath and then started to glide toward him "You knew I was coming. I thought you might. That one-step-ahead thing again? Were you waiting for me?"

"I was trying not to. I saw how emotional you were yesterday. Hell, you were positively aching with sympathy for me. I should have locked the door to keep you out."

"But I'm so good with locks. You wouldn't have stood a chance. Besides, you want this." She chuckled. "You even warned me the other evening. I didn't quite understand it at first, but then I put it together. I may not be your idea of exactly what you want in a woman, but you do want me. And all that other crap about not taking anything from me because I was some kind of victim was pretty lame. I went into that in detail later, but I think some of it still lingered." She took off her sleep shirt and tossed it on the floor. "I may not be good at this yet, but I learn very fast and you'll be surprised how quickly I'll pick it up."

"Are we talking about Maria again?"

"No." She climbed on his lap, unbuttoned his shirt, and pressed her naked breasts against him. He inhaled sharply. "We're talking about how I have trouble trusting, but I trust you. And how I like to touch you, and wish you'd stop pushing me away. It makes it difficult for me." She tucked her head in the curve of his neck and whispered, "And we're talking about how I've never felt anything like this for anyone else before and I keep getting confused. But it still feels right…"

"So damn right," he said hoarsely as his arms tightened around her.

She stayed there for an instant longer and then got off his lap. "But maybe I'm wrong and I shouldn't push myself on you. So I'm going to go lie in your bed over there, and I'd like it very much if you'd hold me all through the night. You don't have to do anything else. But I think we might discover something good if you did. What do you think?"

"I think you're *killing* me." He watched her climb into the bed and push the covers down. Then he was on his feet and taking off the rest of his clothes. "And I think that you've started off right and that's the way we'll keep on for a while. I *want* to hold you. There's no hurry, we'll take it slow…" He was in bed now and drawing her against his body. "You feel so good. We'll have the music and then the dazzle and then we'll see what else is waiting for us out there…"

———◆———

"It was all extraordinary." Lara sat up straight in bed and then turned eagerly to face him. "At first, I thought the music was best. It was like Grieg or Debussy, all clear and gentle and beautiful. But then you brought in the dazzle and that was different and exciting. I could hardly breathe, but I didn't want to breathe. I was on *fire*." She bent down and kissed him exuberantly. "Thank you. Thank you. Thank you."

"You're welcome. Thank *you*." He chuckled as he kissed her again. "You were a little absorbed in the process and you might not have noticed that I was fully engaged at all times."

"Oh, I noticed." She was rubbing her cheek catlike on his chest. "That's what made it so extraordinary. I believe you must be quite wonderful at this. Or it could be that the way I feel about you makes the difference." She looked up, her eyes twinkling. "Though it might be that I don't have enough experience to tell yet. I remember you said something like that."

"It's unkind of you to throw it back in my face." He kissed her again. "When I was trying to be one of the good guys."

"You *are* one of the good guys," she whispered as she nestled closer. "I can tell. I don't need much experience to know that. And I might not be as good as you at this, but you just wait until Maria finishes with me. I'll be fantastic."

"You *are* fantastic." He lifted her chin to look into

her eyes. "You're perfect in every way. You'll always be that way because you're constantly reaching out and changing. You don't need Maria."

He meant it. She blinked back tears. "Then I must be extraordinary, too. It's good to know." She swallowed hard and then said lightly, "But you're wrong, I'll still need Maria. What if you become more extraordinary than I am? I'd have to keep up."

He gave a mock groan. "Impossible. Pressure. Pressure." He suddenly turned her over on her back and smiled down at her. "So I'll just have to go back to the basics. Which were not totally completed."

"Of course they were," she said flatly. "Nothing could have been more complete."

"I beg to disagree." His tongue was on her breast. "You mentioned dazzle, which was very close to reaching that point. But I admit I purposely rather shortchanged the music." He bit down teasingly on her other nipple. "I'm not really into Grieg and Debussy, but I wanted it for you. Now I think we should go for the fireworks."

"Fireworks?" She was trying to work out what he meant, but it was difficult when his hands were now between her legs and she could only feel. "What do you—" She gasped!

"What do you think I mean?" he asked softly. "Tell me."

Then it came to her. Of course, what else could it be? And what else could be happening to her body.

Fireworks!

"Tchaikovsky!"

TAJ SAFE HOUSE
6:05 P.M., NEXT DAY

Lara braced herself and then opened Maria's door.

Maria was working on her computer and didn't look up as Lara came into the room. It wasn't like Maria to be this cold, dammit. "Are you still upset with me?"

"I'm not upset." Maria looked up and then drew a deep breath as she saw what Lara was wearing. "The white gown. The one Tanner sent me a picture of. You look…beautiful."

"No, I don't. I don't think it suits me at all. The only reason I'm wearing it is that it might be a distraction. Tanner said that distractions are always good during a game. Volkov isn't used to seeing me in stuff like this."

"Neither am I. I don't agree. I kind of like it." Her lips tightened. "But I don't like him seeing you in it. I don't want you there at all." She held up her hand as Lara opened her lips. "I've given up trying to dissuade you. You shouldn't be going. Mallory came by and told me that Tanner had assigned him to take care of me this evening and that I shouldn't worry. That means Rennell will be at that casino to back up any play Tanner makes. He doesn't need you."

"He needs me," she said quietly. "Because nothing will happen if I'm not there."

"And that doesn't sound bad to me, either."

Lara sat down on the bed. "I trust him. He's not going to let anything happen to me, Maria."

"If he does, I'll cut his heart out," Maria said.

"That will keep him in line," Lara said dryly.

"I hope so." Then Maria pulled Lara close. "Take

care," she said huskily. "Don't let that son of a bitch Volkov do anything to you. I'd have to go after him myself." Then she pushed her away. "Get out of here. I have to get back to my computer."

"I'm going. I'll see you after the game." She forced herself not to look back as she went out the door and down the staircase.

"Beautiful." Tanner was standing at the foot of the staircase dressed in his tuxedo. He reached out and touched her damp cheek as she reached him. "Am I supposed to ignore this?"

"Yes, it's nothing. Maria was upset."

"But not you?" He answered himself. "Of course not, this is just another Trial to you. Piece of cake." He paused. "You could skip it. I could wing it."

"No, you couldn't. You're not nearly as distracting as I am." She grimaced. "I've held the bastard in thrall since I was eleven years old." She forced a smile. "But you'd better make sure there's a poker handy."

"There will be. Not the kind you used on him before." He took a deck of cards from his jacket pocket. "But it might do just as much damage…"

CHAPTER

15

The Mountain Casino was located on a road off the interstate deep in the mountains. The casino itself was a large building but totally unimpressive, even shabby. Still, the mountainous landscape on which it rested was rugged and powerful. Rough, rocky slopes led up to a high ridge that towered over the boulders below. The area was isolated, and even the rocky parking lot looked a little deserted. Tanner made no attempt to enter the lot but parked across the road some distance away.

"It doesn't look like a happening place to spend an evening, does it?" she asked lightly. "I can see why any tourist would miss it entirely."

"I think that's why it attracted Volkov," Tanner said. "You said he liked to be the center of attention, but I'd bet he also liked to have his own space. It's all in what you do with the space."

Lara shivered as she remembered Volkov's use of the space at his mountain home. "No bet."

He nodded. "I told you I wondered why he built that house in the middle of nowhere. Sandrino liked his privacy, too, but there wasn't anything dark about him."

But this conversation was becoming dark. She quickly changed the subject. "It's still almost deserted. Are we early? Or is there some reason you wanted to get here before anyone else?"

"Yes, we're early. And I did want to get here a bit before you had to face the rest of the world so that I could talk to you." He paused. "Things might get a little wild tonight, and I don't want you to feel lost or that you're not able to keep up. Sometimes I go full speed ahead and don't stop to let anyone catch up."

"I've noticed." She chuckled. "And I feel I keep up very well. If I didn't, I'd just rein you in and put you in a corner until you stopped thinking and started explaining. You can be maddening at times, but it's nothing I can't handle."

He grinned. "I knew that. But you're going to have to face Volkov tonight. I wanted everything clear for you. No matter what I have to say or do."

"Everything is clear between us." She smiled as she shook her head. "And I'm not afraid of Volkov, or anything he tries to do to hurt me. Been there, done that. My fight, too, Tanner. Now will you stop fretting?"

"Fretting?" He made a face. "You make me sound like your grandmother."

"I don't know if I have a living grandmother. Maria made no effort to contact her parents after everything that happened to her. They wouldn't have understood. She thought it would only hurt them."

"It might be time to take another look," he said gently. "I think they'd be proud of both of you."

"That will be up to Maria." She took his hand. "We're proud of each other, and I'm proud of you. So that may be enough." She leaned her head against his shoulder. "But a grandmother might be nice..." She chuckled. "If she didn't fret." Then she sat up straight. "But now if you're through with that nonsense, you can fill me in on what's going to happen tonight. I know you've had Rennell and Mallory both out here. I know there will be a poker game, but no real details."

"It's better that way, much more entertaining. Much more dazzle. We'll just play everything by ear."

She looked at him suspiciously. "But you won't do that."

"Maybe a few things. It's more fun for me if I set a few traps along the way." He tilted his head. "But what should you know? That this mountain is full of deceptions of one kind or the other. Both Volkov's and Rennell's. That beyond that ridge is a canyon where they've hidden the helicopter in which Anton brought his thugs from Russia. That Volkov had a considerable force here before he yanked them out to keep his word to me. He lied, of course. There are probably some of them out there in those rocks watching us now."

"Comforting."

"It doesn't matter. Unless you want to do something with me that you don't want them to see. In which case I'll have to go up there in the rocks and forcibly remove them. It would be entirely worth it."

She started to laugh. "Tanner."

"No? Just a thought." He was rubbing the back of her neck. "Relax. We have a little time before we have to go face the dragons. Close your eyes and think of Maria and fretting grandmothers and Tchaikovsky."

"What a mixture." She'd rather think of Tanner and she thought he knew it. She was feeling all the tension and sadness of her disagreement with Maria flowing away from her. He had wanted that to happen. The edginess and uncertainty were vanishing, too. That was probably why he'd brought her here, so that she could have this time to gather herself together before the storm. She drew closer to him. "I adore the idea of fretting grandmothers, and Maria, and Tchaikovsky." She kissed him. "And there's an excellent chance that I might positively love you, Logan Tanner. Thank you for coming into my life." She kissed him again. "Now we'll stay like this for another few minutes and then we'll go face those dragons. If that's all right?"

He didn't answer. He just drew her even closer.

And that was fine. That was more than enough.

TAJ SAFE HOUSE
7:05 P.M.

Rennell was backing the Land Rover out of the garage.

No more time to wait. In a minute he'd be gone.

Maria stepped out into the driveway and blocked his way.

Rennell put on the brakes and got out of the car. "You're having trouble? I don't have time for you right now. Go find Mallory."

She made a face. "That would be awkward since I just sent him to the music room to adjust Lara's keyboard. It would only confuse him. I won't keep you long if you'll be reasonable."

"You won't keep me long, period. I have a job to do. Get out of the driveway."

She shook her head. "I'm going with you. You're not going to get rid of me. You shouldn't even try. I'll help you."

"Bullshit. You don't know what you're talking about. If I'd wanted help, I could have drafted someone who knew what they were doing. You'd just get in my way."

"No, I won't. I'm only here to protect, and to even some scores. And you didn't really want anyone who might think they knew how the job should be run and might question you. You don't want a partner. You need someone who will do exactly what you say. That's me, Rennell. I believe you know what you're doing. If you want to kill anyone out there, I won't blink. I'm strong, and I'll never say no." She paused. "Unless you tell me to do something that might hurt my daughter. That's out of the question. But that's not on the agenda tonight, so I don't have to worry about it. You're going after the bad guys, and I'm going to help you." She looked him in the eye. "Aren't I, Rennell?"

Silence. "What about Mallory?"

"It will take him a while to fix the keyboard. I thought you could call him later and explain that he'd be more useful coming to Muddy Mountain and joining the action than trying to chase after me."

Another silence. His expression was impassive. "Tanner would really be pissed off."

"But you don't care. It might amuse you. Though you do care about him. Yet right now you're hurting, and all you want to do is hurt everyone who has hurt you."

His lips tightened. "And Sandrino."

"And Sandrino," she repeated quietly. "So are you going to let me help you?"

He stared at her, his expression impassive for another moment. Then he smiled recklessly and opened the passenger door for her. "Why not? It's your neck on the line. Get in. You've already taken up too much of my time. I still have to pick up the dynamite."

———◆———

MOUNTAIN CASINO, MUDDY MOUNTAINS

Lara unconsciously tensed as Tanner helped her out of the Mercedes and led her toward the front door of the casino. *Don't let him know that this first moment of facing the dragons is still a little scary.* The front facade of the building was still as unimpressive as when they'd arrived here earlier. She glanced at the rocky slope of landscape beyond it that appeared totally deserted. But then so was the casino area. Only a few vehicles in the parking lot. "You told Volkov that you'd be on the lookout for anyone who might interfere with the game, and evidently he took you at your word." She glanced at him. "Or did he? It's a little too quiet."

Tanner shrugged. "I'd like to say he was intimidated by me, but it wouldn't be true. But he was impressed by the deposit I made in that Cayman account. He didn't want it to be canceled. Still, that didn't mean he was going to keep to the terms of our agreement. This area may appear deserted because he ordered his men to back off and make it look that way, but it's as phony as the casino facade. I've had Mallory and Rennell both scouting out the other areas for the past twenty-four hours and they've both seen troop movement."

"Where?"

"Those rocks on that upper slope behind the casino hide a multitude of sins. Rennell said that he'd spotted at least seven potential snipers in that area."

"Charming."

"But that shouldn't really be a problem for Rennell. However, the Bell helicopter that generally carries fifteen that's hovering behind the south ridge might give him a little trouble."

"I'd think so." She glanced up at the rocky slope again. "He doesn't intend us to get out of here alive."

"But then we feel the very same way." He smiled at her. "And we know what we're facing, and just how to get around them. All it will take is a little dazzle." He took her hand. "Ready?"

She smiled back at him. "You're the dazzle expert. But give me a cue and I'll try to follow you." They'd reached the doors and he was swinging them open for her. "I did say that I wanted—" She broke off and inhaled sharply as she saw the man coming toward her. "But you're in for a treat, Tanner. I don't believe you've ever met my father." She took a step inside and felt Tanner move closer to her. "How nice of you to come to greet us, Anton. I've told Tanner so much about you. But some of it was hard to believe."

"You bitch." His face was flushed with anger. His hands were grasping her shoulders and he was shaking her. "Do you know how much trouble you caused me with Volkov? I told you what to do and you didn't do it, or Tanner would never have been able to get hold of you. Do you realize how Volkov's been treating me? Wait until I get hold of Maria. You'll be sorry that—"

"No, you'll be sorry," Tanner said coldly as he plucked Anton's hands off Lara and shoved him against the wall. "Evidently you haven't had the new orders from Volkov. Unless you want me to seriously damage you, there will be no putting your hands on her again. Do you understand me?"

Anton opened his lips to speak and then closed them again. His voice was surly as he said, "I understand. Volkov said that you were coming, Tanner. Some big game… That's why I'm here, he said he wanted everything running smooth." He added viciously, "But that doesn't mean he won't change his mind about Lara the minute he sees her. I wasn't the only one who wanted to choke her when we found out she was gone." He gestured to the door leading to the casino. "Go on inside. He's waiting for you." He glanced at Lara and his lips curled savagely. "I'll see you later."

"Yes, you will," she said. "By all means, run and see if Volkov wants you to run any errands for him." She heard him swear as she passed him and went toward the door.

Tanner caught up with her. "Did he hurt you?"

"No, and you shouldn't have bothered with him. Anton is nothing. I've told you that before. Most of the time I could just avoid him."

"It was hard for me to remember that when he was shaking you," he said dryly. "It made me want to make him truly 'nothing.'"

She suddenly smiled. "That would not have been unpleasant. But that's not why we're here. Anton was a surprise. But he said Volkov wanted him here. Anton usually deals with the men for Volkov. I suppose we should be wondering why he would want Anton here tonight."

"No, we should only keep an eye on him. Your father impresses me as a man who will reveal anything we need to know if we just give him the opportunity." He opened the casino doors. "Let's let him do that."

———◆———

"This is incredible." Lara glanced around the casino floor. The carpeting, lighting, and décor wouldn't have been out of place in any of the world's most extravagant gaming establishments in Monaco, Macau, or Las Vegas. Red-uniformed servers stood by with drink carts, and the similarly attired dealers manned the dozen or so tables. "This place looked like a condemned old shack from the road."

"Tanner!" Volkov was moving toward them from across the room. "Welcome to my playground."

"Is that what you call it?"

"Why not?" Volkov smiled at Lara. "Good evening, my dear. You honor my establishment with your presence. I can't wait for you to become more accustomed to it. If Tanner hadn't been so hasty about taking you away from me, I might have brought you here myself."

"I've seen enough of your playgrounds. This is just another." She lifted her chin defiantly. "It's boring. I'm ready for a new start."

"But I'm not. I prefer to linger awhile before I show you the place where we'll have our grand finale."

"I'm glad you're happy to see Lara," Tanner said. "But I only brought her here at your request. I don't want to hear you talk about old times. Her present and future are up to me, unless I decide otherwise." He paused. "And do I have to remind you that we have a game to play?"

"I haven't forgotten." Volkov brushed a long finger under Lara's chin. "Tell him, Lara. The way I play, they're never games of chance. They're psychology. And I'm as good at them as I am at life itself."

She suppressed the shiver that ran through her. Mustn't give him the satisfaction. But she hated his hands on her. Well, she knew how to handle that problem. "He's as good as he says, Tanner. But he has a blind spot you can drive a truck through."

Volkov jerked back his hand. "Blind spot?"

"What Tanner calls a tell. It's always been there."

Volkov was clearly incensed. "What are you talking about?"

"Your weakness. That fatal flaw. It's been obvious to me since I was a child."

"Enlighten me."

She smiled. "Play him, and maybe I'll point it out to you. Or maybe Tanner will point it out to you when you lose."

He spat out, "There's no tell. You're just trying to goad me."

"Keep telling yourself that, Volkov."

He stared at her for a moment longer. "You're lying. I don't have time for this, bitch."

"Then maybe you'll have time for this." Tanner reached into his pocket and produced a small key. He tossed it to Volkov, who caught it.

"What's this?"

"Look at it."

Volkov turned the key over in his hands. He

stared at the distinctive logo on its head. "Talbot Automotive."

"That key fits into the ignition of a 1948 Talbot-Lago Grand Sport. Luxury Edition, of course."

Volkov stopped breathing for a moment. "You're lying."

"No. And what's more, I own it. As I'm sure you realize, there were only twelve ever made."

Volkov still looked stunned. "I've been trying to get that car for years. I almost bought one in Sao Paulo last year, but the owner changed his mind at the last minute."

"So I understand."

"How—? How did you—?"

"I found another one and worked my powers of persuasion on the owner." He repeated Volkov's words: "It's not a game, you know. It's psychology."

"Is it here?"

"No. I had it delivered to the Hammerstein Luxury and Classic Cars dealership in North Las Vegas. They should be finished detailing it anytime now. After that, it will be on display in their front window showcase. If you don't believe me, you can send one of your men to go take a look." Tanner pulled out his phone and scrolled through a folder of photos. He showed one to Volkov. "Here it is shortly after they took delivery. It's beautiful."

Volkov gazed at it with more longing than Lara had ever seen him express toward any human being. His eyes flicked up to Tanner. "How much do you want for it?"

"It's not for sale."

"Everything's for sale, Tanner. It's just a matter of price."

"That's almost true. And I am a little short right now. So maybe I'll give you a chance to win it from me. We'll play here. Right now."

Volkov's eyes went back to that photo on Tanner's phone. "It's stunning."

"It can be yours by the end of the evening."

Volkov stared at the photo for a moment longer. "Where did you find it?"

"Alberta, Canada."

"Part of the Duffer collection...I'm familiar with it. It's in remarkable condition. The Duffers had no interest in parting with it...They won't even return my phone calls or emails anymore."

"Like I said, it's a matter of psychology." Tanner put away his phone. "Are we doing this or not?"

He was still hesitating. "What's your game?"

"Today I'm in the mood for poker."

"Five-card stud?"

"I'm thinking Pai Gow. At that table right over there."

Volkov turned toward a red-felt-topped table in the center of the room. An elderly Asian woman was dealing cards to four male players. "I'd have to move those customers."

"Do it. We'll wait. Oh, and Volkov..."

Volkov turned to face him.

"My key, please."

Volkov tossed the key back to him and walked toward the table.

Lara smiled and spoke quietly. "When did you have time to track down that car?"

"It just took a phone call. I have very talented associates."

"Obviously. But do you realize how good he is at

almost every game he plays? He may not be a superstar like Sandrino or you, but everyone says he's excellent."

"I know what you told me, and I did some additional research on him. I'm surprised by your lack of faith in me."

"He's good, Tanner."

"So am I."

She rolled her eyes. "Dammit, I knew you were going to say that. So what's this game you're playing?"

"Pai Gow. It's based on a thousand-year-old game played with Chinese dominoes. It's been transposed to playing cards with many of the rules of poker."

"And how good are you at this?"

He shrugged. "I've played a few times."

"A few times?"

"But I've played poker all my life. In Pai Gow, each player is dealt seven cards. From that, the object is to create two poker hands: a five-card poker hand and a two-card poker hand. The object is to beat the dealer, who will have two hands of his own."

"And Volkov is the dealer." She moistened her lips. "Watch him carefully. He's not only a skillful player but an even better cheater."

"Stop trying to take care of me. Trust me, I know who I'm dealing with."

Of course he did. She looked at him for a long moment. Tanner was clearly in his element here, engaged and totally in the hunt. "What's your endgame?"

"What do you mean?"

"I'd forgotten I even mentioned antique cars were one of his passions. You wouldn't have gone through all the trouble to track down that car if you didn't have a plan how to use it."

"Of course not. Passions are important, but it's just

the lure. That car means a lot to him, but it still isn't enough for him to give me what I really want. It will, however, bring him into my game."

"Or you into his."

"We'll see, won't we?"

"So what do you really want from him?"

He turned toward her and raised an eyebrow. "You helped me make out the list. It hasn't changed. Can't you guess?"

"Not at the moment."

He smiled mischievously. "Then I guess you'll find out the same time he does."

"Tell me."

"And ruin the surprise?" He placed his hand on the small of her back. "Oh, it looks like our table is ready. Shall we?"

"Tanner…"

But he was already moving her toward the cleared table. The players, obviously puzzled by their sudden eviction, stood to the side holding their chips and drinks. The croupier was hastily trying to move them out of the casino.

Volkov sat in the dealer's chair and motioned for Tanner and Lara to sit across from him. As they took their seats, Lara glanced around to see that they were attracting a crowd. Several gamblers from neighboring tables had left their games and were taking positions nearby.

Tanner had also noticed. "It's to be a private game, Volkov."

Volkov shrugged. "I know. But I'm very good, and I don't mind letting them watch me for a while. I'll send both them and the croupiers out of the casino after a hand or two."

"I've heard about your ego." Tanner smiled. "Then let's give them a good show."

Volkov cut the seal on a deck of cards and moved to place it in an automatic shuffler.

Tanner raised his hands to stop him. "No. Hand shuffle only, please."

"You don't trust my machine?"

"I don't trust anything I can't see."

"Very well. Do you have a preference? I can do overhand, Hindu, weave or faro, corgi, or a basic riffle."

"Any of those is fine."

"I'll give you an assortment."

Volkov showed himself to be astonishingly adept with the cards, manipulating them with a mastery that obviously impressed the crowd. Tanner watched the cards closely as the flourishes became increasingly elaborate. Volkov finally finished with a smooth fan on the table.

"Satisfied?"

"It'll do."

"Do you have the car title with you? You may throw it and the key into the pot. I'll, of course, match it with cash. What amount do you think is fair?"

"Let's start a bit smaller." Tanner unzipped an inner pocket of his jacket and produced a thick stack of cash. "I'll buy in for fifty thousand dollars."

He frowned. "I agreed to play you for the car."

"And I promise you we will. But it's going to be a long night. We'll begin this way."

Volkov glared at him for a moment, but finally nodded toward a red-jacketed croupier standing nearby. The croupier took the cash from Tanner, speedily counted it, then placed a large stack of chips in front of him.

Tanner smiled. "Let's begin. A thousand dollars a hand?"

"As you wish." Volkov dealt seven cards each to himself and Tanner, then dealt a short stack of four cards to the side.

Lara had watched Volkov and Anton play standard draw poker since she was a child, but she was surprised how different this variation made the game. The men played their five-card and two-card hands quickly, with little time between new dealt hands. Within minutes she could see how the game revealed the true character of its players. Volkov was increasingly fiery and aggressive, while Tanner showed intelligence and precision. Both approaches benefited the opponents; Tanner won more hands, but Volkov tended to eventually make up his losses with bold and risky bets.

"You play well," Volkov said. "You've earned your reputation."

"As have you." Tanner leaned forward in his chair. "Shall we step things up a bit?"

"In what sense?"

"Ten thousand a hand?"

Volkov thought for a moment, then nodded. "Do you wish to increase your stake? For you I can extend credit, but of course I'm also equipped to make a wire transfer from your financial institution."

"That won't be necessary. At least not yet." Tanner reached into his inside jacket pocket and produced a stack of crisp thousand-dollar bills, held together by a brown paper band with a bank logo. "That's a hundred thousand."

Volkov waved over the croupier. "Do you always travel with that much cash on your person, Tanner?"

He smiled. "Just some walking-around money."

"Be careful where you walk."

"No worries." Tanner nodded toward Lara. "I have her to protect me."

Volkov regarded Lara with a stare that was chilling. "But we've already agreed to have that discussion. She may not be around to serve that function."

"Just deal the cards, Volkov."

Volkov waited as the croupier took Tanner's cash, counted it, and gave him another stack of chips. He then dealt Tanner and himself another seven cards each.

Tanner looked at his cards and arranged them to create the five-card and two-card hands. He put the cards facedown and moved a large stack of chips to the center of the table.

"I put in fifty thousand."

Volkov raised an eyebrow. "You wouldn't be bluffing, now, would you?"

"Only one way to find out."

Volkov stared at the two sets of cards. He shrugged and moved a stack of chips into the center. "I'm a curious fellow."

"How curious?"

"I'll see your fifty and raise it ten."

Tanner considered this, then flipped up the edges of each of his hands to show Lara. Why had he done that?

Because he had nothing, she realized.

A pair of garbage hands.

What in the hell was he thinking?

Trust him. Go with it. He'd shown her his hand and that must mean he wanted her help. She'd had years of keeping Volkov from reading her, and it was never easy. This time she must make it impossible. She allowed the faintest smile to touch her lips and then she looked quickly away. Had she reacted fast enough or had she given away Tanner's bluff?

Tanner finally nodded. "Then I'll raise you…thirty thousand more." He placed another stack of chips into the middle of the table.

Anton, who was acting as croupier now, inhaled sharply.

Volkov's gaze narrowed on Tanner. Lara remembered that she'd once overheard him tell Anton that he could always tell more from a man's hands than from his face. She wished she'd mentioned that to Tanner, but it was too late now.

No matter, she realized. Tanner's hands were rock-steady, and his face was totally relaxed.

Volkov smiled. "I fold." He tossed his cards down faceup to reveal he was holding a pair of fours with his two-card hand and pairs of Jacks and Kings in the other. Far better than what Tanner had. "Perhaps my sixty thousand dollars earns me the right to see what you were holding."

"It's now my sixty thousand." Tanner pulled the chips over to his side of the table. "If you wanted to see my cards, you knew the price, Volkov. Deal, please."

Volkov was clearly annoyed, but he dealt again. In the games that followed, Volkov continued losing. Badly. Tanner's controlled, steely strategies in the early rounds had given Volkov a false sense of his opponent's strengths and weaknesses, Lara thought. Which, she realized, was Tanner's plan.

Volkov realized it, too, but any adjustments he tried to make only added to his woes. Tanner was always one step ahead, anticipating Volkov's moves and countermoves with almost uncanny ability.

After an hour, Tanner leaned back in his chair.

"The fates haven't been good to you tonight. Perhaps I should let you off the hook."

"Stay where you are," Volkov snarled. "It can all change on a dime, as you know."

"Yes, as we've seen tonight. But the stakes are still too low to hold my interest. I'm getting bored, Volkov."

"I can promise that things will soon get much more exciting for you." Volkov spoke it as a threat.

Tanner tilted his head. "Is that right?"

"I guarantee it."

"I see." He looked down at his chips. "By my reckoning, I have almost one point two million dollars of your money here."

"Almost."

"But these are just chips. I'd feel more comfortable if I had cash, rather than these pieces of wood."

"You don't think I'm good for it?"

"We both know men who claim to be billionaires but can't afford to pay their gardening bill. Let's just say I'd feel more comfortable with a bit more evidence."

"You insult me, Tanner."

"I wouldn't want to do that. But you don't have the most ethical reputation, and I told you that I have to recoup my finances. I need you to show me proof." He paused. "Maybe we play for something other than money."

"What do you propose?"

"Freedom."

Volkov frowned.

"Whose freedom?"

Tanner glanced at Lara. "The original prize that cost me a great deal of time and trouble to obtain. I believe we were going to use her anyway, but I seem to have gained an advantage and I might as well throw her in with the pot."

Volkov wrinkled his brow. "Freedom? Do you think I'm a fool? You want her for yourself. You're crazy. Do you know how much time I've spent on that bitch? She has to learn the lesson I've been planning all these years. I won't let her go."

Tanner gazed at him impassively. "Perhaps I used the wrong word. You're right, of course, I do want her for myself. I can see why you're so intrigued by her. Though the word *freedom* would also include not having to look over my shoulder for the rest of her life. I can't always be there to kill the ridiculously inept men you'd send for her. I'm sure Lara would be happy to have a go at them, but she's had enough Trials in her life." His voice lowered. "But since you're being so stubborn about her, I guess I'll have to raise the pot to make it irresistible."

Volkov tensed. "What are you proposing?"

"We play again. I'll add another million to the pot. Plus sign a waiver to allow you to take my deposit in your Grand Cayman account that we were supposed to be playing for tonight. Winner take all. If you win, you get the entire pot and I promise to turn Lara over to you."

"You can't do that to me. I won't go anywhere without Maria," Lara said fiercely. "You can't make me."

"Well, it seems we have to add the mother." Tanner shrugged. "But you can't beat the deal."

Volkov's cheeks were flushed, his eyes glittering as he looked down at the chips. "It might be possible."

"I'll throw in the Lago Grand Sport," Tanner said.

"I'll play you," Volkov said immediately. "Winner take all."

"His word means nothing," Lara said. "Don't do this, Tanner."

"Oh, I have no intention of just taking him at his word," Tanner said softly. "For starters, I want to see him produce a financial instrument to guarantee that he can pay me for my winnings so far. An electronic bearer bond should do the trick."

"This is ridiculous," Volkov fumed as he pulled out his phone. "I can have one for you in ten seconds."

"Do it."

Volkov impatiently held up the phone to allow it to scan his face, thumbprint, and eyes. "This is humiliating. I'm going to remember how you treated me. Once we finish here, you'll never be—" He froze as he stared at his phone screen. "What in the hell?"

"Problem?" Tanner asked.

"No." He performed the biometric scan once more, then appeared even more puzzled. "I don't understand."

Tanner grabbed Volkov's wrist and angled the phone screen toward him and Lara. "Balance zero? What are you trying to pull?"

"Nothing." Volkov raised his hands. "Wait! I have other options." He pulled up another page on his phone. He signed in, but again a bewildered look crossed his face. "What the hell…"

Volkov waved frantically at a slender man dressed in a stylish gray suit.

Lara leaned toward Tanner. "That's his finance director, Vincent Kael. I didn't realize he'd have him here."

"I did. That's why I set up the Grand Cayman bank transfer over the phone," he whispered back.

"I needed him to have a money man on duty for authentication."

They watched as the two men worked on the phone together, trying several more sites.

Volkov dazedly shook his head. "I can't believe it. Every account, gone. Move everything," he rasped to Kael. "Now. Before I'm totally wiped out."

"But sir, I—"

"Now!"

"Yes, sir." Kael pulled out his own phone and began frantically working.

"Hurry! I told you, do it before I'm totally wiped out."

Tanner smiled. "My, it's an old-fashioned bank rush," he murmured to Lara.

Volkov suddenly looked balefully up at him. "You did this."

"How? I've been sitting here with you. Though if you need some cybersecurity experts, I have some of the best in the world on my payroll."

Volkov was still glaring at him. "I'll bet you do."

Tanner stood and waved his hand over his chips. "Mail me a check once you get things worked out, will you?"

"Tanner!" Volkov screamed with rage.

Tanner pulled Lara to her feet and moved her toward the exit.

She leaned close. "Did you just wipe him out?"

"Not yet. It takes a little time."

"What just happened?"

"It's called an Adler move."

"Is that a poker strategy? I'm not familiar with it."

"It's not a poker strategy. In one of the Sherlock Holmes stories, Holmes tricks a character named Irene

Adler into revealing the location of a letter by making her believe her home is on fire. She goes right for it. I just updated it a bit."

"Updated how?"

"I made Volkov believe his financial house was on fire. He doesn't know it, but he was just connecting to dummy web pages he thinks are his financial institutions. I created those pages myself. His accounts all appear to have been zeroed out. He's now frantically going to every account he owns in order to move his fortune to safety. He doesn't realize that my associates are watching every virtual move he and his financial manager are making, every account number, every biometric reading, every password. He'll be cleaned out within minutes."

"The Adler move..." Lara said. "I didn't realize you were such a man of letters."

"I'm more comfortable with numbers, but I've been known to crack a good book now and then."

"Too bad for Volkov."

"Yes. Too bad."

"Though I refuse to feel sorry for him. He was only considering taking your deal after you threw me into the pot. It was that blasted car that sealed the deal for him."

Tanner smiled. "The man clearly has no taste. But you have to remember that he intended to have it all anyway." The smile faded as he opened the door for her. "We'll have to tread carefully out here. This isn't over yet. We're keeping Volkov busy, but I'd judge he's almost ready to explode. I think it's time we got a little head start before Volkov decides to take off after us." He took her elbow and started to run toward the Mercedes across the road. "We'll jump on this road that connects to the interstate. Then we'll double back and circle until we reach the ridge road that leads to the canyon. I'll drive this time. Unless you can tell me that you've had experience driving in the mountains. Those roads can get pretty rough."

"You can drive. I don't have that much experience with mountains, and I've watched you drive at Sandrino Place." She slid into the passenger seat. "Where in the mountains? I thought you said something about snipers."

"So I did, but I think we'll be able to avoid them." He tore out onto the road. "We're going in another direction." He reached for his phone. "But just in case we can't..." He dialed Rennell. "We're on the move. I'll be heading up the mountain toward the ridge. You might have to run interference. The card game went splendidly, which means that Volkov is in a very foul mood and might want to castrate me."

"If it wasn't Volkov, I'd empathize," Rennell said. "I've felt like that about you many, many times even when my mood was just fine. How close are they?"

"I'm doubling back now and heading up the mountain. I don't want to go too fast. I want them to be able to see the headlights to follow me. No sign of them leaving the casino yet."

"Then call me when you have to worry. I'm busy right now."

"I'll do that. Are the charges set?"

"We probably had the ones on the upper ridge set before you were halfway through your poker game. The lower ones required more time and thought, but we're getting there. I just wanted to orchestrate something more interesting in case we got a visit from

Volkov. I didn't want him to feel that we didn't appreciate him."

"We? I thought you were handling the charges alone. Who did you pull in to help?"

"Just some bozo who doesn't know squat about dynamite, but knows enough to keep quiet when I need to concentrate. We're getting along all right."

"That's an amazing compliment in itself. But are you sure that the ridge charges will do their job? If we're going to lead Volkov into a trap, I don't want to lure him with a dead device."

"They're not as interesting as the ones down here. But they'll do the job...I think."

"Could you be a little more reassuring? I have Lara in the car and she's already had a more complicated evening than she was prepared for."

"But she can handle it. And she's probably sitting there resenting you thinking she can't. She knows I don't make mistakes. She doesn't need me to tell her. Isn't that right, Lara?"

"Absolutely. On all subjects," Lara said. "But it's good to hear it from the expert."

"Which Tanner is not, except in a few minor categories. Did he really pull off making Volkov blow his mind?"

"Any minute now." She smiled at Tanner. "He handled that minor category very well, indeed."

"Then we'll have to see if we can stop playing around and go the distance." Rennell's tone was suddenly dead serious. "I'm ready, Tanner. Give me the word and it will be the Fourth of July." He cut the connection.

CHAPTER

16

Rennell immediately turned to Maria, sitting on the ground beside him. "Satisfied? I did what you wanted. You heard her voice and she's fine."

"As fine as she can be when they're going to be chased up the damn mountain at any minute." She nodded jerkily. "Yes, I'm as satisfied as I can be, considering. Though I was half afraid you'd tell her I was here."

"Why would I do that? It would disturb the balance of the operation. You're not doing too bad so far."

"I'm doing exceptionally well," she said dryly. "If I wasn't, you would have gagged me and tied me up somewhere to get me out of your way."

"True. But don't let it go to your head." He was focusing his binoculars on the casino. "You've only set the one charge so far, but you did well enough for me to trust you with the others. Just be ready to move fast when I tell you."

"Of course. I want this over. When you tell me to jump, I'll ask how high." She grimaced. "Like a humble bozo should."

"You didn't like the 'bozo'?"

"I would have liked it better if you hadn't enjoyed it so much."

"One has to take pleasure wherever it appears," Rennell murmured. "I've been cheated of the joy of killing Volkov all evening, so I just had to make do…" He lowered the binoculars and turned to her. "Are you ready to go? If you're too scared, then don't do it. I don't want you screwing it up."

"I won't screw it up. I'm not scared. It's just a job to be done. You're the one who would probably screw it up if you tried to plant those charges. I'm small and I can move fast and light. You're huge and you'd probably stumble over those men."

"I wouldn't stumble, but I might be more visible." He shrugged. "Then what are you waiting for? Grab the charges and get moving, bozo."

Maria grabbed the backpack and slung it over her shoulder. "I'm out of here. As long as these blast charges don't go off in my hands."

"It's not the charges I'm worried about."

"Volkov's men? They won't see me. I'll be in and out before you know it. You'd be surprised how living with an ass like Anton can give you the skill to fade into the woodwork whenever you choose."

"Still, keep an eye out. There's at least eight of them on the ridges surrounding the casino. There's only two of us."

"I've no choice but to take those odds, do I?"

Rennell smiled. "No. Forgive me for stating the obvious. Good luck."

Those last words surprised her. He was usually so noncommittal. "You, too. See you back at the car."

Maria crouched and ran into the brush. She kept low, looking out for Volkov's men as she made her way across the ridge. She stopped, unzipped her knapsack, and pulled out the first of the radio-controlled blast charges. It was tiny, scarcely bigger than a bottle stopper. But she knew it wasn't meant to cause major damage, like the monstrosity Rennell had planted in the box canyon down the road. Still, it would serve their purpose.

She raised the small antenna and pushed the device into the bush. She ran and repeated the process four more times, spacing the charges about fifty feet apart. She was about to place the sixth charge when she heard a snap behind her.

She froze.

Snap.

Twigs breaking. Brush rustling.

Someone was coming!

She rolled behind a tall boulder and crouched low.

The footsteps grew louder, and she could see a man with an assault rifle making his way toward her. She recognized him as one of Volkov's bodyguards, a red-haired man the others called Pinky.

He was now less than six feet away. Another few steps and he'd be right on top of her. She glanced around. Nowhere to go without him seeing her, and in any case she couldn't outrun the bullets from his gun.

Pinky stopped. As he looked around, Maria could see that his eyes were scanning across the patch of brush where she'd left the explosive charge. Shit. He was going to see it.

His walkie-talkie beeped, and he abruptly turned

away. The radio blared something she couldn't understand. He responded, "Copy. All clear down here."

He turned and walked away.

Thank God.

She waited another few moments to let out the long breath she'd been holding. She slowly moved back around and finished setting the charge.

She looked into the knapsack. Four more to go.

She could do this.

———◆———

MOUNTAIN CASINO

"Don't you tell me that I've lost everything!" Volkov's voice was almost a screech. "It can't be true." He whirled on Kael. "You were supposed to protect me from things like this. What do I pay you for?"

"It was an expert hacking job," Kael said frantically. "Absolutely faultless. You saw me call and check on the bigger accounts to verify that it had actually happened. The bank executives couldn't believe it."

"But you still can't get my money back?"

He shook his head. "It just…disappeared. You know I'll do my best."

"Your best sucks," Volkov snarled. "What good are you?"

"It's not my fault." Kael was backing toward the casino door. "No one could have stopped it. It was…faultless."

"It was Tanner," Volkov said. "He was sitting here and mocking me, and all the time he was stealing me blind. I could see it in his face. I'll kill the son of a bitch."

"Yes, it must have been him," Kael said quickly. "It wasn't me, sir."

Anton threw open the casino door and ran into the room. "I checked the road and Tanner didn't leave by the interstate. And I just saw headlights on the upper ridge road. He might be trying to head west for Arizona. He's got to know he can't get away with this."

"Might? You're as much an idiot as Kael. You and Maria and your bitch of a daughter. You're all idiots and trying to get me. Call some of the men at the helicopter and find out where they are on the property."

"I was just going to suggest that," Anton said. He was backing away. He'd never seen Volkov in a rage like this. "Just give me a little time." He was looking for a way out, some way to distract him. "Do you want me to get rid of Kael? He's no use to you now."

Volkov whirled on Kael. "I'll get rid of him myself." He took out his gun. "You did your best to save my money?" He shot him in the head. "Not good enough, you asshole." He turned on Anton with the gun still in his hand. "Now find me Tanner and that bitch from hell or I'll blow your head off, too."

Anton didn't doubt he'd do it. He'd have to play along until he could get Volkov to quiet down. "We'll have to be smart about this. We have to catch them, not just shoot them. If it was Tanner that took your money, then he's going to be the one to know how to get it back. And you're angry at Lara now, but when you get over it, you're going to remember what a fine time you had with those Trials. You had plans for her."

"I'll tear her apart," Volkov said coldly. "I'll tear both of them apart. They can't do that to me. Don't try to convince me I should keep the whore because it's over. You only want to wring me of every dime you can."

"Whatever you decide," Anton said. "I only want what's best for you. But you agree we should try to capture them? That way you have a chance of getting some satisfaction." And Anton might stand a chance of reaping more money from Volkov or at least keep himself alive. "I'll gather the men and we'll hunt them down."

Volkov was frowning. "Hunt...I like the sound of it." He smiled savagely. "And they may be playing into our hands by taking the west exit from the mountain. They're on the ridge road, and the helicopter is still in the canyon. I'd rather get the helicopter and attack them from the air. I could really chew them up." He was heading for the door. "That's what we'll do. Call the helicopter and alert them I'll be in the canyon in fifteen minutes and to be ready for me. You go up the mountain road and grab some of the men, then join me."

"But it would really be better to—"

"Don't tell me what's better," Volkov said. "Just do what I order, and you might survive what that bastard Tanner did to me." He was striding out the door. "But I doubt it."

———◆———

"I think that Volkov might have just found out that all his money went up in a poof of smoke." Lara was looking in the rearview mirror, which was reflecting the casino in the valley. "I see two trucks leaving the casino area at breakneck speed. They're heading in this direction."

"I'll let Rennell know it might be time to run interference." Tanner added sarcastically, "Though I wouldn't want to bother him." He phoned Rennell. "I can't promise you Volkov is in either one of those trucks coming toward us, but they're in a big hurry if it interests you."

"Oh, yes, it definitely interests me. Get up on that ridge and put Mallory and our guys on alert. Volkov or not, it's time to start the action anyway." Rennell ended the call.

Rennell quickly adjusted the sights of his Barrett MRAD sniper rifle and rolled over onto his stomach. With the gun barrel extended before him, he shimmied under a bush and surveyed the ridge. It was a good spot. Maximum visibility with minimum exposure. He looked though the scope. Volkov's men were doing a fairly good job of staying out of sight, but he knew they were scattered across the ridge.

Time to draw them out.

He pulled out his phone to make sure Maria had finished her job. A one-word text from her was on the screen: CLEAR.

He activated the app, which showed him the placement of the explosive charges. Each point glowed green on the screen.

He pressed the first one.

BLAMM!

Just as he hoped, it sounded like a gunshot. The first one was to put Volkov's men on alert, a moment to wonder: *What the hell was that?*

Rennell pushed another dot on the screen.

BLAMM!

And another.

BLAMM!

That should send them diving for cover, taking positions.

He peered into the scope. There was no wind, so any movements in the brush were surely the men.

He smiled. Three swaying bushes on the hillside.

He squeezed off three quick shots.

BLAMM! BLAMM! BLAMM!

Two men tumbled from their hiding places.

He made another go at the third. BLAMM!

The third man stood and slumped over the bush, holding a gushing wound on his neck. He lost consciousness.

Rennell set off two more of the charges. BLAMM! BLAMM!

Come on, guys. Fire back…

He set off another one. BLAMM!

Suddenly shots were coming from all directions.

That was more like it.

Rennell's tactical sunglasses made it easier to see muzzle flashes on the hillside. Zero in, and…

BLAMM-BLAMM-BLAMM-BLAMM!

Four more guys down.

He set off a couple more charges to keep the others from homing in on his location.

Another volley of gunfire, which only served to reveal more muzzle flashes and more moving bushes. He took aim.

BLAMM-BLAMM-BLAMM!

At least two more down. Maybe a third.

He fired again. BLAMM! BLAMM!

Definitely a third. The man slid down the hillside headfirst.

Rennell looked over the scene once more. Had he gotten them all?

"Don't move."

Shit. The voice came from behind him.

"Drop the gun now or you're dead."

Rennell dropped his rifle.

"Now turn over and stand up."

Rennell rolled over. A red-haired young man was holding an assault rifle in one hand and a walkie-talkie in the other. He spoke into the walkie-talkie. "I got him. What do you want me to do?"

No reply.

"Your friends are dead," Rennell said.

"Shut up."

The kid was starting to panic. He spoke into the radio again. "Guys, I'm at the bottom of the ridge. I got the shooter. Where should I take him?"

No reply.

Rennell stood. "I told you. They're dead."

"Maybe I should just kill you." He spoke into the radio once more. "Guys, if I don't hear from you, I—"

Rennell dropped a knife from his sleeve scabbard and, in one smooth motion, threw it at the young man's chest.

FFFFT.

The blade went right into his heart. The young man dropped his walkie-talkie and gun, then staggered backward. He dropped to the ground, dead.

Rennell grabbed his rifle and ran.

The two trucks that Tanner had warned him about were barreling up the road toward his location. He fell to his knees and aimed at the first one coming over the hill. BLAMM! The windshield shattered and the driver screamed as he lost control of the vehicle and went off the road, crashing into a boulder. The second truck was right on top of Rennell now, and he didn't have time to aim. He rolled out of the way of the truck's tires and tried to get off one shot as he struggled to his feet.

BLAMM!

The driver screamed and then screamed again as the truck turned over, pinning him beneath it.

Rennell froze.

What the hell? That hadn't been Rennell's shot! It had come from behind him. He went into a crouch and whirled, gun pointed.

Maria was standing there with a gun in her hand. "I heard the shooting and came running." Her voice was shaking. She looked down at the gun in her hand and drew a deep breath. "I picked this up on the way. I probably could have picked up half a dozen more. It was a lot of shooting, Rennell. How many...No, I don't want to talk about it. You did what you had to do, and I helped you."

"I did the killing," he said flatly. "All you did is bozo work. Stop trying to steal my thunder."

"Why, Rennell, I believe you're trying to save my tender feelings."

"Bullshit."

"Too late. You've already shown me that minuscule amount of softening. I won't tell anyone." She smiled shakily. "But it was a waste because I deliberately killed that man and we both know it. In fact, I caught a glimpse of his face before I pulled the trigger." She moistened her lips. "And now I'm going to go over and make sure he's dead." She moved over to the truck. "Though I aimed for his throat, and he was pinned under the truck so I'm almost sure."

"I'm very sure," he said harshly. "You don't have to look at the bastard."

"Yes, I do." She was kneeling beside the truck and shining her flashlight on his crushed head. "Yes, quite dead." She got to her feet. "Thank God!"

"Maria?" His gaze was narrowed on her face. "What's going on?"

"I told you, I saw his face." Her lips were curved in a bitter smile. "And I knew his name. It was Anton Balkon, my dear departed husband. You might have heard a few stories about him. They were all true. So I won't pretend to be sorry about the bastard. He was probably on his way to torment Lara. He and Volkov had a habit of—" She stopped. "I didn't think—what happened here might change things. Why are we standing here? Shouldn't we go and help Lara and Tanner finish this?"

"Yes, I was just waiting for you to stop talking so that we could get on the road. We should probably head for Mallory and his guys and see if those charges are really going to work." He gazed at her, deadpan. "If you're truly finished mourning…"

"Bastard." She headed for Rennell's car. "I'm definitely finished mourning."

———◆———

Lara held tight to the seat belt as Tanner gunned the Mercedes over the rough, rocky terrain of the ridge road. "I'm glad I didn't volunteer to drive," she shouted over the rattling noise of the metal. "Mercedes are supposed to be very sturdy, but this doesn't feel like it."

"It's a good car. I'm punishing it," Tanner said. "I

want to get to the pass where we'll be able to see the copter. If Volkov took the bait, then the timing should be just about right in another three minutes. He'll be arriving at the pass about the same time as we do." He grinned. "Of course, he'll be driving up to the copter pad, which will be about a hundred feet below where we are on this ridge road. And the point will be to encourage Volkov to come up and join us, preferably in that helicopter."

Lara was bounced against the side of the door again. "I wouldn't want to insult that great numeric gift you have that everybody keeps telling me about, but I may end up outside this car before we get to the pass if you keep jouncing me around."

He nodded. "One more minute. But I can make the call to Volkov now."

"I want to make the phone call to Volkov," Lara said quietly. "You closed me out the last time and I gave in. But not this time, Tanner. I want him to know that it's ending for him, and it's partly because of me that it's happening. There's no slick card game nor even your very impressive gift of gab. There's just me and the man who's hated me most of his life…and made me pay." Her voice was low and emphatic. "How he made me pay."

He looked at her for a moment and then reached for his phone. "I hear you. In the end, it only matters that we get Volkov on that helicopter. Then we'll leave it to Rennell to do his job. I'm just checking to see if he's reached the pass yet." He dialed. "Rennell, are you at the pass? Is Volkov there?" He hung up the phone. "Volkov took the bait. He's driving up to the helicopter pad now." He smiled at her as he handed her his phone. "Just press the button. It will bring up

Volkov's number. And it will show my name as the caller. I believe that will goad him to answer since he was ready to behead me when we walked out of the casino. But I'll be glad to share it with you. I don't want to be selfish."

He was joking, but Lara realized it was an unselfish act. His hatred for Volkov must be as deep as her own, and it was natural he wanted to control every facet of his removal. She smiled. "I appreciate your generosity."

"You're welcome. I'm sure that you know what you have to do."

They were at the pass now and she could see down into the canyon where the gray helicopter was sitting some hundred feet below the ridge. Volkov was getting out of his car, and he looked…stressed. That was a good sign.

"Stoke the fires," she said softly. "Mock him. Make him want to chase us to hell and back." She shrugged. "No problem." She punched the number.

It rang only once before Volkov picked up the phone. "Tanner! Where are you?" His voice was harsh with malevolence. "Do you think you can get away with this? No one gets away with cheating me. When I catch you, I'm—"

"It's not Tanner," Lara interrupted. "It's Lara. Tanner was busy driving and didn't want to bother with you. We're through with you, and on to good times. But I didn't get a chance to say goodbye to you, and I always like to put a period to a relationship. Particularly when it's turned out to be so profitable for me."

"Profitable?" he repeated. "What are you talking about, bitch? You're dead to me. After I've killed

Tanner, I'll send my men to hunt you down and cut your heart out. I'd do it myself, but you're not worth my time. I'll just tell them to make sure the rape is long and painful before they even start the actual torture." His voice fell to a hiss. "Just as I would have done. You've always known that's what's been waiting for you, haven't you? I was going to treat you as I would have your whore of a mother before I ended you."

"Are you finished? Yes, I always thought it would end that way if you had your way." She added mockingly, "But aren't I lucky that you're not going to have your way? Because you're a loser, Volkov. I wish I could have seen you when you found out that Tanner had taken you for every nickel. Did you scream? Did you moan and cry like a baby? Yes, that must be what you did. You must have cried, and everyone around you in that casino was probably laughing at you."

"Shut up! No one was laughing." He was screaming. "They were all afraid of me. Everyone was afraid."

It was almost too easy to push him toward hysteria. "I don't believe you. They were all pretending. I've watched people pretend to be afraid, and then laugh at you behind your back." She chuckled. "And you didn't even know it. I did it myself. Because you were such a pitiful human being."

"You were afraid of me. I know you were. I'm not a loser."

"Yet I was beginning to win every Trial you set me. So I was the winner, and you were the loser. And when I found Tanner, we built on that. Look at you now. Everyone laughing at you. No money. No fancy cars. All the families will be feeling sorry for you until they decide to devour you. That will come soon, won't it? Like the way you pounced on anyone too weak to fight you. I've watched you and wondered when it would be your turn."

She could see the tension in his body as he spat at her, "You're lying. I'm strong. I'll never be weak."

"Then how could Tanner just take me away from you? I'm sure all your men were laughing at you when they found out. Weak. So very weak."

"Lies. I'll hunt you down. I'll shut you up so that you can't lie about me."

"Hunt me down?" This could be the moment. She could see that his rage was searing and growing white-hot. "What a fool you are." She was opening the passenger door as she spoke. "Do you think we'd be afraid of a weakling like you? I just dropped in for a chat before we got on the road again."

She heard Tanner mutter a curse, but she was already out of the car walking toward the edge of the ridge overlooking the canyon. "Look up, Volkov. Wave goodbye. Because this is the final Trial and I've won it big time."

He stared up at her in rage and disbelief, and then he made a sound that was like a cross between pain and madness. The next moment he was frantically climbing up the boulders of the canyon wall to get at her.

"Enough." Tanner was beside her and jerking her toward the car. "If you hadn't taken them by surprise, his men might have started taking potshots at you." Then he was pushing her into the car and jumping into the driver's seat.

"But I did take them by surprise," she said as he pressed the accelerator and the car leaped forward. "And I think I took him to the edge. I knew there wasn't any chance of him climbing up that entire cliff to get to me. But I bet he'll be frustrated enough now to jump into that helicopter."

"We'll see. We should know soon enough. In the meantime I've got to put distance between us and that canyon." He called Rennell. "Action?"

"Action," Rennell confirmed. "Ever since Lara appeared on that cliff like an angel from heaven. But that's not what Volkov is calling her. And he's cursing a blue streak at everyone else on the helicopter team. I think they're going to take off any minute." He paused. "Look, I have an idea. Let me try to distract them away from you once they're airborne. I'm heading up toward the ridge now. Kill your headlights. If they mistake me for you, I might be able to lead them back down to the box canyon. I've been trying to think of a way to do that."

"Any particular reason?" Tanner asked.

"Only a little problem, nothing to worry about. Just kill those headlights as soon as you see me, then get off the high road and go down and around to the other side of the box canyon. I'll stall a little to give you time to make it. And then I'll lead the copter to your location…"

CHAPTER

17

Y*es.*" Rennell grinned as he looked in the rearview mirror at the night sky. "They're doing it. They're following in the helicopter."

Maria looked back. "And that's a good thing?"

He stepped on the accelerator. "Yes. Strap yourself in. It's going to get bumpy."

She pulled her seat belt taut. "Maybe because we're not using that nice smooth road up there. I liked that one best."

"Not an option." Rennell swerved to avoid a clump of bushes. "We need to go through that box canyon up ahead."

"Box canyon as in 'boxed in'?"

"There's an outlet on the other side, but we need to get through it before the copter gets there."

She looked back. The helicopter was gaining on them, kicking up a cloud of sand and silt from the desert floor. "This canyon is where you planted the rest of the explosives? You think it'll be enough to bring down that copter?"

"Not directly."

"What does that mean?"

"Kaskov's contact wasn't as good as I expected. I didn't have as much explosive material as I'd like, so I had to improvise. If we set it off in an open field, no way could we generate enough explosive energy to bring down a copter a hundred feet overhead. But here we can use the rock walls of this narrow canyon to focus the blast wave. Simple physics."

Maria nodded. "But that also means we need to be out of this canyon when it blows."

"You know it." He pointed to his phone on the dash. "Take that. It's already open to the triggering app. When I give the word, press the red button."

Maria grabbed his phone.

The copter's roar grew louder as it approached. Rennell gunned his engine and roared through the box canyon, dodging boulders and clumps of brush.

RAT-AT-AT-AT!

Volkov and his men were leaning out of the helicopter's side doors, firing on them with their automatic weapons.

"Shit!" Rennell put on an extra burst of speed.

"They're gaining," Maria said. "We're not going to make it."

"It's going to be close. Be ready with that trigger."

As Rennell navigated the canyon's twists and turns, the helicopter roared even louder. He looked in the rearview mirror. "I can't see it…It's kicking up too much sand."

RAT-AT-AT-AT!

"We're almost out," Rennell yelled. "Get ready!"

Maria raised the phone.

Rennell put on an extra burst of speed and roared out of the canyon. He cut the wheel hard right. "Now!"

Maria punched the button.

BOOM!

The explosion rocked the canyon behind them. A moment later the helicopter's roar gave way to a grinding sound and the screeching of metal against rock. Pieces of the broken blades shot from the canyon.

Tanner and Mallory's team were waiting there with their assault rifles.

RAT-AT-AT-AT!

Gunfire erupted from the canyon.

Rennell grabbed his gun. "It isn't over yet."

They took positions behind their cars and aimed for the helicopter's wreckage.

"Two survivors," Tanner called. "They both have guns. One's behind the rock at two o'clock, and—"

BLAMM!

Rennell fired his rifle, effectively blowing away the man behind the rock.

"One survivor," he said dryly.

Tanner nodded. "The other is behind the tail section."

RAT-AT-AT-AT!

Rennell's back windshield shattered.

Tanner returned fire, then turned to the others. "Be ready. When he pops back up from behind that tail, let him have it."

The gunman jumped up with his rifle, but before he could even squeeze off a single shot Tanner, Rennell, and the team hit him with over a dozen rounds of ammo. He flew backward to the canyon floor, dead.

Silence.

And then they heard another metallic scraping coming from the canyon.

"Maybe one more survivor," Tanner said as he reloaded his gun.

"We made sure that Volkov was on that helicopter." He started for the canyon. "Wouldn't you know the bastard would live through it?"

"Not for long," Rennell said as he moved after him. "I've been waiting for this…"

A bullet pinged the rock beside his head!

He fell to the ground and then wriggled to the nearest boulder.

"He's behind that propeller," Tanner said, moving quietly through the brush. "I'll get him."

"The hell you will. He's mine."

But Volkov was crawling on the ground, groaning with every breath. "Stupid. You can't hurt me. I'm too smart for you." His arm was bleeding badly, but he still managed to lift his automatic. "She was wrong. I won't let that bitch be right."

Tanner knocked the automatic aside. "She was right. You're beaten, and soon you'll be dead. Like Sandrino. You remember Sandrino, Volkov."

"I remember him. He kept calling me a loser. I made him pay for it." His smile was ugly. "You should have seen what I did to him. He kept talking about you. He said you'd never stop."

"I never did. That's why you're lying there bleeding to death." He turned to Rennell. "Leave him like this? Or do you have a better idea?"

Rennell raised his gun and aimed at Volkov's belly. He pulled the trigger. Volkov screamed. "Sandrino," Rennell said. He aimed at Volkov's penis. "Sandrino." He pulled the trigger. He aimed at Volkov's chest.

"Sandrino." The bullet exploded his chest. Then Rennell looked down at him and shook his head. "I think that last Sandrino killed him. Pity. But I never could win an argument with Sandrino."

He turned and walked away.

———◆———

Maria stopped Tanner as he was coming out of the canyon. "How did you keep Lara from coming with you?"

"With great difficulty," he said dryly. "But when I talked to Mallory on the phone a little before you showed up with Rennell, I realized the last thing I wanted was to have her there when you'd be in danger. I pulled one of Mallory's men and told her to stay with him. She wasn't pleased."

"I'm not surprised. It could be the end between you."

"No, it will only mean anger and adjustment. She knows me. She trusts me."

"I'm not so sure." She shrugged. "She's going to be even less pleased with me. But I had to do it." She gazed at the canyon. "Volkov is dead?"

"To Rennell's regret. But he got some satisfaction out of it."

"Anton is dead, too. I killed him." She shook her head. "Things are changing...It's what we wanted, but it's still strange."

She straightened. "I guess I'd better go and be with Lara. Can you give me a ride back? Rennell forgot about me."

"He has a lot on his mind."

"Do you think I don't know that? I wasn't complaining. I understand him...I think." She ran her hand through her hair. "And he gave me what I wanted today. I have to see if I can help him." She turned and headed for his car. "But Lara first."

He got in the driver's seat. "By all means, Lara first."

"Maria?"

Tanner had just told Lara what Maria had done, but she was still having trouble believing it. Yet there was no doubt it was Maria, though her shirt and jeans were dirt-stained, and there was a bruise on her left cheek. Maria looked up and smiled, then waited for Lara to come to her. Lara fought her way across the rocks to where Maria was getting out of Tanner's car. "Are you crazy?" Lara enveloped her in a quick hug before she pushed her away. "What are you doing here? Are you all right?"

"Where else would I be? Did you actually think that I'd let you go without me? You've been on too many Trials over the years and left me behind. Not this one. I wasn't going to sit back there and wonder what was happening to you. I needed to *keep* it from happening." Her lips twisted sardonically. "But first I had to convince Rennell that I wouldn't get in his way."

"Tanner said you were with him. That was pretty weird, Maria."

"He was the one who was going to be in the action. It seemed the place for me to be." She glanced down the hill to the casino at Rennell, who was now in deep conversation with Tanner. "And it still does." She started the Land Rover. "My job's not finished yet. I'm going to follow Rennell out to Volkov's place and see if I can help him."

"Volkov's place? What are you going to do?"

"Whatever I can. Probably not much." Her gaze

was still on Rennell and Tanner. "Rennell said this entire area is probably going to have law enforcement crawling all over it soon. We were a little…loud. Rennell said he and Tanner had talked and they want to get Sandrino out of that cave and take him home to Sandrino Place before that happens."

"Of course they do. I'll go with you."

"No, you won't. Rennell is going ahead. That's the way he wants it. Tanner will follow us after he gets all the team safely away from here and on the road. You help him." She paused. "After Tanner comes and they get Sandrino ready to go home, I'll start making anonymous calls to the police, sheriff's department, and Immigration. I'll tell them what we found there. That way perhaps we'll be able to send those poor victims home to their families, too. It shouldn't take that long, and it might answer some of the questions they'll be asking when they find what we did here to Volkov, Anton, and party."

"And when should I come and help?"

Maria didn't answer. She was looking Lara up and down. "You know, it's a good thing that you didn't like that gown. You've made a complete mess of it." She switched to another subject. "Did you give Tanner a hard time? He thought he might get by with minimum punishment because you trust him. Was he right?"

Lara's lips tightened. "Yes, but he'll think long and hard before he pulls that bullshit again."

"Don't be too hard on him. He couldn't have stopped me." She paused. "And we both know that being able to trust someone like that is a rare and precious gift." She pressed the accelerator. "I'll talk to you later." She looked back over her shoulder as she started down the mountain. "It's almost over, Lara. Just a little longer…"

By the time Lara had walked down to the casino, both Maria and Rennell had taken off in their separate vehicles. But Tanner turned away from talking to Mallory and said, "Maria said she'd filled you in and you were going to give me a problem about this. Don't do it. You've already gone through your particular hell there. I know you want to help, but it's something Rennell and I have to do by ourselves."

"Maria will be there."

"She's in agony because she doesn't want Rennell to be alone out there when he sees Sandrino. She's actually feeling maternal toward him, which is fairly incredible considering their combustible relationship." He made a face. "It must run in the family." Then his phone rang, and he glanced at the ID. "Kaskov. I just talked to him fifteen minutes ago and gave him a progress report." He answered and then was silent for the next few minutes. "Yes, I hear you. Yes, I owe you. Yes, I know we should get her out. I was already planning on doing it. I didn't need you to tell me." He cut the connection and turned back to Lara. "You heard it. Wasn't I meek? I wanted to break his neck. But the bastard was right. Not only smoothing the way with the Albanians, but sending us extra men and explosives. We do owe him."

"Yes, we do. What does he want?"

"You and Maria out of Las Vegas, away from any possible investigation. Those documents I gave you wouldn't hold up under close inspection, and we don't have time to bribe someone at Immigration or Justice to get sets that would. If they checked with Interpol, they'd bring up Volkov's and your father's records, which could cause you problems."

"And Maria was saying it was almost over," she said wryly.

"It is. There's nothing that we can't handle. All it takes is a little time and more than a little money. There are good people we can tap to help us. But we don't have that time. So I'm sending you out of here right away to New York with Mallory, where I have the contacts to make it happen."

"What about Maria?"

"I'll pick her up myself tonight and take her to New York in the Gulfstream. There's no way she was going to leave Rennell right now anyway."

"I don't want to leave her. Why can't I wait?"

"Because I want you out of here. And because Kaskov wants you to make a stopover in Atlanta on the way to New York."

"Why?"

"How do I know? He didn't say. So you can thank him personally? He just said he wanted to talk to you." He whirled her around and kissed her. "Stop worrying. Nothing's going to happen to either of you. I promise. By the time you get into New York, I'll have this little hiccup managed. Trust me."

"I do. I just don't like leaving you here, either." She was looking around the wreckage on the mountain. "You might say I contributed to this chaos. I shouldn't leave you to deal with it by yourself."

"I'll let you make it up to me when you reach New York." He was motioning to Mallory. "Right now all I want is you out of here, so I won't have to worry about you." He grinned ruefully. "And I guarantee that I'd much rather deal with this chaos than have your job of dealing with Kaskov."

EPILOGUE

W hat am I doing here, Nikolai?" Lara wasn't at all sure she liked what was going on. There might be nothing to worry about. But with Kaskov, one could never be entirely certain. "I was supposed to have a meeting with Kaskov at the airport and you whisked me into this limo and took me into the city. You're disobeying his orders."

"I never disobey his orders," Nikolai said. "Well, almost never. Only when it is better and safer for him not to do something. That is not what's happening now. You are mistaken, I'm not taking you into the city. See? There is a lake right ahead." He pulled the limo over beneath some trees and stopped. "I believe you're supposed to get out here. He's waiting for you." He left the limo and ran around the car to open her door. "Here she is, sir," he said to Kaskov as he strolled into view. "She thought I was being disobedient. I explained that was most unlikely."

"But not impossible." He smiled at Lara. "And it's my fault. Were you afraid I'd kidnapped you?"

"Not afraid." She made a face. "Maybe a little wary. After all, you did it before."

He chuckled. "That should have reassured you. I'd hesitate to repeat such a splendid venture. It could never have the same success ratio."

"Which is why I'm only a little wary," she said quietly. "It *was* a success, and I'd be grateful if I felt I could trust you. But that's difficult for me. Why am I here, Kaskov?"

He smiled. "I made both you and Tanner a promise. I had to fulfill it. I think perhaps Tanner would prefer I stayed out of your life from now on, but I'm accustomed to that response. Actually, I applaud it. But I did make another promise and I won't break my word. First, I've made arrangements at Juilliard so that you can acquire that polish I mentioned might be beneficial. It's in New York, so Tanner won't be too displeased that you'll be at school and ignore him."

"He's already mentioned that he wanted to be the one to send me. So he's ahead of you, Kaskov." She frowned as she remembered something else he'd said. "*Another* promise? What do you mean?"

"I told you that there was a multitude of reasons why I decided to hire Tanner to get you out of Russia. One of them was more important than the others." He shrugged. "I have a granddaughter whom I allow myself to see for one month a year at her discretion. Mine, too. I prefer no one be aware of our relationship. During one of those months I played one of your CDs for her. She was very upset when I told her that there could be difficulty getting you out of Russia so everyone could hear you. She can be very determined and doesn't understand or care about my business problems." He met Lara's eyes. "All she cares about is the music."

Her eyes widened. "You promised *her*?"

"And it was a promise I couldn't break. She wouldn't have understood."

"I believe I'd…like to meet her."

"That's why you're here. I had to show her that I hadn't broken my word. I expect you to get along famously." He nodded at a charming cottage a little distance away. "They call it the Lake Cottage. Not exactly my style, but my granddaughter loves it when she comes to visit here. I think you'll enjoy it, too. She'll probably want you to join her when you're on a break from school."

She shook her head. "She doesn't even know me."

"She knows you. And you know her." He showed her the photo on his phone. "You might have even heard her play. She's had a lot of airtime recently."

Her eyes widened in shock. "It's Cara Delaney, the violinist. She's *wonderful*."

"She said the same about you. Before she made me give her that promise." He frowned impatiently. "Now stop waffling. Do you know what I'm giving you? So you have a lover and everything is bright and shining in your world. But Cara could be a friend who knows how you're feeling when you play. It's something you both could share and be enriched. She *loves* the music. And she has a family that she'd also share with you and Maria. That's something you've never had. You'll meet them today. Eve Duncan and Joe Quinn and their son, Michael. Cara is crazy about them. Absolutely no more loneliness. Ask Tanner if he can match that."

She smiled. "You speak as if it's a competition." And

maybe it was, she thought. The two men had always been contentious and driven where this mission had been concerned. Completely different motivations, but the combativeness had been there. Though perhaps not terribly different. Lara hadn't known about Cara. She felt a rush of warmth. She was grateful for Kaskov's help, yet she couldn't let Kaskov think that she was on anyone's side but Tanner's. "It would be hard. But if Tanner tried, he might be able to do it. He's made a habit of being the best. Of course, he doesn't have a family, either." She was looking back at the cottage. "I think I'm definitely going to meet your granddaughter, Kaskov. Are you coming to introduce me?"

He shook his head. "They're expecting you. I'm tolerated but not welcomed." He turned back toward the car. "I'll have Nikolai take me to the airport. I think you'll be here awhile. I'll phone Tanner and let him know Nikolai will put you on a later plane." He glanced back at her. "Don't think I'm soft. It's not as if I cared. I did it all for Cara."

"I know." She smiled gently at him. "And for the music."

<hr/>

NEW YORK CITY
8:40 P.M.

"Well, you do *look* happy." Tanner's skeptical gaze was narrowed on Lara's face as he took her duffel and headed for the limo stand. "Kaskov said that he'd already taken care of a number of your problems, and I wasn't to interfere. I told him to go to hell. Is everything okay?"

"I believe everything may be very much okay. I'll tell you all about it later." She chuckled. "I got the impression that Kaskov was a little annoyed that you'd seen fit to take over getting me settled here in the U.S. He particularly mentioned Juilliard. I think he was outraged you'd interfered with his plans. I decided he may be regarding it as a competition."

"Too bad." He stopped her before she got into the limousine and pulled her into his arms and kissed her. "Did you tell him I always win?" He kissed her again. "And I've no intention of losing this one. It's too important. The stakes are too high. Kaskov doesn't stand a chance."

"I told him you like to be best." She reached up and caressed his cheek. "I didn't tell him that you were definitely the best for me because that would only have irritated him. He was sure I couldn't ignore what he was offering me." She shook her head in amusement. "He researched me very thoroughly. He made it almost irresistible."

"Almost? That never wins the game." He opened the door for her and nudged her gently into the limo. "Not when I've got an ace in the hole." He leaned inside and kissed her again. "I'll join you later. Turn on the video-conferencing. Maria wants to talk to you." He slammed the door shut and motioned for the driver to take off.

Lara sat there stunned for a moment before she found the videoconferencing app on the console monitor screen and punched it. Maria's face came on the screen. "Thank heavens you're here, Lara. What's Tanner up to?" she asked. "Ever since I arrived here this morning, I've felt like I've been in the middle of a tornado." She added, "Not a destructive tornado. Some exceptionally good things, but difficult to assimilate and take in. I decided I'd wait for you instead of trying to dig deep into Tanner's psyche. That could be very time consuming."

"I've no idea what you're talking about. Tanner made all the flight arrangements to get us here, and the only thing he told me was that he'd take you to New York to get you settled." She drew a deep breath. "But I think that you'd better begin telling me about the tornado. First, where are you?"

"Our apartment. Very nice. Not like the Taj, but you'll like it. Tanner brought me here to okay it before he took me to the office."

"What office?"

"Tanner has an office on Wall Street. Very sleek, but I think I can make it comfortable."

"What are you talking about?"

"The first time I met Tanner, I hadn't been with him for thirty minutes before he was talking about hiring me for a managerial position. He said I was a natural." She grimaced. "And I thought it was bullshit. I never thought about it again until he took me to that office today."

"And what did you think then?"

"I could *do* it." Her face was lit with excitement. "Give me a little training and I could do a damn good job of anything Tanner's executives could throw at me. Anything *Tanner* could throw at me."

"And you want to try it?"

"I want to try it. I felt *alive* today."

And how long had it been since Maria had felt that excitement and hunger for life? Lara wanted to reach out and hug her so that she could physically touch that excitement. "That's fantastic. Of course you can do it. You can do anything. What else did you do today?"

"Tanner took me for a tour of the city. I liked it better than Las Vegas. That was nice, all gloss and make-believe, but New York is real, sometimes wounded, but always strong. I like strength."

"I know you do." Lara added lightly, "But I bet Tanner can find us some glitter that we'd enjoy to balance that strength. He has a talent in that direction." She changed the subject. "I imagine we're going to head your way for dinner, if you're not too tired."

"I'm not tired." She hesitated. "What about the tornado?"

"Nothing to worry about. Tanner was just excited about being right about you. I'm glad you got along well together today. I'll see you soon." She cut the connection.

It was only a couple moments later that Tanner called. "Ace in the hole?"

"Maybe. You've made her very happy. But do you value her? Do you realize what you have?"

He said soberly, "I realize that she's a unique personality who made you the person you are. I like her and respect her, and I feel closer to her all the time. I will care for her and honor her. Value her? I think she's brilliant and will probably run that office like a brigadier general. Is that enough?"

"That's quite a bit."

He grinned. "Then do I win the competition from Kaskov?"

She laughed. "You're very persuasive. He had only one thing to offer me you didn't." But that one thing had filled her day with warmth, laughter, hope, and togetherness. It had opened a new world to her. Her eyes were suddenly twinkling. "Now, I don't want you to panic. It's not what you think." She paused. "But how do you feel about families?"

ABOUT THE AUTHOR

IRIS JOHANSEN is the #1 *New York Times* bestselling author of more than 30 consecutive bestsellers. Her series featuring forensic sculptor Eve Duncan has sold over 20 million copies and counting and was the subject of the acclaimed Lifetime movie *The Killing Game*. Along with her son, Roy, Iris has also co-authored the *New York Times* bestselling series featuring investigator Kendra Michaels. Johansen lives near Atlanta, Georgia. Learn more at:

  IrisJohansen.com
  Twitter @Iris_Johansen
  Facebook.com/OfficialIrisJohansen

For a complete list of books by
IRIS JOHANSEN

VISIT
IrisJohansen.com

 Follow Iris Johansen on Facebook
Facebook.com/OfficialIrisJohansen

 Follow Iris Johansen on Twitter
@Iris_Johansen

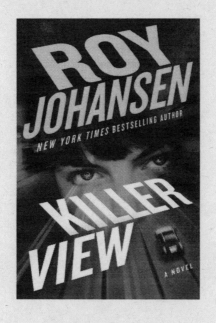